Savior

The Shattered World Saga
Book 3

by
Dennis K. Hausker

Published by
Melange Books, LLC
White Bear Lake, MN 55110
www.melange-books.com

Savior. The Shattered World Saga, Book 3 ~ Copyright © 2013
by Dennis K. Hausker

ISBN: 978-1-61235-709-6 print

Cover Art by Caroline Andrus

Savior
Dennis K. Hausker

In the stunning conclusion of the epic story of Aron and his post apocalyptic world, Damien poses the threat of a society of his rabid followers bereft of rational values and concerns. He's faced with the impossible in leading the rebellion with primitive arms against a nightmare enemy armed with fearful weapons from the ancient war that destroyed the world. His personal angst continues, as again love remains elusive with the obstructions of endless setbacks and interference from others. Can he find a way to prevail and warrant the faith his friends have in him or will the world sink into Damien's dark reality?

Chapter One
~ Panic ~

The warm pleasant day faded into dusk and the lamps were lit at the palace in Nephora. As people went about their normal business, there was no sense of trouble. The fact Aron and Cherine hadn't returned yet from their romantic excursion didn't concern anybody. Palace denizens made assumptions about the couple's possible choice to spend time alone together in light of their recent announcement of a relationship. The union was a happy surprise, unexpected, but nearly universally approved. Aron was finally smiling after what seemed an eternity of galling setbacks and Cherine was certainly seen as a worthy companion for him.

Granor sat in his room curious about Lilith's absence. It wasn't like her not to at least check in with him each night in case he had plans for her.

"That woman is getting to be a little too headstrong," he muttered in annoyance. "I think she forgets who's in charge and who the vassal here is."

He went to pour some wine in a wide mouth chalice and took a deep swig, some of which spilled down his cheeks and dripped onto his shirt.

"Now see what you've done, Lilith," he snarled. "You made me spill this expensive wine with your rude behavior."

He heard a knock at his door.

"Enter," he yelled sourly.

Lilith stepped in his room with a smug smile.

"You're late," he challenged, trying to wipe away the spill from staining his white shirt.

"I had my reasons," she cooed. "I have great news for you."

"What news?"

"We've ambushed Aron and Cherine returning from the royal gardens and kidnapped them. We hold them prisoner."

"What!" he shrieked. "Lilith, what were you thinking? We're not ready for that."

"When would we be ready, Granor?" she replied in an acid tone. "They're expertly guarded surrounded constantly by the fiercest fighters in the realm, people who make no mistakes. There would have been no better time than now to capture them when they let their guard down. It was ridiculously easy. They were besotted with romantic passions and paid no attention to their surroundings. Frankly, I'm surprised. With all the legends and grand stories about them, I expected much more. I find they're just a simple man and a woman, no different than any other."

Granor frantically paced the room, trying to collect his thoughts.

"Lilith, you've set something in motion we can't undo. Once the authorities realize they're gone they'll leave no stone unturned looking for them. There will be no place in the city to hide. The Black Fist and the masters will be feral in that pursuit. Where do you think they'll look first? You may have signed our death warrants."

"You don't think I know that? This is why you've always been a secondary figure here at court. You fear to take bold steps. Do you think sitting here in a dither and doing nothing will impress Damien?"

Granor fought his panic, but his fear was too strong. Lilith watched him clinically, assessing whether he was fit to follow any longer as a leader, or if she needed to go in a different direction. She felt no panic, instead feeling giddy at her success in capturing the greatest names in the kingdom.

"No one knows they're in our hands. We have time to take action. I hadn't planned on keeping them in the city. There's a station outside of the city limits where we can safely keep them in the short term. I have some ideas about a more permanent home. They'll give us huge bargaining chips with either the crown or with Damien."

"Damn you, Lilith," he hissed. "If I go down, you'll go down with me."

She shrugged. "Life is opportunity and its chance. I saw a golden opportunity and I took it. If it leads to my demise, so be it. I feel no regrets for what I did."

"We'll see how you feel if we're discovered and they take you to the dungeon for torture. Being a woman won't protect you there, in case you didn't know that. They'll tear your flesh apart the same as they would a man."

"They'll never take me alive. I'll fight to the death first," she replied frostily.

He paused and glared at her.

She smiled insolently, went over to the pitcher, poured a full chalice of wine, and sat down at his table. She crossed her leg evocatively and smiled, drinking slowly savoring the high quality of the beverage. She eyed Granor mirthfully cognizant she could affect him with her feminine wiles, as if daring him to say anything about her affront.

"Ah!" she said expansively. "Delicious. You do have excellent taste in wine."

"Where do you have them?" he asked softly, his attention affixed to her attractive legs.

"In two separate locations, they're close enough we can gather them and be on our way in no time at all."

Granor scowled again. "If we leave the palace now there'll be no doubt about who's responsible for the kidnapping."

"I can send our people ahead. Your weak demeanor is unbecoming for the type of person you purport to be. Did you think never to risk anything on behalf of Damien? If you wish to cower here, I'll do what must be done about the situation, but the credit will go to me. Damien will know who showed genuine courage and who was timid."

A murderous look spread over Granor's face. "I can see I was too lenient with you. If you think to take my position and power away from me, you'll see a side of me as ruthless as you. Don't forget your place. You're still a woman and whether in the kingdom or in Damien's world, women do not rule. Their roles are clear. Is that what you want from me now to remind you of your real duties?"

He seethed and shook with anger. She hardened her glare in response.

"If you wish to test your prowess against me, I invite you to do so. If you think I'm so easily dispatched, there's an easy way to find out. Do I look to be in fear of you? Is it possible there's a good reason why I feel confident? I told you to come and see us in our training. You should've done so because you'd realize who you're dealing with now. I spoke the truth when I said Cherine is no longer the only woman to fear in a fight."

He continued to glare at her.

"Thank you for the excellent wine. I believe it best I leave you now to see to our prisoners. I'll have them sent away to start their new lives and then I'll return here. As you say, when the alarm is sounded, we both want to be here to avoid instant suspicion. I'm sure you can find others to warm your bed. That's a role I won't be performing any longer, by the way."

He watched her leave the room closing the door. Granor was at a loss about what to do. He trusted no one enough to confide in them. The contingencies of the situation were mind boggling for him. So many things could go wrong. He was in an imminently precarious position.

"Okay, Lilith, let the contest begin. You say you're not so easily dispatched? Neither am I. We'll see who is the greater between us. I haven't ascended to my position with only pure luck."

Frustrated, he slammed his fist into his hand with a loud smack.

"I'll see you humbled and groveling at my feet begging for my forbearance, woman. We'll see if you still eschew my bed with your misguided arrogance. I'll show you I can take risks and I can be a person of iron will and brutal responses to your insolence. You've made a huge mistake trifling with me."

* * * *

Lilith left the palace immediately and rode into the city heading for the first of her stops, an old empty tenement wood house in a poor section. From the outside the structure was dilapidated and seemingly vacant. She'd stationed guards in the ground level to turn away squatters while she kept her prisoner below in the basement.

Cherine was immobile, trussed up with a sack over her head lying helpless on a bed stinking of mildew and urine. An ample number of Granor's guards were in the house, but Lilith's trained servants attended Cherine, so she only received contact from females.

Cherine lay unmoving.

"I know you're awake, Cherine. You need not pretend to be unconscious."

Cherine moved her head in the direction of Lilith's voice.

"You need not pretend I don't know who you are, Lilith."

Lilith chuckled and pulled the hood off Cherine's head. Cherine blinked and focused her vision before looking directly at Lilith. She winced in pain from the head blow she'd taken.

"I regret we needed violence to subdue you, but there was no way around it. Had I asked you to surrender, I think you would have rejected my request."

Cherine simply looked back at her.

"I also regret the poor state of your accommodations, but take solace in the fact we'll provide you with better lodging soon enough. This is a stopover point and nothing more."

"What do you want? You're not a stupid woman. Surely you realize what a colossal mistake this is. What could you possibly hope to gain?"

"It depends on your point of view. I don't see it as a gaff at all. If you're looking for gaffs, perhaps you should look back at your foolishness allowing us to catch you unarmed and inattentive."

Cherine sat up and shrugged. "I can't disagree with you on that point. I put myself in a vulnerable position. That fact can't be debated, but it's not important now. Do you realize the position you've put yourself into?"

"I'm fully aware of our position. I made a calculated choice. Granted, there was great risk, but also great reward."

"Reward from whom? Do you hope to barter with his majesty for our return? You'd have a price on your head which would bring out every manner of man looking to claim the reward for your capture. I'd suspect they'd make it dead or alive. If they caught you, your torment in their torture chambers could be endless. What possible prize offsets such a dire ending?"

Lilith smiled smugly. "You and your little band of allies have no idea what's coming for you. The world you serve is about to change radically, and I intend to be a part of what will be, rather than what was."

"You're talking about Damien," Cherine replied. "Actually, we do have an idea. We were in his camp. We're not making judgments on hearsay like you are. We know all too well what he offers the world with his jaded pronouncements and pathological nature. If you think to strike some bargain with him, you'll rue that decision and I would say sooner rather than later. Damien has no incentive to honor pacts with underlings. He uses and discards without conscience or concern."

"We shall see about that. In the meantime, you're my guest. I'm afraid I can't offer you the deference you're accustomed to. You've been a great example for women wishing to throw away the dominance of men, but you're no longer the only woman who can deal with them on an equal footing. My maidens and I have schooled with the best of trainers we could find. I demanded they show us no quarter and force us to our limits with hard lessons and unsympathetic attitudes. We didn't want to be seen as or treated like women. We wanted to become warriors and we've done that. If you think you're singularly invincible and that no other woman could achieve your competence, I think we'll show you the error of such thinking in the days ahead."

Lilith gazed into Cherine's eyes and saw what she expected, disdain and dismissal.

"I understand your skepticism. It's true none among us has proven ourselves in real combat with men like you have. It's simply because we haven't had the opportunity, do you see? I'll ask you your opinion later once we've had a chance to display our progress for you to witness. That's a process I so look forward to. We'll come to know each other very well, darling, better than any living person you know in this world and that includes your new lover, Aron. That part of your life is over."

"Where is Aron? Is he injured too?"

"His injury is the same as yours. No, he's not here at the same location, and I don't think he ever will be in the same place with you. Don't plan on seeing him ever again. It would be imprudent on my part to allow that vulnerability. You're here alone and on your own. Your new life will not include Aron."

Lilith smiled at a momentary glimpse of emotional distress shown in Cherine's eyes. Cherine quickly hardened her expression.

"We're going to feed you, wash you clean, and then we'll be moving on to better accommodations. Say goodbye in your heart to those fanciful dreams you had. You were never meant to be a wife and a mother. You're a woman, warrior and your true life is not that of other women. Your true worth is wielding a sword. I'll be back later to join you for the journey. Welcome to our little sorority. We're a very select group. We'll see to your needs, Cherine."

Lilith stood up with a triumphant look, almost haughty. She turned to leave with Cherine helpless on the bed, but paused to watch a large number of stocky women come in promptly to untie Cherine as Lilith directed so she could eat and bathe. They were imminently attentive to her every movement and were reinforced with backup so Cherine had no chance to try to overpower her captors and make an escape. She closed her eyes a moment to suppress the pain of her captivity and especially the separation from Aron.

* * * *

Lilith next rode to her other captive site where the guards were among Granor's best. They were equally competent and attentive to details about their prisoner.

When Lilith walked into the room where Aron was being held he was awake, sitting on his bunk glaring at any who came near him. She felt a twinge of excitement, just as she had with Cherine. Aron was a universally renowned figure and not without good reason. On a primal level, Aron was a very attractive man that evoked a woman.

"Greetings, Aron," Lilith said as she walked up to him. "Welcome to you. I'm sorry for the unpleasantness, but I'm sure you understand the reason."

He eyed her grimly.

"I completely understand your feelings, but I hope we can get past that in the near future."

"Where is Cherine?"

"She has a small headache, but otherwise just fine. She won't be joining us here, by the way. As I told her, it would be unwise of me to have you both kept in the same place for a number of reasons. You would do no less if the roles were reversed."

"I'm sure Cherine asked you why you're doing this. The obvious answer is you've gone insane. This move can't possibly have a happy ending for you and

6

your cohorts. If you think you'll escape consequences for this idiotic decision, you're sorely mistaken."

Lilith laughed. "Perhaps I'm a bit insane, but I don't take that as a problem. This is so much better an experience than I anticipated. I find it downright stimulating."

"Enjoy your time while you can. It will be short lived."

She chuckled again. "You've lived a life of the miraculous, though I know you wouldn't see it that way. What you've managed coming from peasantry to such renown, facing down the mightiest powers in the realm, even standing before Damien himself and defying him is remarkable. I'm awed every time I come into your presence."

"I can't tell you how honored I feel to hear that," he replied snidely.

"Oh Aron," she said, chuckling cynically. "This is going to be incredible for me, although for you, perhaps not so much. I'll explain to you as I did with Cherine. Your old life is over. Who you were has ended. I'm sorry to tell you your romantic dreams of Cherine as a wife will never come to fruition. She wasn't meant to be a wife and mother, and she was never meant to be with you. I know how painful that is in light of your other romantic losses first of Coraline to the crown prince, and then Tasha to that rogue, Radigan. You haven't been lucky in love up to this point, but perhaps you can look forward to better days. I have some ideas I'll share with you when the time is right. You've aimed very high with the women you pursued. Perhaps they thought too much of themselves as it's my opinion it was never a flaw in you which caused your failures. With time I think they'd have greatly rued their choices. Your fate has intervened now. Your new course will go in a much different direction. It doesn't have to be the lonely path you've traveled. You're highly respected here, though we have our duties to follow."

"What are you talking about?"

"I know you're curious, but I must keep my surprises. As I said, at the proper time, we'll have a nice talk when you're in a better frame of mind to hear me rationally. Right now your emotions are clouding your judgment."

"I've been a captive before. Whatever you think you'll accomplish with me is not going to work. Although I don't agree with them, many people hold me in high esteem. They won't be idle while you perpetrate your schemes. Since it's you here, I've got to think Granor is not far away."

"The last time I saw Granor, we had a frank discussion. He has a point of view, as do I. I wouldn't plan on dealing much with him."

"If this is your plan, you're far crazier than I thought. This goes beyond insane. I've been in the royal prison and I can tell you you're not going to enjoy your time there."

"I know the risks and yet here we are. I hold your life and that of your former lover in my hands. If I decided to discard my plan, it would be the easiest thing to leave your bodies in an alley to be discovered by royal patrols, hapless victims of thieves and scoundrels."

Aron shook his head dismissively. "You can dream you've got all the answers. I guess it remains to be seen. I've had plenty of practice being patient."

Lilith walked over to Aron, grabbed his face in her hands, and kissed him passionately. He merely sat immobile.

She sat back and laughed heartily.

"Yes Aron, this is going to be so good for me, my love."

* * * *

Both Aron and Cherine were taken from their temporary holding stations tied up and supine in the back of wagons, covered under blankets in a column of supply trains. They both were heading away from the palace in different directions. Away from their friends and unable to leave any sign of their plight. This happened at Lilith's direction, as she had to return promptly to the palace to maintain her ruse of innocence in the kidnapping.

The next day when Aron and Cherine didn't show up at the palace, Galean went to the crown prince.

"I don't want to cause a problem, but I'm worried about Aron and Cherine. We assume they're holed up somewhere in love's sweet embrace, but I tell you neither of them would stay away without sending us word of their plans. They're not thoughtless adolescents and wouldn't choose to act foolish about this. Having a romance wouldn't mean discarding good sense. I fear something dire has happened."

Agar looked at Galean with concern. "Can it be right here so close to the palace, with our patrols all about in the city?"

"I think we need to start a search immediately. If we come upon them in a delicate situation, it's much better than the alternative."

"I agree with you. I'll send out the alarm and begin the search. It's hard to imagine Aron and Cherine being waylaid. They're the last two people who could be caught that way."

"We can't make any assumptions. We don't know what happened to be able to make any judgments."

After the order from the crown prince, word spread like wild fire. The Black Fist and the masters both were enraged and looking to exact retribution on someone. Brock spent every waking hour in the saddle as they scoured every building and inflicted considerable property damage looking for hidden or secret rooms. The royal army joined the search, blanketing every part of the city and closing the exits, but it was too late. The supply trains already left the city after arousing no suspicion at all. Aron and Cherine were on their way to the next leg of their journey.

* * * *

Consequently, Coraline spent considerable time with Aron's agonized mother, along with her own mother and even the queen trying to comfort her.

"I'm sure they'll be found soon. The entire army is looking for them. We'll catch the miscreants and deal with them severely."

"My son has faced so many horrible times, I wonder if this is yet another terrible test. A person shouldn't face such misery. He's paid such a price already, and his spirit is so badly wounded. I thought at last he could find happiness with Cherine. How can this be happening?"

"Bad circumstance isn't something which happens because we've shown weakness and made mistakes. It's random chance. I truly believe it," said the queen.

No one in the group argued with her, though there were a variety of divergent opinions which they opted to keep to themselves.

* * * *

As days passed with no sign of them Brock grew increasingly desperate along with the other searchers scouring the city. His father Barmon, reticent in the best of times, grew foul tempered and acerbic. Aron's father rode with them everywhere, stoic but also depressed. It became obvious the couple had been spirited out of the city before they could seal it up. Helplessness gripped the pursuers like a tightening noose around their necks.

"This is a big country," Trent mentioned as they sat at the city limits and looked across the vast horizon. "We'll continue to search, but it will be a slow process. We have no idea which way they were taken."

"I think we should start by taking Granor to a wine press and squeezing the truth out of him," Brock replied tersely.

"Granor has an alibi. He's the logical suspect, but we have nothing pointing to him having a hand in this. If the villain is another, perhaps someone came to the city we don't know. We would be wasting our time on an innocent man."

"Granor will never be an innocent man. He's guilty of something even if not this, but I understand what you're saying. If Damien sent a team to do this, heading for the wilds would be a logical path for them to follow. We can send fast riders spread out across the flatlands to search them out. I've already sent word to the Uripeans and also to Belisa and the Arreck."

"Galean is very upset by this whole sorry event. He saw Aron as our great hope against Damien. With Aron gone, Galean sees us having no chance to prevail and it seems to have shackled him with despair."

"I can't disagree," Brock replied grimacing at the adverse turn. "Aron has a quality that draws people. He's genuine. There aren't many people around who are sincere and it makes him stand out just for that alone, not even considering his other noble attributes."

"I'm worried who would be so brazen as to take such steps against Aron and Cherine in the midst of our might," Trent continued. "Equally, I'm very worried about Galean. He doesn't seem able to function and we can't afford to lose his help. He fills a role no other person can. Apparently the fate of Aron is the pivotal support to Galean's psyche and his optimism. I have no words to heal his distress. I'm told he stays in bed now much of the time."

"I don't know who we can call on about this. Tasha, Belisa, Liani, and now Cherine are all gone. Enna and Biala were friends to Galean, but they're fighters and spent little time in his company. If they speak to him, I don't think it will affect him."

"I wonder what else can go wrong. Is it our fate to suffer doom? Will we never have a favorable turn of circumstance?"

"I'm a simple man. I can only deal with what comes before me. Anything else is beyond my capacity. I don't ponder fate. I punch it with my fists and knock it down."

Trent chuckled. "That's because you're a bonehead, as Aron says. I am also."

"Perhaps some ale will crystallize our thoughts."

"It can't hurt. At the very least, it will be numbing."

* * * *

It was Coraline taking on the task of visiting Galean. She went to the library and down to his quarters. The room, recessed deep in the ground under the palace, was dim even in daytime. Galean closed the door even though it was just past noontime.

Coraline tapped on the door. She heard no response so she spoke.

"Galean, may I speak with you? It's Coraline."

She heard rustling about beyond the door.

"What do you want?" he replied hoarsely.

"If I could have a moment of your time, I would be grateful, Galean."

He muttered sourly, something Galean wouldn't normally say to a woman. This wasn't the person she'd come to know and respect. This version of him was irritated and annoying.

He opened the door a disheveled mess. It didn't appear he'd bathed recently and his face was blanched. Galean wasn't known as a drinker, but the odor of alcohol was unmistakable.

"How may I serve you, Princess?" he spouted acidly.

She was taken aback, unsure what she should do.

"I, eh…"

"You came to rescue me? Did I need rescue?"

"Will you talk with me, Galean? Let me make you breakfast. I'll get coffee."

He glared at her.

"Am I not allowed any solitude?"

"No, you're not," she replied. "Go bathe, please, your stink is offensive."

Chapter Two
~ Leadership Vacuum ~

Aron's followers were left with a difficult dilemma. No one was willing or able to step forth to fill his role in the interim, or longer. Galean not only refused the job, but continued to flounder in his life and research. Trent, Brock, and any other possible candidate quickly declined the position.

This vacuum of leadership left the rebels with some difficult choices. The idea of kneeling down to and seeking out the crown prince as their leader was a step no one would take. They looked at any other alternate and even had a brief campaign to entice Coraline to step up. She also refused.

Granor offered his services and was nearly skewered on the spot. His status sunk to the point he was barely tolerated in any room and the king no longer included him in his deliberations despite loud proclamations of innocence concerning Aron.

Lilith traveled frequently, between time spent in the palace and trips out to see her 'guests', publicly advising everyone she was assisting with the search. It amused her to perpetrate the ruse with impunity and added to her increasing disdain for anyone other than herself, or Damien—a man she'd never met.

Lilith paid infrequent, uncordial visits to Granor.

"Lilith, you may feel great pride in your actions, but I tell you again this will not end well for you. You may drag me down too, but that will be no buffer for you when the truth is finally known."

"You sound like a small man. I wonder I how ever saw anything worthwhile in you. Your threats don't frighten me. The risk I'm taking is worth it. I strive for a better position and I'm willing to let my deeds speak for me. I've done what no other person could do. I've taken down two of the greatest enemies to Damien's cause. He will not ignore that, in spite of what you say."

"When you're a mindless slave in his harem, we'll see if that's a better position. I'll be there to see it."

Lilith glared at him. "If you're there it will be to mop the floor."

Granor eyed her murderously. She looked back, undaunted, her hand resting on the hilt of her sword.

"You can try," she hissed.

"That day will come."

"This is not that day," she replied.

"Leave me. Enjoy your brief delusions. Doom is waiting just around the corner for both of us."

She smirked and left the room. She went directly to the stable to claim her horse and rode away briskly heading back to her 'guests'.

* * * *

Tasha watched the vast spectacle of Damien's army on the march. They'd faced the first battles of the new world war and had averted defeat. A clear victory hadn't been won on either side, but greater battles were ahead. Nations of the world were slow to realize the extreme threat Damien posed, which gave him a huge advantage in deploying troops, capturing the initiative and controlling where battles were fought.

Without weaponry of the ancient world, this war was different—Damien could smother an opponent with numbers without fear of lethal devices easily wiping them out *en masse*. Gathering followers had always been easy for Damien. The new world was proving to be easy meat. With very little sophistication in the general populace, he stoked their raw emotions with fiery rhetoric and daunting videos of past destruction. And with no competing entity for their loyalty, they followed his call with messianic fervor. Their home countries did little to evoke patriotic feelings. Damien gave them dreams of escaping lives of dominance and abuse from the prevailing authorities. What they would get in return from him he obscured. Damien's society would be no less nightmarish than what they already had, but they didn't see it.

As Damien's armies spread out across the globe, he had no trouble replacing them from the flood of converts arriving on a daily basis. The influx of conscripts was shocking to Tasha, like it was the inevitable fate of the world to bow to Damien in the end.

"There you are, Tasha," said Radigan, embracing her from behind.

She responded to him much less these days and knew he didn't fail to notice.

"I know this seems overwhelming, darling, but it will work out for us, I promise."

"You promise?" she questioned skeptically. "How can you promise anything when it comes to Damien? You have no influence over him. Daily he grows bolder and his behaviors deteriorate correspondingly. You know what I mean. You know the ending he has in mind for Sirina and me. Is that what you want, husband? I've asked you before and you've never answered me. I expect poor choices from Straga, but I expected better from you. He's barely more than an animal. If Sirina is mindless and compliant he wouldn't care, but you pursued me, Radigan. You've already made promises to me of a best life possible, of your worship and undying adoration. You said Aron wasn't the man for me. I loved Aron, but I was fixated on my bond with you and what we'd shared in the past. As I look at it now, I wonder how I could have been so blind. I knew you had flaws of character, but this? I live each day in terror of Damien taking away my mind. Surely you can see the life poor Liani lives at his hands. If she could recover her faculties, she'd be quick to end her life rather than endure further. If you truly love me, how can you stand for this?"

Radigan turned her around. She saw sadness in his eyes.

"Tasha, I do love you. I'm not unaware of your worries and I'm not saying there isn't peril for you and Sirina. No, I don't want you subjected to his mind control machine. Our defense is we must not give him a reason to punish us. Don't you think I'm galled at what he wants from my wife?"

"Are you?"

"Of course I am, but if I took foolish action to salve my ego and it led to dire consequences for both of us, how would that help us? If I was taken down, you'd be alone to face him, Tasha."

"You truly are blind, Radigan. There are obvious answers to our plight, but you can't see them because you choose to be here. You choose to follow Damien. It doesn't occur to you to take us away back to the kingdom. If this world is meant to fall to Damien, I would choose to die in its defense with my comrades and my family. My mother and father stayed here solely for me. They hate this life and hate that lying maniac, Damien. It's no better for Wu Hang. He stayed to succor Liani back to health. He has no hope because I don't think she can be changed back. When you conspired with the prince, I could rationalize you were doing your duty. When you pursued me and rubbed Aron's nose in it, I foolishly dwelled on things that really weren't important. Because you're highly skilled and well practiced in love, I let it sway me. I'll pay the price for that stupidity for the rest of my life, but when it comes to the bigger picture, the world Damien is trying to create, I can't sit idly by. I know I've lost Aron from my life, but I must do something for good and for the people. Do you understand?"

Radigan stood silently. "What would you have me do? Are you saying you no longer love me?"

"No, Radigan. That's a perfect example of what I've come to realize. You have this eternal competition going with Aron in your mind. Your greatest fear seems to be losing my affection back to him. He was never on an intimate footing with me like you, but your ego is your abiding concern. I'm your wife! You won me. I get the feeling you want me to comply with Damien's urges to mollify him and protect your standing in his hierarchy. How can you not see the outrage of such a stance? What about me, my feelings, my shame? I'm the one enduring the offense without the protection of my husband."

Radigan looked daunted.

"Did you not tell me how it burned in your belly the idea of me being with Aron? It was never truly a factor. He was shy in the areas you were bold. Now you simply concede me to that charlatan who should have died back in his own time."

"You know circumstances aren't that simple. This situation isn't the same as between Aron and me. Damien has no qualms about taking deadly action if he thinks he was wronged. He isn't like Aron, or any other living man. He can take what he wishes because there truly are none to stop him. I suspect we haven't seen all of the powers he can call forth. If he can take away your mind, who can say he can't also read our thoughts, or some other impossible thing? You may not believe me, but I do weigh our options. If we had a better choice, I would certainly consider it. Damien has troops everywhere now. We couldn't simply get on our horses and ride away. His forces question everyone, they take nothing for granted. They would stop us and send word to Damien before we could escape. We have to face reality, wife. If we're forced to make distasteful compromises, that's the nature of life now. We make the best life we can and work around Damien and in the process we survive."

Tasha's eyes smoldered with anger.

"I understand. If that's what you want for me, I have my answers. I've been there before back at the palace, remember? If enduring and coping with Damien's abuse is this 'best life' you promised me, know I will cope in every way I must. You may not like the person I will become. Say whatever you will, this is your choice."

"What are you saying?"

"I'm saying you have choices to make, and so do I. Now leave me. I need to be alone."

He started to speak, but thought better seeing her rage. He turned and left in turmoil.

Down below her balcony at ground level, the seemingly endless parade of troops shouted loud chants and martial cries. They were eager for battle. Equally provoked by her talk with her husband, Tasha watched them darkly.

Her musings were as dark as her feelings as she played out in her mind revenge against Damien. They weren't realistic plans but in her current mood, she wasn't disposed to think rationally. Briefly, she pondered going off the balcony. It would be a fall she couldn't survive and the thought of ending her life had a certain appeal.

"Oh Aron, I miss you so much," she whispered painfully.

* * * *

At that moment, Aron was in no position to help her. He was a captive again. This time he wasn't consigned to a forgotten prison cell alone deep under the palace. Competent guards, who kept him under constant watch and at bay, surrounded him.

Lilith arrived from the palace and entered the low wooden building. It appeared deserted from the outside. The structure wasn't near any travel routes so people would not happen past this remote location.

"Aron, it's always a pleasure to see you," she chirped brightly. "Your new accommodations are so much better than the prior ones, wouldn't you agree?"

He turned his head away disdainfully.

"You could at least thank us for improving your lot," she added snidely.

"Come over here. I'd be happy to show you my appreciation."

She laughed heartily. "You give me a reason to get out of bed every morning. I think your show of appreciation at this point might be too painful for me. I'll keep some distance for the time being, but I expect to be in closer proximity with you in the near future. Circumstances change and you're a smart man. You'll soon realize it serves no purpose for you to sit brooding and glowering at us. Your new life is before you. All you need to do is take the first step, my love."

"You have a strange notion of love. Perhaps this is why you're unmarried. I find your approach to the idea to be unrealistic and annoying. Do you think a man simply surrenders out of defeat and accedes to your wishes? Did that approach ever work for any men pursuing you?"

"It did not, Aron. I'm not intending to wear down your resistance. My thought is with time you'll see things much differently. Your romantic history hardly warrants mention. You're defined by your failures. I've already told you I blame those women a great deal, but it doesn't mean you have no room to improve."

"Why would you think I could ever have any romantic feelings for you? I barely know you and our dealings have been adverse. You're not what I would look for in a mate."

Affected by his statement, Lilith glared at him, but then quickly cooled her

16

ire.

"I'm not expecting too much too fast. I really do understand your feelings. I've had my share of hard knocks in my life. What I can offer you is something no other woman has. I can offer you honesty about my feelings and I will care about you like none of them did. Even with Cherine, you weren't the universe to her. She's only recently decided to explore a relationship, inventing her feelings for you as she goes. She can say all the right things, but how do you know they're true? They're self serving for her. She gains unmatched status as your consort. She has ever been about power. Seeing the truth in women has never been a 'strength' for you. Women sense they can use and manipulate you and they have. You've suffered because you never found the right woman for you."

"That woman is supposed to be you?"

"Why not? I'm pleasing to the eye, intelligent, strong willed, and I would be faithful to the death for my mate. I've never found a man worthy of me, at least until now. Are you so closed minded you can't look about you? Perhaps your romantic troubles were because you were looking in the wrong places for love. Imagine the children we would create. There'd be no limit to what they could accomplish."

Aron looked at her skeptically.

"I'm not one to hurt another person, but I must tell you your argument has failed to persuade me. That's a good thing for you. Stories told build me up beyond reality. I'm just a man, no different than any other."

She looked at him tenderly. "Aron, the love of some men is the measure of all other men combined. You don't see yourself clearly, but we do."

This struck him for reasons he couldn't grasp. He offered no sharp retort to her. She smiled like she'd scored a great victory.

"As you know me better, you'll understand, my darling."

Again, he offered no reply.

As was her habit, she walked over to him and kissed him gently. He never cooperated nor resisted her. His thoughts were on the other women in his life, Coraline, Tasha, Liani, and Cherine. This was a much different imprisonment, but in some ways very challenging. Hopelessness was the enemy, but he wasn't a man to lose his optimism. On this night he even thought about Belisa, Enna, and Biala. He smiled at the dogged loyalty of the two Uripean women—a great comfort when he was going through his frequent bad times with Tasha. They were both attractive women, but he'd never really thought of them in a romantic sense. At this point, he couldn't really comprehend why not.

* * * *

Lilith's visit to Aron was brief, as she had limited time. She continued her trek, traveling to where Cherine was kept. Cherine was in a foul mood when Lilith walked in. She was glaring at Lilith's servants as if they'd just had a confrontation. They all looked at Lilith.

"Good evenings, ladies," she chirped happily. "Cherine, I'm happy to see you again. You look fit, but your mood seems spoiled. What's happened to anger you?"

"You already know. I think part of your goal is to take away my dignity in addition to wearing me down in captivity. Do you think I'm so weak such a plan could work? Your guards offend me. I'm sure it's by your commands they do such things. I tell you again, you're destined for doom. I will not break under any of your imposed indignities. There will come a time when you must pay your price."

"There will come a time for every single living soul to pay their price. How am I different from any other? What real harm has come to you in our care? You know this time spent with us could be a great deal more unpleasant. Imagine being in the custody of this man you call 'the interrogator'. Stories of him fascinate me. I've never come across any person who makes such an impression, other than possibly Aron. What would you experience in his hands? They say he was a master at extracting information from his victims. His touch was so frightening, fierce warriors soiled themselves at the prospect of his methods. We've done nothing on such a scale. If you object to our ways, I think you're too critical. What you call indignities aren't the same as utter pain and torment. I understand 'the interrogator' resides in the camp of Damien. It's one of my hopes to meet him some day. He's a legend."

"If you seek the interrogator, you're more a fool than I thought. He's an imminently dangerous man, even with the peaceful façade he put on to dwell with us. What simmers below the surface isn't something you can harness and control. Would you take an ice cat into your home to make it a pet? It would slay you in an instant. You're only food to it. Wu Hang is a unique person and has a unique view of the rest of us."

Lilith laughed. "You have your perspective on the situation and so do I. My plans and my goals remain the same."

She smirked and then turned and went over to pick up a piece of wood hewn in the shape of a sword. She came back and handed it, hilt first, to Cherine.

"This will be an interesting way for us to pass the time. We will have wooden swords also."

"Why would I do that?"

"You have nothing else to do and this will keep you in fighting shape."

18

"I will never be your trainer. If you hope to learn from me, you're wasting our time."

A large woman gave a shout and struck Cherine from behind with her wood sword. Cherine pivoted in an instant and countered the stroke with a blinding swipe. Only the size and strength of the powerful woman allowed her to keep the sword from being knocked out of her hand.

"You see, Cherine. You have your own pride too. You can't abide defeat and that's what fascinates those women of us who aspire to emulate your prowess."

"I don't care, Lilith."

"Ah, but you do. If you fight us and prevail, we'll lessen your indignities."

"If I don't...?"

"Your path wouldn't be pleasant if you lose your fights, or if you simply refrain from defending yourself. There are far worse indignities available to us if need be. Would you like your beautiful hair shaved off your head? I have a creative mind about consequences. There are far more odious prospects waiting for you. Test me if you wish, but you can't win and you'd quickly find out about real indignities."

Cherine eyed her darkly, realizing she was in a no win situation. Raising her wooden weapon, they closed in to attack her from all sides. She didn't know what to expect from them in their fighting skills.

Battling with wooden weapons removed the element of mortal peril so as much as they desired it, these were not real fights. Lilith and her maidens were very determined to impress the captive warrior. Cherine sparred defensively, doing her best not to betray her best moves and immense talent. Keeping them at bay, she assessed the level of their development. They were competent and in some cases such as Lilith, even good. While being careful about the moves she used, she employed every opportunity to land body blows if they grew too risky using her elbows and fists.

Some of the women fell to the floor gasping for breath. Lilith watched the proceedings very closely, attacked sparingly and never gave Cherine a chance to punish her as she did her followers.

Suddenly Lilith simply stopped and her maidens backed off.

"Excellent, Cherine, this was a fine start for all of us. I won't ask for your opinion of us as fighters. We all know you're the superior at this point and what you would say would be meant to belittle us. I'm pleased with our first match against you. Though you didn't intend it, I learned a great deal from you. We'll continue to learn, though you would not choose it for us. Does it not feel good to exercise your muscles? We're happy you're here among us."

"Whenever you want to use real swords, I'm available, Lilith."

They all laughed, except Cherine.

"There may come a day we can cross swords. We have much work left to get to that day."

"Do you truly believe what you're doing will impress Damien? You have a fantasy about many things. I think this one might be the most absurd. You're thinking only about you, your own feelings, and your actions. You're not considering who you're dealing with. You sanitized Damien to coincide with your aspirations. He's not a worthy object for your adoration. He's just a man as flawed as any other and probably more so. He has no better opinion of women. He uses them and discards them as easily as an old shirt. Honestly, I don't waste my time pondering your fate. I'm just telling you the truth because what you do affects me. I have stood before Damien and I have no wish to repeat the experience."

Lilith eyed her thoughtfully, and then Cherine continued. "You should think about what you plan to do in the future while you still can. You choose for more than just yourself. They'll also pay the price of your mistakes. That's part of the price of leadership."

Her maidens all looked at Lilith who got a look of concern for a moment.

"Thank you for your opinion. I know what I'm doing. We can agree to disagree."

Cherine shrugged her shoulders. "It's your funeral."

Lilith turned and went back up the stairs. She decided to dine with the male guards both to ponder Cherine's words and to be apart from her maidens' doubts. Cherine shook her confidence. The more she thought about it, the angrier she got.

Lilith went back down the stairs later in a foul mood glaring at Cherine who smiled smugly.

"Hello, Lilith."

"You've managed to annoy me, Cherine. It's earned you a long and difficult night tonight. Ladies, we've discussed what to do to see to her contentment and rest. I suspect you'll not be refreshed in the morning. You gave me your unsolicited opinion. Now I'm giving you your reward for your impertinence. Perhaps you'll think better of trying to corrupt our resolve in the future. As I said, we have all the time in the world. You can craft your life among us to be as easy or as challenging as you wish. By the way, we'll grant you no respite tomorrow. You're required to fight at the highest level, still. If you falter, you'll face the consequences."

Cherine's eyes narrowed with ire. She had a good idea what to expect from her captors.

It was a long night as Lilith's followers constantly interrupted Cherine's sleep. They were able to rotate guards to get their sleep. Cherine awoke in the morning tired, cranky, sore and bleary eyed. The only concession Lilith allowed her was drinking plenty of strong coffee.

When the fights began Cherine was highly motivated. Even with a wooden sword, she went after the tormenters with a vengeance. She approached it like a real battle and punched, kicked, knocked down as many maidens as possible, but there were just too many. Swarming, they tried to overwhelm her. She fought off each attempt, but fatigue started to take a toll.

Lilith closed on her, fighting determinedly. Cherine fought Lilith and the circle of maidens surrounding her with strength waning. She decided to try a ploy, dropping her arms as if she was totally spent. Lilith smiled in triumph and tried to take a final swipe against a supposedly defenseless Cherine. She stepped close and Cherine reared up and blasted her with a fist to the face knocking her to the floor. The maidens roared in rage and jumped Cherine, beating her down to the floor.

"Stop!" shouted Lilith, her mouth, and nose bloodied. She sat up and looked at Cherine.

"That was remarkable, Cherine. You well deserve the stories told about you. I'm awed by what you could do under these trying circumstances. The fighting is done for today. You've paid your price for your error yesterday. You may bathe, eat, and then go to rest early to recover your strength. You have all of our respect. You may not like our methods and some of the severe things you force us to do to you, but you must admit my maidens and I have improved under your tutelage."

Cherine glowered. Maidens pulled her to her feet, they led her away.

"Allow me to treat your injuries, Lilith," said one of her maidens.

"I'm fine," she replied tersely as she went to cleanse herself.

"This was a fine lesson today."

Cherine eyed the guard darkly. "I'll have more fine lessons for you if you enjoy pain so much."

"Yes, ma'am," said the woman.

Cherine was allowed an entire night without stress or interruption.

* * * *

Coraline returned to the library, unwilling to admit defeat trying to salvage Galean from his self-imposed torment.

Galean was sitting in a stupor, which had come to be his usual state. Coraline walked into his small room and began to clean and tidy up the mess. Galean sat oblivious. She took her time, giving him a moment to adjust to her presence. When she'd finished her task she turned to see him looking at her.

"Greetings, master librarian, are you feeling well today?"

"I feel the same every day. I'm not more or less well. I just vary my state of alertness as much as I can."

"That's very courageous of you," she commented derisively.

He smiled ruefully. "Have you come to school me in my behavior?"

"You don't need to be schooled by anyone, Galean. You're no idiot. Your actions are unbecoming of you, Aron, Cherine, and anybody else I can think of. I'm tired of your childish petulance. Do you imagine you're the only one in distress with the adverse turn in our fortunes? Does sticking your head in the sand protect you in some shrewd way we simple minds can't perceive?"

Galean chuckled, as he saw the wrath in her eyes accompanying the terseness in her voice.

"I'm glad you find this so amusing, Galean. If your goal is to achieve the life of a hermit, shunned by others, you're well on your way. I certainly have had enough of coming down here to see your sloth and smell your stench."

He chuckled again.

"Oh Coraline, your majesty, what a delight it is for me to hear your constructive criticisms. You have no grasp of the root of my distress. Losing Aron is so much more than you realize. I maintained hope against all odds with the appearance of Damien because Aron, alone, could give us a path to survival where defeat seems inevitable. Do you see any other alternative? We can't reason out some savvy defense, gather our courage to miraculously prevail, or any other result you could hope for without Aron. Something in him finds a way to defeat Damien. He can't be replaced. If he's truly gone from this world, our doom is sealed, and I will not live in Damien's hell."

His sobering pronouncement chilled Coraline.

"I don't believe Aron has been killed," she replied softly.

"We all have that wish, your majesty. There's been no word since they were taken. Whoever perpetrated this crime didn't do so for ransom. The only other motive would be to aid Damien's cause. He could well be in Damien's hands now for all we know. I'll guarantee nothing good can come from that. Damien would either kill him immediately, or damage him with machines so he's no longer Aron. You never saw what was done to poor Liani."

"You're hopelessness is taxing, Galean and drags us all down? We all know what you're saying and share the same concerns, but should we all get drunk? Should we lay about every day in our smell?"

Galean smiled. "I can't imagine you ever having a hair out of place, your majesty. An unwashed Coraline could never happen."

"I could wish that an unwashed Galean will never happen again."

"Are you trying to shame me into following your wishes?"

"Of course I am. The question is why should I need to do it?"

"Cleaning my body won't solve any of our problems, Coraline."

"It will solve one for me, Galean. What do you want, an incentive?"

"What did you have in mind?"

"Cleanse yourself and you'll find out."

"Clever," he replied, "a nebulous offer where you leave me to fill in the blank. As if I couldn't discern this, but at this point I have nothing to lose. The probability is you're offering nothing at all, but I'll take the chance to give you your moment. Excuse me while I go to bathe."

"My nose thanks you, Galean."

He muttered a response as he walked away, but she couldn't make it out.

When he came out later, he looked like himself again, but Coraline saw the same torment in his eyes.

"Are you willing to consider interim leadership until Aron is recovered?"

"No," he answered flatly. "I won't do it."

"There are no others. Nobody wants the prince."

"I realize that. I'm still not interested. You refused the job too."

"I'm a woman and I have no training or experience. That's simple enough to deduce."

"Then you must live with compromise. I wasn't the author of the rebellion and I'm not the successor either. Perhaps you think I have an answer to our troubles I choose to withhold from you. I don't and I suspect there is no answer to have by anyone. If your anticipation is that I'll suddenly change my mood to meet your needs, you're not being realistic. I'm not one to foster a façade of optimism when there is no reason."

"If we're fated for doom, so be it," she replied. "I realize we're not always at our best, but Galean, I must say you disappoint me. Aron was faced with failure and strife, yet he never gave up the fight. Why do you allow this in yourself? Would it not be better to go down fighting?"

"Those are brave words, Coraline, coming from a woman who's been coddled and pampered all of her life. You've always been the darling. What hardship have you ever faced? Do you suppose the infidelity of your husband gives you insight into the sorry lives of the citizens of the kingdom? What of the wretches who follow Damien. They'll soon come to understand what they've decided to support. Of course it will be too late for them then. You made a poor choice coming down to see me for I'm no longer of a mind to sugar coat the truth. If you ask me a question, you'd better be ready for the answer."

"Galean, do you presume I'm daunted by your foul moods and irascible spirit? I'm not fragile. I was raised as the daughter of a villager. Did you forget that fact? I'm here because there's a need for you even in a doomed kingdom. If you continue this attitude and this waste of your life, you'll be seeing plenty of me. I'll come down here every day if I must until you resume your duties in defense of the realm. Is that plain enough for you?"

Galean laughed. "Your words are very plain, madam. I understand you perfectly."

"Can I assume you'll discard this childishness and act again like a man?"

He smiled slyly.

"I can enlist Brock, Trent, and the others to assist me, if you like. They have short tempers these days."

"That won't be necessary. I prefer they continue their search for Aron and Cherine."

"Good, then we have an agreement, Galean."

He shrugged.

"What will you do now? Should I send for your staff so you can resume your researches? Perhaps there is no answer, but I prefer to make the search nonetheless."

"As you wish, Coraline..."

"Then I'll leave you now as I have other matters to see about. I'll speak to your clerk as I leave. Your people will be here shortly. You may wish to organize your thoughts so you have something useful to say."

Galean laughed again and bowed. "Yes, your majesty."

Chapter Three
~ Skirmishes ~

While the kingdom's masses searched for Aron and Cherine their leadership remained deadlocked. The prince made what he thought were prudent moves in deploying forces closer to the wilds, but divergent opinions quashed any unified plan to marshal all of the forces. The Arreck stayed in their mountains and the Uripeans in their swamp. The frontier villages barely tolerated royal forces sent to protect them. Old memories didn't die out quickly of prior royal abuses.

Meanwhile, Damien's fast growing army moved against the nations of the world, singularly playing on their animosity toward each other. Devouring the enemy one piece at a time proved to be a shrewd choice. As a nation fell, Damien absorbed the populace into his 'one world' message and incorporated their military into his structure. He was also wise enough to pick the smaller nations for invasion first.

* * * *

Living in Damien's evolving world, Tasha felt completely hopeless about her future, managing to avoid Damien only because he was completely absorbed in his vast worldwide political undertaking. Her only confidant, Sirina, was unable to get free of Straga to spend time with Tasha leaving her with no outlet for her dire emotions and no one to give her reassurance in her distress.

Tasha's marriage was at a point of stress, as Radigan couldn't resolve the problem of Damien potentially taking away her mind. Her refusing to be 'compliant' for Damien threatened Radigan as well as her but his spineless rationalizations failed to persuade Tasha to change her course in spite of the risk.

She was miserable. Sitting in her room brooding one afternoon, she heard a

25

knock. Since Radigan wouldn't be home this soon, she was curious. Opening the door she was surprised to see Liani.

"Hello, Liani, what is it?"

"Greetings, Tasha," she replied mechanically with no inflection. The old Liani seemed missing altogether. "My husband requests you join us for dinner this evening. He regrets he's been unable to allocate time to you and fears you may feel slighted, that you've ebbed in his esteem. That could never be the case."

"My husband is away. I'll speak to him when he returns and extend your kind invitation."

"This invitation is for you, Tasha. Your husband is away overnight on an important mission. Damien regretted his duty required this. He didn't want you to suffer being alone while he's gone."

A cold chill gripped Tasha as she realized time had run out for her avoiding the inevitable.

"When should I tell my husband you'll join us this evening?"

"I, eh...I'll come at the usual dinner hour."

"My husband advises you to wear this new dress, his gift to you."

Liani handed Tasha a package containing the flimsy garb. Tasha bristled, but took the parcel.

"We'll look forward to a pleasant evening." Liani turned abruptly and left Tasha to stand fuming in frustration.

Tasha returned to the bedroom to ponder her options but there were none. The thought of jumping off the balcony crossed her mind again, but dying that way didn't sit well with her in spite of her feelings.

"What's the problem," she muttered tersely. "You've been through this before. It means nothing."

Coolly considering the prospect, she concluded this was going to happen regardless of her helpless feelings. Moving forward with what seemed she couldn't avoid, she spoke her fears, "You must not provoke him to take away your mind. You can do this, Tasha."

Her emotions were astir, again. Dormant distressed feelings awoke about her time in the palace at the mercy of the prince.

"Damn him," she growled, on the verge of being a victim again.

Waiting until the last possible moment to put on the new dress, she looked in the mirror and saw too much of her body exposed. The new dress clearly was a message from Damien. She walked resignedly to Damien's quarters to attend the evening meal. When she approached, the guards opened the door for her. Damien was smiling when she entered. Liani was sitting at his side with a neutral facial expression.

"Oh my, Tasha, you look so lovely. Thank you for coming this evening."

She nearly replied with harsh words, but managed to keep her mouth shut. Glaring a moment, she plastered a phony smile on her face.

"Thank you for the invitation," she answered softly, averting her eyes from his frank stare.

"Please sit down with us. You've been such a good friend to my wife over the years and shared so many experiences. How could we not invite you to spend time with us?"

Tasha looked at Liani who had her usual expression of a placid thoughtless ornament for Damien—from his perspective, the perfect woman.

"Hello, Liani."

She looked at Tasha and smiled. "Hello, Tasha, you look fetching this evening."

"You look very nice also, Liani."

Tasha sat down beside Liani instead of Damien who wore a brief annoyed response before resuming his confident smile.

"How goes your war, Damien?"

"We're making good progress on every front."

"Casualties...?"

"Yes, people die in war, very regrettable, but an unavoidable consequence. We must fix our eyes on the end prize which requires sacrifice."

Tasha eyed him coolly.

"You think me a monster, Tasha, but once we achieve the final victory you'll understand. Our new world will be a marvel, a paradise. There will finally be equality for all."

"I suspect some will be more equal than others," she retorted.

Damien chuckled. "Oh Tasha, you're such a delight. You inspire a man with your great beauty, but your mind is as great a lure. A man in my position seldom gets the pleasure of this exchange of ideas. I so much looked forward to this evening to share personal time with you."

"Liani had such a fine mind, Damien. What a loss for all of us that you took it away. If you truly valued female thinking, you should see what a great crime that was?"

She immediately regretted her words and looked at Damien to gauge if she was in peril.

"Not every decision I must make can be seen as a boon to each individual. Sometimes the needs of the whole outweigh the needs of the individual. You fear this will happen to you. I understand, Tasha. It was courageous on your part to bring it up. I can't explain every detail to you as I travel my difficult path. Yes, I wish Liani was like you. She would be a great joy and yes, she had a fine mind. There may come a time when we can make some changes about that."

"Does that mean Liani can be recovered?"

Damien smiled like a Cheshire cat.

"We feared this state is permanent," said Tasha, pushing the issue. "Can you not tell me the truth?"

"Liani is in a condition of being a different person, a new entity. Her condition can be adjusted, that's true."

"Does that mean she could return to normal?"

"Normal," said Damien with a laugh. "I guess we'd need to define normal. Life is a continuing state of flux. Change is a part of living. You're not the same person you were last year or the year before."

"Damien, I have my faculties, Liani does not. I understand why you like her current incarnation, but taking away our choices, is this the new world we're supposed to relish? Is that a state you'd wish to be living in?"

Again, she knew she was playing a dangerous game as anger crossed his face.

"There's a great deal you don't know, Tasha. As I said, if I tried to explain everything, I would need to educate you for months in knowledge from the past and you would need to have had experiences then. To an extent, I must ask you to trust me. My abiding desire is a fulfilling life for all, no matter their status."

Tasha eyed him skeptically. She thought better of what she really wanted to say.

He raised his eyebrows. "Was there something further you wished to say about this, Tasha?"

"No, Damien. I'm no fool. You have power over me. You're not interested in evaluating your actions. You have self serving goals, just like the prince."

"You equate me to the prince?" he snapped.

Tasha shrugged. "What does it matter? We both know why I'm here tonight."

"Is that so," he huffed. "Do you think I must force a woman to do what she will? What a woman does around me is her choice. I'm a married man. You may not understand the situation of Liani's state, but my marriage vows are true."

Tasha looked at him in shock at his lie. The unending parade of young women into his suite was common knowledge.

"Speak, Tasha," he growled. "You seem to have something you wish to say."

"No, Damien, I don't have anything to say to you."

"If you feel you've been coerced here this evening on a pretext, you're wrong. Feel free to return to your quarters if you think I have ulterior motives. My invitation was honest and without guile, but you've managed to sully an enjoyable dinner with seamy implications."

"Then I'll bid you good evening," said Tasha rapidly standing up. "Good night, Liani. Enjoy your meal."

She quickly left the room and hurried back to her quarters. She worried Damien's guards would be close behind her, but that didn't happen and she was mercifully left in peace that night.

When Radigan returned the following day from his 'mission' he was uncharacteristically quiet with Tasha. Finally she spoke.

"Yes, husband, I feared I'd be subjected to Damien's lusts, but it didn't happen. We spoke for a time and I think it didn't sit well with him. He gave me leave to return home early and unscathed."

"Tasha, did you create a new problem for us?"

Tasha shook her head. "This is so telling, Radigan. You supposedly worried I'd been used because it would bruise your male ego for another man to take what you consider is yours, yet when that sorry fate is averted, you worry more about ramifications from Damien, because he didn't have his way with me. Incredible, husband how can this not scream at you as it screams at me!"

"Tasha, you're distorting my thoughts. I'm happy he didn't touch you in that way, but all of my original concerns are there. Damien is a major factor in our lives in so many ways. If his fixation on you gains us a special place, what's the harm of it?"

"I can easily return to his quarters, Radigan. I can remove your fears with my compliance. Would that put your mind at ease?"

"Tasha, don't be argumentative. I love you unconditionally, but I must always be aware of our tenuous status in Damien's presence. You're too quick to dismiss his revenge. Yes, I worry about him taking action against both of us. No husband wants his wife to be with another man. Why do you throw such things at me when you know it isn't true?"

"Let me say something before I forget it. In my conversation with Damien, we spoke about Liani. I asked if her condition is permanent and he said her condition can be adjusted. That says to me it's possible to recover our friend."

"That's good news, wife. Did he mention how that could be done?"

"Of course not, Radigan, now it's you being argumentative."

"I'm not. That's a good piece of information to know, but it's only partial knowledge. Without knowing the rest of it, it's useless to us at this point."

"It's not useless to me and to the others who love Liani. I don't want to talk to you right now. I'm going for a walk."

She walked determinedly into the settlement with a destination in mind. She

Dennis K. Hausker

searched for a while before she saw him towering over everyone around him.

"Wu Hang," she said as she stopped before him.

"Tasha."

"I have news for you. I've just found out Liani's state is not permanent. Damien told me her condition can be changed. I know nothing more than that at this point, but I thought you should know."

Wu Hang's total countenance changed and he eyed Damien's compound grimly.

"You can't do something rash, Wu Hang. It may be that only Damien can make those changes. We don't know enough at this point."

"You forget that I'm a man who has particular skills. I can help Damien to desire to change Liani."

"Please, Wu Hang. There are few enough of us here. We need you. Please promise me you'll continue to bide your time. I'll continue to seek out the information we need. There may be a time in the future when we can rescue Liani and escape from this madhouse."

"You have my word, but know that my patience has limits. If I feel there is a point where you can go no further, I will take action. No man is immune from me. I regretted nearly all that I've done in my work, but in his case I have no qualms. He is an evil man who has earned his doom."

"I understand, but you must realize too that Sirina and I, my parents, Liani, and I suppose even my husband Radigan are a tiny enclave precariously floating in this sea of the insane followers of Damien. We live with the knowledge we can be lost at any moment. You're our greatest deterrent. If there is any chance to escape here, it's with you."

Wu Hang turned his face directly at her. He was still a chilling sight, like the angel of death.

"I acknowledge your words, Tasha. Be careful in what you do, but also be swift. I can't abide the current state of things. Also, regarding your husband, I don't see him in a positive light. I have always thought of him as an adversary and he's never done anything to prove otherwise to my satisfaction. Be especially careful with what you say to him. He puts you at great risk."

She steeled her courage and embraced him. He was surprised by the gesture and for a moment his facial features softened. He was only slightly less frightening though.

He patted her benignly before she returned to her rooms. She made one further detour to talk to Sirina briefly on the way.

* * * *

Meanwhile, Brock rode steadily at the head of the patrol as they continued

30

their broad sweep across the countryside. In particular, he was looking for isolated places where Aron and Cherine might be held, or buried. He was systematic and thorough, just as they'd been in searching the entire capital city of Nephora. With as much time as had passed it was easy to feel discouragement. He kept a brave face in front of the men, but he'd heard them grumble frequently about the waste of time chasing corpses. Even his comrades of the Black Fist were stoic about the search.

They came upon tracks going off toward a heavy stand of trees near a rock outcropping. Just as Brock was about to follow the tracks a shout came from behind. A rider was galloping toward them.

Brock turned to wait.

"Lord Brock, I have word recalling you to the city. There's word from the frontier."

"What word?"

"I don't know the details, but the enemy has entered the kingdom. The war has begun."

Brock took a glance back along the path of the suspicious tracks before leading his patrol away unaware that not far away was their prey.

* * * *

It happened that Lilith was there at the captivity site talking to Aron.

Her sentries hurried back to tell her about the near miss.

"Our time here has expired, men. Prepare the prisoner to move immediately and meet me at the designated point. I'll go to our other site to prepare them also to move away."

Lilith returned to Nephora and went to see the prince. Galean was there along with the others of importance in the realm.

"Is it true Damien is coming?" she asked.

"We don't know the extent of his foray, but there have been probes and some skirmishes in the borderlands near the wilds," Agar answered.

Granor stared directly at Lilith.

"I feel great urgency about this," she said. "I'm going to mount a force to travel to that region. If the captors plan to take Aron and Cherine to Damien, I want to be there to intercede on their behalf. At the very least, we can lend our strength to the defense of the kingdom."

Agar looked at Galean.

"I see no reason to deny the plan, Galean. What do you say?"

"I'm not a military tactician, Agar. I leave strategic decisions to you and your generals."

"You have my permission, Lilith. We wish you Godspeed and good hunting."

"Thank you, sire."

Lilith smiled at Granor as she left. He glowered back.

Lilith went straight to pack her things and leave the palace with the idea to join Damien's army. She gathered all of her remaining corps of maidens who'd been training under the royal tutors. She also assembled those soldiers exclusively loyal to her and they all rode out of the palace grounds. She'd been briefly tempted to capture Coraline and drag her along with them, but that would've been too difficult and would've put their escape in jeopardy.

Lilith felt giddy again. Each time she managed to perpetuate stages of her plans without negative consequence she grew more confident. Outwitting the prevailing authorities of the kingdom salved her ego.

Lilith's assemblage was decently sized and that men of the kingdom would choose to follow a woman, as their leader was a surprise. Part of her credibility in their minds was her ongoing success with holding Aron and Cherine and also thumbing her nose at Granor, who. He seemed impotent.

Riding away she felt on the verge of great destiny as the pivotal piece of the equation. In spite of what she'd been told about Damien, her imagination painted herself as highly regarded and much esteemed in a welcoming meeting with him. He couldn't help but be awed by what she'd accomplished. Smiling in pride, she anticipated the great moment of triumph where a woman ascended to a position of great leadership, second only to Damien and becoming a factor across the entire world.

Riding at a steady pace, they left the kingdom behind them.

It happened that she passed Brock's patrol returning to the palace.

"Lilith," he said pulling up beside her. "I understood we're all recalled to the palace. I heard Damien has sent forces across the border and the war has begun."

"This is true, Brock."

"Why are you riding away?"

"I advised the prince I'm concerned the kidnappers plan to deliver Aron and Cherine to Damien, so we're going on a fast moving mission to stop them before it happens."

"You have far too few troops for such a mission. You can only spread out so much and if you found the criminals, I doubt you could overcome them. If you'll delay briefly, I can gather sufficient force to man the operation properly."

"I don't want to give them the advantage of time on the move while we sit idly by, do you see? You can certainly follow us and perhaps you can give assistance if we corner them."

Brock eyed her suspiciously and she worried there might be a fight.

"I'll make haste," said Brock finally.

Lilith nodded and they rode off. She felt his eyes on her and had to fight to keep from looking back.

* * * *

Brock rode rapidly to the palace at Nephora and went straight to the prince's chambers.

"Agar, did you send Lilith out on a mission to the frontier? We saw her and I didn't get a good feel about it."

"What do you mean?" asked Coraline.

"She acted strangely. I didn't get a sense of truth from her. Is Granor still here?"

"Yes, he is."

Brock scowled. "I may be wrong doubting her, but we've uncovered nothing after all these months of searching. I wonder if it was an inside job. Did Granor send Lilith and her forces on his behalf to perpetrate this crime? I want to go after Lilith, in force."

"What could she possibly hope to gain?" asked Agar. "If she wanted treasure, why haven't we heard any demands?"

"Money would have done nothing for her. Where could she have gone if we knew it was she who was responsible? She would be hunted down in short order."

"She became a close friend to me and to the queen. We never got a sense of anything dangerous," Coraline mentioned.

"That doesn't mean there wasn't anything dangerous," Brock replied. "You're closely warded by Marin. She probably never got an opportunity to work ill against you. Brock glanced at Marin who was watching from close by. He smiled slightly, as if Brock had paid him the highest of compliments.

Agar looked at Marin. "You've fulfilled my charge admirably. I'm going to raise your status in the kingdom so that all might know I reward those who do their duties."

"That isn't necessary, Sire. I'm content to be a simple man of little renown."

Brock chuckled. "You're not unknown, Marin. We've often talked of how you could fit nicely into the Black Fist, or the masters."

"Thank you for the kind words. I'm happy to continue my duties to safeguard Princess Coraline."

She looked at him appreciatively, but quickly turned her face to smile at Agar. "Your servant has given me a sense of safety in this dangerous world. Thank you, husband..."

Agar nodded to her and then took her in his arms. Brock watched the look on Marin's face. It was easy to see the turmoil he felt about loving another man's wife. Brock also saw Coraline in the embrace of her husband look back at Marin with more than simple gratitude in her eyes.

Similar to Tasha, the little darling from his village had grown into a woman coveted by all. What those women truly felt about the universal adoration, he could only imagine.

"With your permission, I'll go to speak to Trent. I suspect he'll refuse to be left behind in this pursuit."

"Granted," said Agar.

"You realize the entire Black Fist and the masters will demand to go also, Agar."

"I understand. Go with my blessing."

"If Lilith is responsible for all of this and we catch her, I can't guarantee her return unscathed. There's a great deal of rage about this matter. Being on the verge of a great war, to do this is inexcusable. She's taken away our great symbols of courage and compromised our leadership."

Agar looked momentarily upset, as if Brock was belittling him, but quickly plastered a smile on his face.

"I only require you return her alive. If she must face retribution along the way for her misdeeds, that's understandable."

Brock bowed to the royalty.

"Be careful, Brock," said Coraline.

"I will, my lady."

"Brock, I caution you about one thing," Coraline added. "Your suspicions may prove to be unfounded. If Lilith isn't responsible for this, you mustn't wrongly punish her with misguided prosecution. She may be a loyal subject of the crown doing exactly what she said."

"I'll give her all the rope she needs to hang herself," Brock replied. Marin laughed along with the prince. Coraline eyed him reproachfully but said,

"Go and find them, Brock."

He left to implement his plans and went to the library first to advise Galean.

"I'm tempted to go with you, Brock. Sitting here gives me no peace or contentment any longer. My former studies seem now like a waste of time. There's nothing more to be gleaned from the ancient texts. With so many of our friends imperiled, I find mouthing platitudes to appease the royals useless."

"I would suggest you stay here, Galean. We still need you and I anticipate a battle on this mission. You're not young and not a soldier. Out there in the field isn't the best place for you."

"It's true I'm no warrior, but there could be other uses for a scholar on this venture. You may encounter problems which I'm uniquely able to resolve."

"I suspect your staff would like to remain here in safety and also have you remaining here with them. The field is no place for scholarship."

"They're entitled to their opinions and I'm entitled to mine. Having a brain along for your trek isn't a bad thing."

"If you're determined to go, we'll leave very shortly. We won't be able to coddle you along the way."

Galean glowered. Brock chuckled. "Pack light."

"I'll take care of myself, Brock."

"So be it."

Slyly, Galean made a point to tell no one else he was going. They only found out when they saw him riding away in Brock's force—by then too late to stop him, which was his intention.

Agar stood shaking his head at his wife's side watching Brock's precision troop riding away at the gallop, the fate of the realm in their hands.

"What a different world we have now," he commented. "My word and my authority were absolute not so long ago. Now I'm routinely ignored and challenged. Do you think Lilith is behind this crime? I had Granor questioned and it appears this may not be his doing. We didn't know to ask him about Lilith at that time."

"I find it as distressing as you, husband. She duped me and the queen. I can't imagine what she hopes to gain. Whatever her goal, she's doomed to fail. It may be her life issues were greater than she could cope with and this is how it affected her."

"She's in for a grim ending, even with her being a woman, if it's proven she's responsible, she'll suffer the same consequences as a man."

"I understand, Agar. I'm just saying it's a shame to have come to this. She was a woman who had great potential."

"Granor had nefarious plans and you can see where he is now, one of the least trusted and most despised men in the realm. Lilith should have learned from his example."

Coraline shrugged her shoulders. "True, she should have paid attention to his sorry fate. She may be trying to escape to join Damien."

"If that's true, she didn't factor in the ferocity of Brock and his elite forces. They'll drive themselves to exhaustion to catch her. She will be doomed at that point and might not make it back to the palace for a trial for her crimes. Frontier justice could be enacted on the spot."

"She took an extreme risk with her strategy. I'm sure she knew the price of failure, but what she's not is experienced in such momentous decisions. I think she may have fallen victim to her own optimism thinking about the best possible result for her and thinking too little about the worse that could happen."

He furrowed his brow. "Aron once told me he plans for the worst possible outcome so that what actually happens will probably be better than what he anticipated. It's a good outlook and the ultimate in preparedness. Nothing happens which is worse than you planned for with that strategy."

He looked in his wife's eyes before he continued.

"I must admit, grudgingly, I have great respect for Aron and I've had that respect for a very long time. Even when I was my old self and he endlessly defied me, I think internally I was rooting for him, as silly as that sounds."

Coraline smiled. "That's one of the reasons I stayed with you. If you had truly been an incorrigible cad with no goodness within you, I would have found a way to sever our relationship."

Agar looked surprised at her statement. "I never realized that. I've been so self-absorbed for so long, I never thought to see things through the eyes of others. It's distressing to think of you leaving me. Honestly Coraline, I look back and wonder how I could have been consumed with those foolish meaningless intimate encounters with strange women. They weren't really satisfying. I think there was a sense of conquest as a lure and of course the women were beautiful, but it wasn't worth it. I would reverse everything if it were possible."

"Hindsight is always best, is it not? I survived and as I've told you, I made some mistakes too in that area. I say we forget the past. The future will be challenge enough."

* * * *

Meanwhile, Lilith gathered her prisoners and sent two separate groups forward heading toward the wilds. She opted to ride in the group with Cherine who continued to fascinate her.

Cherine watched constantly, looking for any chance to free herself, but Lilith rode directly beside her each day. At night she placed her bedding close to Cherine and they were always surrounded by her vigilant maidens.

"Cherine, can you not conceive of us being close friends?" asked Lilith during their ride one day. "If circumstances were different, you would have been a person I sought out for training and for inspiration. You are all of those things for me now, but under adverse circumstances. Can you see no interesting qualities in me?"

"Do you need validation so badly, Lilith?"

Lilith laughed.

"It's easy for you to say humbling things to us. You've achieved what we can only dream of. Yes, we're very jealous of you, but this is your life now.

Can you not seek to find peace and accept what you can't change? I want to be on a much better footing with you. Perhaps friendship isn't beyond the realm of possibility."

"You do this to me and ask for my friendship?" Cherine retorted sharply. "Your idea of friendship varies a great deal from mine. There's nothing I can do for you or for the issues that drive you. The path I took was painful and a lifelong struggle. That isn't something you and your ilk can simply put on like a cloak. If you imagine I'll wear down and eventually come to embrace you and your plans, you're mistaken. If you think I'll forget Aron you're badly mistaken."

Her words struck Lilith who had her own ideas for Aron. "Aron doesn't seem to have that same loyalty for you, Cherine. I've sensed he finds me alluring though I haven't explored such an option, at least not yet. Do you think you're prowess as a lover supersedes my own? I've had ample training and experience with what pleases a man. If it was my desire, I could easily woo him away from you. It's the one area where you're deficient and vulnerable. You're a near invincible warrior, but for a man, you make yourself weak."

Cherine shook her head dismissively. "You live in your delusions, Lilith. It's your weakness and will be your undoing. It's no different with Aron than what I told you about Damien. They're not puppets bending to your will. If you choose to continue following your dreams instead of facing reality, you'll drag us all down. Aron would never choose you for a mate no matter how great your skills as a lover. He seeks the truth of a woman, what's in her soul, and her heart. He could have had countless beautiful women. They fall all over him. You're a fool."

"With you to counsel me, I'll never need to fear my pride."

"You're welcome. I'm happy to teach you about reality if you're still capable of rational thought. If you're too comfortable living in your dreams there is nothing anyone could do to save you."

Chapter Four
~ Pursuit ~

Brock's forces rode swiftly with an air of urgency to the mission. The idea Aron and Cherine were in imminent danger was pervasive. Now focused on Lilith as the perpetrator, they followed her trail doggedly. Usually, Lilith didn't stop at villages and towns along the way, nonetheless they were spotted by villagers, and travelers in the area—much like a trail of bread crumbs for skilled hunters to follow.

Brock had no idea how far behind Lilith's group they actually were. He watched Galean closely for signs he couldn't maintain the grueling pace. The old man had a grim look on his face, but showed no sign of faltering.

The farther Brock rode away from the palace and toward the wilds, the more stories they heard about skirmishes.

They stopped sparingly only for brief meals.

On a rare occasion for the fast moving allies, a local fleeing peasant family joined them for the meal. They were poor, hungry, and in retreat.

"We left our farm some time ago," the father explained. "There were frightening stories about the invaders. I didn't want to take any chances alone on the frontier with a wife and little ones. It's been difficult with too few supplies and constantly moving, but I feared being caught there would be worse. The day we left our home to escape, a force of raiders marched across our land headed toward our little village. Sounds of fighting erupted soon afterward. I'd heard they're merciless with captives, worse than what dwelled in the wilds before them. The fighting ended quickly. We raced off and had three harrowing days eluding their patrols. They were dressed in all black uniforms. I think there was some emblem on their chests. I wasn't close enough to tell what it might be."

"It's remarkable you got away on foot," said Trent.

38

Savior

"I think I was merely lucky. There were many trying to flee, too many for them to catch us all. The misfortune of those other poor folk led to my being able to escape. I'm happy for my family, but I feel guilty I couldn't help our friends and neighbors. There are many other families in our position. We're going toward the kingdom because it couldn't be worse than what is behind us."

"It was beyond anything you could do. If you'd tried to intervene it would've led to your capture, or worse," Galean added. "Be thankful you have your family here safe."

"I am, and I'm so grateful you shared your food with us. We have nothing left to eat."

"We'll give you provisions," Brock advised. "Continue toward the kingdom. You'll find royal patrols that will safe guard you. They're not the hazard to the people they once were."

"All of my life we've feared and avoided the royal host. Now they're our protectors? What an amazing change in circumstances."

"In these strange times, we all need to get past the problems of the past to work together," Galean explained. "None of us could have anticipated these turns of events."

Brock gave them two horses so each parent could ride and take a child with them to facilitate their escape from danger.

"We're forever in your debt, my lords, safe journey and good hunting to you," the peasant wife uttered as they rode away.

Brock, Trent, and Galean all nodded to the family, mounted up, and resumed their pursuit of Aron and Cherine.

* * * *

Well ahead of them, Lilith rode alternately between the two separate columns of her followers and slept alternately in both camps. They were moving rapidly each day too. She wanted to take no chances with the pursuit. It was a long journey to get to Damien's forces and to the wilds and she knew Aron's friends would be driven to catch her.

Aron was silent when Lilith joined his column. He knew where they were going and that was worry enough to consume him. When Lilith went to the other column Cherine, too, had little to say. Neither Aron nor Cherine had any hopes if they were delivered back into Damien's hands.

Lilith ratcheted up her romantic pursuit of Aron. Each night she was bolder in proposing an alternative life with her rather than his facing Damien. She failed to get Aron to respond.

"Do you think it better to bravely march into the lion's den with no chance of survival? Will you not at least look at other possibilities? Would a life with me be so bad? Perhaps I'm not the type of woman you'd choose for a wife, but I'm not so bad a choice. I know I can make you happy."

"Define happy?" asked Aron. "I think in all of our cases, we have a fate and I doubt we can escape it. If I'm meant to die at Damien's hands, I can't choose my way out of it. I'm not intending this to reflect on you. I barely know you. It may be you'd be an excellent wife. What I'm saying is that's not an option for me. Galean thought I was destined to defeat Damien. I never believed it before and I don't believe it now. If you have a plan to connect with me, you're simply going to go down in flames along with me. Every woman I've tried to be close with has suffered terribly. I think you should get me out of your head. There are a lot of better men for you to choose."

Lilith laughed. "You truly are unaware, but that's fine. I can decide for both of us. I don't fear the specter of your fate, Aron. Perhaps your being with me will give you a new fate, a much better one."

Aron shook his head dismissively. It was useless to discuss it with her. She only wanted her own answers. That wasn't what bothered him. Though she proclaimed her love for him, they continued traveling toward the wilds. Nothing good awaited him there. It was clear to Aron she planned to join with Damien. Seeing him again was a chilling thought, this time without the Black Fist and the masters at his back. As much as he tried to put it out of his mind, he could not. The additional thought of seeing Tasha, Radigan's wife, again left him feeling ill. Liani was there too in her compromised state. He felt uncharacteristic discouragement.

* * * *

Meanwhile, not far away, Cherine was similarly distressed. Each day in Lilith's control wore at her resolve and spirit. Where Lilith regaled Aron with the lure of a romance, she plied Cherine with sisterhood, friendship, and a shared goal of female ascension to prominence. This failed to impress Cherine, who concerned herself less with acting civil. In each of her daily fights with the wooden swords, she struck at her multiple opponents savagely trying her best to injure them. In some cases she managed to inflict large bruises, some cuts, and knocked a number of women unconscious. She could never overcome their numbers. There were always too many of them for her to defeat.

When she lay down to sleep, she thought about Aron and their brief but intense courtship. It fueled the fire of her flagging spirit to continue to resist in spite of her poor future prospects. Holding out hope wasn't so easy for her, by nature not an optimist like Aron. Also as each day passed they drew closer to an enemy guaranteed to be feral against her and Aron. This increasingly gave her a feeling of unease.

"If I could just get my hands on a sword," she whispered.

* * * *

Brock's unit drove forward relentlessly. They'd closed some of the distance between them and their prey but word of battle was spreading. The initial probes by Damien's forces seemed to be over as word of larger scale operations across the entire frontier replaced stories of single groups of raiders.

Increasing their pursuit wasn't an option. They were already pressing their mounts to the limit each day. They talked about their prospects.

"We may face some serious fights before this is all over," Trent commented.

"I expected as much," Brock replied. "What do you say, Galean?"

"It's logical with the course of things, Brock."

"If we can catch that damn Lilith and get back my brother and Cherine, I'd like our chances a lot better in this war."

"You already know my feelings about that," Galean answered.

"It still boggles my mind a woman could pull this off."

"We don't know for sure it was she."

"I'm convinced."

They all chuckled.

"Brock, you've never been a man to let a few facts get in the way of your opinions."

"I admit I'm a blockhead. That's what Aron said about me and I can't disagree."

"What do you think about sending fast riders ahead to try to spot them?" asked Trent.

"It's an idea, but I'd rather the fast moving riders be all of us. We don't know how close they are to Damien's lead units. We may not have time to wait for riders to return to tell us what we already know."

Trent shrugged his shoulders.

"As fast as we're moving, I say we go faster. It's pretty clear to me from what we're hearing they're split into two groups. It's smart on Lilith's part to keep her prisoners separated. We can split our forces too, if we can get close enough. I don't think they have enough distance between the two groups. Are you up to such a pace, Galean?"

"I'll do what's necessary to catch them. It's not me to worry about, it's the horses."

"Good. You impress me with your stamina, and I am paying close attention to the horses."

"Don't think it isn't painful for me, son. I'm pushed to my limits, but I'd rather I personally suffer some discomfort than lose the chance to save them."

They rode forward with greater haste the following morning. On this day they started to see smoke rising on the horizon ahead of them. The fighting was closer than they anticipated. They rode the whole day without seeing any fights, but knew danger was drawing close.

* * * *

Lilith rode with the unit holding Aron when they first saw movement ahead of them.

She raised a white flag as they neared a large force riding straight toward them. The unit was dressed in all black uniforms.

"You're about to lose your options, Lilith," said Aron as they neared the enemy army. "You can still escape."

"Have you reconsidered my offer?"

"What do you think?"

"Then we're both about to lose our options. You could have chosen otherwise."

"Don't blame me. This is not going to be good for either of us."

She scowled but rode stubbornly ahead anyway.

The black clad soldiers increased their pace and quickly circled Lilith and her command.

"My name is Lilith," she cried out. "We've come from the royal palace to join with Damien on his crusade. We bring with us two prominent captives. This is Aron and I also hold Cherine."

The soldiers stared at her and waited. Before long an officer arrived. He was a former resident in Aron's camp.

"My, my, this is a great day. Welcome home, Aron. Damien has left specific orders about you. Is it true Cherine is captive in the vicinity too?"

"It is," Lilith replied. "I captured both of them. I wish to offer my services and that of my followers to Damien. I wish to be taken to him immediately."

The soldiers laughed.

"You name yourself Lilith? Let me explain to you it's not wise to try to dictate to me or any other of Damien's army. We'll take you behind the lines, but whether Damien will see you, I very much doubt. Your guests however, that's a different matter. Damien very much wishes to see you again, Aron. We all do. You thought yourself our better. You never were and now you'll face our wrath."

"Is that right, Korak?"

Aron snorted derisively and turned his head away in contempt. This angered the officer and he rode over to slug Aron in the face.

Aron looked back at him dismissively, as if the blow was weak.

"We'll see if your arrogance remains when you face your death at Damien's command. I'm sure parting your head from your shoulders will impress Tasha that she made the right choice of Radigan. You're nothing."

Aron simply looked at him.

"Have you met with my other unit, the one guarding Cherine?"

"You ask many questions, woman. I think it wise if you keep your mouth shut."

Lilith glowered at him. He returned a smirk.

"I told you," Aron whispered.

"Shut up, Aron," she hissed quietly.

Lilith's force followed the soldiers for a day before they reached a large camp. Cherine's group was already there.

Korak led Aron and Lilith into camp custody and then went straight to her.

"Ah, Cherine, it's truly a pleasure to see you. I regret the circumstances, as I have no control over what will happen to you. If I did, I'd offer you an opportunity to avoid execution. I doubt Damien has any long term plans for you though I could be wrong. He does have means to render you compliant, as you know. Perhaps you'll join Liani in noble service to the leader. You'll dine with me this evening. We can at least have this one night to make pleasant memories before you go into Damien's custody." He smiled at her, but she totally ignored him.

Aron was brought over to her looking at her sadly. They were both in restraints. She felt tears at the edges of her eyes at seeing him.

"I'm sorry about this, Cherine," he whispered.

"I'm sorry too, Aron."

She looked at Lilith. "Is this all that you hoped for?"

Lilith stared straight ahead.

"Come, Cherine," Korak ordered. "We have business to attend to."

They hauled her away. Aron stood helpless shaking with rage. Again he was forced to endure humiliation and shame about a cherished woman in his life. He couldn't protect her—a familiar theme.

As if to rub his nose in it, Korak also bedded Lilith right beside Aron that night, unshackled. She lay quietly for a time after Korak got off of her to return to Cherine. In the darkness Lilith rolled over to embrace Aron.

"This may be my final chance to hold a man I love," she whispered. "Perhaps you're right I've sealed our doom in coming here."

Aron said nothing. He felt sorry for her in spite of her poor choices. Her outlook appeared to be as dim as his. She snuggled against him and they fell asleep in her embrace.

Morning wasn't a welcomed sight. They were abruptly mounted onto their horses to begin their journey to meet Damien.

Aron rode over to Cherine. Her facial expression was grim.

"Cherine," he whispered sadly.

"Don't speak of it," she retorted tersely. She wouldn't look at him. He looked back at the smirking Korak, responsible for her hatred. He wanted to fix this man's face in his memory to never forget who he was. If Aron survived the ordeal of Damien through some miracle, he promised himself Korak would not long survive.

They traveled through familiar territory. Lilith rode over to Cherine.

She started to express her regrets.

Cherine glared and cut her off. "No, Lilith, I warned you. If you think this one heinous act has destroyed me, know that I'm not so fragile. I've faced the evil in men before. This will be the least of our troubles. You should look to your own self as I suspect your road ahead will not be a pleasant one. Beauty was a curse for a woman in the empire. It's probably a worse malady in Damien's realm. We may be living our final days. You should have listened to me."

The journey into Damien's lair went by too fast. With word of Aron's capture, Damien had returned from his other camp to the wilds. He brought all of Aron's acquaintances to observe his triumph over his key adversary.

As Aron was brought before them along with Cherine, Damien smiled. Aron glanced up to see Tasha standing beside Radigan. They both looked sad to see him. Straga was animated shouting derision at Aron and held Sirina near with a handful of her hair in his fist. Liani stood beside Damien, his arm around her shoulders. Her face was blank of expression.

The guards hauled Aron and Cherine off their horses, dragged them up the small hillock, and forced them to their knees before Damien.

"Greetings, my friends," he shouted for all to hear. "Welcome back."

The crowd laughed scornfully.

"I hope your journey wasn't unpleasant."

He turned to look at Lilith kneeling beside the prisoners.

"They tell me you claim responsibility for capturing them. Is this the truth?"

"Yes, my lord."

"Aron, how is it you could allow this to happen? Oh, that's right. You were swept up in love's sweet embrace. You lost track of everything around you seeing only the face of your lover. Frankly, I'm shocked. It's a flaw I never expected in you. I know about your romantic travails. It seems any man who wishes to take away your woman has an easy task."

Aron felt shame at the humiliating statement. Tasha put her hands over her face. Liani had a strange expression. The crowd continued to laugh and shout further insults.

"Cherine, the consummate warrior woman, you chose to weaken and take a mate. I'm more surprised with you. Surely you knew the consequences of such actions. Now here you are on your knees, your lives in my hands."

Cherine stared ahead stoically.

"Stand up, Lilith. Let me have a look at you. They tell me you did this to impress me, to join the cause and seek the conquest of the world. They also say you have ambitions to be a leader in my army."

"If that plan suits you, my lord, I aim to be your servant in whatever capacity you wish."

"Achieving what you have does gain my notice. Certainly I'm not one to waste opportunities or the talents of my followers. I think I'll grant a private audience for you where we can discuss your role here in detail."

"I would be very grateful for the opportunity, my lord."

"Take her to the bath house to be prepared," said Damien.

Lilith looked at Cherine as she stood waiting. Cherine shook her head sadly.

Lilith started to follow his servants away, but stopped.

"May I inquire about my people, Lord Damien?"

"Your people...?"

"Those who chose to accept my vision that coming to you was the right choice for all of us, that you would give us a better life, a life with dignity at last after the abuse of the prince?"

It was a dangerous ploy for Lilith, a calculated risk here in front of his adoring public.

He eyed her shrewdly. "Of course your compatriots are welcome amongst us. They tell me you have trained women to fight."

"We do our best, my lord."

"Perhaps it would be interesting to see these warrior women. I'll see they're cleaned up also. We'll discuss their future later. You may go now. I have Aron and Cherine here before me. This is a delicate matter I must ponder."

They led Lilith away. Damien smiled at his two prisoners.

"I'm sure you're very happy to see your dear friends again, Aron. As you can see, they're prospering abiding with us here. Radigan has achieved a high rank amongst my leaders and Straga has proven to be diligent beyond reproach. He fulfills his tasks completely. I'm very pleased. Tasha is beautiful as ever. Radigan is indeed a happy man with such an esteemed and a stunning wife. She lends us great presence, but you already know that. Their wedded bliss warms our hearts."

Aron kept his eyes on the ground in front of him. He gave no reaction to

Damien's taunts.

"Our sweet Liani is the joy of my life. I too am blessed to have a spouse of such merit. She is everything a husband could wish for. We've never exchanged a cross word."

Out of the corner of his eye, Aron noticed movement. He cautiously glanced over and saw the interrogator who'd inched his way to the front of the crowd. Tasha's parents were beside him. He made a slight gesture so Aron wouldn't look at him directly and draw Damien's notice. Obviously, it was impossible to miss the towering Wu Hang in any crowd.

Aron smiled ruefully. He cautiously touched Cherine. She glanced over and saw them too. She touched his side as an acknowledgement and to share her feelings.

Damien was absorbed in his moment of victory.

"Oh, I'm sorry, Aron, Cherine. Where are my manners? There's no reason to have you on your knees. Please stand up."

Aron glanced again at Liani. She wore a confused, puzzled expression. She blinked her eyes and glanced at Aron questioningly.

He wanted to speak to her, but that wasn't possible here in public before Damien.

Aron glanced over at Tasha. She was staring at him intently. She made the slightest of gestures toward Wu Hang. He wasn't sure what she was trying to impart to him. It set his mind to work. If there was help at hand, perhaps there was also hope.

Damien drew Liani into his embrace and moved close to his prisoners.

"I think we should have a feast tonight to celebrate this auspicious day. My wife and I invite you to join us. Of course all of our friends must come too. Radigan, you must bring your wife also."

"Certainly, Damien..." Radigan looked at Aron, but his facial expression wasn't boastful. He looked concerned.

"Straga, you and your wife will attend also. Tasha, I think I'd like your parents to join us, and perhaps that giant of a man called the interrogator. I've meant to carve out time to get to know him. I think he has unique skills which could be useful for the cause. Yes, it's time for a party."

* * * *

Brock looked all around. The battle had been brief but intense. Their progress chasing after Lilith slowed considerably as they neared the wilds as the number of Damien's patrols increased in size and range.

When Aron emerged so long ago from his prison cell beneath the palace, a hundred brothers in arms formed the Black Fist. Since that day, the ranks swelled as the most skilled were accepted into the corps, so the unit now numbered over a thousand men. Equally, the master's ranks had risen to similar totals. Now, when Brock led a charge, two thousand of the finest fighters in the world were at his back.

They were virtually assured to win every battle, but weren't facing the masses of an army. These were patrols.

Word spread quickly about their approach and soon their fights began to change. The enemy started to set ambushes and traps, which didn't change the outcome of the battles, but did increase the difficulty for Brock. In the middle of a serious fight Barmon and Abdurka suddenly rode into their midst to join them.

As always, Barmon was driven in battle, a consummate fighter, and a completely changed man from his former self. He was fearless, but also reckless in charging into impossible situations with no thought for the danger. With no abiding desire to live, he sought death in battle, which distressed Brock greatly.

"Father, you must not take these risks."

"Why, Brock."

"Perhaps you wish to die, but you're still my father and I'm not ready to lose you after all the time we lost before."

Barmon didn't reply, but Brock could tell he wasn't going to be convinced to change his ways.

"I'm sorry about mother, but that wasn't your fault. We're going straight toward her, and Straga. Perhaps we'll still have our chance to right that wrong and get her back."

Barmon's eyes smoldered with hatred.

Trent approached walking beside Abdurka.

"I'm surprised to see you, Abdurka," Brock commented.

"If Galean can make this ride, so can I. He needs me around to protect his old bones."

Galean walked up, heard the comment, and chuckled. "If my bones are old, what does that say about yours? You could be my father."

"If you were born as my son, I would have punished my wife."

They all laughed. Even Barmon smiled.

"What's ahead for us?" asked Abdurka.

"I'm afraid we'll soon face Damien's army," Brock explained. "We've been fortunate thus far to only see patrols. I suspect they've been massing inside the wilds to start the invasion of the kingdom. They may have huge numbers of troops so we can't simply fight our way through."

"What do you plan to do, Brock?"

"I was hoping Galean would tell us what to do."

"Don't drag me into this," Galean retorted. "I'm just a companion on this mission. I can't help you with battle tactics. I'm useful in other areas, as when we face Damien's machines and so forth."

"So you're merely taking up space and eating up supplies," said Abdurka. They laughed again.

"Something like that, you great oaf," Galean replied mirthfully. "We'll see what value you have, if any, soon enough."

The reunited friends sent small scout teams ahead to determine what they faced and the best route to avoid the most trouble. This didn't speed up their progress—large camps of enemy soldiers impeded their path.

They skirted trouble as best they could, but total avoidance was impossible. The former members of Aron's camp that sided with Damien undoubtedly realized who was coming in their midst and sent out forces in all directions to attack them. Although formerly barbarian thugs, they were adept fighters, especially after being trained by these same elite members of the Black Fist and masters.

Facing fights, they gave away their position and gradually a net of hostile swords drew up all around them, which left Brock and Trent with very difficult issues.

"We're going to face a significant battle where we're terribly outnumbered if we continue as we are," said Trent.

"Do you have an alternative?" asked Brock.

"Let them come," said Barmon viciously.

"Father, we can't sacrifice ourselves," Brock replied, shaking his head. "We're the only hope for rescuing Aron and Cherine. We've got to come up with something to get us through the trap."

"I'll lead a diversion," Barmon answered. "It will be all volunteers willing to die to allow the rest of you to break out. We'll give our enemies a fight to end all fights. Maybe we'll kill them all."

Brock worriedly stared at the nearly insane look in his father's eyes. The others in attendance said nothing, but were equally disturbed.

"We appreciate your courage, Barmon," said Galean finally. "We don't wish to sacrifice any brave souls if it can be avoided. If your desire is to confront Straga and reclaim your wife, this suicidal plan is not a good idea. We can do better."

Waiting for a solution, everybody looked at Galean, who just shrugged his shoulders. "That's my thought about the matter. You may not agree."

"Of course we agree," said Brock. "I have no intention of allowing my father to lead a pointless attack into the teeth of enemy might with virtually no chance to survive. We're in a desperate situation, but sacrificing part of our numbers isn't the answer. Aron never wanted to lose even a single soldier. If we're going to fight, it will be all of us, together, protecting each other. Damien has numbers, but we've fought against the best he has and they're nowhere near our abilities. Everybody needs to think. There must be a better way."

Brock looked at Trent. "You're the best strategist amongst us. At least you had some training with tactics."

Trent looked back ruefully. "There isn't really a tactic for our situation. We're outnumbered and unfortunately predictable. They know why we're here and where we're going. It's just a matter of time before we're cornered and must fight a major battle. Perhaps we should have brought the royal host with us."

"If that's the case, I say we take the fight to them," Barmon piped in. "If we must, let's do it on our terms. Let's drive right into their heart and rip it apart."

Nobody agreed with such a risky plan, but they could all relate to the fire in his eyes which evoked all of them emotionally. Barmon looked around at their faces, like they were all cowards and shook his head contemptuously.

Barmon was a complete new being compared to the person they'd rescued from captivity. He'd worked continuously hardening his muscles and body, perfected his fighting skills to an elite level, and was driven by emotions to deadly efficiency. Struggling with shame in his adverse comparison to Straga in the past, he was now the embodiment of chaos and war. He displayed no fear in any battle and sought out the best fighters amongst the enemy. In his mind, that pivotal point was the reason Sirina had initially displayed hesitance to return to him. This wasn't true, but didn't matter to him—his dark feelings and perceptions defined him. Revenge against Straga was his abiding goal. Damien fit into that hatred as a peripheral component connected to Straga.

Brock knew all of this and felt helpless he couldn't influence his father. Barmon was traveling a road he wouldn't abandon. He had no plan for the future, just destruction of his enemies. Without Aron, Brock was increasingly distressed by helpless feelings. Aron's father was a comfort, but Barmon had an air of inevitable destruction not only for his enemies, but himself too.

Normally Brock would have looked to Galean for help about the matter, but Galean seemed overwhelmed by his own doubts and issues. He had nothing to offer. All of the women were gone, Tasha, Liani, Cherine, Belisa, and Sirina. Enna and Biala had never been close in the sense he talked with them about such personal things. They were fellow fighters in his mind and with the other key women gone the pair maintained a low profile in the camp—their version of Galean's discouragement.

The lack of a defined plan stymied the allies, so they plodded along at a slower pace. When meeting resistance, they attacked mercilessly. Additionally, they varied their path meandering instead of a straight course. In spite of their tactics, the size and the frequency of the opposition grew markedly so each subsequent fight was bigger than the last.

Another problem which developed was their supplies began to run short with no supply lines from the kingdom.

"We have no choice," said Trent. "We need to assault one of their base camps and harvest supplies to sustain us."

"That puts us in a difficult position," Brock replied.

"We're already in a difficult position," Barmon snapped angrily. "You're too cautious, son. I know you want to emulate Aron and his compassion for his own troops, but that doesn't mean you can never take risk. There isn't another choice here. People die in battles. It can't be avoided."

"If you're killed, Father, I won't bury your body. I'll keep it tied to your horse so I can beat it daily."

Barmon chuckled. It had been a very long time since he'd laughed.

"You have a deal, Son. If I lose my life, I concede my body to you to punish as you see fit."

"All right then," said Trent. "I'll send scouts to find the nearest enemy camp."

Brock grasped his father in an embrace before they went to give the orders to the troops in the camp.

Within an hour they were mounted and riding rapidly toward their next fight.

The sentries saw the allies coming too late to mount a successful defense. Their two thousand soldiers swept over the startled enemy of five thousand and routed any opposition. Most of the enemy fled, abandoning the camp and everything in it-a shockingly easy triumph.

"Load up everything we can carry, this will restock our food and water," said Brock. "We need to move quickly."

The allied force rode away chasing the hope it wasn't too late to save Aron. There was no force capable of stopping this feral band. Word of their approach couldn't supersede them as they either wiped out all opposition or rendered them unable to carry ahead a warning.

Chapter Five
~ Deadly Encounters ~

Aron sat in a solitary holding cell, where he tried to think of a plan. Shackled and without weapons, there was nothing he could do. His brief encounter with Tasha and Wu Hang gave him hope that help was coming.

Cherine was taken away. What fate awaited her bothered him. Seeing Liani again in her condition stirred him up, but he was helpless to do anything for her, or Cherine. If Damien chose to subject Cherine to the mind-control life alteration, Aron promised himself he would find a way to avenge them. Then he thought about Lilith, and wondered about what awaited her. He regretted any woman could be put into mindless subjugation.

"Damien, you will pay for your crimes," he muttered. "Somehow, I'll find a way."

At dusk, they came and hauled Aron to Damien's dinner gathering.

Damien was in high spirits with his successes. Liani sat at his side smiling benignly, but absent of her faculties. Tasha was there with Radigan, a phony smile plastered on her face. Lilith and Cherine were there too. All of the women were dressed in scanty clothing, dresses none would have chosen to wear in public.

With a pained expression, Cherine looked at Aron as the guards dragged him past.

He tried to appear strong and reassuring to her, nearly impossible under the circumstances.

"Ah, Aron my friend, our premiere guest for this august evening, welcome. Please come in and join us."

Aron glanced around the room quickly. He noted the number of guards and their positions.

Damien chuckled. "You're eternally the optimist, Aron. I've always

51

admired that about you. Even where you stand, you look at escape strategies and imagine you'd succeed in a foolish attempt. This wouldn't work and would only hasten your fate, my friend. Instead, you should savor your life, or what remains of it. You have excellent food here tonight, the finest wine, beautiful women to admire. Let that be enough for you, and put away your foolish thoughts. I'm afraid that you've earned a terrible ending which can't be put aside. I wish it were otherwise, I truly do. I could find a prominent place for you in the new life of the world, which is coming. You have great attributes that could serve the people well, but you've chosen defiance instead. I can't make your choices for you, Aron. You've taken it out of my hands."

Aron said nothing.

Damien nodded to a place at the table. The guards hauled him there and chained his legs to the chair. He was seated beside blank faced Liani. On his other side they sat and chained Cherine beside him and Lilith beside her.

Aron reached underneath the table to touch Cherine. She touched his hand tenderly.

"I'm sorry I failed you," Aron whispered.

"We'll die with dignity if we must," Cherine replied stoically.

Servants came into the room and laid out the sumptuous meal with multiple choices of meats, ample vegetables of all sorts, fruits, cheeses, and other treats.

Aron ate his food woodenly, as if this was his last supper.

"Does the meal meet with your approval, Aron?" asked Damien with a smirk. He leaned over and kissed Liani's cheek.

Aron eyed him darkly.

Damien laughed and clapped his hands. A troupe of dancers swept in the door to entertain the dinner guests. They too were scantily clad, just the style Damien liked.

Aron paid no attention. He glanced over at Tasha, who watched the dancing women. She must have sensed his glance for she turned to peer at him. He didn't see reassurance, only distress.

This wasn't encouraging for Aron. He tried to move his legs, but they were tightly bound. He wouldn't be breaking those chains.

Meanwhile Damien basked in his glory, while subtlety taunting Aron in a variety of ways. Having control over the significant women of Aron's life pleased Damien immensely.

He signaled to the musicians who started to play. Damien got up to dance individually with each of the women, twirling them directly in front of Aron. He freed them from their chains under the close watch of his guards. Aron stared straight ahead ignoring the attempted affront. Damien bent them over the table where Aron sat to hammer his point home that Aron was helpless.

Savior

Aron silently mouthed a prayer, steeling his courage. He had a sense that this was a fatal evening.

Damien completed his circuit of dancing with Tasha, Liani, Cherine, Lilith, and Sirina, and sat down to stare at Aron. Aron's eyes were closed and his lips were moving.

"There is no escape for you, Aron," he hissed viciously. "You were given a chance and you squandered that chance. Did you really think there would be no retribution for defying me? I'm sorry you've forced this on me, but I do what I must. Tomorrow morning, you'll be brought before all of the people so they may see the fallacy of this mystique you've built around you. You're a misguided man too taken with your delusions and self importance to recognize that I'm the future for mankind, the only future. Your life of rebellion will end. Your body will be fed to the beasts and your head will decorate the entrance to my home. You have only yourself to blame. That is my command. Let my will be done."

An audible moan broke out in the room from all of the women as soldiers yanked him out of the chair and dragged him away. Aron couldn't look back at the women. Shamed and disgraced that Damien had defeated him, impending death seemed a mercy rather than continuing on his life of misery.

Tossed into a cell in darkness, and left to exist in his final hours alone, Aron thought about his happy days as a boy on the farm, the traumatic day the prince arrived and changed his peaceful life forever. He thought about the hopes he'd had as a youth, and about the succession of his women. First, beautiful Coraline, aloof and seemingly untouchable, destined for more than a farm boy. Tasha was a dark haired firebrand that evoked his feelings for her still, even with her choosing marriage to Radigan, gentle Liani, intelligent, sweet, and petite, now a lost person in Damien's control. Belisa was another memory, a woman who he could have made a life with but for her royal lineage. His recent flaming passion he'd shared with Cherine, unexpected but completely valid. Again, he'd dared to dream of a happy marriage with an extraordinary woman.

None of it was going to come to fruition. He felt regret he'd never be a father to delight in his children and grandchildren. It was easy for him for find blame for his imagined shortcomings. It wasn't reasonable conclusions he reached, rather his emotional pain at work. The unfairness he'd faced in his life, the indignities he'd endured, there could be no satisfaction he could exact from his tormenters. Radigan would live to dance on his grave, if he even got a burial. Damien would be free to warp the world into the living nightmare only a maniac could conceive of and hunger for.

Aron could find solace in nothing at all. Only misery seemed to be his companion. He wasn't particularly afraid to die. That part would be over with quickly. He couldn't escape the punishment of his own mind. He would die with the knowledge he hadn't freed his friends and all of those who'd believed in him, which was mortifying and humiliating.

Aron emitted a primal scream, but there was no one around to hear him.

His torment eventually evolved into depression. He sat in silence thinking back of divergent memories, fishing with Brock as children, their mock fights with wooden swords, his father's firm hand about the error of their dreams of war and glory. It nearly brought him to tears to think about his mother, and how she would react to news of his death. He could visualize the agony on her face and it punished him terribly. He felt inconsolable grief for her. Never seeing her again, not being able to say goodbye, these were the thoughts that plagued him late into the night.

* * * *

Brock signaled to attack. With no way around this large camp and numerically at a disadvantage, the allies had greater skill and determination. His forces swept silently ahead striking down sentries in a wave of mayhem. The camp was slow to sound the alarm and mount a defense. Black Fist and elements of the masters zeroed in on the command tent and the leadership of the rival camp.

The fighting turned savage quickly and for a time appeared the superior numbers of the enemy might survive, but Brock's forces would not be denied. Enemy troops dropped frequently while the allies suffered minimal casualties. They drove through the hastily established skirmish line of the enemy and battered down the defenders protecting their leaders. The battle ended quickly after that.

Brock and Trent confronted the very same officer who'd briefly held Aron and Cherine.

The captured officer, Korak, looked at the pair defiantly.

"You think you've won?" he taunted. "They were here. Cherine warmed my bed for an evening and fell in love in one night. She pleaded to stay here with me. We've gotten word Aron will be executed tomorrow morning before a gathering of all of the people. There's nothing you can do to save him. Your little resistance will collapse with him dead. Killing me means nothing. I'm ready to die. Damien will prevail in the end and kill all of you and your families will bow down to him."

The masters were feral after hearing what this man had done to Cherine. Korak tried to maintain a courageous expression, but seeing death in their eyes rattled him badly. His brave posturing had been nothing more than empty words to them.

Cherine's second in command stepped forward. Trent and Brock stepped back to allow him to take the officer away. Korak's deliberately slow and painful execution occurred moments later. His cries of agony echoed across the entire terrified camp. Damien followers who'd surrendered knelt in fear after watching Korak separated from his head in the end.

"What about them?" asked Barmon. "We shouldn't leave them behind to attack us at a later time."

"We're not butchers," Trent replied.

Brock walked over to the kneeling captives. They eyed him fearfully, the fate of their Korak fresh in their memories.

"If you're dedicated to Damien and wish to die on his behalf, stand up and we'll release you from life on this planet. If you wish to continue living, we'll give you a chance to switch sides and join us in fighting Damien. He believes he's invincible. We intend to show him otherwise."

No one stood.

"So be it, stand up because we're going to move fast. If they intend to execute Aron, we must arrive there as fast as possible. In our army, defeat is not acceptable. You will no longer be allowed to lose a fight."

They left the camp at a gallop. Brock's army was now doubled in size with the addition of the camp survivors. Brock interspersed them amongst his original troops so they couldn't change their minds and launch a surprise mutiny at some key time.

Flashing through the remaining territory like blurs and exacting a deadly toll in bodies, they won every battle they faced along the way. None could stand against this collection of the best fighters on the globe.

To cover the distance to Damien's great camp, they rode all through the night, but as the sun peeked over the horizon, they weren't close enough to that camp yet to save Aron.

* * * *

Aron had no way to know his forces were trying to ride to the rescue. For him, this day was his end.

The prison guards brought Aron breakfast, his final meal.

Aron looked at the food and felt nausea at what was at hand. He waited a time before eating. His sadness swept him, along with regret and further shame.

When the guards came back to take away the breakfast plates other guards came with them.

"It's time, Aron."

The guards looked regretful.

Aron nodded stoically, stood up, took a deep breath, and walked resignedly out of his cell. The guards led him up and out of the prison area. They stopped before leaving the building.

"We're truly sorry, Aron," said the lead guard.

"You have no fault for this," Aron replied. "You've decided the best way for you and your families to survive is to follow Damien. I understand completely. I had a good run for as long as it lasted."

"I think your run isn't over yet."

Aron turned around in shock.

"Wu Hang, what are you doing here?"

"I heard about Damien's verdict and I decided it wasn't acceptable, so I'm instituting a verdict of my own."

Aron smiled. "What can you do? We're surrounded."

"As you can see, there are those amongst Damien's forces who've decided to see things in a different way."

He nodded to the guards who all smiled at Aron.

"Do you have a plan, Wu Hang?"

"In a manner of speaking..."

"Uh-oh, this sounds like one of my plans."

Wu Hang smiled and removed Aron's chains. "I have a couple of different options to choose from. I haven't made my final choice."

Aron hugged the big man. "It's really good to see you again."

Aron felt hopeful, though their situation was still tenuous. Aron smiled broadly when Wu Hang handed him his weapons.

"At least I can go down fighting if everything goes south Wu Hang."

"Things can't go south, Aron. There are others depending on us. We must not fail."

"Sure, Wu Hang, whatever you say. You've put me back in the game after I foolishly allowed myself to be taken unaware."

"Women can have a profound effect on a man," said Wu Hang thoughtfully. "I could never have foreseen me being here pining away for a woman who fears me, a woman who could never feel love for me. I'll never escape my monstrous past, but perhaps I can do something positive about my future and save her life."

"That's the spirit. What do we do now?"

"We must free our friends. Liani can't be allowed to endure such a life any further."

"Have you learned anything about his spell over her?"

"I haven't, but we've noticed she's starting to have responses. Perhaps within herself she's found a way to fight back against the curse. If we can get her away from Damien perhaps she'll regain her mind."

"Is Radigan still dedicated to Damien's cause? He gave me a strange look when I was brought before Damien."

"I can't say. I've gotten some contact from Tasha. She wants to flee. Whatever she's seen on the inside troubles her and I got a sense of her urgency to escape."

"This is going to be really difficult to pull off, Wu Hang. We don't have the masters and the Black Fist here to help us."

"The camp has recently been preparing to move. I don't know if Damien intends to start his invasion or if there's some threat developing from the kingdom. The war elsewhere is going his way. He continues to receive huge infusions of converts. His message is alluring to strangers who want to escape their mundane lives. They don't realize until they get here that Damien's world won't be an improvement, quite the opposite."

"Your nation is mighty, Wu Hang. Are they warring against Damien?"

"I don't know, Aron. I think if they are at war, Damien wouldn't be having these great successes."

"Maybe there's still hope."

They crept out into the dim light on a beautiful crisp morning. Wu Hang led them quickly past a guard shack. Aron glanced in and saw the guards, unconscious on the floor.

Hurrying past the large area where Damien's grandstand was built, Aron quickly thought about the arena, the intended site of his demise. It gave him a cold chill looking at the apparatus on the stage for his own public beheading.

Slowing their pace as they approached the residence, Aron was shocked to see Tasha standing beside Radigan waiting for them. Sirina was standing beside Tasha. They both embraced Aron.

"Thank god," Tasha whispered. He returned her embrace and then turned to Radigan who was looking away. Aron took his hand and shook it, which surprised Radigan.

Wu Hang faced them. "I will not leave without freeing Liani. I caution you that if we're surrounded or cornered, leave it to me to create a diversion. You must escape this place. Damien can't be allowed to prevail in this fight. Don't try to save me. I have only one desire. Without her, I have no reason to flee."

Entering the building, they raced into guard post after guard post to knock the startled enemy soldiers unconscious.

Approaching Damien's sleeping area they burst in the door to find fortune was with them. Liani was sleeping alone in the bed. This was a night where Damien visited other bedrooms.

Wu Hang scooped Liani up out of her bed and covered her mouth, preventing her from shouting in alarm. The women grabbed some of Liani's clothes and they raced outside to where more of Wu Hang's friends waited with horses. Tasha's parents were there along with a large number of others who wanted to leave Damien too.

All of the sentries in their path had been taken care of so they quickly rode away toward the kingdom.

Aron glanced around and spotted Cherine. It surprised him she was riding beside Lilith. He veered over to her. She looked at him and smiled.

"Ho, Aron!" shouted Lilith happily. She hooted and shot her fist up into the air.

Aron chuckled.

They rode steadily to put distance between them and the camp.

Damien discovered the escape hours later when he returned to his bedroom to find unconscious guards strewn all about. Shouting in rage, he mounted the chase and personally rode with them. Along the way, he gathered armed followers from their camps and his force grew rapidly into an army racing after the fleeing allies.

Ahead of Aron an intense battle raged and he immediately realized who one group of the combatants was when he saw their standards.

"Cherine, it's Brock!"

The Black Fist and the masters were engaged in a savage fight against a larger force, but when Aron led a charge into the enemies' rear, Damien's forces were shaken and broke ranks. The fight turned into a rout of Damien's forces.

Wu Hang was a beast in the fight wading into the opposition and felling them like wheat. Nearly an hour of fierce fighting raged before Aron and Brock could have their reunion.

Surrounded by the masters, Cherine beamed.

"Never again," they said. "You'll be warded day and night and you'll no longer face the risk of capture. This we swear on our lives."

"Thank you," she replied.

Galean made a bee line for Liani. She stared in confusion, as if she couldn't collect her thoughts.

"Thank god, child," he said wrapping his arms around her. "I'm so sorry for what happened to you."

After quick embraces, including a shocked Barmon accepting the tearful hug of his wife, Aron addressed the unified group.

"Damien is going to be extremely provoked. He'll come at us even worse than the prince did. This time we have nowhere to hide. We're going to need to fly back to royal lines to make a stand there."

"What about Lilith?" asked Trent, eyeing her grimly.

"Leave her be for the time being. I think she's had a serious change of heart after her personal time spent with Damien."

Brock nodded at Lilith. She walked over to them with a defiant look on her face.

"What is it, gentlemen? Did you have a question for me?"

Brock, Trent, Barmon, and the other men glared at her coldly.

"Do you wish to express your opinion about my decisions? It isn't necessary. I've learned the error of my ways in no uncertain terms. I admit I was a fool to trust only my aspirations when it came to Damien. He proved to be merely a man, and not such a good one at that. I found nothing in him to inspire me or any other person. He thought a great deal more of himself than was warranted. I've made my choice to return to the royal fold. If the prince chooses some measure of retribution, so be it. I'm a valuable ally and I think he'll acknowledge it."

They all looked at Aron who smiled.

"Lilith, I can't say I can dismiss what you did. On a personal level, you ruined the best time in my life with Cherine. I'm willing to let it pass since we seem to be on the road to redemption."

Aron noticed the pained look on Tasha's face, but he also saw just behind her Cherine smiling warmly at him. Cherine looked to be herself again, dressed in her uniform, armed to the teeth and self-confident.

"Men, this isn't the time for brusque judgments or field justice. We must concentrate on eluding Damien's noose. We're not in the clear by any stretch of the imagination."

They all quickly dispersed to get ready for the journey. Aron watched Barmon walk with his son, Brock. Sirina was waiting with her other two sons.

Aron heard them say, "You're our real father. We've learned a terrible lesson about our other father. He doesn't warrant our respect. Do you accept this and do you accept us?"

"Of course I do, welcome home."

This warmed Aron's heart after seeing Barmon suffering for so long, and was the first time he saw Barmon soften his harsh exterior and show his emotions.

He turned slowly with the idea of having a moment with Cherine, but she was fully occupied with leadership of the masters who surrounded her completely and protectively. Cherine and her force mounted up and rode away shortly afterwards, Aron's poignant time was delayed again.

* * * *

Damien's wrath was what Aron anticipated and that's what happened behind Aron's fleeing troop. Damien launched virtually every troop he had into the pursuit. In essence, it started the invasion of the kingdom.

After Aron's harrowing escape, the initiation of hostilities with royal forces was just a matter of time. Aron raced away as rapidly as the horses could tolerate, but Damien drove his forces maniacally and they started to close the gap.

"I don't think we can get to the royal lines before Damien catches us," said Aron as they conferred at evening camp.

"We can make a detour, Aron," Enna piped in. "We can go to my people in the great swamp. This will cut off a great deal of time from our journey and we'll be safe there."

"Excellent idea, Enna, I'm sure you'd like to see your people after so long a time riding with us."

"Yes, thank you, Aron."

"Tomorrow we'll veer away. Hopefully Damien will try to follow us into the swamp."

Everybody chuckled.

Enna and Biala hugged Aron after the meeting.

"Do you want to ride ahead to warn your people?"

"If that wouldn't be a problem for you, Aron..."

"Of course not, we'll see you again soon enough."

"I'm so happy you're with us again, Aron. We were worried that..."

"It's behind us now. Things are bound to get better."

The Uripean women left immediately headed toward their homeland.

Aron noticed Radigan was particularly quiet during the ride and made no attempt to join the camp leaders in council. While Tasha stayed with him and tried to keep a low profile like a protective mother hen, this was impossible because the other women sought her out.

Cherine was the first to talk to her.

"I hope you don't take offense, Tasha. I've long had feelings for Aron, but I didn't feel he was free, so I kept my feelings in check."

"Cherine, you know I love Aron, but we were never meant for each other. Much of it was my own foolishness, and I'm the wife of another man. I have no claim over Aron."

Cherine eyed her skeptically. "I was referring to Aron's feelings for you. We've chosen to marry, but I know I'm not his first choice. A part of him will always belong to you."

Tasha blinked. "If that's true, I regret it. Aron made a poor choice. Everything I've ever done proves it. I've been nothing but trouble for him. I look back and wonder how I could've been so stupid."

"This is just my opinion, but I think you made more of your connection with Radigan than was warranted. I'm sure he's a fulfilling husband in those areas where he has great skill, but a marriage and a satisfying life together involves so much more."

"I know that, Cherine. I've been living with that reality."

"I searched for the right man most of my life. I knew Aron was the one for me, but I wasn't able to express myself, so I bided my time. I didn't wish ill for you, but when you went away with Radigan, I didn't regret it. I think if Liani hadn't been throttled, she would have been Aron's next choice."

"I see Wu Hang is at her side constantly. They say she is showing signs of change…that she's starting to regain her old self."

"I haven't had time during our flight, but once we get into the swamp, I want to sit with her for a time to see for myself."

"Cherine, I'm not your competition. You have my blessing with Aron. I want him to find happiness and I can think of no better wife for any man than you."

"Tasha, I'm touched. I don't know what I expected, but I feared you couldn't release Aron."

"It's time that I do the right thing for him and that would be you."

The women hugged warmly.

"Thank you, Tasha."

"I love you both, Cherine. I know you'll give Aron a good life as his wife."

Lilith and her people were kept loosely under control during the trek as a precaution at Aron's direction. Though they didn't present a serious threat within the camp, nonetheless, nobody was willing to forget what they'd done hauling Aron and Cherine away to Damien.

"Aron, I've told you I learned my lesson and I've switched sides," Lilith complained, chaffing at the suspicions.

"The others are not so forgiving, Lilith. What do you expect?"

"I'm a great asset that you're wasting with this needless vigilance. If I still wanted to support Damien, I would've stayed there."

"I'm sorry, but this isn't much of a price to pay for your transgressions, Lilith."

"Perhaps, but they need to get over it and move on. Damien will be all the trouble we can handle. Who can say any of us will still be alive next year at this time."

Aron shrugged.

"You're missing the point. You've ruined the trust we need to have in all of our allies. You may be right about being an asset, but if you change sides with the tides of battle, how can we trust you to be in our midst at critical times when battles are still in question?"

"That's a good question. I can only say you must trust me. What else can I offer but that?"

Aron eyed her skeptically. "Trust you, Lilith. You don't see that's a heck of a stretch?"

"During our private time, Aron, you know that if I was evil, I could've caused you serious harm. What did I actually do? I praised you, shared my high regard for you, and I gave you a new option of a life with me, one which is still available to you."

Aron chuckled. "That's true, Lilith. I hope you don't take offense when I reiterate that I'm going to marry Cherine."

"It's your loss, Aron. You'll never know the wonders we could've had, but that alone should give you an idea of what's in my heart."

"Honestly, Lilith, this isn't fully my decision and it shouldn't be. Maybe you need to make your case to the others."

She eyed him thoughtfully. "Perhaps, but you think you're very good at shifting decisions onto others. You can't avoid your role in this world. You're a person of great import."

Aron shook his head in denial, looked over toward Cherine who was enmeshed in a knot of the masters surrounding her protectively. Cherine looked back at Aron and walked over.

"Is there a problem?"

"Not any more, Cherine."

Cherine looked at Lilith without malice. She put her hand possessively on Aron's powerful shoulder.

"I've conceded that contest," Lilith said with a sly smile. "You have that life back for now, at least until Damien gets here."

"You don't have much optimism about our chances, Lilith," Cherine commented.

"I'm a realist. The numbers are not in our favor. If we win this war, it will be a surprise to me, that's true. Nonetheless, I'm not one to give up. Aron has inspired me in that way. He's escaped so many impossible situations, why not me also?"

"If I'm your example, Lilith, you're in big trouble because trouble has been my shadow." Aron smiled.

"If we fall, I will not fail you. I'll be one of the last protecting your back."

"Thank you, Lilith, that's a nice thing to say. I appreciate the good thought."

"I'll leave you to have your private time together."

Lilith turned and walked away.

Savior

"I feared we would never hold each other again," said Cherine. "This was a great torment for me."

"I was ashamed I couldn't protect you, but I've had plenty of that in my life."

"You must stop creating blame for every possible thing which happens. Our capture was out of your control. There was no blame, other than that of the perpetrators. It's behind us now. Can't we put it out of our minds, Aron?"

"It's easy to say, but for me it's not so easy. I'll never feel the measure of these aspirations other people put on me."

"Aron, forget those things. Just be yourself. That's enough for me."

They embraced and he kissed her tenderly. Afterward, he noticed the masters staring at him, as if he'd broken their rules.

"I think there is at least one group who don't relish our affections for each other."

"It's none of their business," she replied, smiling warmly.

"They don't seem to agree with you, Cherine."

She chuckled. "Don't worry about making them happy. Keeping me happy is your task."

"Yes ma'am."

"Perhaps we can steal a few moments together later."

"I'd like that, darling."

Brock walked over. "I'm sorry to interrupt you. I know you want time together, but we've got to be going. Damien won't be pausing to suit our needs."

"Of course, brother, thank you."

Aron's force mounted their horses and resumed the rapid ride toward their allies in the great swamp.

Limiting their stops, they ate quick meals in the saddle, rode late into the night before stopping, and left early in the mornings as the sun came up.

* * * *

Damien pressed his forces mercilessly in the pursuit, but couldn't catch Aron's band before they reached their destination. By the time Damien got to the borders of the bog, Aron's people were well into the swamp.

Damien sent a probing force in, but between the Uripean sentries and feral creatures that dwelled there, they were quickly slaughtered.

Meanwhile, Aron's unit moved rapidly to the Uripean city to restock supplies and resume their dash toward royal battle lines.

The Uripean King was gracious to them, as always, and he was still shocked to see Tasha married to Radigan instead of Aron. He stared at Tasha and Radigan in confusion and then at Aron who was noticeably trying to ignore them. Aron and Tasha both reacted to the scrutiny. This was the first time Aron saw Tasha act as if she was embarrassed about her choice in husband. None of this escaped Cherine's notice and she was prominent at Aron's side leaving no doubts she intended to possess her man and any other female beware. Her territorial display was satisfying for Aron. On some level, Aron was gratified that at last he wasn't humiliated in the area of love, but couldn't ignore the emotions he felt watching Tasha. His feelings for her were deep in spite of the direction things had gone. Hiding his underlying distress watching Tasha with Radigan was a daily challenge, and he tried to focus his attention on Liani, Wu Hang, and their attempts to revive her mind out of bondage. It was a frustrating task as no one had any idea what to do, or if there was anything that could be done to reverse her malady.

Aron got the impression the Uripean King was more than confused, he was actually upset at Tasha's choice of a spouse. He made a point to devote a great of time and attention her, basically romancing her without totally crossing a line to torment Radigan. Although some would see his actions as harmless flirting, Radigan took far dimmer view.

However, he was in no position to do or say anything. He could only depend on his wife to exercise proper decorum and restraint. His unending paranoia and jealousy about her left him imagining the worst at all times. The king recognized it immediately and this fanned the flames, so to speak.

Tasha, for her part, enjoyed the attention and in light of her dour experiences living near Damien where her husband didn't react to protect as she felt he should have, she did too little to salve his wounded feelings or the ally his fears she would seek out another lover. She had no real plans to dishonor her wedding vows, but at the same time, this was an opportunity to punish Radigan and she took it. She overreacted to the compliments and adulation acting girlish and coy to the king.

Aron saw it all, as well as anybody else with eyes. He couldn't manage to feel sympathy for Radigan who was getting a dose of the misery Aron had experienced. The best he could manage was not to participate by approaching Tasha. She was still alluring to him so it wasn't an easy task.

He made a point of trying to romance Cherine and she spoke to him about it. "Aron, this isn't necessary on your part. I know what you're doing. I'm not a blushing adolescent. I know you still have feelings for Tasha. I understand and it's not a problem. I'm confident in your feelings for me. We don't need to put on a façade."

"Thank you, darling. Maybe part of it was in me. Tasha moved on, but I was worried I hadn't completely."

Savior

"I had a first love too. Those are precious feelings none of us forget. Put it out of your mind. I don't want to lose my warm feelings and you don't need to lose yours either."

"Wow, Cherine. I am so lucky to have you."

"That is so true."

They both laughed and hugged warmly.

They noticed Tasha looking at them. Aron led Cherine over to speak.

"Tasha, I hope Cherine and I being involved isn't a problem for you."

"Aron, I have the same feelings you have. I've got regrets, but that is in the past. Of course you should be happy, and you also Cherine. I think you're good for each other and I'm happy. If I have to deal with pangs, what did I do to you, Aron? I earned this pain with my choices. It isn't something for you to worry about. We all have trouble enough without thinking about things that don't matter now."

Chapter Six
~ Hopeful Signs ~

Reclaiming Liani was the most difficult task anybody had ever attempted. No one knew what to do, or if there was anything that could be done. Taking her away from Damien produced subtle changes in her countenance. She was only slightly less vacant in expressions and awareness of her surroundings, but she did react noticeably to seeing Aron and Wu Hang. Other than them, she remained suspended in a fog.

Galean spent all of his time with Liani assessing her state and experimenting with various methods to try and impact her absent mind, with very little success.

Wu Hang was Liani's constant companion, refusing to allow her out of his sight for any reason, unwilling to give up his hope for her restoration to normalcy. No one chose to argue with him in lieu of a painful lesson at his hands.

Tasha opted to assist Galean with his efforts, even choosing to place her bedding beside Liani each night. This didn't please Radigan which did please Tasha in her current mood, but he wasn't in a position to argue with his wife as he was still highly mistrusted in the allied camp. His presence was barely tolerated and many looked for reasons to pick a fight with him.

Cherine, on the other hand, overruled the wishes of the masters and moved her bedding beside Aron. The masters only partially accepted her verdict. Their answer was Aron was merely included in the circle of the masters protecting Cherine. There was nothing she could do about helping Liani so she moved to her next priority.

"Do they snore?" Aron whispered sourly to Cherine.

"Not that I have heard," she said chuckling. "I think this isn't so difficult a problem for you to endure. We've been through much worse."

"Well, I didn't get a say in it. This is familiar ground for me."

She laughed.

In spite of their conversation with Tasha and her assurances, Aron saw her glance at them, like they were intentionally punishing her with their affections. It saddened him a great deal.

It bothered him, but he could say nothing. He did love Cherine and had no desire to hurt her with his stubborn residual feelings for Tasha.

Aron shook his head in frustration at the dilemma.

He looked at delicate Liani lying prone staring up at the sky. Galean was trying to reason with her and coax her back to her former state. Wu Hang sat watching the process darkly—his wrath toward Damien palpable.

Radigan was nearby, but didn't attempt to force his way to Tasha's side for the evening. Her uncharacteristic disdain disturbed him, shaking his self-confidence and this was not the time or place to try to sort it out. Their troubles were obvious to Aron as he watched them, he who'd experienced those same feelings at Tasha's hands so many times, but he couldn't bring himself to feel any sympathy for Radigan who'd been the author of so much strife in Aron's life. Equally, he didn't feel any self satisfaction at Radigan's distress, which did nothing to balance the ledger between them. Tasha was still his wife.

* * * *

The Uripean king threw a large banquet for his guests that night, although nobody felt particularly festive. The king seated Tasha near enough to him that he could talk to her, and savor the displeasure he saw in Radigan.

"Ho, Tasha, you could have been a wife to me. I think you can see you made a mistake letting that opportunity slip away." He gestured to the bevy of his beautiful wives.

Tasha looked to be particularly amused with him on this evening and played along to an extent.

"Is that so, your highness?"

"It is so," he huffed. "I'm legendary amongst the ladies."

"Legendary for what…?"

His wives all chuckled, which didn't amuse the king.

"Silence," he growled at them, which failed to quell their amusement, looking back at Tasha who was smiling triumphantly at him. "You think to bandy words with me, Tasha. I can rise above your pitiful attempts to humble me. The truth is the truth and you can't soil it with your contrived scorn."

"I can see that," she smirked, glancing mirthfully at the royal wives who chuckled again.

The king scowled. His verbal contest wasn't going well. Tasha remained an untouchable temptation, aloof and superior, like she couldn't be impressed by any man. If she had issues with her husband, it wasn't something which could be exploited.

Tasha glanced mirthfully at Aron. Aron tried not to react to the lopsided contest and maintain some measure of proper decorum. He liked the king, though the king seemed intent on more embarrassing gaffs, which were obviously doomed to failure.

"Aron," Cherine whispered after a time nudging him from his focus on the verbal jousting.

He knew there was a great deal of import in that single word. Was she gauging if he could get over Tasha? He turned his head and smiled.

"Yes, darling...?"

"I was just checking to see if you knew I was here beside you, Aron."

He chuckled and embraced her.

"The past is over, Cherine. I won't pretend Tasha is out of my feelings, but I chose you to be my wife. That isn't going to change."

"Good answer," she replied as they both chuckled. "I would hate to have to skewer you here in front of everybody."

"I would hate that too."

"I know Tasha is exceptional, Aron. I don't hold that against you."

"Somehow, I think you do. I hope we can get to a place that you understand you're my woman."

"That sounds a little barbaric, like you're going to drag me to your cave."

"If that's what it takes, I can do that, Cherine."

"Good luck with that. I'm not so easily beaten, silly man."

"Maybe later we can spar."

"That is so romantic, Aron, wanting to fight with your fiancée."

"With me, what you see is what you get. I'm not a sophisticated guy."

"That is a true statement. Strangely, I love you anyway."

"I'm a lucky man,"

"You're a very lucky man."

"I admit you could've done a lot better than me, Cherine."

She looked at him seriously. "No Aron, I couldn't. You're who I wanted. You need to start looking at yourself like everyone else does, or else I'll need to knock you out."

He laughed heartily. "Is that your idea of being romantic, Cherine?"

"It's as romantic as your idea to spar, Aron."

"You've got me there..."

They gazed back at Galean and his steady ongoing attempts to intervene with Liani. He stopped and gave her a pensive look and said something to Wu

Hang who shook his head in disagreement.

They appeared to argue quietly before standing up, pulling Liani to her feet and leading her toward a large tent. Aron was curious and got up to follow. Cherine got up with him.

"I think Galean has an idea although Wu Hang didn't seem to like it at all."

Tasha joined the pair in following Galean and was surprised when they entered the tent to see the interrogator laying out a large pouch of his former implements. Galean was tying up Liani.

"Galean, what are you doing?" asked Aron sharply.

"We're going to try to shock her memories back, Aron. We're not looking to hurt her, but we need something drastic. I think her fright in the Chenese camp with Wu Hang made a deep and an unforgettable impression. Perhaps resurrecting it can help break this inner barrier holding her prisoner. I want you to be nearby, Aron. You were a key person in her life. Seeing you after we scare her may be the perfect tonic to draw her back to reality."

"Are you sure this will work?"

"No, but I have nothing else. I'm not willing to simply give up on her, Aron."

"Okay, what do you want me to do?"

"Stay out of sight with me while Wu Hang works."

Even though this was just a ruse, being there and watching Wu Hang prepare implements of torture was unsettling, like he could lose it at any moment and revert back to torturing people.

Wu Hang was clearly in distress with the task, but business like. The inner callous he'd developed to protect his own feelings from horrific sessions inflicting suffering emerged and his face fell into a frightening mode. Everyone in the tent felt as though Liani was in grave peril. When Wu Hang approached her, she jerked in fear in an attempt to free her arms and legs. They heard her moan.

"No," she whispered, "please don't hurt me."

Wu Hang stepped close and extended an instrument toward her eye. Liani screamed in abject terror trying to turn her head away, but she was fastened in a case holding her head firm.

Aron was afraid Wu Hang was going to damage her eye and started to lunge, but Galean held him back.

"Wait Aron," he whispered.

Liani cried again, but this time she yelled, "Oh my god, ARON HELP ME!"

Galean released him and he rushed to face her. Wu Hang stepped aside.

"Aron?" she wailed with tears streaming down her cheeks. "Can it be you?"

"You're okay, Liani, I'm here."

Aron quickly unfastened the bindings and she collapsed into his arms sobbing.

"It's okay Liani, you're safe now. We've got you."

Aron took her face in his hands. She eyed him lovingly and suddenly kissed him passionately, throwing her arms around him. Unsure of what to do, he let her control the moment before stepping back and gazed into her eyes to assess her state.

Galean hurried over.

"Liani, do you remember us?"

She blinked like she was trying to focus.

"I, feel strangely. I need to sleep."

She collapsed again, but this time she was unconscious. Aron picked her up, took her to bed, and gently placed her down.

"We'll take care of her now, Aron," said Tasha gently. The women pushed the men back.

"I'm going to stay here, Aron," said Cherine. "I want to help Liani."

"I hope you know I didn't…"

"Aron, I'm fine. We all want Liani back, and we all knew how she felt about you. Go. I'll see you tomorrow."

He left regretfully and looked at Wu Hang on the way out. Wu Hang put up his hand before Aron could attempt to apologize.

"Aron, it isn't necessary. If we have her back from Damien, I am content. She never shared the feelings I have for her. I know that."

"I'm sorry anyway, Wu Hang. I know how hard that must have been to scare her like that."

"I'd never thought to array those dire implements ever again. It was a shock to me also."

The Uripean king walked over.

"Will she be able to travel? I think you shouldn't delay any longer than you must or Damien will surround our entire perimeter to bar your escape. She's welcome to stay with us until she recovers."

"I'm hoping when she wakes, she'll be returned enough that she can function and travel with us. I don't know what's going to happen when the royal forces meet Damien's assault. I don't know that we'll ever be back here."

The king eyed him soberly. "Regardless of how the battles go, you have a refuge here. If there are any you wish to leave behind to be protected from harm, we'll safeguard them."

"Thank you, your majesty."

Brock, Trent, Barmon, and even Radigan joined them.

"What of Liani?"

"We'll know when she wakes up. Galean decided to try to shock her back. We're hoping he succeeded. At the very least, I think we got through to her on some level. She'll be different than the vacant woman Damien created. We've got Wu Hang to thank for any progress we made."

They all looked at Wu Hang with admiration, but he just stared back stoically.

With the women occupied elsewhere, Aron decided to spar that night. Exercise always helped him relax and get his mind off his worries. Brock was always happy to oblige.

"I think we need to be ready to move. We'll see how Liani is tomorrow. The king is right we can't get mired down here. We need to be back with the royals for this war."

"We can move as quickly as we want, Aron. We're always ready. Don't worry about us."

"I guess I'm just saying my thoughts out loud. You're right there is no force more ready than we are, brother."

"Just so you know, Enna and Biala want to stay with us, Aron. They said this was just a visit to their families, but their duty is to you."

"I feel responsible when people say things like that. I don't like to feel responsible."

"Well, try this," Brock replied with a sudden heavy attack.

Aron chuckled and fought off the lunge. He tried to batter Brock and drive him back, but Brock wasn't someone he could overpower any longer. After so many battles, Brock was a superb fighter in his own right.

The brothers leaped, parried and bashed at each other for over an hour before stopping to eat dinner and clean up.

"Very impressive," said Enna, easing up to Aron's side.

"I think you may be getting a handle on this fighting thing," said Biala with a smirk.

"Hey darlings, it's good to see you," Aron said, embracing them tightly.

"We've had time with our families and now we're ready to return to duty," said Enna.

"I think you should stay, but I'm glad to have you with us."

The single question in the entire camp the following morning was the status of Liani. Galean kept her sequestered in a tent to keep away the curious.

She opened her eyes and blinked before she sat up and turned her head towards Galean.

"Liani?" he questioned.

She focused her eyes. "Galean, I feel strangely. What happened?"

"What do you remember?"

"Everything is foggy in my mind. I seem to remember my dreams. They were very vivid. I don't understand."

"Liani, you were taken captive by Damien. He used one of his infernal machines to rob you of your mind. It left you in a pliable state so he could control you. Do you have any memory of that?"

"Just these dreams, Galean…I feel much different. How long was I under his control?"

"It's been quite some time I'm sorry to tell you. Actually it's been almost two years since we lost you. I don't know if you're ready to hear what transpired in the interim, or what you went through."

"I want to know everything, Galean. I gather there were bad things happening."

"Damien took you as his wife."

"What! That can't be. I don't love him. You mean to tell me he…"

"I'm sorry, dear. There was nothing any of us could do to spare you."

"Oh no, now Aron won't want me. I'm spoiled."

"A great deal has changed, Liani. When Tasha married Radigan, it crushed Aron. He struggled for a long time. He and Cherine came to a point where they began a relationship and it blossomed to an engagement."

Liani was devastated. She put her face in her hands and sobbed silently.

"Liani, I'm so sorry for you. I'll give you time if you wish."

"No Galean, tell me what else I need to know."

He sat down on the bed beside her, a look of sympathy on his face.

"Damien began amassing followers and has created an army. He's intent on conquering the world."

"Does he expect me to act as his wife?"

"He's a madman. I don't consider what he thinks. None of us accept his sham marriage when you were mentally incapacitated. We will defend you, Liani."

"For some reason, the interrogator was prominent in my memories."

"When we were forced to flee Damien's camp, Wu Hang stayed behind for your sake. He sought to safeguard you and never stopped believing you could be recovered from Damien's cruel grasp. He cares for you very deeply, Liani, with no expectations of anything in return."

Liani was in shock. "I understand how he sees me. I struggle with the idea of having a relationship with him. He terrifies me still. I can't forget what he did for his people. I fear it's like a malignant creature chained within him that could escape at any time, do you see?"

"I understand, Liani. Wu Hang has done nothing but good amongst us as he strives to make amends for his past. As I said, he has no hopes about you and strives only to protect you and give you a good life. A person can't simply ignore their feelings. I believe he loves you, Liani."

"Love?" it seemed like an incomprehensible term.

She stood up from the bed, shaky and weak. Galean grabbed her to keep her from falling over.

"Oh my, I'm so fragile."

"You'll recover your physical strength quickly, Liani. Let me help you."

Liani and Galean walked out of the tent to find the entire camp gathered in silence. Liani looked around at the sea of familiar faces and spotted Aron who was smiling warmly. She nodded to him and Cherine who was standing at his side. Liani saw Wu Hang and started toward him. His expression was passive but his cheeks were flushed red.

"I'm told of your many kindnesses toward me during my captivity, sir. I wish to thank you from the bottom of my heart. I hope you'll find that acceptable."

"It was my honor to act on your behalf, mistress. I require no recompense from you. Your return to health is sufficient."

She thought for a moment before stepping close to give him a hug, with her petite stature she could only embrace a part of his massive frame.

"Thank you, Wu Hang."

She turned back to Galean and went back to the tent with his assistance.

Aron glanced at Wu Hang after seeing Liani's unexpected hug. It was strange to see the look of wonder on his face. He was lost in his thoughts, but his happiness was obvious.

"Good for him," Aron whispered to Cherine.

"We shall see what comes from this, Aron, but we must make a quick decision. We have no time to dally further here in the swamp. Each day that passes allows Damien to move his forces closer to cutting us off in here."

"I understand, darling. Let's go talk to Galean, and Liani. If she can't travel it's a moot point."

Liani was talking with Galean when Aron and Cherine entered the tent. Liani turned her head toward Aron, her eyes were pained.

"Are you okay, Liani?" he asked, with concern.

She forced a smile.

"I'm fine, Aron. It will take me a little time to get back to normal. Don't worry about me."

"I wanted to tell you we have no more time here. We need to move right away before Damien can pen us in. Can you travel?"

"Yes, Aron..." She glanced at Galean.

"Physically she's fine. She can travel safely."

"Good, because we need to gather our things and be on our way, yesterday..."

"I'll be ready, and by the way, congratulations to you and to Cherine."

Aron felt badly and could think of nothing to say.

"Perhaps we can talk later, Liani," said Cherine.

"It isn't necessary, Cherine."

"I think it is necessary, Liani."

"As you wish..."

Aron watched the two women closely, trying to understand fully what they were thinking. He loved them both and didn't want animosity to develop between them.

"Go, Aron, you have duties in the camp," said Liani, turning her back.

Aron wanted to say more, but Cherine pushed him into motion. "She doesn't want to talk right now," Cherine whispered.

Aron's forces had been antsy so they were already packed and preparing to leave took virtually no time at all.

Aron watched as the king made a point to stop Tasha for his "goodbye." She looked to be amused. Radigan sat beside her on his horse looking away awkwardly.

* * * *

The column moved out rapidly. Enna and Biala took the lead. Nearby, fearsome creatures of the swamp bellowed ominously, but Aron's troops were never threatened.

Traveling in a slight arc toward the furthermost border of the swamp from where they'd entered. They covered the distance in two days and paused only momentarily before emerging back into the empire. None of Damien's soldiers were there to obstruct their progress so they moved rapidly riding straight toward the far distant imperial city of Nephora.

Although they managed to escape Damien's snare, he wasn't far behind them. Already there had been skirmishes with royal patrols. They could see smoke rising on the horizon in numerous places.

The allies traveled until nearly dark before making camp. Aron sought out Liani who was traveling with Galean with Wu Hang nearby.

"I want for you all to stay near me, share meals with us, and participate in our decisions. Liani, as you feel able, I'd like for you to resume your old duties as my assistant."

For a moment he expected her to reject the idea, and him in the process.

"Okay, Aron, if that's your wish."

"It is," he replied firmly.

She looked at him darkly before she nodded.

"Good, that's settled. Wu Hang, I want you to resume your prominent role here also. You're a valuable asset in so many ways and right now I think we'll need every ally we have."

"Of course, Aron..."

"I want us to get back to our old routine, okay?"

Liani looked at him, but said nothing.

"I'm going to ask Radigan and Tasha to join us too. We've got to get over the past or else we'll never have a unified team when we fight Damien. He doesn't need any extra help from us."

"I said I would be there, Aron," said Liani, betraying a slight twinge of irritation in her voice.

He nodded and left to resume their trek.

A rapid pace was set after leaving the protection of the swamp. Each day the allies continued as quickly as the horses could tolerate. Their exodus was similar to the flight from the prince - their enemy always seemed to be gaining ground.

* * * *

A week passed before they started to encounter royal patrols. Aron directed them to join him in returning to the imperial lines. With Damien approaching, there was no further need for patrols to be put at risk.

With the change of seasons coming, they faced a steady drizzle and sloppy muddy roads. This dragged on the mood in the camp. No one had any false visions of a glorious war against Damien. Even the formerly bellicose Barmon mellowed considerably with the return of his wife and Straga's boys. He truly viewed them as his own sons.

Abdurka joined Galean spending time with Liani. Her progress back to normalcy was accelerating as facets of her old personality emerged. She was tolerant of Wu Hang being near to her unlike she ever had before, which was imminently gratifying to him.

Meanwhile the sounds of battles grew each day as Damien's push encountered royal resistance.

"We may face fighting before reaching the royal host," said Brock, as they watched the horizon behind them during their ride. "Who would have ever thought we'd wish to get to the prince instead of away from him."

"Fate is fickle," Aron replied. "The young farm boy I was could never have anticipated any of the things which have happened to us. We dreamed of adventure and glory. If we'd known back then what we know now, I think I would have hidden in a cave somewhere."

"It hasn't been all bad, Aron. You have Cherine as your woman."

"I don't think I'll call her that, at least not to her face. Somehow I don't think it would go over well."

"You never know, Aron. Maybe she'd like the caveman approach."

"Or not, Brock..."

The brothers chuckled which drew Cherine's notice. She rode over.

"What are you snickering about?"

"Nothing, dear..."

"Now I know it's something stupid. Why are men such oafs?"

"It's part of our charm, honey."

"That's charm?" she questioned, eyeing them skeptically. They both laughed and bumped fists. Cherine shook her head. "Men..."

This was a rare moment of satisfaction for Aron having a positive romantic relationship after his rocky history. Cherine was a new treasure in his life, his feelings for Tasha and for Liani notwithstanding.

They covered the remaining distance to the royal lines without conflict, although Damien's forces drew closer with each passing day.

Liani's improvement accelerated and she appeared to be mostly recovered from her malady by the time they entered the royal camp. What that meant for Aron was another taste of disappointment. She was friendly with her female circle, but with Aron she tended toward reticence, she barely tolerated him and wished he would leave. In spite of his connection with Cherine, this adverse turn bothered him a great deal. He got no sense she was trying to be malicious but the message was clear in his opinion, their old relationship was gone. They needed to create a new version.

At the same time Aron felt a little jealous when Liani made an effort to be amenable to Wu Hang, though it hardly qualified as warm and from her side it certainly wasn't romantic. Wu Hang was impassive, like her actions couldn't deter or affect him. As Aron watched though over time, he started to notice little things which implied otherwise. Wu Hang was stung by Liani's emotional coolness.

Cherine saw this development through her own perceptions and finally spoke with Aron one evening about it.

"I don't want you to take this wrong, but you're pre-occupied with Liani. I'm not saying I'm jealous..."

"But you're jealous," he replied, cutting her off.

"I don't like how it makes me seem, like a silly, weak girl instead of a grown woman. We've all been through too much for me to act like that, yet I can't pretend I don't have feelings about the issue."

"When you see me reacting, you're getting a glimpse of what you got yourself into. I'm a faulty person. I'm not pining away for Liani, I miss our close friendship. Some might think it was too close, but neither of us ever crossed that line. I don't want to replace you as my fiancée, darling. I'm the lucky one. You agreed to marry me. We're on the verge of a war that could decimate this world and this is what we worry about? We're a good pair for each other."

"Now that I've said it, I feel embarrassed. It was foolish of me. I do trust you Aron. Can you forgive me?"

"There's nothing to forgive, Cherine. I should be begging for your forgiveness just on general principles."

"Thank you, Aron," she said gently.

"Maybe we should speed up this wedding."

She chuckled. "This isn't a good time or place for a honeymoon, but I'm glad you still want me."

"Of course I want you, how could you not know that?"

"I think women need reassurance in some areas, constant reassurance." She eyed him playfully.

"Yes ma'am."

Brock walked over to them with Trent.

"What are you up to now, Aron? I know that look on your face. Did Cherine finally realize what a toad she's going to marry?"

"Pretty much," said Aron.

Cherine laughed with the men.

They all went to claim a place in the large royal encampment. Agar and Coraline came over to greet them.

"We saw Liani. It is such a relief to see her recovered from her tribulation," said Coraline. "I'd feared the worst in that regard."

"It is a blessing," Cherine replied. "We shared your fear that Liani was lost to us. I think she is still recovering to an extent, but it's very hopeful to see her functioning normally."

"It seems you stirred up a hornet's nest, Aron," said the prince. "I'm told Damien's forces are pouring out of the wilds in a steady stream. The war is at hand. We'll soon see if we're adequate to the challenge."

"We have to be, Agar. We can't allow Damien to institute his vision for the world. It would be endless hopelessness and would be degrading beyond your conception. We've seen what he does, and that's only with partial control in the world. He cows all his enemies with the threat of his weapons, though we wonder about that. To my knowledge, there have been no battles where he used those fearsome weapons. This may mean he's saving them for serious battles, or perhaps with the lengthy passage of time, there is a reason he can't use them."

"Interesting theory, Aron, if we must fight him only with conventional arms, it comes down to the masses and determination of your armies. I like our chances. I realize we have no way to investigate which is the truth, but I feel better already."

"I wouldn't feel too confident yet. Damien is amassing armed forces at an alarming rate. Our hope partially is in what happens elsewhere in the world. If the mighty nations, like the Chenese are able to weather the storm and throw back Damien's forces, it takes pressure off us. What I fear is his attention is abnormally focused here due to our interactions. As you said, I believe we garnered his full attention stealing away Liani, and with Radigan defecting, it adds to our troubles."

"Of course, Aron, I suspected such. I've talked to the general staff about that very thing. Regarding Radigan, do you trust him? Obviously, his actions have ruined his relationship with me. It may not be important at this point, but I will never extend any level of trust to him. He's fortunate I don't punish him for the myriad of his abuses. Actually, if we survive this war, I may still look into that matter. He's done things which I can't abide. Even my wife was an object and a recipient of his untoward affections. I don't take kindly to that. I'm sure you understand."

"At this point, Agar, I can't worry about issues like that. People make choices and suffer the consequences. That's true for females as well as males. Radigan may have been the instigator of a great deal of mischief, but his accomplices went along with it. From my point of view, there's plenty of blame for everybody."

Agar looked at him thoughtfully. "You have a point there, Aron."

"I had no other choice, I had to move on. That's how I coped with the issue."

Chapter Seven
~ War ~

Aron studied the long straight ranks of the royal host gathered at a staging area before their deployment. To see them in their dress uniforms and polished boots with battle pennants flapping in the brisk breeze was awe inspiring.

As impressive as the physical sight of them amassed in one place was, he was more impressed by their sheer numbers. If he didn't know about the size of Damien's approaching army, he would have felt confident.

Unfortunately, Damien had no problem matching numbers and could call upon vast reinforcements worldwide in addition to his daunting invasion force.

Galean counseled at length with the generals at their request. His main worries continued to be what weaponry Damien could bring to bear. The fact he hadn't used ancient weapons didn't necessarily mean he had none. With no answer to such might, that could tip any battle against the allies who were limited to primitive weaponry, trying to create contingencies for that threat was nearly impossible.

Aron was surprised that Liani, instead of returning to service as his aide, spent her time working for and with Galean. She never actually told Aron she was done with him. This was just an evolution she chose to make. Galean was the new focus in her life.

This bothered Aron far more than he let on. Cherine became very much attuned to his moods and picked up on it. In spite of that, he denied it to her even though they both knew he was lying.

It was no comforting factor for Aron coping with his irrational feelings that Wu Hang kept a steady vigil around Liani and made no overt moves toward her in any romantic way. She never gave him anything but courtesy and civility, but that was also true for how she treated Aron. Wu Hang remained an acquaintance and nothing more to her. In general her mood was migrating toward sternness and severity which was a polar opposite of her former self.

Although he was distressed about Liani, Aron noticed Tasha never looked happy. The only time she relaxed was with her parents. Radigan he paid no attention to. Emotionally, Aron's life was a boiling pot.

Aron only saw happiness around him from Cherine who beamed being at his side. Being recognized as Aron's 'woman' was important to her, and provided social validation she'd never achieved before. Being the foremost 'warrior woman' was a role that hurt her chances to be a potential wife and mate in spite of her great beauty. At the same time, belonging to someone romantically didn't diminish her battle readiness. She commanded the masters with a stern hand, allowing no complacency in their ranks.

Her example helped Aron to an extent as he worked out with the Black Fist. Having thousands rather than a hundred under his command was different, but he was adjusting to the change. They were a potent force by any definition of the term and added numbers hadn't decreased their expertise.

* * * *

An impromptu assemblage of the combined military awaited the address of the royal heir on the eve of the coming war.

The prince began his remarks to the army.

"Men, we're on the verge of a great threat to the kingdom. Before us stands evil. We can't allow them to prevail for it isn't only we fighters who suffer the consequences of defeat, it's also our families." He looked at Coraline. "There has never been such danger for our land. We thought ourselves safe from outside forces. That misconception is no longer the case. They come for us with malice in their hearts to work wickedness the like of which we've never seen. They can't be allowed to prevail. Fight with the utmost of your strength and never stop fighting because you are all that stands between them and the heartland. This is the time to stand up for your country and make a statement to Damien that we will not accede to him and his hordes, we will not kneel to him, and we will not surrender our loved ones to his vileness. Who stands with me?"

He was answered by a deafening roar that ran chills down Aron's spine as he stood nearby.

"He's a good speaker," Aron mentioned to Cherine. She smiled at Aron. "I'm ready to go fight for him. I would never have thought that possible."

"Likewise," she answered. "Time heals old wounds. Past grievances have no place now. I'm again a servant of the crown. It doesn't mean I'll ever forget what he's done, but now I'll concentrate on allowing us to survive as a nation, and I'll concentrate on the man I'm going to marry."

Aron put his arm around her. "I'd like that."

Savior

His commitment to Cherine and his feelings were crystallizing at last and deepening. Though he still had affection for Tasha, and Liani, and even Coraline, he could honestly say, Cherine was his focus and his choice. He looked forward to getting married and that evolution was something else she picked up on.

Drums started along with the martial music of the bands as the units marched away in multiple directions to establish the defense against Damien.

"It's time for us to go too, darling," said Cherine.

"I still don't like this idea of us in different places. I wish you'd reconsider."

"You already know the reasons, Aron. Our units perform different functions in battle and as such it causes us to go where we're needed. I don't like it either. Aron, we've been through battles before. This one is no different."

"I hope that's true. If Damien opens up on us, I don't want us to be separated."

"If that happened, if he used those horrible weapons, there's nothing you or I could do at that point anyway. Being together or apart wouldn't change our fate."

"I wish we'd never found him. We should have let him rot in his tank."

"There was no way to know back then. Don't second guess now, Aron."

"Cherine, I know you want a great wedding, but I'm really tempted to have a quick service to tie the knot. I've thought about this more and more lately. I really don't want to wait."

She was distressed at the implication they might not be around long.

She shrugged. "If that's what you want, Aron, I'll not stand in the way. I think every woman dreams about their wedding. In reality, I can live without all of the formality. I can talk to the prince about it. It's the king's place to rule on it, but the prince is his authority here in the field."

"Whether the prince goes along with us or not, let's do it."

She smiled. "I like that you're anxious for me. Some men have a goal with women and then discard them a short time later."

"Nobody would ever discard you, Cherine."

She eyed him skeptically. "Because I could slice them apart with my sword...?"

"Well, there is that."

She smacked him on the arm while he chuckled.

"You men think you're so clever."

"We're definitely not," he retorted facetiously.

She eyed him sternly. He tried to embrace her, but she pushed him away.

"You don't deserve me, sir."

"On that we can agree. I'm an incredibly lucky man."

She smiled. "Yes, we can agree on that point."

She turned and walked away toward the prince's tent.

Aron went to find his brother and his parents.

He was lost in his musings when he came upon Liani on her way to meet Galean. She was talking with Wu Hang who walked at her side.

No matter how benign the interrogator tried to act, he was always intimidating and frightening.

They looked at Aron as he approached.

"Hello, Liani, Wu Hang."

"Aron," they answered.

"Cherine and I have decided not to wait to get married. With the war coming, I can't be sure what's going to happen. In my life usually things tend to go south, so I'm not taking any chances."

"Congratulations, Aron," Liani replied evenly.

"I feel like I should apologize to you, Liani."

"Why, you owe me nothing. You've saved my life numerous times. It's I who owes you. If you can find happiness with Cherine, how could I not be pleased? We weren't meant to be together, Aron. Whatever is my fate, I'll cope with it. Don't waste your time worrying. I'll be fine. Come, Wu Hang."

Wu Hang bowed to Aron and they walked away.

The announcement to Liani left Aron feeling sad. He continued on his way to his parent's tent in a far less buoyant mood.

Brock happened to be there talking with his father.

"Can I talk to you, father? Is mother inside?"

"Yes, son, what is it?"

"Please come inside."

His mother was putting away implements from breakfast.

"Aron...Hello son..."

"I'd like to tell all of you that Cherine and I have decided to marry. The future is too uncertain."

"Aron, you don't look happy about this?" asked his mother.

"I ran into Liani on the way here. I told her and Wu Hang. I cherish her, mother, but somehow it never worked out between us. She puts on a smile around me, but down deep I think I've hurt her terribly. It bothers me a great deal. Everybody tries to rationalize away the problem, but it doesn't answer the hole I have in my heart."

"Aron, you can't solve every problem for every person you know. You can't take on that responsibility," his mother replied. "Those people have responsibility for themselves. They must decide what they want for their lives and they must take action. You've got so much on your shoulders already, don't add more stress needlessly. Liani had her hopes like anybody else. Not everything you wish for in life comes true. That's a good thing. She's a remarkable young woman who will be fine."

"I've been such a failure about women, mother. I'm surprised you haven't disowned me."

She chuckled. "No, Aron, I'm proud of you. Your inner goodness shines through in everything you do. That's what's important to me. Much of what happened in your life revolved around other people and other events. You weren't the cause of their strife. They made their own decisions and they've had to live with the consequences."

"You think Tasha regrets picking Radigan?"

"I think she has regrets, but what you don't realize is she never felt worthy to be your mate. She felt she'd be a fatal distraction, a drag on you. In her way, she wanted the best for you and believed it would be with a better woman."

"That's so wrong, mother. I'm not better than anybody. I worry I'm a mistake for Cherine. She could have any man she wants and there are plenty of them better than me."

"Aron, there's a point where you cross over a line from humbleness and self deprecation to pointless self castigation. You harm more than yourself with that sort of behavior. You must take control of that aspect of your life."

"I understand you with my head, mother, but my heart seems to travel a path of its own. I wish I could control it."

"Don't dismiss this, Aron. There may come a time when it becomes a critical factor in our circumstances."

"Yes, ma'am, I'll work on it."

"When do you plan to have this wedding?"

"Cherine went to talk to the prince. I guess I was leaving the date up to her."

"Even in speeding up the event, there's a great deal women will want to do. You can't simply dismiss our desires, son. We want to have a nice celebration."

Aron smiled meekly and glanced at Brock who was smirking.

"You're going down, brother," he chuckled. "Your life is over."

"Brock, shut up," said his mother. "Go away and find something useful to do."

He laughed as he turned and walked away. "Mr. Cherine!" he shouted, laughing heartily.

"Real funny, Brock," said Aron sourly.

* * * *

The horizon was hazy with the approach of a cloud bank. Royal forces were arrayed across the entire front behind quickly constructed breastworks of wood and earth. Contemptuous of the royal host, the enemy made no attempt to hide their approach. They were singing anthems Damien taught them, tunes Aron and his friends heard on Damien's recordings.

Galean was closer to the front than Aron would've liked, but he wanted to be able to react quickly to Damien's moves. If there would be a weapon of the past unleashed, Galean wanted to minimize the effect. He was stationed at the general's stand perched high off the ground.

Aron glanced at his Black Fist brothers. They were attentive, but quietly confident. They'd never faced a foe they hadn't beaten and their demeanor calmed the royal army soldiers. No one knew what to expect. This would be the first major war in anyone's lifetime.

Aron looked in the direction where Cherine was assigned with the masters, knowing she was too far away to be seen from his position. Aron's wish for a quick wedding didn't get resolved before battle intervened.

The civilians had all been sent far back away from the lines. Liani insisted she stand at Galean's side, so that meant Wu Hang was with her on the general's stand.

Sounding trumpets, drums and singing insanely, the cacophony of Damien's army increased as they drew nearer. Not close enough yet that Galean could discern their battle formations, the enemy still looked like an amorphous dark mass oozing out of the cloud of dust they kicked up.

Waiting was nerve wracking. Trent stood on Aron's left and Brock stood on his right. Both of their faces were intent and determined.

"They make a lot of noise," Aron muttered.

"We'll see how much noise they make after the battle," Brock replied.

"By the way I was curious, how did you convince your father to stay back to protect the women and children, Brock?"

"The same way you did, we're young and they're old. Besides, my father doesn't want to be parted from my mother even for a moment. That was the biggest factor. He lost her twice to Straga. That will never happen again. He'll die first."

"Do you have any regrets, Trent? You've made choices that put you here standing beside us."

"No, not at all...On my old path, I would've just been one of the meaningless faces in the royal army waiting to be sacrificed. I'm better off standing here at the head of the greatest fighters in the world."

"I guess we're about to find out if we're the greatest fighters. Damien has been able to mesh men from all over the planet so they may be our measure."

"No, Aron, they're not. I can guarantee you of that."

They chuckled.

"We'll never lack for hubris. I guess that's not so bad."

"We can back up our words with our deeds," Brock interjected.

Aron shrugged. "I really don't like not being able to keep an eye on Cherine."

"I'm sure that was the idea of the prince. He doesn't want either of you distracted watching out for the other. The slightest loss of focus can cost you your life in the confusion of battle. You know that, Aron. This is why we've been so successful; we focus totally on the task at hand."

The approaching army made no progress in closing the distance. Though they were moving, there continued to be a sizeable gap. As the day passed, they came to realize the sheer size of the massive army. Behind the front line they saw no end to the ranks of oncoming fighters - a sobering sight.

"We're going to need extra cemeteries to bury all of them," Brock joked.

Aron smiled, but didn't feel confident. This would be a daunting task if they got every possible break. The enemy didn't need competence and could overwhelm with sheer numbers.

"It's amazing they can feed all of them," Trent observed.

"Damien is probably depending on sacrificing huge numbers to help solve two problems. He can cull his vast army and wipe out ours in the process. If he's all that remains standing afterwards, he achieves his goals. Supplying them is the least of his concerns."

As the sun slid down toward the far horizon, the march of Damien's army came to a halt. Their hastily erected camp was no less raucous than their field march. The royal generals decided to send out probes to test the enemy camp defenses.

In the gloom they heard the sounds of fighting erupt up and down the front. The royal raiding parties returned later carrying their dead and wounded.

"I don't think we can call that attempt successful," said Trent.

"Bloodying their nose doesn't seem too much of a coup," Brock replied. "What were they trying to accomplish? I guess that's why I'm not a general. I don't grasp the higher understanding of battles."

"You're not a general because you're a blockhead," Aron retorted.

"Yes, I am, and proud of it," Brock replied chuckling. "That makes two of us."

"I can't disagree, brother. Tomorrow we need to have a plan for us and the Black Fist. Right now we're supposed to support the front line and jump in to staunch enemy breeches. I have a feeling things could go wrong. If they just keep pouring over our walls and pushing us back there could be too many breeches to stop. If we're routed and fall into retreat, we need to stay together as a unit. Of course we'll try to do our mission, but I'm not going to let Cherine and the masters get pinned down and trapped."

"That's a tall order, Aron," said Trent.

"I'm going to send word to the Brutan chief to be careful about getting bogged down in any fights. I know they're itching to tangle with the Erati in Damien's army, but I want to be able to call them to link with us. At that point we'd have enough of a force to be able to scythe through any resistance we meet while we chase down Cherine."

"I don't want to disagree, Aron," Brock interjected. "Cherine and the masters could be ten or twenty miles away from us. The course of the battle might continue pushing them farther away. I feel for your motives, but we still need to be practical too. If we suddenly pulled out of a fight at a critical time, it could cause a rift Damien could exploit to tear through our lines and disrupt our defenses. You need to have some faith in her and her men. We also have to think about our families behind us. We'd put them in jeopardy with rash moves."

Aron was irritated, but there was nothing he could say. Brock was right.

"I feel like slugging you, brother."

Brock and Trent smiled.

"I'm still sending word to the Brutans," Aron grumbled.

"Whatever," Brock replied.

"Drang-ku has moved the Chenese to join Wu Hang in defending the generals. Actually they're defending Liani, and Galean," Trent mentioned.

"Good," Aron answered. He stared out into the darkness deep in thought. The noise from their enemies continued unabated.

"Don't they ever sleep?" asked Trent.

"There's a rumor Damien has some sort of drug that keeps them going like crazy people. He's not worried if they burn out. He only needs them as fodder in the short term at this point."

"I guess we should try to get some rest," Brock commented.

"You can sleep through anything, Brock. The rest of us aren't so lucky."

"I can't help you with that, brother. Just close your eyes. I'm sorry Mommy's not here to rock you to sleep, baby boy."

They both laughed and Aron slugged Brock hard on the arm.

* * * *

The royal camp arose with the sun. An eerie silence pervaded from the enemy camp after an end to the continuous bedlam. The smell of cook fires spread as the prevailing wind drifted gently toward them. The day was cool with a clear sky. Damien was in no hurry to commence the action. His forces moved about disdainful of the nearby royal host.

Aron gobbled down eggs, bacon, toasted bread, and coffee, as did Trent and Brock.

"It could be a while before we have a good meal again."

"Battles are like that," Brock replied. "We've been through it before."

"The Brutan chieftain sent back word he's ready if I make the call. They're stationed about a mile to our north."

"Just think before you act, Aron. Don't forget what I said."

"I will, Brock. I'm not a total dummy."

"That's debatable," Brock retorted.

They were surprised to see the prince walking briskly toward them.

"Sire," said Aron.

"Are you in agreement with our plans, Aron?"

"Sure, why do you ask?"

"I know you. You're priorities aren't always what's best for the whole. I know you don't like that I sent Cherine and the masters far away. It had nothing to do with you. We couldn't have our greatest fighters all in the same place. If something dire occurred far from here I needed to have quick reaction forces in the area. The same is true with the Brutans. They didn't like being separated from you and the Black Fist, but this is a time we must all put the concerns of the whole army ahead of our personal agendas. Cherine understands this, Aron. Do you?"

"Why is everybody so doubtful about me?" he answered defensively.

"It was Galean and Liani that suggested I come over here, Aron, You are who you are. We all must take that into consideration in our planning. I'm trying to protect the entire realm, all of those innocent citizens. Do you see?"

Aron scowled to see Brock and Trent step to each side of the prince as if ganging up on Aron.

"Why don't we put Brock in charge," Aron replied petulantly. "I have no problem with that."

"I'm not amused, Aron," said the prince in response. "This is too critical. I must know I can depend on you and your elite forces to fulfill their duties in this battle."

"You have my word, prince."

Agar looked at him skeptically. He turned to Trent and Brock. "I put this on your shoulders."

The prince turned and left them.

"Thanks for the support," Aron groused.

"You've earned our doubts, brother," Brock replied. "You have a long track record."

"Brock, if you ever get a woman who says she'll marry you, perhaps then you'll have a basis for understanding how I feel. This is no small thing to me. My fiancée could be lost through pure chance, no matter how skillful she is. That's a contingency I'm not willing to gamble with. I'm not going to put the defense of the kingdom at risk, but the battle won't be won or lost by my hand. We're just little pieces in the big puzzle."

Brock looked at Trent, who shrugged, before he answered.

"Aron, whatever you choose to do, we will be there for you."

"Thank you, brother."

* * * *

Circumstances seemed strange to Aron as the morning unfolded. The royal army moved casually to their assigned positions. Damien's army was doing nothing to indicate a massive attack was imminent. This caused a strange lull and a feeling of apathy in some. Aron, however, did not feel apathy. He was sharper than usual, focused, and attentive to even the smallest of actions.

Damien's mob appeared to be occupied with cleaning up from breakfast. Their skirmishers had yet to appear to form the assault line.

"What kind of army is that?" asked one of the Black Fist.

"Be cautious men. This may be a ploy. We can't be caught off guard."

Aron sent word up and down their lines to be vigilant, which was a wise move because suddenly from the seeming sloth of the enemy camp they mounted a massive charge from just behind the visible camp area. Roaring in a deafening tumult, they drove forward in unending waves. Damien's forces struck the defenses savagely pushing to scale the dirt wall breastworks and the obstructive barriers at the top.

The fury and near insanity with which they fought was frightening. The line held initially as royal forces pressed close to block any breakthroughs. Aron felt nervous and anxious looking for surges he needed to engage.

All of the pomp and circumstance as well as the courageous words were gone in this mayhem. This was primal, a simple kill or be killed. No one thought about anything but surviving minute to minute.

Soldiers on both sides dropped to the ground frequently taking their last breaths of life in a litany of waste as Damien sought the conquest of the world heedless of the cost. Where Damien was at that very moment, Aron couldn't be sure. He suspected his opponent wasn't far away.

The royal army requited themselves well as the long day ground on.

Damien's army was relentless, but the defensive edifice held against every surge. The ground became so littered with dead and dying it inhibited the attack. Just before dusk, Damien called his forces off. His staffers sent forces to drag away the dead bodies not out of reverence for the sacrifice of their men, but simply to clear the way for the next attack. It showed colossal contempt from Damien as though he considered himself the only person on the globe that mattered.

The captain of the closest section of the defense wall came to talk to Aron.

"I'm speechless, Aron, there were more than men in the force that attacked us. There were also women and some older children. They weren't skilled fighters, just grist to clog the way. This Damien is a ruthless dog. What sort of person could do such?"

"He's a maniac," Aron advised. "I'm sure he's got them convinced a brave death is a ticket to heaven or something like that. Add in these drugs he's supposedly giving them and it shows you why we can't allow him to win. This is sickening work slaughtering innocent pawns, but there is no other way. You must be strong, Captain. Those people are probably barely aware of what they're doing."

"It haunts me, Aron. I wonder if I can live with myself after such actions, assuming I survive this war."

"We're all in the same boat. I've faced compromises all of my adult life. Things don't often seem to go in directions you would choose."

The next day the fighting followed the same script as Damien spent lives elaborately to bleed the royal army. Fatalities mounted on both sides of the line.

Toward the end of the day Aron was forced into his first action as a sudden breakthrough saw Damien's soldier's pouring through a small breech in the line. They met the Black Fist in what was little more than butchery. With no skills to contest an elite fighting force, it took about an hour to close the breech and wipe out those invaders who'd made it behind the lines.

"Not much of a fight, brother," said Brock.

"I hate Damien. I should have killed him with my bare hands."

"Maybe we'll have another chance, Aron."

The Black Fist was called to action more frequently the following day. The opponent's incursions popped up in numerous places. Though none of them threatened to shatter the defense, enemy soldiers were increasingly free behind royal lines.

Wu Hang and the Chenese had their first action as a determined knot of invaders tried to attack the general's stand. As always, Wu Hang was a singular force of his own. He battered away attackers like insects. Drang-ku and his countrymen did little more than protect his back.

He returned from the fight meekly as Liani eyed him thoughtfully. Aron had gone over in case they were needed so he overheard their exchange.

"I don't choose to kill for any reason except necessity, Liani. I realize you'll always see me as a monster. There is nothing else I can do."

"Wu Hang, why do you have these thoughts? I appreciate the protection you provide to me. This is war. Your involvement in the fight is no different than any other soldier. I don't hold you accountable alone. Who am I that I'd even matter? I have a problem with war. Any killing disturbs me. You're personalizing it mistakenly. It isn't my intention."

"With the misfortune of our first meeting and you seeing me in a role I despised, I'm at a loss how to eliminate that nightmare memory to get to a better place in your esteem."

"I believe you place too much importance on that time. A great deal has happened in both of our lives since then. Apparently I've been a bride to Damien himself though I have no memory of it. If I wish to take umbrage, it would be with him. From my point of view, there's peace between us. Actually I owe you a great deal for all you've done for me."

Wu Hang glanced at Aron.

"I didn't think you needed me, but I had nothing better to do. I hope you're listening to Liani. I understand her completely. I think part of your issue is dealing with your own feelings of guilt, and your other feelings."

"Other feelings…" he groused.

"You can't pretend, Wu Hang. Everybody in the camp understands your feelings." They both looked at Liani. She betrayed nothing of how she felt.

"I must return to my work with Galean," she said. She left them standing watching her.

"Aron, you don't help my cause with this interference."

Aron smiled. "Wu Hang, you're the most ferocious man in the world, yet you cower at the prospect of telling that petite little person how you feel about her."

"It's not an area of strength for me, Aron. I'm not a man who draws favorable looks from any woman. If I ventured a request for her companionship, I risk being shut out totally. Of course I'd like a relationship with Liani, but being her friend and protector is better than being nothing and being shunned. Do you understand?"

"I'm hardly one to advise you about romance. I'm the consummate failure with women, but I say there are times you must take the risk. Cherine was a great risk, but it's ended up being worth it. I never thought she'd consent to marry me. I'm still worried she'll come to her senses."

Wu Hang actually looked sad, like the idea was impossible.

"I feel badly seeing both of you suffer needlessly. Liani shouldn't be alone."

* * * *

Aron had to hurry away as another enemy thrust spilled forth a new flood of soldiers for the defenders to corral and eliminate. The enemies never surrendered and always fought to the last man.

The war thus far followed the same routine every day. This gave Aron a queasy feeling he was missing something - maybe Damien had some secret plan in play.

"Brock, Trent, I don't like this. It's terrible the loss of life in these battles, but it's too easy. Damien outnumbers us, even with the entire royal host at our backs. His strategy of just wasting casualties on our defenses is senseless. What's he up to?"

"So far, the soldiers we've faced have been brave and willing to die, but they haven't been elite by any stretch of the imagination," Trent answered. "It seems Damien is holding back the real fighters in his army. Perhaps he hopes to wear us down and cull our numbers before he brings in the real attack."

"He's devious, but he's not stupid," Aron mused. "There must be a way we can discover his plans."

"What did you have in mind, Aron?" asked Brock. "Even if we could send secret patrols out into his camp, how would they discover anything useful, if they could avoid detection and annihilation? Are you thinking we should take chances?"

Aron shrugged his shoulders. "The only thing that I feel is we're making a mistake just sitting here. I don't know what we should do."

"Perhaps we should talk to the prince?" Trent suggested.

"Perhaps," Aron answered.

The allies were forced into action with another of the continuing incursions through the royal defense line. This surge was particularly galling for Aron as there were women and children amongst the enemy troops. Rather than slaughter them, Aron cut them off and his forces beat them into surrender. They were led back away from the lines where Aron could interrogate the prisoners. Galean and Liani joined his efforts to glean out Damien's plan.

One young woman stood out to Aron as they approached the huddled prisoners. She had two boys, clearly her sons, pressing against her.

Aron stopped in front of her and she cowered.

"We mean you no harm, madam," he said gently. "Circumstances have put you in the army of our enemy. We'd like to know how that could happen. These are your boys, brave and faithful to you, but they're barely old enough to wield swords. Surely all of you knew it was suicide to attack the royal army dug in behind these defenses. I don't understand. What has our kingdom done to warrant your devotion to Damien?"

She looked around at the others of her group. Their expressions were sad more than anything else, most looked downtrodden.

"We didn't really choose to be in that army," the mother replied tentatively. "Our men were drawn to him by the stories we could find a better life, freedom, and dignity. Damien said we could have it all, but there was a price. We're now all widows. Our husbands were lost early and Damien wouldn't allow us to live in his camp without making a contribution. I think most of us saw a brave death as preferable to the other alternatives he offered. Being, well…"

"I understand. I don't want to speak for the prince. He has authority here, but as far as I'm concerned, your troubles with Damien are over. If you're agreeable, I believe we can find places here in the kingdom for you. We're far from perfect, but there will be no appalling choices for you to make. We also can't guarantee we can prevail against Damien, but for as long as we remain, we'll provide you a safe home."

"My lord, I have no words to express our thanks for such generosity. It's beyond belief you could show us such kindness after we came here to make war on you."

"You didn't come here with that intent," Aron replied. "Damien came here to conquer the world to impose his hell on all men. We know him well and would never hold you accountable for his choices and his actions. I'm sorry you've lost your spouses. I hope we can all look forward to better days in the future. Can I ask you about what you saw in his camp? We feel there is more in play than we see? Do you know of his secret plans?"

"We're fodder, my lord. He never told us anything other than to be brave in the fights, that there'd be a special place in heaven for the brave and we could rejoin our husbands there. I will say, he has considerable troops behind the camp. I got a glimpse once when I was sent to carry a message to the generals. These were fierce and deadly looking troops. I think if you face them in battle, it will not be a good day. They were numerous in their camp. It went on for as far as I could see. I don't know what he plans for them though, I'm sorry, my lord. If I knew more I would gladly tell you. I would also say, of the troops you are fighting, there are many such as we who are widows. I think Damien doesn't like having so many low level mouths to feed. If we're killed and take a few of you with us, he sees that as a good thing. I never knew men could be so evil."

Savior

"I think he is a man unlike any other," Aron answered. "Reborn, he is a special evil cursing our world."

Chapter Eight
~Broken Stalemate~

The prince left the decision to Aron about captives willing to surrender and switch sides. In nearly every case, there were none of value as fighters for the royal army and they were simply more mouths to feed, so they sent them back into the kingdom proper to refugee camps being established to deal with the problem in the short term.

Galean and Liani were a major part of the plan.

"Aron, this is another good thing you've done," Galean explained.

"I couldn't just kill them. They're helpless and homeless. Without their spouses, they're in for hard lives no matter what happens in the war."

He glanced at Liani who was staring at him.

"Don't you agree, Liani?"

"Of course I do, Aron. I'm continually amazed at you and your life. All men should be as thoughtful as you are of the innocent and the helpless."

Aron shrugged. "It seemed like the right thing to do. It's nothing of me."

Liani smiled. "Right, Aron."

"It's nice to see that smile again, Liani. It's been too long."

"I do what I can. I haven't felt much reason to smile in quite a while. Nonetheless, somebody should express thanks for your good works. In the middle of a battle it's not easy to do."

"My lord," said a messenger riding up rapidly. "There is trouble to the north of our position."

"Cherine?" he questioned worriedly.

"She is unharmed, but her position is hard pressed. She sends word the enemy seems to be making a concentrated effort there."

Aron looked at Galean.

"Sooner or later they were going to try to break the deadlock, Aron. I would react with caution. If we race up there and create vulnerabilities we play into his hands elsewhere. Did Cherine ask for reinforcements, messenger?"

"No, my lord, she wished you to know the latest developments."

"What should I do, Galean?"

"I can't answer that. I'm no tactician. I can speak to the generals if you like."

"They're too cautious. I agree Damien is making a move, but doing nothing may not be a good answer."

"Be careful, Aron," said Liani. "I know that look. You can't personally deal with every crisis. You've got to depend on others to do their jobs. Your task is here."

"I've got an idea. If he's trying to draw us north, I'm going to check to the south. I'll only go far enough to assess if he's trying to launch a surprise attack down there."

Aron hurried back to his command.

"We heard," said Brock. "What are you going to do?"

"We're going in the other direction. I want to see if Damien is looking to weaken us there to make a push."

Brock looked at Trent. "That's good, Aron. You're starting to think. That's very good."

Aron and his friends rode away rapidly a little while later at the head of the Black Fist. They moved as fast as possible through the mass of bodies just behind the lines. Their presence bolstered the mood of the troops they passed who shouted encouragement at them.

As the allies charged a loud boom erupted ahead followed by an explosion. Damien's army charged ferociously, these were crack troops. It would've been a disaster had the Black Fist not arrived to steady the faltering defenders who were knocked back on their heels.

Aron led his force into the surging invaders causing a stalemate of flying swords and whirling bodies. Being mounted gave the allies an advantage over the enemy infantry, but the fighting was the toughest they'd encountered. These weren't soldiers who would surrender and they exacted a terrible toll in royal casualties during the fight which lasted the entire day. The battle was on the brink of going either way, until through sheer effort the Black Fist began to push back the enemy, driving them over the wall into retreat. Everybody was exhausted in the gloom of dusk.

Aron looked over the carnage. Bodies were lying everywhere.

"My god," he muttered sadly.

The area commander came up to him. "Thank you, my lord. Your intervention saved us. We could not have prevailed against them without you."

"Be careful, commander. I don't think they're done. I don't know if they'll strike this specific position again, but I think they'll do more of this to create a break in our lines to get behind us. Be ready to move quickly if you see they're doing this somewhere else. We don't want to have gaps, but we certainly don't want them to break out of containment."

"Yes, my lord."

The commander returned to his men to clear the battlefield and help the wounded.

"Are you a lord now, Aron?" asked Brock snidely.

"It's easier than continuously correcting them, Brock. That's how they see authority figures. It isn't important to me."

"This fight is going to get tougher," Trent remarked.

"We should go back to command," Aron advised as they left the area. "Damien is going to probe everywhere for weaknesses."

"We can't be everywhere," Trent reflected. "I'm sure that's part of his thinking. He can spend troops for however long it takes until he creates an opening he can exploit to get behind us. It's strange, for most of my life I assumed the royal host was invincible. Right now in this environment, I feel overmatched."

"It's a huge frontier," said Brock. "There's no possible way to maintain complete deterrence over so large an area. We're not weak or at fault here."

"It's not a matter of fault," Aron replied. "It's a matter of winning or losing. We're fighting to earn the right to live. Damien isn't the better man. He just has a gift of ensnaring the weak minded."

Trent added, "What we did in taking in those captives after battle, that trend has increased. We've got a growing issue of masses of displaced refugees behind our lines in camps. If Damien forces us to retreat, we're going to have trouble deciding where to make a stand, if that's even an option. Protecting them may put us in untenable situations. They're no more useful to us as fighters than they were to Damien. What if it's Damien plan? What if they rose up against us at a critical time in battle? They couldn't defeat us, but they could cause us to lose to elite enemy soldiers attacking us."

"I know, Trent. I thought about it and just went with my gut feeling. I didn't see them as zealots ready to die for Damien's cause. If I guessed wrong, I know we'll pay a terrible price."

"Aron, I'm not saying I'm right about them. I'm just mentioning it so we make contingency plans."

"Thank you, Trent. I can use good reminders so I don't make some major gaff."

A messenger approached.

"My lord, the prince advises you we've encountered a serious incursion where Cherine is leading the defense. The battle remains in question at this point. The last dispatch from her was you shouldn't race to her rescue. That's what Damien wants. She must counter this threat with her forces alone. Your duty is to protect your sections of the line."

Aron simmered. Trent and Brock stared at him and waited for his response.

"Tell the prince his message is acknowledged and received," Aron replied tersely.

"Yes, my lord."

The messenger rode swiftly away.

Brock started to speak, but Aron put up his hand and turned his back. He stared out across the lines at Damien's camp. They saw his army massing and getting into attack positions.

"This is going to be a big one," said Trent.

Instead of their usual charge they stood in formation, waiting. It got Aron's attention.

"Gather the Black Fist. Do we know where the Brutans are located right now?"

Brock answered, "They're not far away, Aron. Do you want me to call them forth?"

"Yes, I think this is the critical point in this fight."

Within an hour the Brutan chieftain was standing beside Aron, his entire tribe mingled amongst the Black Fist formations. Still Damien's army waited. The usual noise in their camp was gone - they stood in silence.

"This time I think we must stay together as a single instrument," Aron explained to the chief.

The chief nodded, his attention seemingly focused on the enemy army.

As they stood sensing the onset of some momentous event, a terrifying blast of deafening sound spread across the landscape. This was followed by a flash in the sky of something moving at great speed. It was directed far from where Aron stood, but in the vicinity of where Cherine was in battle. A huge explosion and blinding light followed. The concussion knocked them off their feet. The royal army soldiers cried out in terror at the first use of an ancient weapon.

The warning sounded again as another weapon was launched, this time in Aron's general direction. The allies had no time to flee. People at the point of impact had no chance to save their lives. They were killed in the explosion which blasted open a huge hole in the defense line.

Damien's army charged immediately. Aron collected himself and yelled for his men to rally. They charged to block the breech in the line - a hopeless task. The enemy sent soldiers of great skill so it was impossible for the Black Fist, even with the ferocity of the Brutans, to simply overwhelm and stifle the attack.

The allies fought for inches of ground until elements of the royal army could join them, which did nothing more than slow the progress of the attackers. Damien sacrificed his troops extravagantly for any gain and as always, to cull the royal fighters.

The fight became a minute by minute battle to survive the next blow and avoid death. It was a hopeless situation, but Aron had no choice. If he pulled back the entire defense would collapse and it would be butchery afterwards.

They fought for hour after hour as Damien's forces ground inexorably forward. The bow in the royal line was bulging and on the verge of rupture.

Aron glanced back for a brief moment to see the general's stand was abandoned. There was no sign on Galean, Liani, or Wu Hang and the Chenese.

"Hopefully they're safe," he muttered before confronting four enemy soldiers coming at him from all sides.

Aron was already wounded in numerous places. These men were deadly and intent. It took all of Aron's skill to survive their first strike. There were no allies able to save him. His only choice was to win this fight or die on the spot.

Exhausted from the long day of fighting, Aron wasn't willing to see everything end here. He steeled his resolve and went to lightning strikes and effective feints. Once he downed the first of the elite fighters, he attacked them aggressively to maintain the initiative. They tried to rally, but one of them took a chance and Aron ended his life. Against two men, Aron knew he could win, and he did. He looked around after they were dispatched and ran over to save Brock and then Trent.

They called for the Black Fist to rally around Aron. The Brutans also answered the call and together they scythed their way through crack enemy troops and momentarily forestalled the collapse of the defense.

"This battle is lost," said Trent. "We can't hold them off. They've got unlimited manpower pouring through the breech. Make the call Aron. The prince and his generals are long gone. We need to save as many as we can. If they stay here, Damien will simply wipe them out, all of them."

Aron paused only a moment before deciding. The sound of trumpets echoed across the battlefield and the royal host disengaged and retreated according to pre-arranged orders.

The sudden retreat of the allies surprised Damien's forces. They paused instead of taking advantage of the opportunity. They were fatigued also and let the royal army retreat.

Savior

When Damien heard about the battlefield gaff, he was irate.

"I should have the combat commanders beheaded. What didn't they understand about my orders? Was I not clear there were to be no survivors? We outman the royal army and I gave them an opening in their defense wall. I don't tolerate failure. This is the last time my orders won't be followed to the letter. I can find plenty of other commanders to lead my army."

The secondary rallying points for the allies were roughly equidistance. It was impossible to know the status of the other parts of the army. In particular, Aron couldn't get word on Cherine, the masters, or their fate. He could only hope she'd survived. He had his hands full trying to organize the disheartened royal soldiers. They had defeat in their eyes after witnessing Damien's fearsome weapon.

Damien's army was fast in resuming the pursuit. This time they had only flat lands and farm villages in front of them.

Aron sent marauding forces along their entire line to set ambushes, quick strikes, and retreats before they could be pinned down. It effectively slowed the advance of the enemy and gave Aron much needed time to organize the army and retreat in an orderly fashion.

Damien's generals sent their own small quick strike units, but they had far less luck as Aron was ready for their move and they stumbled into traps in unfamiliar territory. Aron ordered they be killed to the man so none could return to Damien to make any reports.

Aron stood talking with Brock, Trent, Barmon, and his own father. "I'm surprised we got out of that predicament."

"We're taking down a lot of Damien's troops," Brock replied.

"Damien doesn't care how many die on either side. Life is meaningless to him. We can't forget that in our planning. He'll always look to overwhelm with numbers to try to pin down and slaughter us. We'll keep moving and avoid pitched battles as much as we can."

Aron sent word back to move the refugee camps and retreated into the heart of the kingdom. He had no other choice.

The allies came upon the site of one of the largest of the camps recently hastily evacuated.

"Where are the prince and his command structure?" asked Aron looking around in surprise.

"I don't know, Aron," Trent answered. "Everything is in flux. I say we continue to make decisions as our circumstances dictate. For all we know, the prince is hiding under his sheets back in the royal suite at the palace."

Aron smiled ruefully. "I doubt the prince is back at the palace, Trent. We have our ongoing issues with him, but he's a changed man in many ways. I don't think he's a coward for retreating from Damien's weapons. He has the responsibility of the kingdom on his shoulders. That includes all of the innocent citizens who are now in harm's way. He did what he had to do."

"Right," said Trent doubtfully. "I never thought I'd hear you apologizing for him."

The fighting surged around them again as one of Damien's raiding parties attacked - a futile and a fatal decision for the enemy. The Brutan's were feral with the smell of blood in the air and cut down the raiders with brutality. It wasn't a good death for any of their opponents.

Aron walked over to the chief. He was agitated with battle frenzy and nearly attacked Aron before he came to his senses.

"Whoa, you got them, chief, they're all dead."

"This is the place for the Brutans," he bellowed loudly. "This is our work, what we were born to do. Let them all come to us. We welcome the chance to spill their blood."

The Brutans all roared savagely, many held up bloody trophies.

Aron could never adjust to this aspect of dealing with the Brutans. He killed out of necessity. That wasn't the case with these barbarians. Some normal part of humanity was either broken or missing altogether from them and they saw no problem in it. They rejoiced in their mayhem. It seemed a miracle to Aron that they would obey him enough to not pose a threat to their own allies.

In a time of war, especially when you're in the inferior position, the Brutans were perfect battle partners.

Aron directed the retreat to keep it from turning into a rout. They continued their tactics of raiding Damien's forces while obliterating the raiders Damien sent in response.

Damien chose to increase the pressure by pouring seemingly endless waves of his soldiers through the gap in the line to press the retreat of the royals before they could establish a new defensible skirmish line.

As Aron passed villages and towns, they were all abandoned. The people were flocking toward Nephora as if there was safety and sanctuary there. It quickly created food shortages and congestion. Sanitary systems were overloaded and diseases began to rise. Hungry immigrants who couldn't find food to feed their families started trying to steal from the city dwellers. With the army in the field, the city guard was unable to maintain order. Conditions in Nephora deteriorated both in terms of material and morale. The city was choked by a feeling of approaching doom. Few people felt the kingdom could win this war as word of Damien's terrible weapons spread like wild fire.

Savior

* * * *

When the prince returned to the city it was in the midst of chaos. He brought key army units with him and they imposed martial law to try to cope with the disaster, leaving the war in the field to Aron. He was shocked at the tepid actions of his father to this crisis.

The king and queen were distraught at the downward spiral, having no answers to the challenge. Each day that passed the king deteriorated.

* * * *

Coraline looked at the latest version of the reigning monarch in shock. He'd always been composed, authoritative, and seemingly competent. Here he was clearly unraveling and it affected the entire royal court. People were beginning to fend for themselves. Some of them considered trying to join Damien if he was the winning side.

Coraline went to her rooms bringing Tasha, and both women's parents with her to safeguard.

"This is a very dangerous situation," she began. "When Damien's forces arrive it will not get better. I think we should look to our own devices to weather this storm."

Coraline looked at her protector, Marin, her husband's assigned guardian. He was steady as a rock in every situation. It calmed her to see his strength and gave her hope there might be a way out of this noose. He was never flustered and acted the equal of every crisis.

He took her glance as a sign to speak.

"I have quietly assembled a troop of highly skilled men," he explained. "We've chosen to make our duty that of protecting you. We all know the outcome of the war is highly in doubt. In the event of the worst happening, we're prepared to take you away to safety. Whether that means a life on the run, I can't say, but it would be life and we wouldn't be under Damien's boot. It's not the life you had in the palace, but it may be that life is over. The problem you must consider is when you choose to flee. We can't wait here in the city until we're surrounded and cut off from escape. I haven't spoken to your husband about this idea. I'll leave it to you to decide. Though many believe he'll want to flee to save his own life because they don't really know him, my opinion is he will stand to the end here. I would take the queen also, but I don't know if she'd leave the king."

"What makes you think we could survive if the kingdom falls?" asked Tasha's father.

"I worry little about Damien's occupying army. As a massive force, they can overwhelm armies in their path because Damien cares nothing about sacrificing lives, but they're poor conscripts. The general skill level of those forces is poor. In open ground on the run, I have no fear of eluding them. We could cause them serious problems with hit and run tactics. Unfortunately what we couldn't do is rescue large numbers of people. We would be forced to maintain a relatively small camp. We'd have no way to feed and house significant numbers. We'd also we be forced to require most of our people be fighters."

They looked at Radigan.

"You have a bad reputation, sir," Marin continued. "Obviously the only reason you're still alive and allowed amongst us is because of your wife. You've been expedient in all of your prior decisions. Whoever had the power seemed to be who you favored. Since you've ruined your relationship with Damien, and no one among the allies would ever trust you again, you have a serious choice to make. If you say you'll join us, it's not enough. It's just words from your deceitful mouth. We must safeguard ourselves, so your alliance must come with a guarantee and a price. It seems to me the only thing you've ever shown any true concern for is Tasha. If she is willing to be your price, we'll give you a place here, but realize the cost of treachery. If you betray us, not only will you die, but so will Tasha. She deserves much better than you as a husband, but that choice was made long ago."

"I agree," said Tasha. "If he betrays us, I will willingly sacrifice my life. That my husband could do such things has been galling to me. I won't allow him to be the author of our demise."

"Tasha, no," said her mother. "You can't take punishment for him. He should've faced his consequences already. You did nothing to incur the wrath he's earned."

"I know, mother, but I married him so I took on that mantle. As his wife, I bear responsibility for his actions."

"Are you going to stand there in silence?" her father huffed, glaring at Radigan. "I never liked your sneaky ways and it's been a daily curse having my daughter tied to you. She's already suffered terribly for your choices. Now you're willing to see her punished for your weaknesses?"

He stared at her father darkly.

"I've had ample time to consider the long list of my failings. Much of what you've said is true. Am I guiltier than your prince? You seemed to have no problem with forgiving him and believe me, his sins dwarf mine. You speak of my past. None of us can change our past. It's done with and over. Yes, I've not shown great character in much of my actions, but you ignore my accomplishments. I've survived at the highest levels in the kingdom, in Aron's camp and in Damien's inner circle. In spite of my personal compromises, Tasha has seen merit in me. She's not unhappy as my wife. Her issues come from the complex dangerous world we've been forced to endure. I'm no more of a threat to you here than you yourself, Marin. I value life as much as any man and I would die to protect my wife and her family. I'm a highly skilled fighter. There are very few who could stand against me in a single combat. I'm worth much more to you as a partner than any imagined risk. I am who I am, so I won't mewl and cower to your threats. Accept me for who I am, or not. It's your choice to make, not mine. If you think you can take my life, I invite you to try. That's not so easy a task." Radigan stared icily at Marin, his hand on the hilt of his sword.

"Brave words," said Marin grimly. "You're not talking to the ignorant here. We neither fear you nor trust you. What you've said doesn't change our perceptions about you. If you fulfill your role and fight in our defense, you'll be allowed to live. That's our offer."

Radigan smiled. "How could I refuse such a generous approach? I'll let my deeds speak for me. For those who wish me ill, beware. I'll not go quietly."

He looked at Tasha's father. "Though you would claim to reject it, you and your wife are under my protection. Only Aron could offer you a better pledge."

Her father glowered at Radigan but turned and went to his wife and daughter. Tasha wouldn't look at Radigan. They walked away to a different room.

"So be it, Radigan," said Marin. "We'll have eyes on you at all times."

Radigan shrugged dismissively. He left the room also.

* * * *

Aron got up while it was still dark. The sun had yet to peek over the horizon. He had a feeling something was amiss.

"Brock, Trent," he whispered. They sat up with a start. "Get up, quickly."

They sent word throughout the Black Fist and the Brutans to be vigilant. Within a short amount of time they were moving as a unit in the direction of Damien's army. They reached their sentry line and found a few of them dozing off.

"We've seen nothing, my lord," one of the embarrassed soldiers explained awkwardly.

"Something is afoot," Aron replied, ignoring the soldier. He stared into the pre-dawn gloom looking for any sign of danger. They knelt in a hastily formed skirmish line suddenly alert.

They didn't see movement, but they heard a metallic sound. Aron used his hand signals to send instructions down the line both ways. They heard another ping of a metal item.

As they waited they started to see shapes in the distance creeping toward them. As they watched, they realized this was a major push from the enemy forces. The size of this force was massive.

Aron sent a warning back to the main camp, so royal forces were rallying and forming ranks in defensive positions.

From above them, they heard that terrible blast of sound which was chilling to the bone. Flares ignited in the sky above their head and the enemy charged.

Aron's archers launched wave after wave of arrows at the attackers felling large numbers of them, but in this sea of humanity, it was a drop in the bucket. The enemy raced toward them intent on wiping out anybody in their path.

Aron considered his best move. Making a stand which could cost him many of his best troops was a difficult option, however pulling out of the fight guaranteed defeat and possibly disaster. He looked around and saw determination as well as fear in the eyes of the royal army. The Brutans, however, were anxious for the fight. They shouted derisively at the approaching enemy.

"Are you ready for this, brother?" asked Brock, as though he expected this could be their ending.

"I'm ready, Brock. If this is it, so be it. We've done our best."

The impact as the two forces met was loud as weapons struck and people shouted. The royal lines bowed under the onslaught of such a large attack. Aron formed the Black Fist and the Brutans behind him like a spear point and he drove forward into the charging ranks of Damien's army. It confused them and it created a sudden problem as Aron disrupted their forward movement in this area. He kept driving ahead mowing down enemies in a bubble of deadly flying steel. The enemy was forced to the sides which slowed the attack in those areas too. The push from behind began to cause trouble for the enemy as soldiers were forced too close to defend themselves and they were easily slaughtered. They began pushing back to try to survive. It stalled the charge.

Aron angled in an arc with his troop leaving a wide swath of dead as they fought back to his lines. There were severe bulges, but no breakthroughs yet. He went to the nearest incursion and attacked the enemy. The royal soldiers rallied behind his courageous example and helped halt the enemy advance. Gradually the line stabilized though the enemy did not relent in the surge. Aron's army couldn't stop the push, they could only slow it.

Savior

The enemy poured fresh troops into the battle and rotated the initial fighters back to rest briefly. The royal army had no such respites. They were forced to fight continually and with time fatigue started to become a factor for them. Aron rode up and down the lines to intercede as much as possible, but there were too many leaks in the dam. Gradually Aron was forced to spend his time riding down pockets of enemy soldiers behind the royal lines. They managed to disrupt the safety of the royal camp and caused food preparation and hospital operations to retreat. This meant royal soldiers couldn't be fed on time and the injured had large distances to travel for treatment.

The royal side had no choice but to disengage and fall back to secondary rally points. Damien's army gave them no quarter racing after them in full attack mode. It was a very dangerous situation as they teetered on the brink of a rout.

Aron arrayed the entire corps of archers in a skirmish line to pelt the enemy soldiers as they came into range. Felling large numbers of them interrupted their headlong attack and gave the royal host just enough time to create separation. They retreated quickly to their assigned places behind the front, exhausted but at least they were still alive and functioning as an army.

Aron felt numb from the continuous battle and with missing multiple meals. It was ironic he could smell food cooking in Damien's camp, like it was another means to torment him.

He looked at his comrades. Even Brock was hollowed eyed with the strain. The Brutans were uncharacteristically quiet. Aron walked throughout their ranks to reassure and laud them for their great fighting prowess during a rare and brief lull in fighting. They stared back at him fiercely loyal. They were willing to die for Aron.

Damien gained territory every day. The royal defense was heroic, but increasingly it became clear the outcome of this war wasn't in doubt. The royal citizenry was being compacted by the noose of Damien's army surrounding and compressing them.

All the commanders along the front sent requests to Aron for what to do. The generals and the prince were long gone as field leaders. Only Aron remained in charge to stand with the army to the end.

"What do I tell them?" he asked.

Brock, Trent and the Brutan chief simply looked at him.

"They already know, Aron," said Brock finally.

"I don't have any answers. All I can offer is to die alongside them. Is this the end of all our efforts, brother?"

"As long as I still draw breath, I'll keep fighting, Aron." It was a brave statement, but Brock didn't exhibit his usual bravado. There was an air of defeat to his demeanor that rattled Aron.

Trent stared vacantly at the enemy lines. He looked to be exhausted.

"I've got to do something," Aron muttered overwhelmed by a helpless feeling.

Chapter Nine
~Difficult Choices~

The king and queen hosted a banquet to celebrate the return of the crown prince to the palace. It was a colossal gaff which shocked the city from the mightiest royals down to the lowliest peasants. Even Agar was surprised and appalled as the city dawdled on the eve of disaster.

Damien's army wasn't in sight yet, which was a miracle in itself of Aron's determined defense, but everyone knew it was just a matter of time. Defeat in the war seemed a foregone conclusion.

The conditions in the city were deplorable and the populace was nearly uncontrollable as starvation was the new norm. Few people ventured out after dark as their chances of returning alive were slim with rabid packs of criminals on the prowl. The city guard and the royal army Agar brought with him were forced to pick enclaves to make their stands. They didn't bother sending out patrols any longer. Were it not for the approach of the enemy army, the citizens would have fled the city. As it was, there was nowhere to go.

"Your parent's are different people, Agar," said Coraline in an attempt to sound diplomatic at their mystifying behavior. "I have no words for this strange decision to have a banquet. There's nothing to celebrate and food is scarce."

"I've been asked to replace my father by many of his advisors. They fear he's lost his mind, darling," the prince explained.

"What are you going to do?"

"I haven't decided. I've dreamed about ascending to the throne all of my life, but this isn't the way I would choose to do it. If I did take the throne, I suspect my reign would be a short one. Damien's army seems to be beyond our abilities to contain. The royal host is fighting bravely, but still he pushes us backwards. I know the field troops think me a coward for not standing with them in battle, but when reports came to me about the chaos in Nephora, I felt I had to return. My father is proving to be a poor war king. I didn't feel I had another choice. I guess whether I died out there or died here doesn't matter."

"Don't say that, Agar. Have some faith. Galean still believes Aron will lead us to victory over Damien."

Agar took Coraline in his arms. "I'd like to be an optimist, but I'm the authority here now. I must plan for the worst. If Damien marches up to this building and bursts down our doors, I can't have you suffer at his hands. I want to make a plan, along with Marin, to spirit you and our parents out of the city before it gets closed off. Though the Arreck don't see us as their friends, I would have you go to their land and ask for their mercy. Perhaps it would only be delaying the inevitable, but I want to see you live free for as long as possible. They'll be a tenacious and a determined foe for any opponent. Perhaps in their mountains they can prevail against Damien. If they're defeated, it will be your choice what to do then. I assume I'll be gone from this world at that point. You know the life Liani lived as Damien's chattel. I fear there's only one way to avoid that, crossing over to join me in the next life, but I can't make that choice for you."

Coraline looked distressed at Agar's grim assessment.

"It isn't something where you have to tell me your decision, Coraline. Life is sweet and we're loath to give it up. Taking such a radical step is a terrible choice. It may be you can accept a life of subservience to Damien rather than die. I can't fault you if you do. As I said, the probability is at that point, I would be dead and buried so my opinions wouldn't matter. It was easy to be proud and haughty when our rule was unchallenged. Too late, I've learned about humility."

"Our marriage hasn't been perfect, but I chose to marry you and I've tried to be a good wife. Being sent away, I don't know if I can do that. My fate is tied to yours."

"I appreciate those words, more than you could know, but while I'm able, I won't cede you to Damien. If he's meant to conquer this world, I vow it won't be with you at his side. I don't deserve such a wonderful wife."

She hugged him tightly.

"Hopefully, it won't come to that."

He went over to where Marin was sitting. He was never out of sight of Coraline as was Agar's wishes.

"You've heard my idea. I want for you to begin preparations immediately. Assemble a fast moving and skillful unit who can flee or fight in any situation. I will speak to my parents and to Coraline's before we have a final order."

"Yes, my prince. I've already done that. You've made a wise choice. I won't allow her to be touched by any man. I pledge my life on it. Damien can pursue us at his peril. Also, I agree with Galean. I've been around Aron enough to believe he won't allow us to be conquered. I don't know how he can do it, but I think he will find a way. The defense he's provided out there has been remarkable."

Coraline spoke, "Agar, can I ask you, is it your intention that only I be sent away? Are there others that should be preserved too? I'm thinking of Galean who's a unique person, possibly irreplaceable, Liani, and Tasha for example?"

"I'll consider it, darling. You have a good point. If there's a way to rebuild after this war, if Damien is defeated, it will be with intellects like Galean. I think Aron would add Abdurka in that irreplaceable category. He's become integral in Galean's actions. It would probably be wise to include Liani, because Wu Hang and his Chenese friends would then be a part of Marin's strike force. I'll talk to them to get their opinions. I'll go to my father now and be back later. Marin, follow my plan in the meantime."

"I'll leave a squad of my best men with Coraline when I'm away, my prince."

* * * *

The battle raged on for the royal army. Damien's progress was slowed even further as they dug in to fight for every inch of ground. The allies were surprised when they received unexpected reinforcements. The local displaced citizenry, who were faced with the choice of the nightmare conditions in Nephora or the war, increasing they opted to venture out and join with the army in the battle. They were much needed bodies against the tidal wave of Damien's army. Although they weren't skilled fighters, neither was many in Damien's army. The considerable number of captives who converted to ally with Aron added their support in the front line also. The royal defense was stiffening by the day.

Unfortunately, it wasn't a development Aron could use to any advantage. It did little more than even the odds, slightly. Damien still had overwhelming numbers and their assault never faltered.

Each day Aron was driven inexorably closer to the royal capital city.

In the capital, news of the war created numerous riots and outbursts with the growing panic. Some people started to slip out into the countryside. It was dangerous, but so was staying in the city. They fled either north or south hoping to avoid Damien's advance. Crime was a daily occurrence. There was no force capable to quelling the unrest at that point. Civilized society in the city had completely broken down.

Aron had long ago sent Enna and Biala to the great swamp to join their people. Although they resisted greatly, he wouldn't allow them to face the end he felt was inevitable.

Eventually, Nephora was at their back. Damien sent his army in nearly endless attacks to tighten the noose and deny escape to his prey,
He drove back the royal defenders who no longer had any positions to make a stand as they were driven into the city. The panicked citizens caused a problem clogging the streets as they were condensed by the shrinking skirmish line. The defense broke down into clumps of defenders basically fending for themselves.

* * * *

At the palace, Agar called forth Marin and those people selected to travel under his protection. The king and queen were initially hesitant to abandon the city but the terrible sounds of the fight in the streets changed their minds.

In an ironic twist, Granor showed up to volunteer his followers to join the protection force. Similarly, Lilith appeared with her maidens with the same offer.

"We're useless trying to fight in the streets," she explained to the prince. "We can use our skills in a fast moving mobile force. Marin wants speed, but I'll guarantee he'll be glad for every sword he has available in his force, my prince."

Agar looked at Marin. "I'll take her along, sire, if it's your wish. I'd say the king's personal guard, my people, and these few volunteers added to my handpicked corps should do well for my purposes."

Agar took Coraline in his arms. There were tears in her eyes.

"Please don't stay here, husband. It's certain death for you. Damien will use you for a spectacle to cow the populace. It's a horrible useless ending."

"I can't, my darling. Perhaps it's time for me to pay for my many sins. I'm not overly brave, but I know if I don't stay, things could collapse, and it might endanger your chances of escape."

The queen walked over to hug her son.

Radigan appeared along with Tasha.

Agar took Tasha in his arms.

"I hope I'm sparing you the nightmare of Damien. We'll take down as many of them as we can before we fall. I'm so sorry for how I wronged you before. Perhaps this is some small step toward righting those wrongs."

"Prince Agar," she replied. "There's been so much happen in my life, I can't even remember those days. It isn't important to me now. I wish you wouldn't sacrifice yourself like this."

"If I thought there was another way, believe me I'd go away with my wife to live in peace."

Granor eyed Lilith, smirking. She smiled back and stepped close to him.

110

"Do you think this is your chance for mischief, to repay me and these others with some devious betrayal?"

"Lilith, how can you think that? I'm at Damien's mercy as much as anyone else. My only choice is to follow this group with the hope of a life elsewhere."

"Granor, I think Belisa hasn't forgotten you. I'm no fool. Going to the Arreck is a poor choice. You have something sinister in mind. I'm warning you, we'll side with Marin and I guarantee you'll lose against him. I respect only Aron more than I respect Marin. We'll have eyes on you at every moment."

"If that's so, you'll see I'm no threat. My issue with you is long over with, Lilith."

"Of course it is," she replied skeptically. "You've been warned, Granor."

They had to go to the library to extract an unwilling Galean and Liani and their staff to join the flight.

There were considerable courtesans and nobles who begged to be included. Agar lined up his personal guards to keep them restrained until the escapees were gone.

* * * *

Meanwhile, the battle for Nephora raged on. Casualties were enormous on both sides. The criminal gangs and scavengers joined in the attack on Damien's army, having no other choice.

The smoke from fires in the city buildings choked the air and obscured their vision. Damien's forces refused to relent with the onslaught pressing on like a vice grip squeezing the city into pulp.

The sheer numbers of people caught in the trap served to stymie his progress. They clogged everything, making it impossible to move in any direction.

Damien himself came to the city after hearing the reports of the stalemate. "Pull back our forces enough to give some separation. I'll create an avenue."

Aron knew what to expect as he watched the maneuver, but was helpless to do anything about it when the enemy retreated.

Brock was on one side and Trent on the other. Their uniforms had long ago been battered and shredded. They all had significant scars and they were all weakened from many missed meals.

"He's going to unleash his hellish weapons," Aron commented.

"We're sitting ducks," said Trent.

Aron fully expected this would be his ending, but when the flash came in the sky it struck to his right in a massive concussion rocking the ground and knocking them to their backs.

The sounds of the screams were deafening. People panicked and trampled the weaker ones trying to flee. Damien's army charged immediately at the breech and through the smoldering ashes of flattened houses and the reek of immolated bodies. Aron was locked in his spot as civilians pushed forward to escape Damien's charge. The Black Fist and the Brutans were forced to be bystanders to the charge on the royal palace.

"My god, how can this have happened," said Brock.

"I guess Galean's trust in me as a savior was misguided," Aron replied ruefully.

"Aron, what else could you have done. If not for you, Damien would have been here a month ago or earlier."

Aron stood sadly watching the carnage before turning to look south.

"I want to try to find Cherine. I don't know if she survived, but I need to find out."

"The masters would not allow her to be killed, Aron," said Trent grimly.

"I pray you're right, my friend. You've been a brave comrade in arms, Trent. I owe you more than I could ever repay."

"We've all saved each other numerous times. Don't get maudlin now. Let's go find your future wife."

Aron smiled in spite of the surroundings. They charged toward the nearest of Damien's attackers and scythed through them easily. The royal army around them followed, having no other orders. It turned into a significant allied incursion driving apart Damien's forces. Damien's elite troops were assigned to spearhead the drive going to the palace so these were common soldiers in Aron's path and far from the best of Damien's army. Aron was able to make rapid progress driving along the line. The remnants of the royal army rallied when he came past so his impromptu assault gathered momentum rapidly. Damien's forces receded in their path and offered weak resistance.

It took an hour of charging and fighting their way before he saw his first member of the masters. He was beset in a heroic fight alone against ten enemies. He was exhausted and fighting on his last legs when suddenly he was surrounded by whooping Brutans slaughtering the enemy in droves. He looked around in astonishment as Aron pulled up to his side.

"Come, my friend, this is not your day to die. Take us to Cherine."

"Yes, my lord," he replied. They gave him a captured enemy horse and he joined their ferocious drive south.

Ahead they saw a stubborn knot of combatants and the unmistakable uniforms of the masters, surrounded by enemy.

The Brutans struck the encircling fighters hacking down any they could reach and driving apart their column.

Aron saw Cherine and charged at full speed. The near death experience evaporated quickly for the masters as they were suddenly in the midst of the Black Fist, the Brutans, and significant of the royal host. Damien's forces were blunted in progress and pushed back with heavy casualties.

The royal army cheered at the rare victory and drove forward savagely to extract revenge for so many of their comrades lost in the war.

Cherine sat in her saddle stunned as Aron rode close and grabbed her in an embrace.

"I feared I would never see you again," she whispered.

"I worried when I couldn't get word of your plight. I trusted your skills and the protection of the masters, but sometimes ill fate intervenes."

"What of the battle? We saw the explosion."

"Damien slaughtered all of those innocent people to clear a way to the palace. I don't know the situation there. If the king chooses to make a stand, his reign will soon end."

"Agar is no fool, Aron. I'm sure he had a plan to save, well, the people that count."

"Hopefully that means Galean and Liani, people who can provide wisdom if there are survivors."

"What should we do now, Aron?"

Brock and Trent rode over.

"Cherine, it gladdens my heart to see you," said Brock.

"Brock, I thought I'd come to the end for me and my men. I'm shocked to be with you again."

"What do we do now, Aron?" asked Trent.

"I'd say the civilians will be racing away from the battle for the palace. I can probably collect the army as we go and drive in behind Damien's attack, cut them off from reinforcements, and then maybe we catch them between Agar's palace defense and us. We can possibly destroy his best units."

"That's a pretty optimistic view, Aron," said Cherine. "We're still beset by superior numbers."

"In our drive to rescue you, we found the bulk of Damien's forces were low quality. He seems to have sent his best units to specific places for specific battles. We just helped you destroy one of his better units."

"They were a test," Cherine affirmed.

"Are you able to return to the fray, wife?"

Cherine looked at him directly. "Have we married from afar? I was your fiancée to my last knowledge."

"In my dreams we married," said Aron. "We'll rectify that matter shortly."

She chuckled. "Yes, husband, I'm ready to fight. We must hasten to save those poor souls trapped in the palace."

Reunited at long last, the masters blended with the Black Fist and the Brutans and they led the royal army in the south toward the palace. Cherine rode beside Aron with Brock and Trent directly behind them.

It was a steady advance as Damien's forces weren't expecting an attack from their flanks and rear. They felled numerous enemy troops, something they had no choice about.

The masters were like a refreshed corps with their confidence returned. No one had had much to eat in a while, but now they felt there was light at the end of the tunnel. They felt rejuvenated being with their elite comrades again.

As they fought their way in the chase to the battle for the palace, Aron tended to stay very near to Cherine warding her. It was the very thing he'd agreed he wouldn't do. She didn't object to his aid though.

They were attacking the rear of Damien's finest fighters so once the element of surprise was gone, they were soon immersed in a serious fight. Their enemy was highly skilled and highly motivated, and there were many more of them to call upon.

The battle forward ebbed and changed into a static battle of attrition. Even with the sounds of battle all around them, they still heard the roar of the charge at the palace in the distance. Agar was on his own trying to survive the attack. There was no way Aron could break through to reinforce palace defenses. The royal host surged behind Aron sensing a critical juncture in the war. They managed to bend back Damien's front, but they couldn't break through.

* * * *

At the palace, Agar looked out from his balcony at the scene below. Damien's army looked like a plague of insects swarming the palace walls. His personal guard, those who he hadn't sent away with Marin, awaited Agar in grim silence surveying the desperate battle.

The royal defenders fought courageously but they were hopelessly outnumbered. Agar took his sword and headed out of the empty royal suite to go outside. The palace servants were long gone.

Agar's hope to see Aron ride to the rescue didn't seem to be coming to fruition. He couldn't be sure who was still alive out in the city. Although there was fighting visible in the distance in most directions, they couldn't tell what was happening out there. Agar assumed the worst.

Suddenly the enemy pulled back from their attack to hold their ground, waiting. After a short time they heard a roar in the sky and saw an ancient weapon streaking toward them. It struck the main gate with a massive detonation blasting it apart and throwing bodies everywhere.

Damien attacked immediately. Agar roared in defiance and personally raced to fill the breech. The palace defenders were in shock, but rallied when they saw their prince's bravery. The two forces met in a clash of weapons and quick death. For a time, the royal fighters held the fight in a stalemate, but as their comrades fell, the defense started to falter as Damien's endless hordes swarmed through the wall to drive them back. Damien could absorb casualties where Agar could not.

The knot of contained enemy attackers inside the courtyard swelled and bulged as the surrounding defenders failed.

Agar sounded a retreat and his forces retreated to the palace steps to make their final stand.

The enemy raced after them giving no quarter. They attacked immediately. Agar went to the forefront to stand at the tip of his defense. His men protected him and fought against the enemy taking numerous of Damien's best men. It was brave but also hopeless. It wasn't a quick battle but nonetheless, the pile of the dead and dying became the single most notable sight.

Damien himself slipped forward to stand there in person at the last.

He watched avidly as the defenders were pounded down to the ground. Finally, he personally stood before Agar as his men disarmed the exhausted prince.

Agar was defiant on the outside, but internally, he was crushed his life with Coraline was over. It was about her he thought instead of thinking about the destruction of the monarchy and the dissolution of the royal society.

"We meet at last, Prince Agar," said Damien magnanimously. "You requited yourself very well in the war. Unfortunately for you, it could have ended only one way. I've heard much about your royal rule of your subjects and your abuses. It's a joyous day for the world to put an end to such villainy."

Agar shook his head. "I've equally heard about you and your stewardship of your followers. We've seen ample examples in the battles with the sacrifice of women and children as fodder of how you view the masses. You're right, I have mountains of my sins to atone for with my blood, but I think when your time comes to an end on this world I'll see you in hell. I suspect they'll have a special place for you."

Damien's smirk vanished.

"Your insolence won't protect you from my wrath. I planned on a quick death for you in honor of your courage, but you've convinced me we should look to a slower more punishing end. Ponder that in your prison cell. You'll never know the day I choose to take your life. Take him down to their palace prison cells."

They started to drag him away.

"Something else for you to consider, prince, I will hunt down your family and loved ones. Your wife or I should say your widow will be in my arms and at my mercy. I understand she's a breath taking beauty. Perhaps I'll take her as a second wife to Liani. They tell me it was one of your many weaknesses, the soft caresses of numerous lovely women. You took the women of other men and now it will be done to you. Think on that and despair."

Agar eyed Damien darkly before starting to whisper a religious chant as they hauled him away.

Damien turned to his lieutenant, Straga, who was standing beside him.

"In all these centuries I've lived, I've seen this so many times. When people stand before their doom, they turn to religious displays, as if it will miraculously save them. It never has, not one single time. How could such a man as Agar think he could warrant salvation?"

"They're weak and they're fools," Straga replied. "His is only the first of the deaths we'll savor from this royal rabble. If you wish, my people are well skilled in pain and torture. We can visit the prince. I guarantee he'll beg for death."

"All in good time, Straga. As you say, we have unfinished business. I will have them all stand before me in defeat, starting with Aron. He's defied me for long enough. I will have Aron's women too, all of those beauties he cherishes. I have all of their names, Belisa, Tasha, Coraline, Enna, Biala, Liani, Cherine, and even this Lilith who turned her back on me. She'll regret that foolish decision as she screams out in agony. Aron's mother, the royal queen, Tasha's mother, I will capture them all."

"I only ask that you forebear your wrath from Sirina, my wife. I ask that you allow me to deal with her in my own way. I still wish to have a life with her afterwards, but trust me, she will suffer at my hands until she kneels and concedes all authority and control to me. I will take off Barmon's head and mount it outside my house until it rots away so she sees it every day of her life."

Damien eyed him with a calculating look. "I'll strongly consider your request, but this matter must be handled properly. I'm the authority and it's my wrath which prevails. Wronging me was their great offense. Your interests are secondary to mine. Do you accept that, Straga?"

"Yes, my liege."

Damien laughed.

"So now I'm addressed as a royal person? That amuses me. Your assignment is to go back out into this city and capture Aron. They're beaten but he's the type who never gives up. I've faced such men before, and killed them all. Bring him before me and I'll be favorably disposed to honor your wishes. Where Aron is, there will be the heart of their leadership. This prince was a figurehead. Aron is the real driver of the resistance. We'll crush them once Aron is brought to justice. I think he'll experience such a terrible ending it will create a new legend. A prominent death before the public of such horror, no one will ever dare rise up against us again."

"Your will is my command," Straga replied, turned, and left.

With the Erati at the spearhead, Straga led the elite of Damien's army out to pursue Aron. What he realized when he arrived on the scene was the large number of remaining royal soldiers who gathered around Aron. Instead of an easy ride back down their assault route, they quickly met their brethren who were being battered backwards by the royal host. It was a situation which was eroding rapidly from the perspective of Damien's side. They continued to have a numeric advantage, but their forces were unorganized and disconnected with the course of the battle. There were no easy victories awaiting Straga.

"At last we'll face Aron and his ilk," Straga shouted to the Erati. They gave a shout, but it was hardly a ringing endorsement. They knew what facing Aron meant. Aron's "ilk" included the savage Brutans who had deadly intentions for the Erati whom they saw as traitors for siding with Damien. It wasn't a fight they relished.

Even Straga had reservations. The allies were a group with numerous skilled and highly motivated men with a grudge who would be looking for Straga on the battlefield. Although he always spoke contemptuously about Barmon, he was no fool about his opponent. Barmon transformed his body and spirit into a fearless near killing machine. He wasn't a man to take lightly. Revenge is a powerful motive.

The allies drove ahead relentlessly.

When they were suddenly confronted by Straga at the head of a deadly unit of fighters, it caught their attention. When the Brutans spotted Erati banners, they went ballistic, charging instantly. It jeopardized Aron's position having his lines suddenly destabilized. They had no choice but to charge after the Brutans to support them. It meant racing into the teeth of Damien's elite without any advantage in position or strength.

The ensuing fight was a titanic battle which became a stalemate as neither side could gain an edge.

The Brutans were insane in their drive to reach the hated Erati. Straga stayed far enough away from the line to avoid Brutan wrath but he was like a magnet to them. They battered against the best Damien had to offer and with time they began to make slow progress. When the Erati met the Brutans in battle it was a savage fight with no rules, no quarter and no limits.

Newly returned to join the defense, Barmon rode into the center of that contest to join with and to inspire the Brutans in the toughest fight of their lives.

He fought with all of the abandon of the Brutan and every bit of their ferocity. Straga pondered his next move. Watching Barmon scythe through his best men gave him pause. His hatred was no less than ever, but beating Barmon was no guarantee. Straga wasn't anxious to risk his life unless he was sure of the outcome.

Brock saw the peril his father faced and quickly rode to try to protect his back. This drew Trent to follow him. Aron didn't join them as Cherine was fighting right beside him, so he hesitated torn between fear for his brother and fear for his fiancée.

"Do what you must, Aron," she called.

"You're my priority," he huffed, panting with the strain of the rigorous fighting.

A determined knot of enemy experts suddenly broke through to surround Aron and Cherine. It was a critical point as they were instantly tested to their limits just to survive. These men had one mission and they intended to take down the leader of the resistance or die in the process.

The Black Fist and the masters reacted quickly, but the enemy was close enough to succeed.

Aron worried about Cherine, but it took everything to avoid his own death. They came at him simultaneously from all sides and cut him off from her. He was nicked a number of times before his men rallied to save him. When he looked for Cherine he saw her limp in the arms of enemy soldiers carrying her away toward Straga. Her horse sat, rider less.

Aron screamed in frustration and charged. Straga gestured at Aron, grabbing Cherine by the hair in triumph before he called a sudden retreat. They allowed their regular army soldiers to fill in blocking the way while the elite dropped back to take their key captive to Damien.

The sheer mass of enemy soldiers impeded Aron and allowed Straga to escape.

"No!" Aron yelled in agony.

They fought fiercely, but it didn't matter. The way ahead was clogged. They were left with the slow progress of driving back the enemy, unable to affect a rescue.

Damien smiled when a groggy and beaten Cherine was forced to her knees before him.

"This wasn't your orders, Straga, but with this you've done well."

"Now Aron will come to us," Straga replied. "We can dictate the fight to our advantage."

Damien knelt down and took a fistful of Cherine's hair to turn her face to him.

"Hello, Cherine. It's so good to see you again. Did you think to never see me again? You should've known you'd be on your knees before me eventually. Take her to my rooms and have my servants clean her up. Put her in more appropriate clothes, perhaps a nice red dress."

The guards dragged her away.

"At the rate of their forward progress they'll be here in a couple of days," Straga continued.

"That's excellent, Straga. I'm of a mind to grant your request, but obviously your wife and boys are not in our custody."

"I'll find them, Damien. Nothing will stop me now."

"Straga, go out there and win this battle. Don't take victory against Aron for granted. Smother him with our numbers so when he gets here they'll be exhausted and unable to prevail."

"Yes, master."

Damien decided to go down to the dungeon.

"Hello, prince," he taunted. "We've captured Aron's woman, Cherine. She's in your former royal suite at this very moment bathing and preparing for the next phase of her life as my consort. What do you say about that?"

"I say your smugness won't protect you when Aron batters down your door. He won't be forgiving of your transgressions. This is a huge mistake on your part."

"You can only see things through your own eyes. When you were in the position of antagonist to Aron, you had superior numbers, but you weren't the leader for such an august moment and you frittered away your chance. I'm not you. I'm the equal of any challenge, Aron included. We look forward to his appearance at the palace gates. It will be nothing more than his ending, and this silly rebellion with him."

"Damien, it's equally true you can see things only through your eyes. You judge him on your past, not on his capabilities. You've never met an opponent like Aron. You can savor these few moments taking advantage of those he cherishes. It will only enrage him further and guarantee your demise."

Damien stared at Agar.

"Your life is in my hands, prince. You could be in for a very short remaining life and a painful and prolonged ending."

"What can I do about that, Damien? Whatever happens is out of my control. I've reconciled to my fate. Do what you will. It won't save you in the end."

Chapter Ten
~The Battle of the Palace~

It did take days for Aron to lead his men within view of the palace. In fact it was over a week of determined fighting before they reached their destination. Damien had been correct, they were exhausted having had too little to eat, and virtually no sleep. They were operating on courage and grit alone against superior numbers. That never changed.

Having Cherine captive in Damien's hands was irreconcilable for Aron. He'd faced this scenario so many times in his life. His women were out of his reach at the whim of evil. His enemy could taunt him with his helplessness to protect them.

What she would be forced to endure was obvious around a man like Damien. She'd been through it before with the prince. What worried Aron to death was Damien doing to Cherine what he'd done to Liani, taking her will away leaving her a hapless pawn to toy with as he wished. Cherine mentally shackled was a nightmare with which Aron couldn't cope.

Aron was no longer an immature spirit about the outrages committed against women. He'd felt jealousy and inadequacy in his contest with Radigan for Tasha where she chose Aron's competitor. Here he was far past that state. Cherine had no blame for this. It wasn't any choices she'd made. He only felt renewed rage against Damien and a burning desire to exact terrible revenge.

None in his collection of elite but exhausted fighters had anything left. There was no swagger. Average soldiers wouldn't have made it this far. As he glanced at the faces of his officers, they knew the impossible task before them of trying to take the palace. Each day more of Damien's army closed in all around them between the invasion force already in the city and the endless flow of reinforcements filling in behind them.

The war in the others parts of the world was going very well for Damien

120

so he had plenty of available troops to call upon.

It was a hangman's noose tightening around Aron's scrappy army.

"This may be beyond us, Aron," said Trent.

"I know, my friend. I can't simply abandon her to him, but it shouldn't cost the lives of everyone else."

"What are you saying?"

"Perhaps we can perform a raid in the palace. Meanwhile the remainder of the royal army can fight their way out of this trap and go north to the mountains to join the Arreck. That's the best chance for them to survive. We can't all die here for nothing. Damien will continue to swamp us with his numbers. We're already past our limit."

"How do you think to get inside the palace, Aron?"

"I'll think of something."

Brock came over with Barmon. He had a concerned look on his face. "Aron, even if you got inside, which is doubtful, how could you get out later to escape? Nephora is flooded with Damien's mob. You're no fresher than we are. Determination can only take you so far. You have no supplies for a lengthy flight."

"Brock, I'll only take volunteers and only just enough to accomplish the mission."

"Aron, every man in the army will volunteer."

"I'll order them to desist, to survive to protect their families. I understand our civilians are away and heading for the north already."

"Yes, it was too dangerous for us to try to keep them at hand, plus we had no way to feed them."

"I'll accompany you, Aron," said Barmon grimly. "I'd like a shot at Damien, and of course I have unfinished business with Straga."

"Brock…?"

"If my father goes with you, I will also."

"Trent, someone must lead the army in my stead. I know you want to volunteer, but this could be suicide. I want your word you'll stay behind to lead the army and the people. Belisa will be waiting with the Arreck army. In their mountains they may be unbeatable no matter how many men Damien chooses to sacrifice attacking them there."

"Aron, you, and Brock have become my family, my brothers. If I leave you to this fate, I'll feel a coward and a failure the rest of my life."

"Don't be so convinced we're going to fail with this, Trent. We've come through some harrowing tests before. Galean believed I would find a way. Who can say what's in our future?"

"One other thing, Aron, we've heard from the city the crown prince was captured when the palace fell. Damien's planning a public event very soon with us at his door. I think he's going to make a spectacle of the prince, and I think he'll display Cherine. You know he's one to create a scene to perpetuate this myth he's invincible and his victory is inevitable."

"Is there any word of the others?"

"I suspect Agar sent them away. The logical destination would be going to Belisa and the Arreck."

"If he had Galean, Liani, Coraline, and Tasha, he wouldn't be secretive about it. I agree with you. This is all the more reason for you to lead the army to safety, Trent. If he thinks he's won, we'll teach him otherwise."

"If I go along with this, Aron, how do you plan to act? If we pull out of this battle suddenly, anyone left behind would be sitting ducks."

"I have a thought to use subterfuge," Aron explained. "If we cloth ourselves in the uniforms of the enemy, perhaps we can simply walk in the front door. Their camp and field security is lax, other than around Damien himself. They're such an amorphous lot. They're all strangers to each other, especially with new reinforcements arriving every day."

"I like it," Brock interjected.

"I think we should start preparations right away, Trent. Each day that passes we're weaker. Send the orders to the army. We're going to take a couple hundred at most so we don't draw undue attention. They'll be volunteers from the Black Fist and the masters."

"Aron, the Brutans won't accept leaving you and they certainly won't agree to have no volunteers in your force."

"The problem is the Brutans have a distinctive look. They're barbarians and look the part. They're easy to spot by our enemies. I'd love to have them at my back, but for this mission it wouldn't work. They must follow you, Trent, with the rest of the army. It won't be an easy fight to break out of containment."

Trent shrugged. "I suspect you'll need to tell their chief personally. I don't think they'll take that order from anybody else."

"I can do that," Aron agreed.

* * * *

Cherine sat on the bed, angry and ashamed at her predicament. Again she'd been forced into compromised circumstances. Damien left a large contingent of guards in close proximity at all times in addition to the female servants so she had no chance to take any action. Going to his bed each night was particularly galling. She knew in Liani's case, she wasn't cognizant of what she endured. Damien left Cherine with her full faculties and for her it was worse than with the prince, and with the dead barbaric officer Korak who'd abused her in camp. That man had paid with his life for his crimes.

Damien came into the suite.

"Good morning, my dear. Breakfast will be ready shortly. Later today, I'm going to have an event of great import. We'll deal with the prince of this realm and put an end to the monarchy and free the people once and for all. Afterwards, I think we'll bring you out before the people in your wedding dress. They'll see Aron is thwarted in love again when you join Liani as my bride. After all, why should only one woman enjoy the honor and the acclaim of my companionship and intimate partnership?"

She glared at him.

"I see that you're overwhelmed with my generosity as a woman who took up arms against me. Of course, that will never happen again. As my wife, I'll expect all of the fidelity, love, and loyalty of any husband. It isn't an option for you. Do you understand?"

"Damien, if you think I could ever love you, or that any woman could love you for that matter, you're more demented than I realized. Obviously I'm in no position to stop you here, but what you're doing is nothing more than rape. There will come a time you'll pay severely for it."

"Do you envision Aron riding to the rescue, charging through that door into the teeth of my finest fighters to save you? I was always the future. It's my destiny. Who else has done what I have, defying time itself. I beat my enemies of old and believe me they were true challenges. Against his ragtag collection of glorified farmers, there will be only one outcome and it won't be with you becoming his bride. Think on that, my love. After time, when he's gone and buried, you'll change your mind in your feelings about me."

Cherine shook her head skeptically.

"Did you wish to say something further?" he asked with a frosty glare.

"No, Damien. I'm content when you leave me in peace. You've been warned. Your delusions of grandeur aren't reflections of future events, just your sickness."

"Take her to the dress maker to pick out an extraordinary wedding dress. I think it should be form fitting to highlight her incredible physique and bright red to reflect her brazen nature. After all, we're not talking about a virgin maiden here, are we?"

Cherine didn't rise to the bait. She got out of bed and put on a robe to go in for her morning bath. Damien made no accommodations for modesty, privacy, or decency. Guards followed her into the bathing room along with the female servants. It was galling but she coped because she had no other choice.

* * * *

Agar awoke that day with a feeling of foreboding. He had trouble holding his breakfast down. Usually the guards ignored him totally, or possibly made a rude comment, but on this morning they all came with sneers on their faces.

"Eat well, prince."

He had no doubts what that meant for him. He didn't dwell on dying. He'd thought continually about his life, his sins, and his wife. Who he'd become compared to who he'd been most of that life were at polar opposites. Too late, he thought about the kind things he wished he'd done rather than squander his life in hedonistic lust shaming so many innocent women. It was too late to atone. What that would mean for him after life ended, he worried about. Was there forgiveness out there in the universe for one such as him? He was emotionally beyond the point of hating Damien, who was beyond Agar's ability to touch. It would fall on other people to deal with him, if he could even be dealt with by any force in this world.

Agar felt overwhelming sadness that Coraline was gone. He could never hold her again. She was under the protection of Marin.

Life is a precious commodity which none of us want to lose and it was no different with Agar. Even in the face of certain death in his despair, he still hoped for that miracle which would spare him.

* * * *

"What is it?" asked Damien of the messenger.

"My lord, the enemy army has changed tactics. We expected them to try to attack the palace, but suddenly they've turned and are trying to break out of confinement to escape northward."

"Have they broken out?"

"Not yet, but the field commander expects they'll do so. We can't get sufficient troops in front of their new assault fast enough. It seems Aron has decided to abandon his woman and flee to save himself. We're surprised by this cowardice."

Damien smirked. "This will be a day of great triumph. I knew it would be so. We'll chase down Aron and he'll kneel before me, just like the prince, before I take off his head. With Aron, it will be doubly sweet because Cherine will be there to see his head roll on the ground. Why are these people such fools that they can't see the logical end of resisting me?"

"It will be a glorious day indeed, my lord."

* * * *

The grim time arrived for Agar. He heard the tromping of boots as they came for him. He eyed them stoically as they led him out of his own prison and up out into the light. There was a great throng assembled of Damien's troops, but also royal subjects who hadn't been able to escape. They stood in silence and sadness at the grim spectacle while Damien's followers celebrated as though it was a holiday. The bright sunshine in a clear sky blinded him momentarily until his eyes adjusted.

They led him over to Damien who smiled imperiously. Agar ignored him, instead looking at Cherine in her gaudy red wedding dress. She looked at him compassionately.

"Can you forgive me for what I've done to you?" he whispered.

"I forgive you, Agar," she answered sadly. "I'm so sorry about this."

"I'm ready," he replied. "It's a comfort to have you here at the end."

Cherine couldn't stop a flood of thick tears from streaming down her cheeks as her distressing emotions surged. This man who she'd despised all her life was going to forfeit his life and she felt no vindication. It was merely tragic and painful to behold.

They led him over to the headsman's block. He didn't resist at all and got to his knees on his own.

Damien edged close to Cherine.

"You will watch the execution, darling, or you will face severe consequences. The same will be true when Aron kneels down there. You will be the one to pick up his head and hand it to me. Do you understand?"

She nodded and wiped tears from her eyes. Agar looked back at her sadly before he put his head down on the block. Cherine couldn't stop sobbing. The killing blow was swift and sure. Cherine spilled blood all her life, but here the sight of Agar with blood spurting from his headless corpse sickened her. She walked over on wobbly legs, knelt down to pat his body before she picked up his head and carried it to Damien. He lifted it in his fist to the roars of his followers.

"Take this and mount it at the entrance to the palace. Take the body down to be consumed by the beasts."

He dragged away a numbed Cherine by the hand and led her to the royal chapel for the sham marriage.

Damien pronounced them married, though Cherine spoke no words at all.

* * * *

The execution, the wedding, and the wedding night were occurrences Aron couldn't stop. They'd managed to get inside the palace outer walls, but it was mass bedlam with Damien's troops packed in solidly. Watching Agar's death struck Aron, just like it struck Cherine. There was no feeling of justice served for his crimes and transgressions, only overwhelming sorrow. Coraline was now a widow. Seeing Cherine before him was a supreme test to keep from taking precipitous and foolish action in an impossible situation.

Getting into the palace proper was the greatest problem. Here Damien stationed crack troops. They challenged anybody who came close.

Straga moved about watching the crowd, so they were forced to recede and to find dark corners to wait for their chance.

"We can't just bust in the front door," said Brock. "Straga is wary in spite of the royal army seemingly retreating."

"I know, brother."

"I know you want to stop tonight, but Cherine is a strong person. She can endure. She probably already has endured…well, you know what. I hate to say it, but she's been through it before."

"Brock just shut up. I'm not naïve and I'm not a child."

"I'm sorry, Aron."

"I'm trying to think of a way to get in. I wish I had Galean here to advise us."

* * * *

For Cherine, after the execution, she was in a fog. What happened afterwards felt unreal in her emotional condition. Though Damien was no stranger in the bed since she'd been his captive, this 'wedding night' affected her as she had trouble hiding her revulsion of him. Agar's slaughter was clear in her memory and it evoked a desire to avenge him somehow.

Damien was very sensitive to the reactions of his women, as though it was a childish vulnerability. The fact so many of his intimate encounters were with women he'd subjected to the power of his machines where they no longer had any resistance or even cognizance of his actions spoke volumes of his lack of confidence in that area.

Cherine understood this the first time he came upon her. He was no great lover, he had no skill in that area, and he wasn't a man any woman would seek out twice for intimacy. It was a deficit he was well aware of which was why Cherine was such a risk for him. In her case, she was aware of it and that she could verbally humble him, if she chose.

Cherine had wisely been neutral and noncommittal but she knew he was keenly watching for signs of her true reactions as his partner. About this, he was vulnerable and needy, seeking for validation he couldn't ever realistically expect, or deserve. Adding to his intimacy deficits was the fact of being artificially preserved over the ages in stasis didn't help his stamina and virility and with his innate lack of skills. He was guaranteed to underachieve with every woman. It was doubtful he could father a child even if he wanted to.

What he was very good at was being vigilant at every moment. He didn't care how his loving appeared to others. He kept guards close at hand even at intimate times so Cherine never had any opportunity to take action against him. Often Damien had her tied to the four bed posts while he took his pleasure for his own safety. He knew she could kill him with her hands if she ever got the chance. Even with her restrained, he still kept his guards close at hand.

The only emotion he was able to create in her was undying hatred and an abiding drive to strike back at him someday and somehow.

She developed an outer façade to mask her ire while she bided her time, ever watching for weaknesses she could exploit. Her comfort was Aron had apparently escaped capture. It gave her hope that someday she might be free of Damien, as Liani had eventually been freed.

In the meantime, she did what she had to in order to survive. It was lonely in spite of being constantly surrounded. All of her friends were gone. There were female servants of Damien with her constantly, but none of them were trustworthy.

It was at that point a new woman was added to the staff, Nala. She approached Cherine aggressively to establish a relationship. It didn't take long to understand Damien tasked her to break through to Cherine emotionally.

Cherine waited a day to talk to her.

"Damien has given you a job to do, Nala."

"Of course he has, ma'am. I don't think he had visions of fooling you."

"If I'm aware of the plan, why go through with it?"

"He thinks I have skills others lack. In this situation where you're isolated I think he believes with time you'll become vulnerable. What person can live endlessly without a companion, a kindred spirit, someone with whom to share their inner feelings? He's told me he will kill your fiancé before your eyes, this Aron everyone speaks of. If that occurred I can see how this might open possibilities from Damien's point of view."

"You don't know Aron, Nala? How's that possible?"

"I'm not from your country. I was brought here from outside very recently. It's not that I particularly subscribe to Damien, but life was bad in my home. Most people around me were happy to rise up against our oppressive rulers. After we came to Damien, we discovered too late the error of our hasty choices. For me personally, I wasn't high born, I had no realistic prospects for a good life. Bowing to Damien to do his bidding was a choice of expediency and nothing more."

"You must be aware of the price of failure in his service. If he's given you the task of bringing me to heel, I think you're in for a bad ending. You're a lovely young woman, but Damien isn't a forgiving person and he has endless lovely women available for his uses."

"I know all of that, Cherine. I'm not a fool. You're doing what you must to survive, but you always plan to take revenge and to escape him. This fact is glaringly obvious to everyone around you and including Damien. He laughs at your attempt at subtle subterfuge as he uses you for his perverse needs. He truly believes he's superior to everyone else in the world."

"You sound as if you have a plan of some sort, Nala."

"I think we can help each other in the interim. If you mimic changes in behavior that he covets, does it change your true situation? If he thinks I'm succeeding in bringing down the walls of your defenses, how does that harm you? What more can he do to you than he's already done? He's a man and therefore we can exploit him. He wants from you what he could never earn. You already know this. He wants you to have feelings for him. We both know that's impossible, but it can be used as a ruse I think we can sell. If he thinks I've become a person you care about, it's a short step to his believing the other things too. I have some ideas about behavior between us we can gradually develop to pique his interest and his neediness. What do you say?"

"I have nothing to lose, obviously. I'm a very skeptical person and you're telling me this doesn't mean I automatically accept it and believe you, Nala."

"Of course, Cherine, I would expect nothing else but caution from you. I tell you let my deeds speak for me. I'm also a woman alone, but I'm in a strange land where I know not another single soul. If you're cut off, you have people about to give you hope. I must prosper or fail on my own. If I die, none of my people will ever know."

"I'll take you at your word, Nala. What do you want for me to do?"

"At this point nothing...It's too soon for me to have gotten past your defenses. It would put Damien on alert. Continue as you have and we'll make subtle changes as we go."

Cherine shrugged. Nala put out her hand. Cherine stared at it for a moment before accepting her handshake.

Cherine tried her best to avoid any feelings about Nala and her proposal, but hope crept back into her life anyway. Even just having a plan against Damien was gratifying. Whatever Nala had in mind for her, it couldn't be worse than this life with Damien. She smiled thinking back of her capture by Lilith and how that worked out for the better. Nala reminded her of Lilith in her confidence and determination.

* * * *

Meanwhile, her fiancé remained thwarted just outside the palace building. Straga was thorough seeking out any means of entry and providing layers of defenders. A month of fruitless searching made it clear they couldn't break in to spirit Cherine out of harm's way.

Brock said nothing but simply waited for Aron to make his decision.

"If we stay here any longer, Aron…"

"I know, brother, I know I'm putting us in jeopardy, and I know you understand why I've stayed all this time."

"At this point, Aron, I can't be sure we can escape the city. Damien's had time to consolidate his conquest and to establish his forces. It'll be a serious fight no matter what way we go, and with the others going north, they'll have that way heavily staffed and reinforced. Can we afford to sacrifice these particular men, the best in the allied army?'

Aron was silent for a time.

"Brock sometimes I wonder why I was born with the life I've lived. Why couldn't I have simply died at childbirth?"

"Your story is still being written, brother. These incredible hurdles you overcome, they give hope to everybody else. Without you and what you've accomplished we wouldn't be here today fighting Damien's tyranny."

"Without me digging him up out of the ground we wouldn't be in the middle of a war. You might be a married happy farmer back home."

Brock smiled. "I don't even think about such things. Until we eliminate Damien, I couldn't bring children into this world."

"A wise choice, Brock, a wise choice indeed."

"If we leave now, we live to fight another day, Aron. No one wants to leave their love behind, but do we have another choice? Damien will face his day of judgment. We'll never give up coming after him, but this isn't the time or the place."

Aron shrugged. Brock didn't wait for a tacit commitment from Aron. He ordered everyone to pack up for the move. Aron simply went along. It was another galling setback and added more fuel to his personal fire of self-doubt and self-recrimination.

Their movement was executed in stages and shifts so they didn't have a single conglomeration of troops to alert Damien and Straga. Barmon was equally loath to leave without facing Straga personally. There was no other option.

In spite of their caution, the net around them had no holes so it was inevitable they would face a fight. Fortunately, they'd covered enough ground Straga couldn't get to them quickly. Rather than go north, they went south to get out of the city. Fewer defenders stood in the way of their flight, but that didn't mean there were few defenders. There initial dispersal pattern soon devolved where they were forced to gather together to handle the serious fights.

Damien's defenders were stubborn because there were so many of them, but they didn't win the fight. Aron led his people to the edge of the city and out into the countryside.

Straga arrived too late to catch them. They were gone and out of his grasp.

* * * *

It was significant for a number of reasons. Damien came straight to dinner that last evening and leered at Cherine.

"What now, Damien?" she asked.

"Perhaps you haven't heard. Your former fiancé has just fled the city with his rabble in a rout. It seems his love for you had severe limits. Trying to rescue you wasn't a stronger reason than his sparing his own cowardly life. You can see you've made the right choice in a husband. I would move heaven and earth for you, darling. I would never abandon you to fate as he has."

It bothered Cherine a great deal. Damien's posturing meant nothing to her, but the idea Aron had been close and was forced to leave burned at her resolve. She glanced at Nala who looked stoic, not wanting to publicly reveal any sympathy for Cherine.

"Have you nothing to say, Cherine?" Damien taunted. "Your false hopes of rescue are dashed. Perhaps you'll finally realize the truth of my words. You're mine and nothing will ever change it."

"What do you want for me to say, Damien?"

She surprised him and for a moment he seemed to be at a loss for words.

"Tell me the truth of how you feel as the true nature of Aron is revealed. You can no longer deny what I've been telling you. He's a lesser man not worthy of a grand lady like you."

Cherine blinked her eyes and thought about Nala's plan to fool Damien.

"I'll admit this move of Aron's surprises me. Perhaps I do need to rethink some things."

She saw out of the corner of her eye a slight smile from Nala.

Damien swallowed the ploy totally.

"This is so good, Cherine. Did I not tell you that with time, you'd come to see things differently? This is a wonderful first step for us, darling. We can be man and wife in reality at last. We can have all the happiness you desire. You deserve it, wife. I offer you the world."

"Thank you, husband," she replied. It was repugnant to say it, but the result was clear. Damien was agog.

* * * *

The battle of the palace never happened. The battles occurred away from the palace in the streets. Damien was smug with the turn of events. In his mind he'd personally faced down Aron. Straga said nothing, but he knew better. This was the worst possible eventuality. Aron was still out there and that meant he was a serious threat. Damien's arrogance always bothered Straga who knew better. He evolved from his barbaric roots with the events he'd experienced and he would never take victory for granted.

In addition to Aron's elite unit eluding them, the rest of the royal army escaped as well. In particular, that meant Sirina and his sons were gone from his grasp yet again.

The new focus had to be the gatherings in the land of the Arreck, but Damien was so taken with his misperceived progress with Cherine, he dawdled in making a plan and going after the survivors. Nightly he went to his suite to the 'bliss' of his imposed marriage and allowed himself to be duped by Cherine's ruses.

* * * *

"Cherine, you're doing so well," said Nala. "Damien is more gullible than I would have believed. For a person who thinks himself the measure of any situation, you have him hopelessly lost in your sway. He thinks you love him. What you've done in pretending he now matters to you, and that magically he now has the skills of a great lover, is genius. He's like a puppy. He's beyond disgusting. Be strong to the revulsion and keep him in the dark. I think we're going to have opportunities in the near future."

"He thinks us great friends now, Nala. You could possibly waggle some reward of your own."

"I'll take no chances because this is still a delicate situation and one which is in flux. I'll risk no mistakes on my part. We're on the right path. I'm content. He's paranoid at heart so we must be very careful in our actions."

"I must say I didn't foresee this. When you first spoke to me of making a plan, I thought it was just Damien taking a new approach, that you were his thing and not trustworthy. I owe you, Nala."

"I may seek to collect on that debt someday."

"What reward would tempt you, Nala? I wonder? You're a secretive woman and I think the obvious types of reward such as riches would not be what you seek."

"You would be correct, Cherine. What I'd want will remain my secret, but believe me, there are definitely things which call to me."

"You have piqued my curiosity, Nala. You must promise to give me your answers someday."

Nala smiled broadly. "Cherine, you'll be the first one to know."

Damien came into the room at that moment.

"What are we talking about, ladies? You both seem to be amused."

"It's just girl talk, husband," Cherine replied, with a crocodile smile. "It's nothing which would interest you."

"I'm interested in everything about you, Cherine. You've made me a happy man. There's nothing you could ask for that I'd deny you."

Cherine smiled ruefully at what she would request, starting with the demise of Damien. So instead, she lied.

"I would ask for a pleasant evening with you and Nala."

She almost laughed at his over-reaction.

"That is my wish too, to spend my time with both of you. Nala, I've come to cherish you and your performance of your duties is second to none. Perhaps we can look at a new status for you. I have another wife, Liani, who will someday be re-joining us. Perhaps we should talk about a third wife. What do you say to that?"

It was a pronouncement neither of the women anticipated. For a moment, startled, Nala paused.

"My lord, I'm stunned that you could consider a low caste person such as me. The honor of being your wife exceeds all possible dreams of any woman. To be offered such an exalted place, I'm speechless."

"Then let it be so," he replied magnanimously. "We'll have the ceremony of marriage tomorrow."

He grinned happily, but his expression struck both women as that of a mewling idiot. The fact he could be so misled astounded them.

"Nala, your mundane tasks are over. You'll join us at the dinner table from this night forward."

"Perhaps I should change into something more appropriate," said Nala.

As she walked by Cherine, she put a hand on her shoulder and winked.

Cherine nearly laughed right out, but managed to contain her scorn.

"Oh, the delights that await you, darling," she whispered in jest.

"Shut up." Nala whispered back and left the room.

When she came back to join them, she'd changed into a form fitting and sexy dress. She was a beautiful woman.

"Excellent, my dear," said Damien.

"I'm glad you approve," she replied glibly, playing along with his fascination. "I thought you'd like this."

Again she winked at Cherine and Cherine fought to keep from laughing at the comical situation.

"Let's eat, my little doves," said Damien. "The chef has promised his finest efforts for our dining pleasure tonight."

The women glanced at each other at his ignorance of their true feelings.

Chapter Eleven
~Welcome to Arreck~

Marin wasted no time in establishing who was in charge when they left the palace. His small group of designees morphed as Agar had been convinced as to who was indispensable and necessary for inclusion in the flight to safety and survival. His carefully selected unit of fighters and critical persons like Galean had also been ballooned with the inclusion of Granor and his people, Lilith and her warrior maidens, the king and queen's other children, and some select friends and advisors to the king and their families. It was right on the verge of being too unwieldy a collection, but he was given no choice.

Technically, the king was still the prevailing authority, and Granor sought to re-establish his role as chief advisor to the king, and therefore leader of the venture in a contest of wills with Marin.

Once they'd fought their way out of the city into the countryside, Marin had his showdown with Granor. He gathered everyone around him.

"Sire, I'm your servant," he began. "If it's your will to put Granor in charge, I must tell you I will not follow him. I was given a critical charge by your son the crown prince to preserve your life and that of these other vital persons. Granor is not skilled in what we must do either in battle experience and training, tactics, or in reacting to sudden situations. If he and his people wish to accompany us, it can only be as answerable to me. I'm not going to get into his divided loyalty. That could be said of Lilith also, but in her case, I trust her motives and I respect the skill she and her ladies have developed. I'd grant her trust that I wouldn't extend to Granor, in battle, or in other matters."

The king looked distressed and undecided.

"Sire, if I may speak in my defense, Marin is a mere soldier. His life has been that of following orders. He has no grasp of the higher place we occupy, pondering matters of import, and making decisions for a nation. When he says

I'm not qualified, I laugh. Who is he to claim competence? What is that based on?"

Granor looked around to gauge the effect of his oratory. Marin looked grim as he stared at Granor. They were surprised to be interrupted by Lilith.

"Your majesty, we don't need to listen to Granor pontificate. What Marin says is true. Granor ever looks for advantage, for an edge over his competitors. I know him intimately. He has never been one to put the concerns of others ahead of his own schemes. Neither I nor my maidens will follow him either. We support Marin."

The queen stepped forward and took her husband's arm.

"What do you say, Galean? You're the greatest mind here."

"My support has always been for Aron for in him is our only hope to overcome Damien, but here I side with Marin also. He's a decent and principled man and he will fulfill his obligations to the prince."

"So be it," said the queen, looking sternly at Granor. "The matter is closed. Marin commands here."

Granor looked at the royal children for their reaction. They were as spineless as ever. They averted their eyes rather than draw attention and possibly make an enemy of Marin.

"I concede the point to you, Marin, but be warned, I'll watch everything you do, and I'll make my thoughts known. You don't have unlimited leeway here. We're all at your mercy if you choose foolishly. I won't allow the royal family to be lost through your poor decisions."

Marin smirked and shook his head at Granor posturing.

"Your concerns are noted, Granor," said Galean dismissively.

Granor then glanced at Radigan. He also looked away. Radigan had been completely non-confrontational in every situation. He gave no potential adversary any excuse to call him out. Granor saw no ally in him.

Tasha noticed Granor's look and took Radigan's hand protectively, scowling at Granor. They turned their backs and walked over to join Liani, Coraline, the queen, and some other women in listening to Galean.

The king remained in a fog, as if his mind was permanently lost. His wife led him around most of the time and cared for him like an infant.

Abdurka saw it all too, but always remained in the background saying little. He accompanied Galean, but left it to his friend to do the talking. When he spoke it was in low tones to Galean or his inner circle, library staffers and the like.

Life on the run was trying, especially with this mix of people. Damien's forces chased after them doggedly. Marin's rear guard frequently faced fights and his forward point ran into hastily arranged enemy traps, though none of them proved telling. His fighters were very skilled and the enemy was only average, but it didn't mean every encounter wasn't dangerous and potentially catastrophic with Marin having limited numbers.

Subsequently, Radigan volunteered to join the forward troops and his immense prowess added greatly to their readiness and their success.

It was a cold and rainy day when they finally reached the border of the Arreck. The mountains loomed in the background like silent dark sentinels spanning the whole horizon partially obscured in the low hanging cloud bank. The entire area ahead was hazy with the rain and mist.

They had no time to dally as their pursuers were close at hand. Marin led them in a rush into the forest and out of the sight of Damien's approaching vanguard.

They didn't go very far before they were surrounded by Arreck army forces.

"Stop and turn around, or die. This is no place for you and your kind," said the Arreck commander.

Marin wisely sent Galean, Liani, and Tasha to speak.

"Do you know us?" asked Galean.

The commander paused.

"I do."

"Then you know our reasons to believe we should come here. We have no wish to embroil the Arreck in this war, but you're no fool. We've been driven here and when Damien's army arrives at your border, they won't stop. This war engulfs the entire world. There is no place to hide from it."

The commander pondered his words.

"We'll stop them from following you onto our land, but it's not my decision if you can stay."

"I understand, commander."

He turned his head. "You're Marin. It seems you lead this force. We know you and your martial deeds. Lead your people after this scout to a place you can make a temporary camp. Please understand we have no control over the ultimate decision of our leaders. We wish you no harm, Marin. You have our respect."

Marin nodded in acknowledgement of the supreme unexpected compliment.

The rain increased instead of decreasing making for an uncomfortable cold camp. There seemed to be no escape from being wet. The royal children were red faced and filled with complaints. None of them had ever faced adversity or discomfort.

Their mother, the queen, looked at their pitiful behavior and turned to

Liani and Tasha, embarrassed.

"I'm sorry you must endure them. They were spoiled early and never had reason to improve themselves as people. Only Agar gave me hope, and that was later in his life after he realized some things. I have little I've done in my life I can look to with pride. I'm a queen in name, but a failure as a mother and even as a person. I regret so much and wish I could go back and change things."

"Your majesty, who of us can't say the same thing," Tasha answered. "We faced what we faced and tried to cope. In my mind, there are so many things I would change, but I made my choices and I too must live with the consequences. Don't revile yourself, ma'am, there are plenty of other people anxious to do it. I've learned that through so many hard lessons. We're your friends. That's what you need to keep in mind."

"That means a great deal to me," the queen answered. "Thank you."

"Is there anything we can do to help you?"

"I know you mean about the king. There really isn't. Coraline has been so kind treating him like her own father. It's been an immense help in keeping him calm. I fear this affliction of his mind can't be reversed."

"We're sorry, your majesty."

"I know you are, though we don't deserve your forbearance with the great distress we caused in your lives. It's one of the many sins crushing my soul."

"Don't think about it that way, my queen. If you want to talk about sins, talk about Damien for he's the supreme sinner and scourge in this world. He dwarfs any of the mistakes of the rest of us."

They could hear the sounds of battle as Damien's scouts crossed the border and were summarily slaughtered by the Arreck army not far away. The screams of the dying was always disturbing, but they were accustomed to the sound with what they'd already been through.

Periodically, fighting would flare up, but the result was always the same. None of the fights were lengthy. It meant the main pursuit force hadn't arrived yet.

They slept the night there and were greeted early the next morning by the arrival of an Arreck delegation headed by Princess Belisa.

Tasha and Liani were quick to embrace her. Belisa came showing a frosty facial expression, but seeing her dear friends warmed her up quickly.

"It's so good to see you again," Tasha blubbered emotionally. "I've missed you so much."

"You must tell me everything," Belisa explained. "This is a very precarious situation. The king and queen, my parents, are enraged against your people for what was done to me. Looking for their forgiveness might be an impossible dream. I spoke at great length before coming here to keep them

136

from wiping out your party."

"I don't know what you've heard about the war, but it's gone badly here, and it seems Damien is winning everywhere else in the world. He invaded the kingdom with such numbers even the royal host could not protect us," Tasha explained. "It isn't just the vast numbers in his army. He's used horrible weapons from the past such as we saw in his camp when he magically portrayed those troubling images of old. It would seem there is no army capable of defeating him."

"Where are Aron and the others?" asked Belisa with concern.

"He was fighting in the city when last we were there. It was a hopeless situation. He became engaged to marry Cherine, but she was captured by Damien. What happened after we left, we don't know, but we fear the worst."

"Aron and Cherine, I wouldn't have thought that," Belisa reflected.

"With my situation with Radigan, Liani being a slave to Damien, and Coraline bride to the prince, I guess it was natural they would console each other and it developed into a relationship."

"How did you cope with losing Aron, Tasha?"

"You know me, Belisa. I have my selfish side and yes I felt jealousy, but it wasn't fair. I couldn't have him and he deserved a good wife and a happy life. What will happen now, I wonder."

"How is it for you, wife of Radigan?"

"I'd be lying if I said it was perfect and I had no issues, but we stay together and I try to be a good wife. Do I have regrets? Of course I do. Coraline would say the same thing, and I suspect you would also."

"I had romantic thoughts for Aron, but I never gave them life. It wouldn't have worked out. Certainly, my parents and my people wouldn't have accepted my marrying an outsider. This brings back so many memories. Being away from all of you, I guess I reverted back to the stoic as is the way of the Arreck. Having strong emotions and displaying them for others to see goes against our ways. Tasha, I've never forgotten you though. You're still my love, closer than a sister. You're a part of the Arreck people with having been through the ceremony."

"I'll never forget it, Belisa, and I feel the same for you. We're kin."

The women paused a moment lost in their thoughts. Tasha looked up as her husband walked over.

"Hello, Belisa," he said. "It's nice to see you again."

She looked at him trying to smother her memories of him and the old unseemly relationship they'd had so long ago in the prince's suite.

"I must tell you, Radigan, my parents know about you and about us. I think it best you not present yourself before them. I no longer hold anger for you, but I can't say that about my parents."

"Thank you for telling me. It may be that none of it matters with the coming of the war. Those indiscretions and old grievances may never be addressed to your father's satisfaction. I think Damien may supersede such concerns with his own agenda. My approach to life lately has been I'm living on borrowed time. For your father, I can offer one of the most skilled swords in the world. I suspect it will be all for naught in the end."

"Those are very sobering words. I've never seen you like this, missing your confidence and arrogance."

"The old days are over, one way or another, Belisa."

"So it would seem."

"What ails the king, Tasha? He's a shadow of his former self."

"The trauma of the battle for Nephora, the defeat, and our flight, it seems to have taken away his mind. Crown Prince Agar took over rule, but we heard he was taken when the palace fell. Coraline has been worried to extreme. Over time, her marriage and her relationship with the prince changed as he transformed. You wouldn't have known him for the man he became. He truly regretted his former life and what he did. My feelings about him changed and I would have thought that impossible."

"It does sound impossible," Belisa replied. "I can't say I've been able to reconcile the past."

"What happens next for us, Belisa?"

"I'm to return to my parents to give them my assessment."

"Would you allow me to come also? I'm one with the Arreck, right?"

Belisa smiled. "If you do this, your husband must stay behind."

Tasha looked at Radigan.

"It's your choice, Tasha. I'll be here fighting."

"I do wish to go. I hope you understand, Radigan. Going back to their holy place is like no other experience in the world. It's the only place I've ever felt truly safe and contented."

"So be it," said Belisa. "Come sister, we must make haste before the sun sets."

Radigan shrugged his shoulders and left them to return to the soldiers.

The women rode in silence for a short time.

"Belisa, I find it hard to believe you and your people have no knowledge of the events in Nephora and of the war in general."

"We have spies there, as we always have, Tasha. The difference is with battle and the mass of soldiers moving about, it's very difficult for couriers to get through. Our last word was the great battle hadn't ended. In fact, Aron and his allies have offered stiff resistance. Although Damien's army swamps the city, they haven't been able to secure it. They take large casualties daily, but Damien is unconcerned. It seems he has an entire world of strangers willing to come and die for him. They tell me it isn't rare to find women and children in his front line assault troops."

"He uses them as fodder to clog up our positions before he brings in his real troops. It's been an effective strategy. We can only assume he's conquering all the other nations outside our boundaries. He's a soulless tyrant."

"He holds Cherine captive. It must be intolerable for Aron. I hope he doesn't do something foolish and give Damien an advantage. I agree with Galean that Aron must be protected if we're to have a hope."

"Are you speaking for all Arreck when you say Aron is important?"

"I speak only for me," Belisa replied with a chuckle. "My father has severe feelings about outsiders. I hope he'll mellow in his stance."

"His scorn is understandable, Belisa. What was done to you was unforgiveable."

"You have the same grievance, Tasha, yet you and the others have moved on. I've done the same, but my father is stubborn, as if his personally taking revenge will assuage honor. He doesn't realize that number one, it's over, a long time ago, secondly it was me that endured, not him, and thirdly, the game has changed so much the old grudges are *passé.* "

"Perhaps I can persuade him, Belisa. I think he holds me in high regard, or at least he did. Possibly my picking Radigan instead of Aron will sour his view of me. I admit I would think little of a woman who would make such a poor choice."

"His view of you is based on what we shared at the ceremony. He saw into your heart as did we all and accepted you for the good person you are."

"I hope I'm a good person. I seem to make too many stupid mistakes, I wonder if I'm inherently flawed."

"My mother is your advocate, Tasha. She sees you very clearly as my friend and as a person of worth. That's important."

"I appreciate it. I like her too."

It was a lengthy trip to get to their destination. Their progress was slowed by the inclement weather as the storm front hung over the area dumping seemingly endless gallons of rain. The narrow ascending winding mountain trails became slippery and treacherous for travel.

Tasha saw Arreck military everywhere, alert and edgy.

When they finally came to the city the following day the atmosphere was radically different than when she'd visited before. The streets were sparsely populated with civilian traffic. Army units were moving above.

They arrived at the palace and walked briskly in for the audience with the rulers.

The king had a severe look on his face, but the queen smiled warmly.

The herald stepped forward.

"Here comes our royal princess and her friend, a member of the people."

The king scowled, especially when the queen got up from her throne and went down the steps to embrace Tasha.

"My dear, this is unseemly," he complained.

"Oh shut up," she replied dismissively.

"How can I rule this realm with such indignities I must endure?"

"This is Tasha, as you well know. She doesn't deserve your scorn and your ill temper."

The king grumbled.

The queen kissed Tasha on both cheeks. "I'm so happy to see you again, child. You must come with me to dinner where we can talk."

"I have questions for Tasha," said the king irritably.

"You may come with us, but only if you act a gentleman."

The women tried to keep the mood light, but the king wouldn't be deterred.

At the meal he focused his conversation on Tasha.

"You know you're always welcome here," he began. "I can't make the same statement for the others of your people. I'm not a fool, I know things have changed. They tell me your king has lost his mind. I give you my condolences, but regardless, my duty is to protect and preserve my people. If I'd allowed the Arreck army to go to join in the battle for Nephora, would it have changed the outcome? With the endless supply of reinforcements, Damien can wear down any opponent. Our advantage is here in our home grounds where we know every trail. We can put them in situations to our advantage and keep them at bay."

"I'm not a soldier," Tasha replied. "I will say Damien's weapons terrify us. He's used them sparingly so we don't know when, or if he can strike again with them. They're remnants of the old war."

"I've thought about that a great deal," the king answered. "I haven't decided making an alliance with the remains of your army is a wise choice for the Arreck."

"Father, how can you possibly believe going it alone is better for us? Disclaiming them doesn't assure us forbearance from Damien. He attacks all in his path. He's bent on conquering the world, all of it, including the Arreck nation," Belisa interjected heatedly.

The king scowled but said nothing.

"Why don't we eat our dinner," said the queen. "I think my husband must think about the obvious before he makes his pronouncement."

"The obvious," he complained. "Now you're taking their side?"

"There's only one side, husband," she replied evenly. "It's just a matter of your accepting things as they are. Their old world is gone, and so is ours. We can't cower in our lair any longer. Death is coming to knock on our door."

The king got up in anger. "I must speak with my advisors. Send food to my council chamber."

"Yes dear," the queen replied, smiling blithely.

The king left in a huff. The women watched him leave the room.

The queen looked at Tasha. "Our last courier said the battle in Nephora is desperate. Damien hasn't defeated Aron, but Aron can't win there either. He stays because he wants to free Cherine. Damien and his lieutenant, Straga, are waiting in ambush. What do you think he'll do?"

"Aron is loyal to a fault. He'll keep trying to rescue her far beyond any reasonable hope to succeed. He'd gladly accept any risk, but thankfully Brock and Trent have always been able to reason with him. I think he'll come to the conclusion to bide his time. He's been through it so many times before."

"I understand what that means for Cherine," said the queen. "We've been told about poor Liani in Damien's custody."

Tasha shrugged. "If women ran the world, I think things would be much different."

She didn't intend it as a joke, but they all laughed.

"I agree with you," said the queen. "I've often dreamed about what I'd do differently. I'd certainly love the chance to try."

"There would still be men to deal with, mother," Belisa added. "Even if we magically gained control, they would still be there to cause us problems. Why are they so…male acting?"

The women laughed again.

"When you're married to a man, you learn how to accomplish your goals," said the queen. She looked at Tasha. "Is this not true with your husband?"

"Yes," she admitted. "What they want from you gives you great leverage over them. About that, they're like children."

They laughed hilariously.

* * * *

Back at their camp, the alarm went up as they heard the sounds of heavy battle. Marin sent scouts to assess the situation. Granor spent all of his time whispering in the king's ear. He hadn't given up his attempt to regain his former position, status, and authority.

It was a considerable time before the scouts were able to return. Along with them rode allied soldiers in the vanguard of royal army fleeing the battle of Nephora.

"What's this?" asked Granor, leading the confused king to the meeting.

"Sire," said the new arrivals, going to a knee. "Aron sent the army north under the command of Trent. They're very close. We've been fighting daily to make it this far. We have with us all the civilians and families. What are your orders?"

Granor started to speak, but Marin cut him off.

"We have no word yet from the Arreck king if they'll allow us sanctuary, but continue driving to us. We can make a unified stand here, if need be."

"The civilians...?"

"We'll send them to the Arreck and hope for their mercy. There's nothing else we can do."

A number of the riders left to carry Marin's instruction back to the main body of the army.

Marin sent an alert to his troops in the camp.

"We'll make a skirmish line near the Arreck border. The army will come to us."

As if on cue the local Arreck commander walked into the camp.

"I'm sure you know what's happening. The war is coming to your door. It won't wait for your king to make his decision. We're going to protect the retreat of the royal army. It's a considerable force approaching to include the families."

The commander looked toward the border. "We'll assist you against Damien. If the king decides otherwise, we'll deal with it then."

"Thank you, commander."

"We'll have supplies ready when they arrive, Marin. There's a place we can take the noncombatants where they'll be safe."

"They've wiped out the force that was pursuing us, but what is pursuing them will be a test for all of us to survive. Damien's army is relentless."

"I must tell you a hard thing, Marin. One of our spies just arrived from the city. The crown prince of that realm, Agar, has been executed by Damien. His head is mounted at the palace entrance. We felt it best that you tell his widow. We had no love for him, obviously, but for her please say we're sorry for her loss."

Marin was shaken by the revelation. He walked solemnly to the royal family. The king had been led back to them and sat in his usual stupor.

Coraline spotted him at once.

"What's happened, Marin?" she asked with concern.

"I'm sorry," he said, looking at her and then the queen. "I've received ill news. Your husband was captured in the fight for the palace. Damien has…"

He couldn't finish before both women broke out in tears crying wretchedly. Agar's brothers and sisters were in shock. The girls started to cry also. For the first time, the king stirred from his mental fog. He got up and walked over to Marin.

"Have they taken my son?"

"I'm sorry, your highness," Marin replied soberly. "Damien made a spectacle of the execution. There was nothing Aron could do to save him."

"I see," said the king grimly. Granor stepped close to whisper to him. It angered the king who pushed him aside.

"Get away from me, jackal. My son is gone and you talk of your petty schemes. I have grim business at hand on behalf of my kingdom, my people, and my slain son…"

He looked at his remaining sons, none of whom instilled his confidence.

"We'll follow you, father," said the oldest of them.

"You're no more warriors than I am," he replied honestly.

They reacted like he'd struck them with his hand, their heads dropping in shame.

The king started to mumble to himself and lapsed back into his malaise. The queen took his arm and led him away. The royal children wandered away but in a different direction.

* * * *

Damien's army increased their pace to try to stop the royal army from crossing the Arreck border. They failed as once the civilians were safely across into the lands of the Arreck, the army could change their tactics, and they too could speed up.

The Arreck brought up significant forces to array along with Marin's people. As the royal army crosses onto Arreck land they were directed and dispersed to predetermined positions in the defense line. When Damien's army attacked they were stopped and rebuffed as Arreck ferocity replaced the exhausted efforts of the underfed and sleepless royals.

The battle was lengthy only because Damien's attackers were relentless, but for them it was a killing field as they were doomed to lose this fight.

Eventually they withdrew and established their camp. The numerous dead bodies of their comrades they left on the battlefield. The Arreck moved in the darkness of the night to clear away the dead.

"This isn't honorable that they have no reverence for the sacrifice of their soldiers," the Arreck commander reflected to Trent, Marin, and the officers.

"They're an army of strangers," Trent explained. "They don't know the people in their own units. They have loyalty to Damien, but not to each other. It's a strange situation not to have comradeship. They prevail only because they have such numbers. If Damien sacrificed the lives of the entire world, he'd have no concern. He'd see it as that many less mouths to feed."

The Arreck commander looked shocked. "I thought I'd seen the worst of humanity with my time in Nephora. This surpasses all understanding. If my king foolishly decides to withhold Arreck cooperation, I suspect the people won't accept it. I can tell you my men and I are in this war to the finish. We won't abandon our families to such a fiend."

"Commander, it's the only decision possible. Damien honors no agreements and respects no other persons. He looks to devour the world and remake it as his servant. I pray for the chance to face him personally, though I know that could never happen," Trent explained.

Battle resumed with the rising of the sun but the outcome didn't change. The Arreck resembled pillars sprung up from the bedrock granite of the world, unmovable and invincible. The enemy sent wave after wave of attackers only to accumulate more stacks of bodies. The stench of blood was so strong it drew predators and scavengers out into the open to consume the easy meat. It was easier to let them clear the field than to risk the arrows of Damien's archers trying to retrieve the bodies.

After a week of battle they received the belated decision the Arreck king decided to join the allies.

Even the Arreck commander chuckled.

"I think leaders should be forced to spend some time with field troops," he groused. "Perhaps they might grasp the importance of prompt decisions. Had we waited for his choice, Damien would be knocking on the palace door."

"Welcome to the allied army," said Trent. "You're much appreciated."

"We won't allow them to come onto our land," the commander reiterated.

"Hopefully we can fulfill your pledge. We've become so practiced at losing battles it's hard to imagine winning for a change."

* * * *

A few days later, Belisa and Tasha returned to the front, this time accompanied by the king and the queen. They went to see the civilian camp first. Sirina was the informal leader there since no one else would take the responsibility.

Coraline was in mourning and had been so since she heard the news about Agar's death. The only thing she would arouse to do was care for the king in his quandary.

Savior

The Arreck king was shocked when they brought him to the royals. The queen was subdued embracing her enfeebled husband. Coraline sat on the other side of the king. The royal children sat behind them, cowed.

Coraline looked up teary eyed at the Arreck king. Belisa and Tasha stepped close out of compassion and concern.

"I've been told the dire circumstances in your city. I'm sorry for your loss, madam."

Coraline nodded. Marin stepped behind her protectively. The king looked at him quickly assessing there was a bond between them.

"You're Marin. My staff tells me good things about you."

"I appreciate the kind words, but we all have a terrible task before us. We can't explain how grateful we are you've offered us your protection on your land and alliance with the resistance against Damien."

"It became clear we're facing the critical trial of mankind. We're fighting to survive but more, we're fighting to prove we're worthy to survive."

"That's it exactly, your majesty. I regret our king has nothing to offer to you. His losses were too great for him to bear. I fear he's lost to us, and now his heir is gone too. Whatever is the result of the war, the world will not be the same."

"Perhaps that's a good thing," the Arreck king mused.

"A world of Damien, we can't allow it, sire."

"I agree with you, Marin."

Next the king went to the front lines to talk to Trent and the royal command as well as his own army command. Belisa and her mother stayed to comfort the royal queen and Coraline.

* * * *

Tasha stayed with the women. When Radigan came up behind her, she touched his hand, a gesture he sorely missed and greatly appreciated. Any love she showed him was like water in the desert for a dying man. The confident and arrogant man he'd always been was gone. He was a shade of his former self. His taste for all other women seemingly gone, replaced by devotion to his wife. It would've been an excellent development for most, but in his case his personality was wrapped up in his behaviors, so he wasn't a more compelling man in this state.

Chapter Twelve
~The Messenger~

Aron led his mobile troop in a wide arc away from and around the outskirts of the city. He realized no one would believe he'd go anywhere other than the Arreck lands.

They had to raid enemy camps to obtain food, water and other needed supplies, so they zigged and zagged a great deal trying to surprise the opposition with where they'd strike.

Straga anticipated this tactic and moved considerable forces to where Aron was eventually going to let him come to their strength.

Aron also knew that and sent ploys in numerous directions to mislead Damien's forces.

Both sides were successful to an extent. Aron and the allies were able to cover ground toward their destination, but at the same time they would be facing a major battle at some point as Straga massed forces in their path.

Damien regaled his 'wives' each night with glowing reports from the field. They'd both sufficiently mastered their feelings to be able to perpetuate the illusion of bliss with their life with Damien. Even the guards started to buy their phony behaviors. Damien wanted to believe the women honestly changed and they thirsted for Aron's head on a pole as much as he did. The effect of beheading the prince had been more powerful cowing the city than he'd thought possible. There were no revolts or uprisings against his rule, though he hadn't been entrenched long enough to install the world of the future yet. The war required singular focus on capturing and defeating Aron, and the rebellious Arrecks.

Damien smiled at the close relationship between the two women, having no inkling of the true nature of it.

* * * *

Lilith, in the past, offered a captive Cherine a friend relationship. Cherine hadn't accepted it. With Nala she was given the same option and this time she did commit to having a relationship with her. She took the chance in giving her sacred trust to a stranger.

They both had to truly trust each other because Nala was taking an equal risk. They looked to the particular needs of their specific situations to support each other in whatever way the situation called for. It quickly moved past being a symbiotic partnership to something much more. Nala succeeded in being the first woman Cherine had ever let in to her trust on any level. Cherine began to care about what happened to Nala. For Nala, Cherine became closer than family. It rivaled the relationship between Tasha and Belisa going deep into their personhoods.

* * * *

Meanwhile, Straga paid close attention to what was happening at the Arreck border and the failure to make progress of any kind in battle. In his current mood, Damien paid too little attention to the war reports in his wedded bliss. His early successes around the world had given him a false sense of the course of the war. He made unwarranted optimistic assumptions about battles present and future.

Straga tempered Damien's optimism as best he could. All the while he was the actual driving force in picking where they fought and when. Damien took only a peripheral interest, as if the war was already over. Straga watched the performance of the women entrancing Damien with scorn and also worry, but he was wise enough not to discuss it with a man out of control.

* * * *

Aron drove closer to the Arreck's mountains and closer to the main battle Straga was engineering. What he did, unbeknownst to Straga, was to slip a small team through enemy lines riding at full speed and avoiding fights at all cost to alert his northern allies of their situation.

When they rode into camp at the gallop they raced straight to Trent at Aron's specific directive.

"Aron needs for you and the Arreck to attack Straga from the rear for us to be able to break through."

"When does he want us to attack?"

"As soon as you can get there, my lord. He's waiting not far from their front line but he can go no farther without facing a serious fight."

Trent called together the officers and the Arreck command. They waited until dark before they sent a vast host of the royal army and the Arreck to surprise Damien's lurking army, caught between two allied armies.

It was a major incursion and when they reached Straga's camp the ensuing battle was titanic. Straga was caught off guard for the first time. He actually saw Aron, Brock, and even Barmon ride into the campfire light to join the battle. Once they reunited with their allied brothers, the fight ended quickly as they fled to safety across the border, but Straga's command was in shambles. Straga narrowly missed death in the battle as three determined and barbaric Brutans fought their way close to him. His Erati brothers arose to save him, but they lost ten lives for each one of the Brutans they felled. It left Straga badly shaken. The possibility of death and his own mortality came to be a thought he wrestled with frequently. Recovering his mutual wife and his sons was his overriding agenda, regardless of what Damien said or did. The fact Sirina still considered Barmon to be her husband was galling to Straga. He never could find relief from that painful reality.

* * * *

Racing back across the border with Aron in their midst led to a spontaneous allied celebration. They took Aron to the camp of the civilians. He saw all of his friends and the families.

Belisa was teary eyed when she grabbed him in a fierce embrace as he tried to get off his horse. Tasha, Liani, and even Coraline nearly dragged him to the ground in their fervor. He could think of nothing to say. They treated him like a conquering hero when he felt the opposite having been driven out of Nephora and leaving his betrothed behind in the arms of Damien. He saw his mother and grabbed her. She alone understood what he was going through emotionally. He craved isolation and solace but he would find none of it here. He'd been in this state so many times before.

"Coraline," he said turning and taking her into his arms. "I'm so sorry I couldn't save your husband."

The queen walked up beside her.

"Did you see it happen, Aron?"

"We'd just managed to sneak into the palace grounds dressed in enemy uniforms, but there were so many of them packed in together we couldn't even take a step toward Damien. I'm sorry to say we saw it happen. Agar was brave to the end. He called out your name, Coraline."

She wept wretchedly as Aron held her from falling to the ground.

"I've failed all of you so many times," said Aron regretfully. "I think this time is the worst of all."

"No one blames you for my son's death," said the queen soberly. "You've done more than any man could rightfully expect from you. We're here away from that deathtrap and alive solely because of your battle efforts, Aron."

Aron happened to notice Marin watching him holding Coraline in his arms. Aron motioned for him to approach.

"Marin, I'm sorry your master is gone. You've fulfilled his charge completely to protect Coraline. I hope I can have your friendship and loyalty like you gave to him."

"Of course, my lord..."

"Marin, I'm not your lord. I'm just a man trying to do what he can, just like you. Are you willing to be an officer in leading this army?"

Marin smiled. "If that's the wish of her majesty..."

"Of course, Marin," the queen answered.

"I know you're close with Coraline," Aron continued. "She's been my friend since childhood. I care about her like she's family, but I know you do too. Aron pulled back and nodded for Marin to embrace Coraline. She looked up hopefully. Marin was torn by what to do. He looked at the queen."

"There is no objection from the crown, Marin. Her husband, my son, is dead. If she can find peace and solace in her grief in your arms, how could I take issue with that?"

He nodded and then embraced the woman he'd secretly loved for so long. Coraline hugged him tightly. She whispered in his ear and he replied softly.

Marin was surprised at the queen's position. Him taking the place of the crown prince as companion of the primary heir to the throne was a possibility he could never have imagined. None of the queen's other children stood ahead of Coraline in the favor of the throne, or the order of succession they'd selected.

"Coraline isn't the only widow in the kingdom," the queen added sadly. "Damien has no conscience."

The royal children eyed the situation critically. Even in the midst of their incompetence, there was a thought about succession to the throne amongst them and the power which went with it. Though they were thinking of the kingdom as it was rather than what it would be after the war, Granor wasn't the only person with ambition. The princes and princesses were equally craven but in their cases they were woefully incompetent for leadership and responsibility. Their childhoods had been spent as users and that was all they knew.

Granor was equally riled by the anointment of Marin as Coraline's companion causing Lilith to smirk at him contemptuously. She passed close by him along with her column of maidens, the ranks of which had expanded a great deal.

"Did you want to revise your threats to me? Thus far, what you've predicted hasn't panned out. I seem to be doing better and I have yet to be humbled before you. I think that was your dire forecast for my future prospects was it not?"

He said nothing to her. His people were greatly outnumbered by her followers. Her ladies stared at them, itching for a fight. Lilith wasn't the only one of them with grudges against Granor and his people. He simmered in silence.

"I suspect your dreams of crawling into the royal bed beside Coraline are over. King Granor is a fantasy only you could have imagined."

He looked at her murderously.

"You're welcome to try, Granor. I and my maidens await you at anytime and anyplace."

He changed his expression. "Lilith, we're allies, remember. We're on the same side. Will you ever move past old grievances? Everyone else has done so. Aron came to a point of treating Prince Agar as a friend. Cherine forgave him his transgressions. I no longer harbor ill intent toward you or yours."

Lilith laughed. "Who do you think you're talking to? I know you down to your deepest and darkest thoughts, and your impulses. You couldn't change that vileness if you wanted to. I will never trust you and we'll be on guard against your schemes every minute, day, or night. I repeat, you're welcome to make your move anytime. We'll be waiting for you."

Granor shrugged dismissively to her threat. "Live however you choose, Lilith. I have more important things to deal with. I'll hold you up no longer from your duties. Please continue on your way."

Lilith smirked but led her troop away.

"Come," he said to his lieutenant.

They left but only to seek out the royal children in secret.

"You know me. I'm your father's counselor. It's a crime how others have usurped our rightful places. You know as well as I do this alliance of the old guard has little chance to prevail over Damien who brings forth the future in might and deadly purpose. They've crushed all opposition in their path and if rumors are true, they've conquered every other nation in the world. We need to look to our own defenses and I offer you my protection in the new order. I'll negotiate with Damien for proper status in his world. It may not be what you're accustomed to, but it will be much better than dead like these fools will be. I fear the king is lost. His mind seems permanently altered so that only leaves Damien as our last choice. I propose we send word to him of your allegiance. He already knows I'm his asset here in the allied camp. We don't have means to overcome them, but we can certainly affect the outcome of the battle."

"How do we know you can negotiate anything with Damien? What does he have to gain from us?"

"The children of the former king...? It's obvious. If you support Damien over the royal side, it will go a long way toward subduing the masses. They've been bred to royal rule. Damien can simply replace the king as their liege. We can stand at Damien's side after he triumphs for the inevitable. Don't follow your brother's path to the chopping block. The bloodthirsty mob will lust for savagery in purging the old regime. You must be a part of the new order. Don't you see? There is no other choice for you."

"Damien has no reason to spare us."

"We'll give him a reason. It may be you'll be forced to live a new life, but at least you'll still be living. Damien has a clear taste for beautiful women. You princesses can ponder your options but I think that life wouldn't vary a great deal from the hedonism you've already chosen up until now. As for the princes, becoming vocal fanatical advocates of Damien would be a good option. This would be after the war, of course."

"We'll talk about it, Granor. Though you think little of us, we can still reason. Simply manipulating us into trusting you isn't so easy a task as you seem to imagine. Also, you think us incapable of loyalty. In that you're wrong too. Life at any cost, a life without value, it appeals to you, but we aren't you."

"Have it your own way. I'll await your decision, but I wouldn't take a great deal of time deciding. Time for the allies is short."

* * * *

Straga waited to bring up masses of troops before he started probing along the border to test the defenses. It would be a different war in the forests, foothills, and mountains. The Arreck had every advantage here even with the large inequity in the number of fighters. Combined with the royal army, they still had considerable military forces they could bring to bear and they could pick and choose the sites for battles.

Straga's probes brought him no usable intelligence and often his patrols met with dire endings. He remained in the dark about a strategy to invade the Arreck nation.

Belisa left to return to her parents' home in the capital, but this time she took Aron's loved ones and friends. His mother and father, Tasha and her parents, Liani along with Wu Hang and his Chenese, Abdurka, Sirina and the boys, Galean and his staffers, they were all removed from the border areas which pleased Aron getting them farther away from danger. The vast civilian encampment was also moved far in country. Only the soldiers stayed behind to mount the defense of Arreck.

Coraline, the queen and her children also went with Belisa, and the demented king. It was over Coraline's objections as she was loath to part from Aron, and Marin only grudgingly acceded. Lilith and her maidens were allowed to accompany Belisa, but Granor was not.

"Granor, it's time you stand up for your country," said Trent, as Granor was brought before a gathering that included, Aron, Brock, Barmon, the Arreck command, and the allied generals. Granor saw a uniform expression of contempt on every face.

"I'm happy to do my duty," he replied evenly. "I'm a loyal subject of the crown."

"Right," said Brock. "You're loyal to whichever way the wind blows. You should be very careful how you act. None of us have ever trusted you and that will never change. If you do what's right, perhaps you may survive. If you try to connive we'll kill you."

"What are you talking about? Damien hunts me as much as any of you."

"We'll see, Granor," said Aron. "We'll judge you on your deeds, not your words."

"Of course, that's as it should be. I'm happy to serve."

"You may go, Granor."

He glanced at the sea of unfriendly faces again before he left. He went to his unit.

"Tonight we'll send riders to Damien. We need to have a contingency on both sides of the fight. I think this collection of allies will be a stubborn opponent, but in the end I believe Damien will crush them. I don't plan on being caught in that net like floundering fish out of water. After dark we should be able to manage this. No line is totally impervious. If there are more public beheadings, I don't plan to be one of them. Let Aron and his arrogant friends have that honor of spilling gallons of their lifeblood all over the ground. They've earned the punishment."

"Yes, my lord."

* * * *

A week later Granor got word from Straga he'd consider an accommodation. Around the same time a messenger rode into Aron's camp.

"My lord," he began. "I bring word from Galean. He's found something important but you need to come to him."

"Where is he?"

"The Arreck monarch took him to a secret place. They wish for you to come and see the sight."

"I'm surprised the Arreck would reveal one of their secrets. They guard their society closely and giving trust to strangers is a rare thing for them."

"What response should I give, my lord?"

"Go Aron," said Brock. "Whether you're here or not won't change the battle that's coming. Trent and I are here. Go along with the messenger."

"If you have need of me, send word right away, Brock."

"I will."

"Stay safe, brother."

"Always, you also, brother..."

Aron rode away curious about a discovery so important Galean would feel compelled to call him away from the front on the verge of a critical battle, and perhaps the critical battle. The allies had nowhere else to go if they were defeated here.

They hadn't been gone an hour before they heard the trumpets and drums of Damien's army moving into action. The shouts of the millions of soldiers on both sides was deafening even with Aron's being away from the scene.

He nearly turned around to head back.

"My lord, we must hurry," said the messenger. "Lord Galean made it clear we must make haste."

They increased their pace. Riding all day didn't take them out of range of hearing the beginning of the battle. It stirred Aron's emotions of worry for his friends and for their defense. Damien never lost these massive battles.

The entire front was locked in a desperate struggle against endless ranks of Damien's troops. In this case, the planning of the Arreck command worked well. They were not a static enemy dug into fixed positions. They moved and remained mobile in spite of the numbers of soldiers involved. They lured Damien's attackers into trap after trap extracting terrible casualties. Straga's push which was basically flooding every possible opening with overwhelming forces didn't fully succeed. Their staggering personnel losses dwarfed any prior battle. When night fell they pulled back from the battle. It was an appalling loss of life. The allies had endured losses too, but they'd been fortunate the Arreck plans saved them a devastating fight. Straga could never use his superior numbers to any advantage. The Arreck wouldn't allow it.

It became a meat grinder which eventually caused Straga to pull back to consider other approaches.

* * * *

Aron was welcomed to the Arreck capital by the king and queen.

"Thank you, your majesties," he answered as they showered him with praise for his battle exploits.

"I'm sorry I don't feel deserving of praise for being chased all over the kingdom by Damien."

"We've watched very closely," the king replied. "You've done a remarkable job. There is no shame in retreating to fight another day."

"I got a message Galean had something he wanted me to see?"

"It will involve something of a journey," the king replied. "It's located in a very inhospitable place. We discovered it long ago purely by accident. A hunting party was lost when they came upon it. You'll rest the night here because you'll need all your strength to make the climb. We have our best guide and mountain specialists to accompany you."

"Did Liani go there?"

"Yes, they insisted. That woman, Lilith and her warriors, Tasha and her husband, and of course my daughter Belisa demanded to go as well."

"I'm ready to leave now, majesty."

"It's not possible. You'd be forced to climb in the dark. Only a fool would attempt that."

Aron grinned. "Well, more than one person has considered me a fool during my lifetime. I can't say I'm known for the best decisions."

"You're not a fool, Aron," said Belisa's mother, the queen. "You're dear to my daughter and we understand why. I also want to say, we've been told Damien holds your betrothed. We know what that means so you have our deepest sympathy. He'll pay the price of his sins, I promise you that. There is no Arreck who isn't pledged to his death, I included. I'd gladly plunge a dagger in his heart with my own hand. What he does to women, abusing them, it's not the Arreck way so it's hard for us to understand how any persons could do such. It seems to be a weakness in your people."

"Possibly the kingdom was allowed to sink to the darkest impulses of people, you may be right about that. I believe it's a function of unchecked power. The royals did such excesses because they could and they had no force to counter them."

"What became of their inner beliefs? Did they lose all sense of decency? The Arreck have our path toward purity. Surely they had it too at one time. I wonder what happened to it. New born babies are all innocent. Evil isn't innate in anybody. I feel it's something learned."

"I'm no scholar, ma'am. Galean would be the better man for this discussion. My opinion is there's light and darkness in everybody. Possibly the Arreck do better than we in controlling their urges."

Both highnesses got a momentary uncomfortable look.

"We've had lengthy talks with our daughter about what she endured as prisoner in the kingdom," said the queen. "More important, we talked about what she felt. She and her friend Tasha both described feeling guilty that they'd worn down to become compliant with their miserable states. They gave up resisting and they regret what came after that. They lost their self-respect for what they became. She was brutally honest about things she did. It was a condition no person should have faced. I think Tasha believes her failures then are the reason she made poor choices later. I know she regrets choosing Radigan. He's another who has a price to pay for things he did. Now isn't the time for that though."

"I don't forgive him those actions, but I can say I've come to the point in my life I can understand things I couldn't previously. Possibly as I cope with my own failures and weaknesses, it's easier to understand the failures and weaknesses of others."

"In that way, perhaps you're a nobler and a better person," the queen added ruefully. "I and my husband are quick to judge and quicker to seek retribution. I don't know what that says about us and our society. Radigan would have lost his life the day he arrived here if we had our way, but he's Tasha's husband as mystifying as it seems to us. It wasn't for us to make her a widow. As reprehensible as was the crown prince, we saw the genuine pain of loss of his wife, Coraline. It moved us both to rethink some things. We were told how greatly he'd changed his ways. Killing Radigan would have robbed him of the same chance to atone for his sins."

"I hated Radigan to my core. I thought he robbed me of Tasha, but now, it was so long ago, and so much has happened since, I really do hope he can make Tasha happy. I had my chance at winning her and I failed. That's the truth I've learned to accept. I had to move on. I love Tasha and I always will. I love Liani, too, but they apparently weren't meant for me. I'm not settling for Cherine. She is another woman way out of my league, but she puts up with me, so that's good enough. With what she's going through right now, I felt the same way when it was happening to Tasha. I was helpless to prevent it then and I still am now. I often wonder if Tasha secretly held it against me I didn't find a way to rescue her."

"Aron, you don't understand women," said the queen. "You have it wrong. You seem to want to place yourself in the middle of every mishap of those around you. There are events independent of you. People face what they face and make their choices. You seem to believe you've been rejected by these women for your flaws. The truth was never that. They never felt worthy of you. Tasha answered dark callings inside her. She followed her impulses, as you say, and I think she regrets it to this day."

"That's interesting," Aron replied thoughtfully. "I understand your concepts of decency and appropriate behavior, but what you just said struck me. No one would argue it's good to do wrong things, and that's not the point. Do you feel it's a mistake to have urges and to answer their call? I wonder if that's correct, or even possible. If we put those urges in what we define as an acceptable context, are we saying they're okay? I think it goes against nature to expect people to have no thoughts about…"

The king and queen looked perplexed.

"I don't expect you to speak about such things that you find borderline. It's just my stupidity at work."

"No, Aron, you're not stupid. These are difficult questions for any Arreck citizen to grapple with. If you think our strict ways mean we no longer feel temptations, you're wrong. You saw how our daughter acted. Failure isn't beyond any of us. It's a daily fight just like yours. We chose not to talk about that side, perhaps feeling we can hide from it, but it remains. My husband and I have chosen to be totally honest in our marriage and we've both, eh, felt urges. It's galling in light of our stated goals to avenge what was done to our daughter. She's railed at us to drop it. She accepts her part in that life. To tell you the truth, when she was telling us the seamy details, I understood fully what she was feeling. I didn't have to go through those abuses to know the feelings."

"If I've overstepped boundaries here, majesties, just say so. I was trying to give you insight into my perspective. Maybe that was a mistake because I'm an idiot."

The queen and king chuckled. The queen hugged Aron firmly. Like her daughter, the queen was a beautiful person and it was stimulating for Aron.

"I think I've caused you enough distress with my addled mind for one night. Good night, your majesties."

"We'll see you have an early breakfast, Aron," the queen replied. She eyed him with a penetrating look before turning away.

He smiled benignly. She evoked memories of the allure of Belisa Aron once felt, and still felt.

Aron went to bed. He thought about all the women in his life. Pondering his meandering and painful path wasn't easy and it led to the thought of Cherine captive to Damien. Thinking about what she was living caused the same angst as he'd felt about Tasha. It led to a restless night tossing and turning before he finally dozed off.

* * * *

Cherine's night was like any other. Her focus was on Nala. Blotting out their life under Damien's control was something they'd mastered. He was comic relief and as they devised ingenious ways to mislead him they laughed in private at this man who believed he was destined to rule the world. What Damien did was inconsequential to them. They found secret ways to cope with their needs and feelings and to protect each other. They were companions as Damien could never be, and he didn't even know it.

As word of the battle impasse at the Arreck border never changed, it started to draw Damien's attention and his wrath. His ongoing contentment in his 'marriages' no longer masked his anger at the continuing failure of Straga to capture his enemies and end the war.

He ranted and railed at dinner.

"You're a general, Cherine. What do you say about Straga's leadership of the army?"

"I'd say you're facing a desperate opponent backed against the wall. If you thought this would be an easy fight, you're naïve. Expecting skilled savvy enemies to easily give up their lives and protection for their families, how can you not see that?"

It was far more honest than she'd intended.

It stopped him, and instantly Cherine regretted saying it. She thought about going back to false compliments but it was too late.

"You're right, wife," said Damien. "You're absolutely right. I have so many yes men around me, I never get the truth. Thank you for that. I've handled this completely wrong. I need to change our approach. The status quo is not a viable plan for us to move forward. Aron is a stubborn antagonist. It's going to take cleverness to overcome him and his ilk."

Cherine looked at Nala. She looked concerned.

"I apologize, husband," Cherine added evenly. "It wasn't my intention to spoil our dinner. Let's speak about a better topic?"

Damien eyed her closely. They didn't see his usual euphoria at their false adoration. He looked away deep in thought.

"I fear I've upset you," she continued. "What can we do to correct this mistake?"

He looked back at her. She smiled seductively. That brought a smile from him and she relaxed. This was an arena she knew she could control.

"Tell us what we can do, husband?" asked Nala. She batted her eyes to accent her point.

"How could any man not give thanks for such loving wives," he answered. "I won't withhold that which you both so desperately require. I will grant you my fulfilling love."

They both nearly laughed right out at his preposterous statement.

"Oh, thank you so much," Nala cooed. "You're truly the nectar of our lives, my love."

"Let's enjoy this feast, ladies. We'll see to those other things afterwards."

Cherine glanced at Nala. She winked and smirked for a moment. Cherine returned her smile.

The crisis seemed to have passed, at least for the moment, though she worried if she'd inadvertently created a new problem for Aron. What Damien had in mind to do, it worried her. He'd proven to be a skillful leader and had yet to be defeated. She thought about her friends' plight in the land of the Arreck. If Damien could find a way to breech their defenses, there was nowhere they could go. It truly would be the end of resistance and the end of the world she knew.

She thought about Aron and how he was handling this situation. Going through what Tasha had with Aron, it wasn't a good prospect. He felt her situation and her choices were his fault. There was no way Cherine could protect from his concluding the same thing with her now. It worried her a great deal. There wasn't any guarantee they'd ever get back together. The allies were holed up and on the defensive. It wasn't a good scenario militarily. They couldn't take the offensive and could exercise none of the initiative which was never a good situation.

She remembered the toll this same situation had taken on Tasha and Belisa, how deeply it had changed them in a negative way. She pondered her own reactions in captivity and how easily she dismissed acquiescence to Damien, as if she was blameless, a position she had trouble believing. As the two women discussed it Nala was in the same helpless state, but she coped differently emotionally. In her case, she truly had no residual guilt over being intimate with Damien. It truly was meaningless to her, but with her former life she was in a different place than Cherine. She'd never been a leader of men and a person of great import in the realm. Her focus in all things was survival and working advantage. Damien was another tool in her world to use.

After Damien visited them each night, he went to another bedroom to sleep. From the very first night, he'd never put his safety in jeopardy even with guards close at hand. That left Cherine and Nala together to whisper in the dark. It was a glaring mistake on his part though he had yet to recognize it. In addition to commiserating together for support, they could discuss plans whether about potential escape, or other actions they could take.

The guards, over the protracted time, tended less toward vigilance watching the women. It was easy to hear the sound of their steady breathing when they fell asleep on duty. Cherine and Nala never did anything to betray their secrets to their surveillance. They posed no threat to alert the guards and Damien. What they did in the deepness of the night remained unseen and unknown by their overseers.

For Cherine, it was too easy to settle into the life. They were given every luxury of food and accommodation. They could soak in a hot bath every night, her tough days in the field a distant memory. Damien's presence though an odious imposition wasn't beyond their toleration. They cared for each other to function well in their roles.

Cherine worried about losing her edge.

"Damien, I'm not a woman who wishes to be soft. I hope you understand I need exercise. This isn't threatening to you. It is necessary for me. I must stay fit."

"There can be no weapons," he said. "Whatever you do outside of that, I agree. I like my women to look good. This is a good idea. I assume Nala will be exercising with you."

"Of course, husband."

Chapter Thirteen
~Galean's Discovery~

Aron enjoyed his breakfast chat with the king and queen. On this morning, they were very mellow rather than the formal and stern approach, an abrupt departure from their usual manner.

"I hope I haven't upset you," said Aron. "You seem a little different today."

"Is that a bad thing?" asked the queen mirthfully.

"Not from my point of view," Aron answered. "I seem to have a knack for spoiling people's moods and beliefs. I don't want to cause problems for you."

"Put your mind at ease, Aron," the king replied. "It was a refreshing talk with you yesterday. It gave us a chance for a lively discussion, the queen and I. Our conversations amongst my people tend to be narrow with little room for speculation. It was an interesting new path for us to follow."

"I hope that's a good thing, sire."

"It was, Aron. We both feel very good this morning."

"I'll be leaving shortly. I want to finish the journey as soon as possible."

"We understand. May peace go with you, Aron."

He bowed before departing to go outside. The guide eyed him thoughtfully, like an assessment. Aron nodded amiably. They could only ride part of the way to their destination. There was a way station at the base of the mountains which took their horses until they returned. Aron didn't particularly like heights and this climb looked treacherous staring up at the mountainous peaks as they walked to the path.

"My lord?" asked the guide. "Are you okay?"

"If my friends could do it, I can too. High places rattle me. I'm afraid of heights."

"I understand, my lord. We'll be cautious on the ascent."

The beginning of the climb was easy but that didn't last long. Their path soon became steep and for Aron, frightening. There were no difficult and dangerous hurdles, like scaling sheer cliff faces. The path wound back and forth and was cut wide enough to afford a measure of safety, but it was open with no safety rails or protective barriers. If a climber tripped and fell it would be the end because the drop off was right there. Aron felt terrible anxiety the entire way up. The debilitating feeling nearly defeated him.

"One foot in front of the other," the guide repeated frequently. "You can do this."

When they finally scaled the mountainside which took several hours, Aron gave a sigh of relief. Ahead of him was a cave mouth.

"In there," said the guide.

Aron went into the passage which was lighted by torches until they reached a great metal door. There was writing in a language no one knew and a great symbol.

The door wasn't closed so they stepped around it and slipped inside. It was like entering a new world. He thought immediately of the building Damien had been in.

They heard sounds ahead and began to walk. It was totally dark inside except for periodic torches.

They came into an open area. It seemed like a gathering hall with the expansive size. Continuing to follow the sound of the voices around the back wall they came to another opening. It was a large door. They stepped through into the light of many torches.

"Aron," said Tasha. "Welcome. Galean is this way."

Tasha went to another room which was filled with equipment, all of which were dark. Galean was sitting beside Liani studying the book, *"Invictus."* There was a lantern nearby issuing flickering light, but the illumination was still poor.

"I think you're right," Galean muttered.

"Do you see this?" asked Liani.

Aron glanced up to see Wu Hang nearby watching the proceedings curiously. He nodded. Wu Hang returned the greeting.

"Oh, Aron," said Galean, noticing him for the first time. "I'm so glad you came quickly. This place was a secret of the Arreck which they guarded jealously, and it's good they did. With the combination of my native curiosity, this strange book, and Liani's experiences with Damien's machines, I believe we've made significant progress. We're nearly ready to do our first experiment. I thought it best you be here to witness our success, or failure, to learn what we've learned, and to decide what we can do, if anything."

"Is this one of Damien's places?"

"I feared that too, but as we've studied here, I think we've stumbled onto a place of Damien's enemies of the past. There are none of them who survived like Damien, but this place seems to be intact. The book has been invaluable in helping me learn. I've made some assumptions which could prove wrong, or perhaps may kill us."

"That's good news, Galean."

Liani looked up and smiled.

"Hello, Liani."

"Aron, welcome to our little project...Galean is unduly cautious. I believe I can assist in accessing these machines. I wasn't in control of myself under Damien, but I remember everything I learned about Damien's devices. These are no different. What we must do is access the power. Damien's machines automatically did it before I sat down when I was there. Here, I must find the way to do it. It's a critical first step."

"Is there something I need to do?"

Liani chuckled. "There's nothing you could do. This part falls on me, and Galean. Only I must find the way to access and activate these machines."

Aron sat down in a chair beside Liani. Tasha walked over to sit with them.

"Where's your husband?"

"He chose to help elsewhere in the building."

"I don't want any trouble with him, I thought he knew that."

"He knows, Aron. He really did feel he'd be useful elsewhere with other tasks."

Liani studied the console before she reached out to a largest lever. It had a large red knob.

She tried to move it, but it seemed struck. They waited while she tried to rock it free. Aron leaned over to help her and with a prodigious tug it suddenly broke free from the ancient corrosion and moved to the open position. For a moment, nothing happened, but then there was a flicker of light in the machines that quickly multiplied. With a sudden flash the control room came back to life. A warning horn sounded before the entire complex flooded with light and power. They heard the whirring of machines activating everywhere in the structure. Air blew out of ventilation screens initially full of dust from countless ages of slumber. The air was purified quickly.

They sat in awe as the system did a diagnostic test and then automatically recalibrated. A large screen over their heads alighted and a face appeared of a long dead female technician. She spoke in a melodious voice. Aron was agog. She was pretty, young and dainty, dressed in a uniform. They could see other technicians walking in the background. It was a snapshot of a day preserved through the eons, just like Damien's.

Of course, they had no idea what she was saying.

Her recording ended and the screen went dark. It was replaced by a different image. It was the darkness of outer space. The stars seemed unusually bright.

"Is that then, or now?" asked Aron.

"Excellent question," Galean replied. "Liani, you've done it. I was hopeful, but I didn't think we could accomplish this."

"Without my captivity, we wouldn't have," she answered. "Some things are similar to what I did to Damien's equipment. I just started them going. Most of it they did automatically."

"Equipment?" asked Aron.

"It's what they call these machines."

"Do you see the symbols are different than the symbols we saw at Damien's building? This is why I think these may have been his enemy's devices."

"Do you think there are still weapons here we can use to counter Damien's?"

"That's my hope, Aron. We have a great deal to do. There's so much we don't know."

"If you meant to dazzle me, Galean, you've succeeded. Liani, you truly are a rare gift to this world."

She smiled warmly as he hugged her from behind and kissed the top of her head.

"Sorry, Wu Hang," Aron added. "I meant that in a friendship way."

Liani laughed heartily. Wu Hang shrugged. "I'm her protector. Your relationship is between you and her."

"I'm engaged to Cherine. That won't change."

He saw a slight smile from Wu Hang.

"Liani, is it possible these machines have automatic actions too?"

"I believe that, though I don't know how to access those actions."

"It's one of our research goals, Aron," Galean added.

"I'd make it my top priority," Aron commented.

"We already know that, Aron," Liani chided.

"I guess I'll get out of your way and let you work."

"Would you let me show you the building?" asked Tasha. "Now with the lights on it will be easy."

"Sure." He glanced at Galean and Liani, lost in the book instantly.

Tasha led Aron away back out of the control room into the main open room. They could now see how large it was. Royal throne rooms would be dwarfed in this enclosure.

"I wonder what this room was for?" asked Aron.

"Radigan guessed it was a staging area of some sort."

"I would agree with that."

Tasha walked close to Aron. He didn't fail to notice and glanced at her, curious.

"I can't believe you're right here standing beside me, Aron. So much has happened to both us of. Do you ever think back of the village?"

"I do, it was a good time in my life, but we were young and everything seems good at that age."

"I was so jealous of Coraline, but as you said, we were so young. Now I see her as a dear friend. Those silly girl spats seem so senseless now. Real life taught me a great many lessons, most of them bitter lessons, but I've learned. I hope I'm a better person now."

"Listen, Tasha, if you're going to apologize again for marrying Radigan, that's not something to worry about now. Yes, I was hurt. I loved you, but who knows how things would have worked out if we got together. I needed to grow up and learn my own lessons. I'm a much different person too. I can't say better, but certainly different."

"Actually, I wasn't going to apologize. My husband is Radigan and I've come to terms with it. I have regrets, but I can't change the past. I do what I can in the present."

"That's the right thing to do, Tasha. I finally found a woman, even though it always seems my women are captives of..."

"I know, Aron. I think often about what it was like for you. It took me a long time to get past my issues and my pain. Now I can appreciate yours. I hope to find a way to make it up to you."

"You don't owe me anything, Tasha. I had my chance to win you. It wasn't your fault."

She looked deep into his eyes. "There are things I'd like to say to you that are better left unsaid under the current circumstances."

"I, eh..." he stammered as his face flushed.

"Perhaps at another time we'll talk about some things."

"Okay, Tasha."

"I do want to explain something though. When I came out of captivity in the royal palace, Belisa and I were wounded spiritually and altered. We weren't capable of much, and certainly nothing good. The compromises we made in the palace defined us then. It was unfair for you to face such a burden for our poor choices, but it was beyond us to do anything good in that state of inner pain. I say this because I hope you learned from it. I'm talking about Cherine. There's a chance she'll have her own version of issues after being with Damien. If he's afflicted her with his machines and taken away her control like with Liani, can you deal with it? Don't make wrong assumptions. You're too quick to create self-blame in situations not even involving you. There is no fault on you for her being captured. Do you hear what I'm saying?"

"I'm older now, Tasha. I think about those very things. I have the intention to handle it better and I want Cherine back no matter what. What she had to do to survive isn't anything I'll blame her for."

"That's good, Aron. I was hoping you'd say that. As you said, if things with us had gone differently, I don't know if we'd have ended up together, or should have. You don't understand it, I questioned if I was good enough to be your wife. If you think you're flawed, what about me? Look at what I've done. You imagine you've made mistakes, I've actually made mistakes."

"That sounds so weird to me," he replied. "Tasha, you're the darling of every man. You, Liani, Coraline, Cherine, Belisa, even Enna and Biala, you're extraordinary women."

She smiled ruefully. "That's because men are all brainless infants when it comes to women."

"No argument here," he answered, laughing.

They saw Radigan appear along with some Arreck soldiers. The Arreck went their way and Radigan walked over.

"Hello, my friend," said Aron. "I hope you can see us here alone together without feeling those all old jealousies. This is your wife and I'm no threat to you. Cherine is my woman."

"I can't say I have no feelings, but I cope now. Those days of old were emotional tests for me, but I can also understand what you felt. Now I feel regrets for my actions I wasn't capable of not so long ago."

"We've got enough current day problems without resurrecting old ones."

"Aron, it isn't those romantic issues that worry me. How can I believe you could forgive me for siding with Damien? I was a highly ranked officer for him. I accept why everyone despises me."

"It's concerning, Radigan but I feel you aren't the threat here away from his influence and power. Also the critical factor is I think you'd never jeopardize Tasha."

"That's it exactly, Aron. Sadly, few others realize that. I'm scrutinized every minute."

"There's nothing I can do about that. It's a price you pay for those choices. We've all still got the problem of Damien to solve."

"Hopefully Galean can do just that with his research here. If Damien prevails, I'll suffer the same end as anyone else. I'm totally committed to the allies."

"Good, we're glad to have you. I hope you can see me as a friend."

"That's never been a problem for me, Aron. I wronged you."

"Tasha and I were just talking about that. I wanted her badly, but looking back, I can't say I would have been the best choice for her. There's a reason she kept turning to you, Radigan. It was appalling to me for a long time, but now I think things worked out like they were supposed to."

"That's remarkable, Aron. I wouldn't have been able to say the same thing. You've always amazed me, even when we were the worst of antagonists. I truly regret the things I've done to torment you. Of course I accept your friendship and welcome it."

"That's fine with me. I'll put out the word I trust you. Perhaps it will help."

"Thank you, Aron. You do so many of these magnanimous things people can never repay."

"I try to do what I think is right. Nobody owes me anything."

Tasha continued to take Aron on the tour of the facility, but with Radigan included.

* * * *

Straga prepared for another round of attacks but he was interrupted receiving a message from the capital city.

"My lord Straga, Damien advises you, he'll be coming to the front to observe the situation. He's not pleased with the lack of progress."

Straga simmered thinking Damien might be looking for a scapegoat to sacrifice to spur the troops.

"When...?"

"He's a day behind me, my lord."

"Return to him and advise we'll be ready for his arrival."

He then sent an order to his camp to resume the full attack. Damien would see a busy camp and an active battle zone.

This time his forces were attacked before they reached the border, but the allies quickly retreated back into cover. There were few casualties on either side, but it slowed the attack markedly. Damien's forces retraced steps to the same impenetrable defenses and the results didn't change. They lost more soldiers and accomplished nothing else.

The following day when Damien rode into camp the sounds of battle was deafening across the entire front.

Straga was shocked to see Damien brought Cherine and Nala along with him. He looked at them skeptically and went to Damien.

"Is it your wish to bring them here so close to our enemies? I don't understand? If the allies get word they're nearby, it could generate a serious raid right into our midst."

"Exactly," said Damien, smiling.

"I see, my lord. Did you have a plan for such a raid? They'll send their finest fighters, the Black Fist, the masters, and the Brutans."

"If they do, we'll have them located in a confined area fighting in a place of our choosing. The Erati desire to meet their barbarian cousins again, am I incorrect?"

"That's true, Damien. We wish to wipe them out, but at the same time we're very careful about how and when we face them. They're devils in battle, as you know."

"Have we no devils on our side, Straga? They seem to have our army at a standstill. We can't allow that to continue. If this is beyond you, say so now."

Straga looked at Cherine who had an amused look on her face. It was strange to see her out of her uniform and without weapons at hand. She was gorgeous as was her new companion in tight dresses.

"You look much changed, Cherine," he ventured. "Marriage to Damien has done you much good. I think you're happy and perhaps at peace? The master is very much pleased with his wives. Congratulations on being on the winning side of this war."

"Yes, I can see how you're thrashing the allies, Straga. And how much ground have you captured after all this fighting?"

He scowled at her. Damien chuckled. "I think it unwise to spar with my wife, verbally or otherwise. She's a force of nature in any situation."

Straga bowed to Damien.

"I think it best if we re-energize our army, wouldn't you say, Straga? They may need additional incentive to push through the hard tasks ahead of them. There is no defense that can't be beaten."

"What did you have in mind?"

"I've always found it's the right mixture of a number of things whether in battle or in governing the masses. Of course cowing them is important. Using awe is an effective tool to generate loyalty. That loyalty is fickle. With changes in circumstances, they can easily revert back to who they were. The greatest element we use is fear. They must fear our wrath more than they fear death in battle. That's not so easy a task. How do you override their native feelings about their families and their lives? This is part of why I use women and children in the battles, to shield the real soldiers and to eliminate the issue of families left behind. Widowers are driven men. They require an outlet for their grief and their rage. If I tell them the allies killed their families, they have no way to know the circumstances. Do you see?"

Cherine was appalled listening to Damien's insane reasoning. Nala put a hand on Cherine's to calm her. It seemed Cherine was pondering a silly move which couldn't succeed.

"I'll speak to the troops tonight," Damien concluded. "Come, my angels, let's get settled into our tent. I have time at the moment for us."

It was Straga's turn to smirk reveling in the looks on the women's faces. Cherine turned stiffly and followed Damien away. She had no other choice.

"This is pleasing seeing her humbled," he muttered to his lieutenant. He was a fellow Erati. "It's been too long a time in coming. She won't be the only one humbled before this is over."

"It will be a great day when we see the rest of the allies humbled too, my lord."

"Yes, indeed."

"Women should never have been allowed such power and position as Cherine had. The sooner we reassert proper authority over them and they yield to their true roles in the world, the better."

Straga shrugged with a smug grin.

* * * *

Damien's arrival at the front was no secret. Brock's spies sent word of his coming along with notice he'd brought massive reinforcements too.

Brock sent a speedy courier to the Arreck capital to get word to Aron. Of course, Aron wouldn't receive the message before Damien could take action.

When Damien stood up to give his evening speech, there were Brock's spies in attendance too along with the throng.

As always, Damien's army was a loosely connected mass populated by considerable rabble. The spies targeted the women and children and funneled them each night in the darkness into Arreck and away from the battle. The enemy officers never knew they were bleeding away battlefield fodder as all of the people they controlled were strangers. One face looked the same as the next to them.

Damien felt particularly animated after his afternoon with his 'wives'.

Cherine and Nala were forced to put on red dresses which left little to the imagination for the public event. They simmered standing on the platform beside Damien, on display as his trophies, trophies he could never earn.

"My children," Damien began expansively. "We've come a long way on our difficult path toward the salvation of the world. Before us stands our final obstacle. These allies, as they call themselves, are no different than any other foe we've already conquered. We faced them all through this kingdom and beat them every time. We crushed them in their own capital city and took off the head of their crown prince. That head is lonely at the entrance to the palace. We need to add the heads of the other leaders of this rebellion to welcome visitors to the palace so they see the price of defiance. They can't win. They're too stubborn and stupid to admit it though. We must take what's ours this one last time. I regret that we must lose lives to accomplish this, but when we cross over, it will be so much better when you go as a martyr. There is a special place for the brave in the beyond. This I know for a fact. The hard life we live here isn't the sum of living. We can aspire to better and know at the end when we pass over there will be utopia waiting. There will no longer be starvation, pain, and denial. We'll get all that we want in that perfect place. Put aside your fears and march bravely against your enemies. They're craven barbarians who pitilessly slaughter women and children. You know this because you've seen it with your own eyes. Avenge those poor souls. Carry your righteous rage with you into battle. Show them no fear and fight with no pity because they'll show you none. Shatter this false aura about Aron and his band of miscreants. They can be killed like any other. Drive the stake into the heart of the beast and end their danger forever."

The crowd shouted wildly.

Damien raised his fists straight into the air triumphantly. He drew Cherine and Nala into his arms, like he was a god, and they were his pretty things. Cherine very nearly grabbed his head to snap his neck in her rage, but the guards were always very close. She didn't bother pretending to smile, nor did Nala.

The allies' spies used the opportunity to spirit away huge numbers of women and children to the safety of Arreck. Unfortunately, it was an unending tide because behind them arrived many more sacrificial lambs as Damien was moving his followers to this specific place and this critical point in the war.

Straga watched the spectacle critically. Damien had a gift to dazzle, but it had become less fascinating to Straga with time. He was left with the ongoing problem to defeat the allies. The speech hadn't changed battlefield dynamics. He also saw Cherine and Nala were showing increasing signs of rebellion.

"Gather the officers to meet with me, Straga," said Damien, as he herded his wives back to the tent.

Damien placed an entire unit of soldiers surrounding the tent while he went for his meeting.

Straga felt some worry. He wasn't sure what Damien would do. He could be capricious and unpredictable and this was not a guaranteed victory over the allies. A great deal can go wrong on the battlefield.

Once they were assembled Damien took control.

"Don't fear this meeting. I know the severe problem you face in Arreck country. They're cornered and a cornered animal is dangerous. Nonetheless, we never accept defeat. I'm not going to say you must try harder. They have geography and positioning on their side. You're not stymied for lack of effort. I know that. We aren't without weapons. I've used them sparingly before, but they remain at our disposal if needed. This is one of those times. We'll continue our frontal assault with the greatest intensity. It will force them to draw up their reserves to plug the holes. At a signal, the army will suddenly withdraw leaving the allies exposed to destruction. I've programmed in the firing command and the attack solution. Their annihilation will be automatic when the remote sensors detect the scene I've created. We'll wipe them out in droves. Afterwards it will be little more than a mop-up action. I'm sure any survivors, especially the Arreck soldiers on their home ground will be a stubborn foe, but the outcome won't be in doubt any longer. All of those traitors will kneel down before me as did the crown prince. I may behead Aron personally. The women, Liani, Tasha, Belisa, and the others who were the beloved of Aron, they'll join Cherine in leading a better life in my custody, one which serves the greater good. After all, a man can never have enough wives."

Straga heard snickers throughout the crowd but he wasn't convinced Damien could simply wipe out the opposition even with his terrible weapons.

"Of course, they'll get word Cherine is here, so we know they'll make their misguided rescue attempt. It will fail miserably. It may make it easier if Aron himself joins the team they send. It would speed up the end of hostilities."

Again there were more snickers. Straga bristled at the idiocy around him, as if Damien's words were reality. If the Black Fist, the masters, and the Brutans came it would be a serious fight and certainly no sure victory.

His Erati brethren looked at him. They were of the same opinion.

"We'll attack at sunrise. Send the whole army into the fray and tell them there is no retreat. Be alert for the signal unless they wish to perish in an instant of flame and death. After I strike the enemy army, they must attack and kill anybody in their path. There will be no surrender, no prisoners, and no mercy. The families of these traitors will pay a terrible price for disloyalty. My men are free to exact revenge on them however they choose."

Damien came over to Straga. "See, my friend. They're a rabid pack of dogs now. The lure of loot and women is overpowering to them. The Erati will get their share too. I think I'll make a new law that every one of my soldiers is required to have multiple wives. I like that. What do you say?"

"If that's your wish, how could anybody object?"

"You don't want a supply of beautiful women to brighten your nights and warm your bed, Straga?"

"I focus on battle. Those other considerations come afterwards. I expect a supreme fight and I believe we must expect setbacks. Nothing ever goes as planned in battle, Damien."

Damien chuckled. "This is good, Straga. I'm glad you're cautious. It never hurts. I stand on my record. I've never lost in war and I won't this time either."

He glanced toward the Arreck mountains before continuing.

"I've set traps within the trap for Aron. I believe the chance to come for Cherine will be too strong for him to resist. We'll be ready. If he sends his whole army, we'll mow them down like grass. I have a good feeling about the upcoming fight."

"I hope it happens as you forecast, Damien. Just in case of those setbacks, I'm setting up contingencies of my own. The Erati will rally to me. I think we might face the fury of the entire Brutan nation and that's no small thing."

"Whatever," said Damien, dismissively.

He walked away toward his tent.

"Straga, he's a fool about this. Has he learned nothing in all these years of fights against them?"

"I think he can conceive of nothing else other than his dreams of glory. He leaves it to us to make it happen. My concern is the Erati at this point. I don't share Damien's good feeling about the battle. I feel just the opposite, like we're on the verge of disaster."

"It was a good idea to tell him we're not going to disperse amongst the rabble. If you're right and we're somehow beaten, we'll be together to make our escape. You need only give us the signal and we'll move instantly out of harm's way."

"Good. I still want to make it as far as their civilian camp to find my wife Sirina and my sons. Once I have them, my part in this war is over."

"Yes, my lord. I'll pass the word to the men. Our women and children are gathering too. They'll be ready to flee and join us, on command."

"Our quarrel with the Brutans needs to happen later at a time and place of our choosing. They're not our superiors. We'll teach them that fact before we wipe them out and take their families into slavery to us."

"May that day come soon, my lord."

"Be sure everyone knows to stay together. That's critical to our plans. We won't wait for stragglers."

* * * *

The all-out attack happened as Damien demanded as the landscape looked like plague approaching Arreck. There were continuous surges of endless bodies screaming and waving their weapons as they raced toward the skirmish line. As many women and children as the allies funneled away, Damien's ranks were still filled with inappropriate fighters at the front of the attack.

The allies stood their ground and met the onslaught with unyielding resolve. It was a bitter fight from the start and it didn't relent.

"This attack is different, Brock," said Trent.

"Damien has a plan. His personally coming to the battle tells me he thinks to end the war here and now."

"He thinks we'll strike his camp to rescue Cherine."

"Damien thinks no one else can match his intellect. We're backwards peasants in his eyes. I hate him, Trent. I can't stomach the thought of him winning."

"We all do hate him, but we have a difficult crisis. We can't afford to make any mistakes or Damien will get his wish."

"Do you have an idea?"

"The Arreck command has a fairly rigid view of what we should do. We don't have much leeway to try any risky plans."

"That's probably a good thing."

"I believe Damien assumes Aron is here close to the front. That's a part of his plan to get Aron to lead a misguided rescue attempt into Damien's trap."

"He's convinced himself he's invincible, Trent."

"I understand since he hasn't lost any battles, but I don't think he can't be beaten. I'm afraid we're going to be forced to call up reserves. He's sending over numbers we can't contain, even with our geographic advantages."

"That worries me, Trent. If we let him pull the strings sooner or later we'll be at his mercy in a battle we can't win."

"I think we're fast approaching the time when Galean's miracle needs to happen. He's had unshakable faith Aron would perform some great feat to destroy Damien."

"Do you think we should work some sort of foray to spring Damien's trap?"

"Brock, I honestly think Cherine is out of our reach. I'd say leave Damien's schemes untouched at this point. If circumstances arise where we can make a move, we can be ready at that time."

"I'm sure if Aron was here he'd have a different opinion, but I think you're right. Our priority should be winning the fight on behalf of our people. I don't want to say we abandon Cherine to her fate, but she's a clever resourceful woman. I suspect she can find a way to deal with her situation until an opportunity arises."

"Do you think Damien took away her mind, like Liani?"

"I honestly don't know."

Savior

* * * *

Aron eventually received the message from the front about Damien coming and bringing Cherine with him.

Tasha, Liani, and Galean surrounded Aron.

"You know this is a trap, Aron," said Galean. "He hopes to provoke you into precipitous action he can take advantage of."

"Aron, I know you suffered terrible guilt when I was captive of the prince," Tasha added. "I survived my time there, just like Cherine is doing. This isn't your fault and you can't single handedly solve every problem. What happened to me there over time were my own weaknesses. Cherine is not me."

Liani added, "When I was held by Damien and had no control, I still had some awareness of things. I just couldn't do anything about the situation. If he's done the same to Cherine, you can see she isn't lost for all time. I was brought back and she can be too. When I was finally free, I could have started up right where I left off. Cherine will be the same woman you asked to marry you. What's happened in the interim is meaningless."

"I know all of that," Aron replied. "Are you saying I just ignore it?"

"Aron, I feel we're so close to a breakthrough. You should be here, not there," Galean answered.

Chapter Fourteen
~Invictus Fatum~

Aron wrestled with his urge to race away to the front in spite of his tacit agreement to his friends to avoid senseless action.

Galean and Liani went back to work feverishly trying to solve the complex issue of alien technology. Every step they managed was virtually a miracle as they had no basis to understand and operate the equipment of the ancients. Getting to this point seemed impossible, yet here they were.

Tasha stayed near them, but Aron walked about a great deal. His strong feelings to do something weren't easily controlled.

Radigan walked up to him one day.

"I wish I could help, Aron. I remember how I felt when Tasha was out of my hands and potentially at risk. Having Cherine a captive and being stuck here, I know it eats at you. Would it be helpful if we spar? Perhaps it will help you relieve some of the stress. I'll try to keep from getting killed at your hands."

Aron smiled. "I guess it's worth a try. I'm convinced this is the pivotal point in the war. I should be at the front fighting."

"You and I are nearly without peer as individual swordsmen, but in a massive battle, one sword makes very little difference one way or another. Your own feelings are your enemy at this point. Perhaps Galean and Liani will give you a weapon to deal with Damien. You must stay the course."

"Do you honestly think he's right, that I'm the one who will find a way where no one else could? I can't say I ever subscribed to that idea. I'm still fighting because I'm stubborn and I won't concede anything to Damien, not because I ever believed I had a higher destiny."

"I didn't believe Galean for a long time, Aron, but I've changed my mind. You've done so many things no one else could do in leading us. I don't find it impossible to think you could find a way to rid us of Damien. I lived in his world, as you know. He's not a god or some magical being. His strength is his continuous caution in addition to having the past at his disposal. He never leaves anything to chance. He makes contingency plans down to the smallest detail. He trusts no one but himself. Taking him down won't be easy. We'll all be here to support you."

They went down into the huge open room to spar. It became a daily habit and a lengthy one.

It did help reduce the stressful feelings. Radigan was incredibly skillful and the two men fought fairly evenly. After they completed the work late one evening, they sat for a moment to catch their breath.

"Aron, I want to say something else if you'll listen. I have plenty to regret in my life. Don't think because I got Tasha in the end it was an outcome without consequences for me. She bonded with me early, when you were unable to interfere being kept imprisoned by the prince which gave me a free hand to win her. I was skillful in areas where I had great experience and you didn't in your youth. That may seem important to you, but believe me, I never got what every man covets, the genuine love of his woman. Tasha isn't bashful in being honest about it. She's a faithful wife, but to her I'll always be a mistake she made, a faulty choice. There's nothing I can do to change that. We'll never reach a point of total union as two spirits joined. She's given me her physical self and that's wonderful, but her spirit is separate and aloof. She still loves you, Aron."

Aron could think of nothing to say.

* * * *

Damien was surprised the allies didn't make a rescue move promptly.

"Damien, I could have told you such," Straga related after a month of continuous battle. "You've listened to your own counsel for so long you ignore important ideas from the people around you. I think it's a serious mistake."

"You're particularly aggressive today. I'm not sure I like it. As far as my decisions, seeing as I've conquered the world, I trust my own counsel, as you say. I hear you and the others, but your thinking is too small. Our ploy wasn't the key variable in ending the war. If they'd taken the bait, it would simply have accelerated their end. I'm not concerned. They're pulling in their forces as I predicted they would do. It will soon be time to roast them."

Straga looked at Damien.

"What is this sudden skepticism, Straga? Have I ever failed? I give you a certain amount of latitude because you've been valuable in leading my army, but you're annoying me with this attitude. It's not a good idea, my friend. It's easy enough for me to find others to take your place."

"That's your choice, Damien. I do my duty. If that doesn't suffice, what else could I do?"

"We're on the verge of the greatest victory in human history yet you fret like an old woman."

"I'm a cautious person by nature, Damien. I'll be happy to celebrate after the war is ended."

Damien smiled. "Celebrate we shall, parading the heads of our enemies on poles all the way back to Nephora."

Straga noticed his second in command standing behind Damien. His expression was one of disdain.

They were greeted by a knot of troops escorting Cherine and Nala.

"Hello, my ladies," said Damien warmly.

It was entertaining to Straga to see the momentary look of loathing cross Cherine's face before she displayed a crocodile smile.

"Husband," she replied.

Nala bowed toward Damien.

"You both look so nice this fine morning. I regret you must wear warm cloaks for this dismal northland. I wonder why anyone would choose to live in such a distressing place. I think this fog must be their permanent weather."

Cherine looked frostily at Straga for looking at her.

"Good morning, Cherine. I must say I never get accustomed to seeing you without your uniform and your weapons."

"I'd be happy to rectify that discrepancy if it's your wish."

"I think arming you may not be a good idea," said Straga with a satisfied grin.

Damien looked at the challenge in Cherine's eyes, a reflection of her old self. She quickly lowered her feral gaze fearing she'd put Damien on guard and herself in jeopardy in the process.

"I'm only verbally jousting with your army commander for sport, husband. You know the true joy we both feel serving you as companions and wives. Fulfilling our duties is our highest calling and we glory in it. It's an honor beyond measure."

His skeptical look didn't go away quickly. Cherine worried she'd opened a serious problem with a simple slip in her demeanor. She felt Nala touch her hand. Cherine smiled sweetly, as did Nala.

Straga smiled at the obvious deception as Damien stood pondering them thoughtfully.

In the background they heard the fighting renew. Cherine looked longingly in that direction. Straga knew what she felt, a hunger to act. He felt the same motivation. Battle called to both of them.

"You may return to our tent, ladies," said Damien dismissively.

They nodded and walked away surrounded as always by a phalanx of Damien's guards.

Damien looked piercingly at Straga. "I'm not the fool you seem to think I am. Do you think they control me, that I'm an adolescent boy agog at their presence?"

"It's a fascinating match, Damien. I think both sides are highly skilled players and each move is exceptional. It'd be easy for many to conclude you're distracted with the women and not paying sufficient attention to the war. It's the key juncture and this is the critical point in time."

Damien smiled. "I think I've been the more skillful player. I get what I want from them willingly while they think me addled with sophomoric fascination. I've lived through the vast ages and I've been with countless beautiful women. I admit these two are enjoyable, but I never surrender control or my faculties. I never leave an opening for Cherine. She's a deadly warrior and a great threat to my life. I take proper precautions every minute of every day. At night when I visit them, they're both restrained and that will always be the case. I haven't survived by making mistakes."

"Damien, I'm glad to hear you say this. I leave your private life to you. I only cared if you put us in danger. It's clear to me now you have complete control of the situation."

* * * *

The women went to sit down on the bed. They talked in low tones.

"We need to be very careful. I sensed something in Damien today that concerns me greatly, Cherine."

"I know what you mean. I noticed it too."

Nala glanced at the guards who were staring at them suspiciously.

"Yes, it's such an opportunity to please our husband," she piped loudly. "What man wouldn't be happy with such devoted friendship from their wives?"

She whispered to Cherine. "I've been amazed at your aura. I never saw you as you were, but the wake you cause in people around you is remarkable. You're revered by your enemies as much as Damien who is their leader. I wish I could see you that way."

"My hope is someday you will, Nala."

"Where I'm from, I never met strong women. We were subjugated and controlled by men, and it wasn't rare to be abused. Even as a captive, it was obvious to me you were different than any woman I knew. You were competent, a barely restrained storm, you weren't frightened. You've fought

177

men as an equal. It's so compelling for me. It's the biggest reason I was attracted to you. I envy you that prowess and the respect that you've earned."

"It was a difficult and a painful path, Nala. I suffered more than my share of setbacks and humiliations. I guess I wasn't willing to stay down though. Maybe that makes me different. I wouldn't wish my life on my worst enemy."

Nala chuckled. The two women embraced warmly.

"Toward the end, once I met Aron, I started to look at things differently. I realized I had short term goals, but I was lacking any great purpose. Aron is a man who lives in the center of relevancy. His participation in anything gives it credence. I thought I'd seen the pinnacle of power with the king and the crown prince, but Aron eclipses any other man, especially Damien. It amazes me Damien's managed to avoid his punishment for his sins. He's not impressive at all. I think he was shrewd and was in the right place. He has certain skills of oratory but there's no true substance to him. He's a façade, an illusion of a great man where Aron is a great man. Damien touts his nonexistent prowess. Aron doubts his worth, though everyone else can see it clearly. He exudes true power without trying."

"I understand you, Cherine. I never thought much about men. They were always such a danger and there was nothing good in dealing with them. You make Aron sound like a person worth knowing, a man I could finally respect."

"I'm sorry, Nala. I'm so self-centered a person. I never thought to ask you about your life."

"There's little to tell, and certainly nothing of great import. I was robbed of my childhood and parents. Early I set about learning to take care of myself. I became good at certain things because I had to. I never trusted anybody before you, Cherine. I couldn't take the chance because if I was wrong it could cost me my life. This may sound very strange to you, but this is the best my life has been. I have a dear friend now, I live in luxury, and comfort, my food is very good these days, and my…"

Cherine laughed. "Don't say it. I think I know what you were going to say. I agree with you but let's not say it right out. If it weren't for your presence here, I don't know if I could've maintained the illusion so long to fool Damien, assuming we have fooled him. I really never trusted anyone before either, except for Aron. I was on a good footing with the other women in his life but I didn't have the bond I have with you."

"That means a great deal to me, Cherine, thank you."

The guards stirred.

"We should stop talking for now. Tonight after he leaves, we can talk again in the darkness. There are a few more things I'd like to talk about, Cherine."

"Certainly..."

"No more talking," said the sergeant tersely. "You know Lord Damien doesn't like it."

The women bowed to him.

"Yes sir."

Nala took Cherine's hand for a moment for reassurance with a gentle squeeze.

* * * *

Galean looked up from the passage pondering a conclusion.

"I think there is an assumption we've made which may not be true regarding Damien."

"Please explain," said Liani.

Wu Hang walked over close to listen.

"We've believed ourselves vulnerable and helpless against his ancient weapons. I don't find a basis to support that assumption. If my readings are correct, I think there may be an answer to the threat. I think there's a way to answer his attacks. Liani have you found anything in this machine that's unknown and unexplored?"

"There's a great deal that fits into that category, Galean. I've stayed away from areas that don't fit the scope of the knowledge I have. What is buried here, I couldn't speculate. Is that what we want to do? Is it safe for us to experiment with the unknown? What if we unleash our own demise out of ignorance?"

"We have no choice but to try. Damien is at our door. Our time has run out."

Liani looked at Wu Hang.

"I want to say this, sir. If what I do next ends our lives I want to speak my mind so you understand. Our first meeting was adversarial and for me, terrifying. You believe I've never forgiven you for what was out of your hands then. That was possibly true for a short time, but I've come to terms with it long ago. I know your true desire. I couldn't give you such a union because my heart belonged to Aron. You've done for me what no one person could. You've had faith in saving me when I was lost to Damien's power. You faithfully safe guarded me in the face of hopelessness. You stand by me against all odds. I'm not unmoved by that, Wu Hang. I've developed feelings for you, true affection. It isn't the same as the love I feel for Aron, but it's significant. I've thought about this a great deal. I'll never have Aron as my husband so it's time I move on. If you understand that and can come to terms with it, I will offer you this. If we survive, I'll become your wife and give you the children and the family you covet. I'll put aside my pointless pining for a man intended for another woman.

I will strive to give you the love and respect you should get from a wife. I don't know if it can work out, but I'll try."

Wu Hang looked nearly in pain as strong emotions wracked his face.

"I'm a blessed man, Liani, to hear these words from you. I'll accept you on any terms. I don't hold your love of Aron against you. He's a unique man beloved by many. Whatever crumbs you throw my way is enough for me. It's a miracle I've dreamed of but never thought possible. I knew you were the one when I first saw you, Liani. I wish I could erase that fright I caused you."

"I've learned the type of man you are, Wu Hang. You've done what you had to, just like the rest of us. You're no guiltier than I am. Remember, I was Damien's trophy to use as he wished."

"You have no guilt for that, Liani. It was out of your control."

"What you don't understand was what Tasha and Belisa said because I went through it too. In such situations it's your spirit that fails you. I gave up the fight as they did. I lost hope. Had my faculties suddenly been freed, I would have been jaded too, like they were. It took me time to recover dignity and self-worth. Guilt is a heavy burden."

"Dealing with guilt has been the curse of my life. I understand what you're saying, Liani."

They both looked at Galean.

"You don't need validation from me, or any other person. If you can find happiness in each other's arms, what else matters? Liani, you've been like a daughter to me. This warms my heart to hear you looking to bond with a man. I'll see your children as my grandchildren."

Liani chuckled and Wu Hang smiled proudly.

She looked back at the console and took a deep breath.

"Just be cautious and take your time. We'll try this in increments, Liani."

"That's if it can be done incrementally, Galean."

She accessed the screen icons. There wasn't an empty space on the screen.

"I'll start with this first one," she muttered. She pressed the symbol and it brought up a face of a young woman droning in the unknown language.

"This probably instructs us on the system," said Galean. "It's too bad there's no one here to understand her."

Liani closed the transmission and went to the next symbol. A man's face appeared with a streaming board behind him which he pointed to. There was a long list scrolling which he was explaining, apparently.

"An inventory?" asked Liani.

"I think you're right. What those are, we don't know."

"I'd say they're weapons," Wu Hang interjected. "I think this was a military base."

Galean nodded.

Liani moved on to the next icon. It showed schematic charts with blinking red lights in the rooms.

"It must be this facility," said Galean. "Remember Damien had a force keeping us out. Perhaps this is a display of similar power."

They continued their tour of the icons and were most of the way through them when they came to an icon which glowed unlike the others. When Liani clicked it, the lights blinked, red lights started to flash everywhere in the building, and warning tones sounded.

Aron was talking to Radigan in the main open area when it started.

"Uh-oh," he muttered in fear.

The entire wall behind them started to shift opening a vast storage area. Out of that darkened area a huge ship slid out on a moving panel. It was sleek, massive, and frightening to see. It looked brand new with no sign of aging.

The ship was inert until the panel stopped. Then it came to life with flashing lights and warning sounds of its own.

"Are we in peril?" asked Radigan.

"I don't know. I think Liani found this thing. I'd say we should probably get out of this room."

They hurried up to the control room.

Everyone else had come up too, in fright.

"Do you know what it is and what to do with it, Liani?" asked Aron.

"I think it is like Damien's weaponry. What it does, I'm not sure, but I think it can act without my controlling it."

"As long as it doesn't attack us, or our army, I guess you can give it a go."

Liani looked at him.

"I can make no guarantees, Aron."

She turned back to the console and typed in a command. It was from her memory of using Damien's machines.

They heard another deep tone and the outer barrier suddenly rotated open to the outside. The ship launched immediately and rose up into the air.

"God help us," said Galean.

The ship slowly rotated, as if getting bearings.

Suddenly all the screens and displays lit up in the control room. They saw views in a number of directions. On Liani's main screen they got a view from the automated ship. A voice recited a preset litany the ancients would have known. Aron and his friends were just spectators.

The ship hovered, waiting.

"Perhaps it needs directions from us?" asked Liani.

"If that's true, our adventure ends here. We have no way to command the thing," Galean replied.

Liani studied the screens and typed in a command, something from Damien's devices.

It generated a massive response as every screen in the control room displayed dizzying floods of data and the machines hummed loudly. They heard other machines activate. One of the machines near them was a printer. It started to spit out reams of printouts, none of which had any meaning to the befuddled allies.

Galean studied them curiously. "Apparently we can interact with it, but what are we saying?"

Liani tried another command. The outside ship shifted position and scanned the sky. Periodically one of the screens in the control room beeped and furiously ran data. It generated another printout concluding with a deep voice speaking for a short time.

Everybody looked at each other.

"Should we continue, Galean," asked Radigan with concern.

"I don't think we can stop at this point. We've started something. Hopefully it will be helpful to us. I fear that ship will defend this facility cutting off all approaches. Whether we'd be allowed to leave, I don't know that either."

Aron shrugged. He noticed Tasha staring at him intently. He remembered what Radigan told him about her ongoing feelings. Aron smiled at her and she smiled back warmly.

The ship completed the aerial scan. The monitor screens began to display various views both on the planet and in space. They saw numerous orbital firing platforms in the darkness of space. They also saw ground installations, many of which were buried under rubble or others blasted open in the ancient war. Some appeared to still be intact though.

The computer began calculating firing solutions, though no one in the control room knew what it meant. They just saw gibberish. The automated voice droned a lengthy explanation when the calculation was completed. There was a pause.

"We're supposed to give an answer," said Liani.

Galean smiled at her, sheepishly.

"Fire," he said as a joke. Everybody chuckled.

"I guess it doesn't respond to our voices," said Liani rhetorically.

"What do we do?" asked Tasha. "Can we leave that thing out there like this? I feel like it's as much a hazard to us as it is to Damien."

Galean shrugged. "Perhaps..."

"Liani, does it follow some pre-arranged orders from the ancients?" asked Aron.

"I believe so, but I've no way to know for sure, or to know what those orders would be. I assume they'd seek their enemy."

"That would be a good thing," said Aron. "I wish we could control these views to spy on Damien."

"It would be nice," Galean agreed.

"I think that thing can do some real damage," Radigan remarked. Everybody chuckled.

"You think?" asked Aron jokingly.

"Seeing a machine like that would have caused a heart attack from terror not so long ago," Aron remarked. "It's strange that now I accept its existence without as much as a glance. How things can change."

"Yes," Galean replied. "I've thought upon that very idea many times. I've spent the bulk of my adult life studying the wisdom in the ancient tomes out of curiosity. I never had a feeling it could lead to this reality. I suspected portentous events in our future, but to have the whole world pivoting on what we do, it's remarkable. It's also daunting that history might judge us very harshly for our failings."

Everybody looked at Aron. He shrugged. "I do what I can with what I've got. I didn't ask for this job."

Liani started to experiment again with the screen icons. At one point her click generated a large image of a button.

She looked at Galean.

"That's probably what we've been searching for, Liani."

"If I push it, we may rain down death on friend and foe alike. I don't think I can control it. I suspect it will begin procedures the ancients created."

This time everyone looked at Galean.

"What do you say, Aron?" he asked, shifting the responsibility for the choice.

"I think I'm willing to go with your instinct, Galean," shifting the choice back.

They smiled at each other.

"Do it, Liani," said Galean.

She clicked on the button image. Again the entire building reacted. Defensive shielding activated sealing the facility, the ship issued a deafening deep tone that echoed across the mountains in a terrifying blast, and the view on the screens changed. The ship started to cruise slowly upwards.

* * * *

Coincidentally, Damien was standing beside Straga as they performed Damien's strategy to lure the allied armies close to the skirmish and then quickly retreat.

"Hear the allies cheer," said Damien smugly. "People are such fools and so predictable, no matter what era. The ancients were equally gullible, believe me. Now they'll get their just reward, they'll get incinerated and sent to the next level of reality in defeat."

Damien keyed in commands to his hand console and transmitted the firing orders to his orbiting weapons stations. As always there was a loud warning tone of the imminent launch. That tone occurred at the same time the alien ship sounded its own warning miles away so Damien never heard it.

The ship locked on the impending attack and reacted immediately. The ship launched into dizzying speed and within moments it was hovering over the allied army.

"No, that's impossible," shouted Damien in shock. "They're all dead!"

When Damien's weaponry fired, the enemy craft responded neutralizing the deadly assault. The ship raced upwards to space and began systematically attacking and destroying the remaining weapons platforms. The explosions were massive as the weapons detonated the sky was filled with sound and light for hours as each battle in space erupted.

"Damien, what was that thing? What happened?" asked Straga.

Cherine and Nala were on the hillock along with the other generals.

Damien looked terrified.

"I must take defensive action," he said and turned to leave. He looked back.

"Bring them along."

The guards forced Nala and Cherine to the horses and they rode away in a huge phalanx of Damien's personal protectors.

"Where are we going?" Nala asked Cherine.

"My guess would be back to the wilds, to that place where he was buried. I think that may be some sort of hub for Damien's operations. I don't know, Nala."

"Why would he take us?"

"There could be many reasons, Nala. We must be alert for any chance to escape. I think what waits at the end of this ride won't be good for us. Perhaps it's one of his attempts to harm Aron if he harms us."

"I didn't think he was so taken with us that we really matter to him, Cherine."

"We need to be strong emotionally and not let him realize we're worried. It will be a tip-off that might accelerate our demise."

"I'll try to use your example as my guide, Cherine. I'm not the person you are. I'm afraid of dying."

"Don't give up hope, darling. We'll fight to the end. We might be able to impact Damien and help Aron in the process, even if we ultimately…"

"Don't think that. If Aron now has such weapons as Damien, I believe he can prevail."

"If it happens, Nala, I want you to know how much I cherish having you in my life."

Nala got a sad look on her face.

They rode rapidly stopping late and departing early each day. It was a long journey back to the wilds.

When they stopped at night, Damien placed the women on each side of him so they couldn't talk to each other. He also had their hands and feet bound while they slept.

All around them, Damien's forces were in pandemonium as their command structure quickly broke down. With Damien fleeing the battlefield without warning and without leaving instructions, Straga was forced to try to keep control of a quickly eroding situation.

The allied army which had been totally defensive up to this point saw their chance and began sending probes and raids across the entire front. Straga still had far superior numbers, but it did nothing more than slow the inevitable. The allies were starting to turn the situation in the field in their favor and make gains on the ground.

The mighty ship took a week to circle the globe destroying what remained of Damien's network of orbiting stations. It glided soundlessly over the battlefield, propelled by powers unknown to the new world. The sight of it broke the resolve in Damien's army, what remained of it anyway. Those forces started to filter away each night until they were a flood fleeing the war. Their officers were overwhelmed and soon joined them in abandoning Damien's grandiose plan.

The heart of that army, those competent fighters like Straga's Erati, made their own alternate plans.

"You must abandon the idea to recapture your wife and sons, Straga," said his lieutenant. "We must go home while we can and make a stand there."

Straga eyed the allied surge morosely before signaling the retreat.

* * * *

Back at the alien command center, completion of the mission to neutralize the orbiting hazard and the return of the ship to home base opened the protective barriers. The ship glided into the vast hanger and was automatically stored back in its berth.

"Are we free to leave, Galean?" asked Tasha.

"It would seem we are, Tasha."

The people cheered.

"I would say we leave a force here to continue researching this place, I'll be happy to stay."

He looked at Liani.

"I'll consider returning, but I have other business to take care of. I made a promise to master Wu Hang. It's time to fulfill that pledge."

"Will you allow me to prepare a proper service?" asked Belisa. "This must be appropriately observed by the world."

"I don't want a big ceremony, Belisa."

"Too bad," said Belisa with a smirk.

All of the women laughed and descended on Liani. She took one last look at Aron.

He walked over to her. "I want to wish you the best, Liani. You know I've got to go save Cherine."

"I know, Aron. Godspeed to you..."

Aron walked away giving instructions to forward to his force commanders in the field.

"I want the Black Fist, the masters, and the Brutans at a minimum. We need enough fighters but we must be mobile and fast moving."

"You'll also include me, and my maidens," said Lilith, suddenly appearing at his side.

They looked at each other.

"We've more than proven our worth, Aron," she huffed. "This isn't negotiable."

He smiled. "So be it, Lilith. Ready your forces. We leave immediately. Damien has a big lead on us."

"Do you know where he's going, Aron?"

"I'd guess back to that place we first found him."

Chapter Fifteen
~Dangerous Pursuit~

It was surprising to Aron and his officers how quickly the enemy front dissolved. Damien's massive army was still in the area but they were moving rapidly away from the fighting.

Straga's Erati spearheaded what remained of the resistance. They were particular as to when and where they chose to fight.

With so many people moving in an uncontrolled way, and with supplies suddenly the key factor they were concerned about, the allies thought progress in their pursuit of Damien should be faster. It wasn't.

Galean and Liani had tried to reactivate the ancient drone to assist in the war, but were unsuccessful in doing so. The ancient programming had been geared to Damien and nothing more. It left the mop-up to the ground forces and the allies were still greatly outnumbered, though that ratio was changing rapidly.

While Liani and Wu Hang had their hastily arranged wedding at the Arreck palace, Aron was still forced to probe ahead cautiously. Straga set up ambushes and traps to slow and to stymie his march giving Damien plenty of time to put distance between them.

Straga dangled temptation in front of Aron's force using the Erati to lure the Brutans. Their natural hatred had grown during the war until each side lived for the total annihilation of their rivals. Aron had to spend a great deal of time riding with the Brutan chief to be sure the barbarians were kept under control. Whenever an unfortunate Erati was captured in battle and dragged to the Brutan camp, Aron had to leave rather than watch the horror of his torture and slow death. His screams haunted all of the camp.

The Brutans were never contrite about what they did.

"Our brothers face similar fates as captives of the Erati," the chief explained, as if it excused their brutal behavior.

Those members of Damien's army who weren't a part of Straga's force were an amorphous mass. They didn't seek out the allies for battle, but they were plentiful and if they got trapped, they would fight back. Those numerous pockets of resistance were an ongoing problem to Aron's attempt to break through and give chase to Damien. Most of them felt they had nowhere to go. The mayhem in their home countries had wiped out the existing society and including the economies. There was no guarantee if they returned home they could survive there.

They were lost without a leader to direct them. It was an opportunity Aron could have used to give them purpose and convert them to the allied side, but his only priority at that point was rescuing Cherine.

Each day they were beset with sudden battles and skirmishes. They varied in size and duration but each one was a serious matter.

The royal army, with Marin in charge, supported Aron's offensive to recapture the kingdom. The Arreck army stayed close to their borders which further complicated Aron's troubles. Though the enemy was in disarray, they were a threat merely by being numerous and being everywhere. Aron was always thrust into fights where they were badly outnumbered.

* * * *

Meanwhile Damien kept a steady pace having nothing in his path to hinder him. With time and fleeing the danger combined with no further appearances of the drone, Damien regained his composure and his swagger. A month of travel opened an insurmountable lead on Aron's pursuit, so Damien slowed the pace to be sure the horses were always fresh.

He also resumed pitching his tent in camp at night so he had time with his 'wives.' Although it was the usual that Cherine and Nala lived with, this time it was like a new wound. Cherine had been physically close to Aron at the border only to see the chance of escape dashed. Being dragged away, again, was distressing and it motivated her to make some sort of move out of the frustration.

"Cherine, you must not," Nala cautioned time after time. "We've no chance here. We must wait, darling."

"If I were alone, I would seek an end, Nala, either of him or me. This has become intolerable. I always had in my mind to hold out until this captivity ended. What's ahead for us now I'm afraid will be worse than we could ever imagine. Damien is sly and resourceful. If his ancient enemies are still alive to threaten him, I think he'll take measures to protect himself as he did before and abandon the world. If his enemies hold malice for us, we're doomed."

"Cherine, you said he was in a machine asleep preserved for the ages? What if he plans to preserve us too? What if he plans to take us with him into the future?"

Cherine looked shocked at the idea. "I won't allow that, Nala. I'll attack him with my bare hands if I must."

Nala looked worried.

"I wish I could be reassuring, Nala, but I can guarantee nothing here. We're in terrible peril. There's no way to disguise that fact."

They'd have had a risk free ride back to the wilds but Damien got careless in straying too close to the great swamp where the Uripeans monitored everything close to their border. Although they'd never ventured out of their realm to participate in the war thus far, they ruthlessly wiped out any of Damien's army that foolishly ventured into the swamp both with their fighters and with the beasts they influenced. Enna and Biala chafed at Aron's order they return to their people to stand with family and friends.

Here, with Damien's camp close enough, they demanded the opportunity to act.

They sat before the king in council, highly motivated.

"This war that was going so badly, something has happened," Enna explained. "Damien's forces are wandering about aimlessly and Damien himself is going the other direction. Aron must have prevailed in the key battle. We burst with pride he could overcome the whole world marching against him, but we're ashamed after having spent so much our lives and our blood fighting at his side that we're forced to sit here cowering because our people fear to take an active role."

It was a severe chance Enna took calling out the king, and her society.

The king simmered with rage, but took a moment before he replied to the affront.

"My role first and foremost is to preserve the people. We were nearly wiped out in war. We were a mighty nation reduced to ashes and huddled survivors."

"We know that," Biala snapped angrily. "We don't need a history lesson, my king. That was a long time ago. Look around you, the people lived, prospered and multiplied. We're a force once again. This is a chance we can't afford to pass by. Damien was the author of that ancient demise and again he's the cause of mortal peril for the world, not just us. How can we rationalize this inaction? It strikes Enna and me as cowardly."

The king rose off the throne angrily.

"You go too far with your impertinence. I've given you extraordinary leeway, but now you demand we put our lives on the line."

"How are we different than any other people? If we permit Damien to escape it might lead to countless new deaths. How many have been lost already in this senseless war? How many more have to die before you're willing to act. If every human being alive out there is killed, how does that help us? Is that the best new world for the Uripeans?"

The king scowled. "You're both still young. You think because you survived by some miracle you're invincible? You think you can't be killed?"

"Of course we know the risk," Enna replied angrily. "That's not the point. We're willing to take that risk. We learned so much from Aron. He didn't make choices based on if he was safe. He chose for his friends and family. He stood firm when everyone else ran to hide. I refuse to sit here any longer. Biala and I are going out to interdict Damien. If only the two of us go, that's the choice of the rest of you. If we die in the process but allow Aron to catch Damien, the world may survive."

The gathered mass of the people murmured.

The king put up his hand.

"I'm not deaf to your call, ladies. If this is the will of the people, we're going to do this properly. Call forth my generals and we'll make a plan. Hear me though when I say, I'm not going to put the army out in the open to be vulnerable. We can't take foolish risks."

Enna nearly argued with his hesitance, but Biala grabbed her arm.

"We can work with this, Enna. If you say something further he could change his mind."

"All right, Biala, but I'm going to that generals meeting."

Biala laughed. "We're not Aron. They still see us as silly girls, though we're full grown women now. We've faced more battle than all other Uripeans combined."

"If they try to prevent us from attending, they'll face more battle," Enna huffed.

They didn't face a fight against their own. When the women appeared at the gathering, they were escorted to seats of prominence without controversy. Men nodded deferentially to the young women.

That evening with dusk Enna and Biala jogged at the forefront of the first foray of the Uripean army out of the swamp, ever. They made their way toward Damien's camp.

They weren't practiced in maneuvers outside of their realm so the sentries heard them approaching. Enna and Biala charged immediately. The commander hesitated before following them. Damien was alerted and quickly broke camp to flee. They were beset with a determined attack and were outnumbered by the Uripeans.

Savior

* * * *

"Is it Aron?" asked Nala.

"I don't know, I don't think so, Nala," Cherine replied. "I wish I could get a sword. This might be our chance to escape."

Damien wasn't far away and looked over at them.

"Don't do something foolish," he told them walking over with his guards. "You over estimate your value to me if you think I'll abide a mutinous act in my own camp. Gather your things, we'll be moving quickly."

Cherine eyed the troops and the odds, which were poor barehanded without weapons. She shrugged and started to fold up her bedding.

The fighting reached the edge of the camp fire light. They all squinted to see who was attacking but it was too dark to recognize them.

"What force does Aron have stationed out here this far away?" asked Damien.

"I'm aware of no fortress or force. To my knowledge all the allies stayed together to defend Nephora. If some were driven away and took up residence here, I don't know of it, Damien. What's the difference?"

"The difference is, I need to know what's ahead blocking our path."

"I can't help you with that. I have no way to know the current deployment of Aron's allies."

"I tend to believe you with that. You've been out of the fight for quite a long time now and things have changed. Come my darlings, let's slip this noose."

Damien mounted up with his trusted elite and left the remainder of his force to slug it out. They raced away in the night with the hazard of stumbling into further peril, or losing horses to unseen obstacles in the darkness.

The Uripeans were on foot, so they couldn't move fast enough to block the path. They did rise to the challenge of battle and defeated the enemy. Damien was now accompanied only by a fast moving skeleton crew. The following day he paused long enough to gather wandering bands of his army.

Damien commanded them to attack and there were enough of them around to be a force against any pursuit.

* * * *

The following dawn at his old camp brought a determined assault on the Uripeans who considered a quick retreat. Enna and Biala refused to do so and stood in the center of the fight forcing their brethren to support them. It was a fierce attack and the Uripeans were outnumbered, but the cause of the enemy dissipated in a short amount of time. The assault faltered and the Uripeans drove away the enemy troops, but it allowed Damien to flee.

"We can't go after them," the commander told Enna. "I also wish to catch that snake, but the orders of the king are clear. We've struck a blow for the allies. That must suffice for the time being."

"You may return to our home. We're not giving up this fight. I think I saw friends who're captives of Damien. We can't abide that. We're going to follow them."

The commander nodded. "Be very careful out there, ladies. We'll explain this to the king and follow his further orders. If he permits it, we'll follow you. I would suspect the king will not be happy with your choice."

"We can't make choices about the king's moods. We make choices based on right or wrong."

"Good fortune."

They raced after Damien. Several warriors refused to abandon them to fate with such danger abroad, so Enna, Biala, and five warriors rode away on captured horses on Damien's trail.

* * * *

Meanwhile Aron slogged ahead at a frustrating pace losing day after day buried in needless battles. Straga sent harassing strikes at various times, some in the light of day and some after dark. They weren't meant to defeat Aron. That wasn't possible, but they disrupted his camp and delayed breaking out of the morass.

With the void in leadership created by Damien's sudden flight, Straga slowly reestablished a level of command. Increasing numbers of Damien's army followed his orders for lack of any other option.

There were increasing numbers of them who once they found their families opted to return to their home countries. With the vast number of them about, it still left a great problem of those men whose families had been sacrificed in the charges of Damien's attacks during the war. Those troops were angry and Aron was the only outlet for their rage.

Aron experienced another issue. Lilith attached herself to him whether in battle or in camp. She didn't make untoward advances, but she was always present. She smiled at him, joked with him, and supported his position, no matter what he proposed in the meetings with the staff.

"Aron, I've got your back," she'd say before they started any battle.

Brock and Trent started to look at Aron askance after a while.

"Is there something we should know, brother?" asked Brock one day.

"No," Aron replied in annoyance.

"Your new companion is persistent. We wonder if that will include her final goals."

"Cherine is my future wife, brother. That will not change. Lilith is just being Lilith. If she has foolish plans for me, it won't sway me."

"Of course not," Brock answered skeptically.

Aron scowled at him. "Brock, I'm not a boy."

Brock chuckled as Trent walked up to them with a smirk.

"These campaigns in the field are very draining," Trent commented. "We know the value of pleasant diversions along the way."

"Speak for yourself," Aron huffed.

"Now I'm really worried," said Brock. "You're awfully defensive about the topic."

"As if I don't have enough to worry about, now I have my closest advisors thinking me weak and vulnerable."

"Are you weak and vulnerable?" asked Brock.

Aron glared at him just as Lilith walked over.

"Good day, gentlemen. You look tired, Aron. Can I do anything for you?"

Trent and Brock chuckled.

"What is this?" asked Lilith, eyeing them in confusion.

"It's nothing to concern yourself with, Lilith," Aron replied. "I appreciate your concern for my welfare. I'm fine. The daily fight is a strain on all of us. I'm no different than any other man."

"Yes, you are, Aron."

"So true, brother," Brock added mockingly. "She's so right about that."

Lilith looked at the smirks on Brock's face and on Trent's. "Am I missing something?"

"Lilith, they're idiots. Pay them no mind."

She looked at Aron and smiled warmly. "If you need anything just send word to me. I'm here to serve you."

She turned and walked away, but there was extra sway as she sashayed. She smiled like her plan was coming together and Aron was taking a romantic interest in her at long last. It wasn't hard to figure out what the men had been talking about.

"This is not what I need," Aron groused. His friends laughed.

* * * *

Coraline completed gathering her things and went to see the queens. Her mother-in-law was talking to the Arreck queen.

"You've been most hospitable with us for which I'm eternally grateful. I regret our prior misfortunes and the pain we caused to your daughter. You extended friendship when it wasn't deserved."

"You needn't leave prematurely, majesty. Your kingdom is in ruins and I suspect it's a dangerous place."

"This is the time we must show courage. Our people are leaderless and suffering. Someone needs to take control and alleviate their misery."

"I regret to say I think your husband is lost to you. Our healers have tried every remedy, but his mind is lost."

"I've talked about this at great length. I know what you hesitate to say is I'm not a strong person to assume the mantle of leadership. I can't disagree, so I've decided I'll abdicate in favor of the crown princess, Coraline. She'll take the throne with Marin being her consort and future husband."

"Your children agreed to this?"

"They said nothing, but I know they're displeased. I'd have picked a successor, but there are none among them qualified or worthy. If they make more poor choices and contest this, I think it will be a serious mistake and they'll lose that confrontation. The people would never allow one of them to ascend to the throne. Actually, at this point we can't be sure they'd accept resumption of the monarchy."

"We're your friends from this point forward. If things don't go well, you're welcome to return here to live in safety. It's our opinion you have no culpability for the poor decisions of your husband and son. Therefore I see no reason for you to suffer needlessly. My opinion is that you should let Marin go first to be sure it's safe."

"I need to be there. I'm frightened but so many others have shown courage, it's time for me to do so also. Thank you again, my friends."

* * * *

The push of the royal army went toward Nephora. They coincided with Aron's path generally but he was gradually angling away toward the wilds. It was also a slow process for them too slogging ahead through legions of Damien's leaderless forces.

Straga didn't engineer any battles against Marin with the forces he retained. He had no interest in the royal capital city. With the command structure of Damien's vast army disintegrated, he couldn't fight on multiple fronts. His focus remained Aron's party for personal reasons. As Straga veered away, the path ahead became easier for the royals and they started to make progress toward their home in Nephora.

Tasha resisted the invitation to stay with Belisa in Arreck. She joined the royal march back to Nephora. That brought Radigan and many of the families. Wu Hang and Liani stayed back to enjoy a honeymoon.

Granor was among the displaced royal citizenry going home following

Savior

Marin. He wasn't content to be idle. His nature was one to meddle and to scheme so he collected the spurned royal children and took them in his group at the tail of the army. He avoided the fighting and spent his time conspiring with the princes and princesses. None of them would have formed a plan on their own. They were sheep for Granor to lead. The queen and the king rode with Coraline under heavy protection.

Marin proved to be an able leader and he inspired his men to become an army again instead of rabble, but there was too much happening for him to pay attention to Granor. They fought each day but the battles never tested them. Damien's residue receded before them with less threat each day. The trickle toward the wilds and therefore to the border and the outside world was rapidly becoming a flood.

Marin had no reason to chase them in their retreat. If they left the kingdom, it was enough to serve his purpose.

Within a month they reached the outskirts of the capital city. It was in ruins, yet they felt relief to be there. The civilian residents who'd fled to escape the battle were already slipping back to reclaim their homes. They worked together and shared their meager supplies communally out of necessity to survive. Some homes had already been rebuilt.

It was encouraging that they cheered the royal army as it passed and to see the progress they were making in rebuilding homes and businesses.

The queen insisted Coraline ride prominently at the head of the procession beside Marin so the people would see who would be their new ruler.

Marin deployed forces to patrol and to protect the citizens along the way. It was a novel concept which surprised the people, an army not to fear. It was a development helping endear the common people to the new leadership. The old military posts were still there. Soldiers started their own rebuilding projects as they reached them and resumed stations throughout the city. It didn't take long for them to exert control over the whole city and provide safety and security for the populace from the criminal element.

The remaining bands of thugs and brigands were easy fodder for royal soldiers. The potential problem of the resumption of chaos was blunted before it could arise.

Granor remained a cancer in their midst, but he made no moves to alert his rivals. Lilith who would have seen his treachery immediately was away riding with Aron in the chase after Damien.

* * * *

Damien sped along each day as rapidly as the horses could stand. He worried about the pursuit although he feared the Uripeans far less than Aron.

He didn't want to relinquish the lead he'd established.

Enna, Biala, and the five soldiers caught up to Damien's force, but merely followed them. They didn't have sufficient numbers to capture him. They watched each night as Damien lorded over Cherine and another woman they didn't recognize.

"Poor Cherine," said Enna.

"She's strong," Biala mentioned. "We'll find a way to free her."

"She seems to have a friend in that other woman."

"That's good. Problems seem far worse when you're alone."

Damien established buffering forces from the remnants of his army to travel nearby in case resistance appeared. They traveled parallel to him both ahead of and behind him.

They'd left the high populace region of the kingdom and entered the formerly sparse farm regions of the villages.

"I think he'll get to the wilds before Aron can get here," said Enna.

"We're assuming Aron survived to be able to give chase."

"Damien wouldn't flee without a serious reason. I choose to believe the reason is Aron."

"I wish we could get a signal to Cherine so she knows we're here for her."

"It would be too dangerous, plus it might trigger her to take action that could get her killed. They guard her constantly."

"We'll continue to shadow them."

"It doesn't appear Damien took away Cherine's mind. That's a good thing."

"Indeed it is."

* * * *

One evening as Cherine sat chatting softly with Nala she thought she saw a glint of reflected light from the nearby brush. It alerted her but she said nothing to Nala. Each night thereafter she checked for signs of help. She saw no other glints, but it heartened her anyway that possibly allies might be close at hand.

Damien's guards didn't make any mistakes though. Their vigilance never wavered or lapsed.

Each day brought them closer to his goal of the wilds and the facility located there and each night brought them the prospect of Damien and his 'companionship'.

* * * *

Meanwhile Aron moved steadily after them. They'd finally extricated themselves from the morass of Damien's soldiers who were fleeing the area and offering little resistance to any allied force. Straga increased his pace and decreased his attacks so the way forward was slightly easier. The allies were able to cover ground now with speed at last.

"I hope this isn't too little, too late," he muttered to Brock as they rode along.

"Everything will work out as it's supposed to," Lilith shouted from his other side.

Aron glanced at her and she smiled broadly.

He'd started sending collateral forces to forage for supplies as they went. That meant overrunning Damien's fleeing forces and stealing their supplies. It worked well enough to keep them moving without sizeable delays, which was Aron's primary instruction.

When they stopped for brief meals, Lilith was always at Aron's side. She chatted amicably and didn't particularly need Aron to respond. It was mildly entertaining for him and it was having an effect. His perennial barrier was softening with her perpetual verbal dialogue.

The anger he'd felt at being her captive so long ago had long since faded away. Now she was amusing and in a fight she and her maidens were trustworthy allies. They held their own.

"Aron, Marin sent word they've taken back Nephora," said Trent. "The city is in shambles but they're safe enough to rebuild and resettle there. Also, the queen has decided to abdicate in favor of Coraline as the next ruler."

"Amazing," said Aron. "I never saw that coming."

"I'm happy for her," said Lilith. "I won't lie I had ambitions, but I could still recognize true worth and she was worthy. The queen made a shrewd choice. If she'd tried to rule she would have been overthrown sooner or later. Coraline is a stronger person and with Marin at her side, she can withstand any treachery coming from people around her."

"She was a villager like me," Aron mused. "I could never have dreamed how our lives would go. It's incredible."

"We have work yet to do," Lilith added.

"We'll keep chasing Damien, but at this point I think his destiny is out of my hands. We can't catch him in time to intercede."

"Unexpected things happen, Aron. That is true for him also. We assume he has a free path to his destination, but perhaps he faces adversity too. I expect the best to happen. Spending time around you has made me an optimist."

Aron chuckled. Lilith started to laugh with him.

Brock looked over shaking his head. "You're both batty."

That particular day Straga set another ambush so they had a serious fight. The outcome was never in doubt, but it slowed them down. Coincidentally, a large assemblage of Damien's army was in the area and joined the fight which meant Aron lost an entire day in battle.

Aron's forces couldn't corner Straga's ambushers. They used the opportunity to slip away when Aron was tied up fighting the others, the stragglers. Once Straga's men pulled out, the battle lessened quickly, but it was too late in the day to cover any ground.

"See, Aron," said Lilith. "I told you we could expect fortunes to go our way."

"Thank you so much, Lilith," he replied facetiously. "Your assessment was technically correct."

"I'm grateful for any good fortune," she added. "I don't worry about what we can't change."

"I guess that's a good attitude."

"Aron, you have too much responsibility. There are too many worries weighing down your mind. You should do as I do. It will make for a much happier life. You need a diversion." She smiled at him provocatively.

"You're probably right, Lilith." He was forced to avert his eyes which caused her to chuckle.

They were able to move rapidly the next day and the next, but again Straga had an ambush waiting just before they were going to stop to make camp. Fighting at dusk and into the dark was a deadly situation. They broke the stalemate by a fierce attack driving into the ambushers in a surprise. It caused casualties on both sides. Straga's strategy changed after that as he couldn't afford to lose significant numbers. With the Brutans riding with Aron, anytime they could tangle directly with the Erati it was a blood bath.

Aron's progress increased markedly and Straga was reduced to sheer flight to avoid being cornered.

Entering the region of farms and villages which was Aron's roots brought back many memories for him, not all good. In this open flat area they raced ahead catching numerous groups of Damien's army but rather than fight, they simply skirted them in favor of speed.

It wasn't good strategy to have enemy troops between them and the royal army, but Aron focused on catching Damien.

Eventually they reached the outskirts of the great swamp. Uripean soldiers were deployed along their entire border. They emerged to greet Aron. The king came in person.

"Aron, Damien passed this way. He had captive your friend, Cherine. Enna and Biala ignored my wishes and gave chase. They only have a small number with them, so I fear they couldn't recapture her. We gave them a fight and greatly reduced their numbers."

"Good, that slowed them down," Aron replied. "We made the best speed we could but it's been too slow. We're going to try to increase our pace."

"I'd like to add soldiers from my army to increase your numbers. We also have enough supplies that you can race along without foraging."

"Thank you, your highness. That will help a great deal. We'll do what we must, but I'll do my utmost to have Enna and Biala return home safely to you."

"They are dear to me," the king replied. "That would be a great debt I would owe you."

"King, I owe you. It's the right thing for me to do. Let's not talk about debts. That's not a footing I want to be on with anybody."

"So be it, Aron. We're curious about the state of the war? It appears things have radically changed."

"Galean and Liani discovered ancient weapons hidden in the Arreck mountains. They were weapons of Damien's enemies which we were able to use to attack Damien's weapons. It sent Damien fleeing. With him gone his army lost heart and are dispersing."

"We wondered at the tremendous amount of traffic going away from the kingdom."

"I just got word Coraline is going to assume the throne with Marin as her consort. The queen didn't feel able to rule and the king has lost his mind permanently."

"What a strange twist in circumstances. What had been our lifetime enemy is now our hope for the future. A villager girl ascended to royal rule, it seems impossible. They royal nobles were vile people. I'm surprised they accept this."

"The royals suffered terrible losses in the war. When Damien took Nephora, punishing and executing royalty was a favorite pastime. I think their ranks are greatly reduced, your majesty."

"Some might see that as justice served."

"That's one way of looking at it. I don't see Damien as a proper instrument to serve justice on anybody. He's the guiltiest man of all time. He's engineered the demise of countless souls in the past and the present."

"This is why you must catch him, Aron."

"We'll happily accept the supplies and the troops you offer, your majesty. We'll leave at dawn tomorrow."

"Good hunting, Aron."

The king glanced to his side where Lilith was planted, smiling amicably.

"I take it this is your new lieutenant, Aron?"

"I am," she piped in before Aron could respond to the question. "Aron is one of the few men alive to appreciate the worth of women and to allow us significant roles. I'm grateful to him, but at the same time, my maidens have held up well under their responsibilities. We're very competent and have earned our place at the table of greatness."

"Are you," said the king, eyeing Aron mirthfully. "Has she held up her end well, Aron?"

Aron's face turned red at the king's playful jab.

"They fight well, your majesty," he answered tactfully. "I feel confident with them in battle."

"She does appear to be capable of giving you a tussle," the king joked.

Aron glowered at him but Lilith laughed heartily.

"Your majesty, you have no idea," she chirped happily.

"On that note, I'll part with you now, your majesty," he replied sourly. "I have a great deal to do to prepare for an early day tomorrow."

Lilith walked at his side.

"Does that idea strike you so terribly, Aron? Am I not beautiful, feisty, and pleasing to hear?"

"Lilith, let's not get into it. We've been down that road before. Nothing has changed for me. I'm still focused in recovering my fiancée."

"Of course you are," she chided mirthfully.

He said nothing to encourage her to continue her annoying banter. He was angry that she could evoke any feelings in him, a young man long apart from any romantic unions.

Chapter Sixteen
~Return to the Wilds~

The way ahead eased noticeably. By this point in their retreat, most of Damien's old army concluded there was nothing here for them, so they were intent on leaving the kingdom and heading back to their home countries. There organizational structure had basically disintegrated and they started to band together by their national origins.

Whenever Aron came upon them, they sat passively by offering no hazard at all. It worked well as he traveled through familiar grounds from his childhood and went through his abandoned home village. Their farm buildings surprisingly at their father's old farm were intact and untouched. Aron and Brock paused and went into their childhood house.

"I wonder if they knew this was our home?" asked Brock. "Nothing is touched, broken, or stolen."

"It's probably just a lucky chance they missed us."

"We'll be in the wilds very soon, Aron. Do you have a plan if we meet Damien?"

"I'm more interested in Cherine, but if I get a chance to face Damien *mano e mano* I'll be a happy man."

"He's a wily *hombre*. You don't want to take him for granted. He's survived because he found ways to conquer the tests in his life."

"About him, I have singular focus, Brock. If he can find a way to prevail, it will fall on you to end his life. I don't intend to fail but things can happen. I trust you to have my back."

"Trust me too, Aron," said Lilith. "I've got your back too."

Brock smiled at Aron who frowned in return.

"Thank you for your faithfulness, Lilith. I'll keep that in mind."

"You should for it's no small thing what I offer you."

201

"I don't disagree."

She suddenly stepped up and hugged him tightly. Aron glanced at Brock. Brock shrugged and chuckled at her gesture of affection.

Lilith stepped back. "I have something I must do now but I'll be back shortly, Aron."

They watched her walk away.

"Do you want a hug from me too?" asked Brock, smirking.

"Do you want my fist bouncing off your head, brother?"

Brock laughed. "You have unique problems, Aron. She might be taking you captive again. It appears you think you might like it this time."

"Now would be a good time to stop talking, Brock."

He laughed at Aron anyway.

They continued their trek and soon saw the border to the wilds. It always looked the same to them: uncontrolled and foreboding. Even with established travel paths, it was no less a dangerous place to be. The predator animals were as numerous as ever. Damien's former army was concentrated here as they traveled to the border. Damien snared many of them to set up a buffer around him. It made Aron's traverse suddenly more difficult.

Damien had no border guards *per se*, but he did have ambushes set up. Straga had abandoned striking at Aron. The Erati were quick to head for their homes. That meant Damien wasn't far away.

The battles Aron fought had none of the usual intensity of Straga and they won easily, but he was cautious nonetheless. There forged ahead steadily and set extra sentries each night to protect their camp. The Uripean soldiers who'd joined them were uncomfortable being away from their friendly swamp. Aron integrated them with his people to minimize any possible problems.

As they neared serious grounds he deployed Brock to lead his spearhead, a job he was very good at. Aron kept close to his vanguard so if they encountered trouble, he could react quickly.

Encountering trouble was a given and it happened soon as they entered dangerous ground.

Here the Erati engaged along with significant numbers of Damien's soldiers. It was a terrible battle that stalemated quickly.

Aron kept Uripeans as a reserve and concentrated the masters, and the Black Fist, in the initial assault. The Brutans were right behind them rabid to get at the Erati.

Aron didn't want any sort of final battle here on grounds the enemy picked to favor them. He maneuvered his attack to make surgical strikes which rotated to different points to keep them off guard.

The battle lasted until dark when the enemy suddenly withdrew. Aron was left with the problem of trying to make a camp for the night in unfavorable terrain in a poorly defensible position. It was Straga's plan to stress them with only bad choices to select from and it was working.

Rather than accept Straga's scenario, Aron decided to forge ahead in the dark, as dangerous as that was. They stumbled onto enemy troops en route sent to harass them in the night, except Aron wasn't where they expected him to be. They had sporadic clashes for hours before they reached a place they knew they could set up a defensible perimeter. It was a short night but there was no way around it.

Each day they faced more serious fights as they slogged their way through the opposition.

* * * *

Damien reached his destination and went immediately inside his command and control building. Cherine and Nala stood nearby as he quickly accessed his controlling machines and performed searches of his worldwide installations and armaments. He was shocked to see his air capabilities totally wiped out by the drone attack. His land based facilities were only damaged if there had been weaponry there.

Damien programmed instructions for his plan into the computer system. Only Damien understood the language when they heard a verbal response transmitted.

He turned to his wives.

"Don't fear, ladies. I've faced worse than this and came out the other end. We'll get past this challenge. The dream I have for humanity can still be saved."

"What does that mean, Damien?" asked Cherine.

He smiled his best crocodile smile.

"I'll make provisions for your safety along with my own, darlings."

Cherine eyed him darkly. His guards were standing close by with their hands on their weapons watching her carefully. She calculated her chances of taking down Damien before they could kill her and it wasn't hopeful.

Nala seemed to sense Cherine was on the verge of a deadly action. She touched her arm. Her gesture staved off Cherine's suicidal attempt.

"Now that we're back in my home I can create any meal we chose and it will be perfect every time. I think perhaps we should have *Filet Mignon.* Enough of this common fare these peasants eat. The guards will escort you to quarters where you can bathe and change into proper clothes for the occasion."

Of course they both knew that meant the skimpy red dresses Damien craved.

Damien whispered instructions to the guards before they led the women away. They stayed very close and very much on guard for any moves by either woman. Cherine's thoughts to act quickly evaporated. She had no time where she was alone, even in her bath. Guards and female servants eyed her constantly and closely. They wouldn't allow Cherine to see Nala until it was time for them to go to the meal.

Damien donned a military uniform from his past. The coat was covered with decorations and medals.

"Welcome, my darlings," he said expansively. "We're on the verge of auspicious events. A regal meal is appropriate to celebrate our impending victory. Your Aron has failed in all his tasks and he will fail again. He sought to make you his bride, Cherine. He wasn't worthy of such an august position. He couldn't protect you. Actually you were your own best defense. This 'refuse pile' of a society isn't worthy of my dream. We'll go to a better time where intelligent ideas can be better received. I'll let these dullards fight over the scrapes of their shattered world. We'll see much better in the future when they're all gone, dead, and buried."

He looked at the women, both of whom eyed him darkly. Neither of them felt compelled to pretend any further about their true feelings. Damien chuckled.

"Sit down. We have a fabulous feast before us. Eat and enjoy. By the way, I've opened a bottle of my best wine. It was a highly sought vintage in ancient times when things were so much better."

Nala poured a tall glass of the wine and drank it down rapidly. Cherine poured wine and sipped at it.

The food was excellent, but Cherine had the feeling her time was about to run out. Whatever Damien had in mind would happen soon.

She handled the dinner knife, again measuring her chances against fully armed guards too numerous for her to overpower. Further, she worried Damien was going to use his machine to take away her mind, and Nala's too.

Damien pretended to be oblivious to the undercurrent, babbling away merrily. He was very much entertained by his own company.

They all looked up when the door opened. Straga strolled in.

"Welcome, my brave friend. You've done well in delaying our enemies until I could get to this place of safety. Please sit down and join us for this wonderful repast."

Straga nodded to Damien, but looked over at Cherine and then Nala,

"Do you like the color red?" asked Cherine pointedly, her eyes ablaze with anger and challenge.

Straga smiled. "As a matter of fact, I do. You both look lovely."

"Through no choice we made," Cherine retorted hotly, staring at Damien as if daring him to respond.

"Ah yes, the real Cherine," said Damien. "You've played a part for so long apparently thinking I could never discover your ruse. You give me too little credit. I didn't act before because you were compliant to my wishes. I had no reason to discipline you. However, from this point forward we move to new ground and your behaviors will need to be corrected. As you know, I have means to do that, so I'll leave it to you how you want to live out your remaining days."

"Thank you for the chance to have a choice," Nala piped in quickly before Cherine could say something destructive to worsen their situation.

Every eye turned to Cherine. She pondered a fatal strike, but that would leave Nala helpless. She had no martial skills. Cherine looked at Straga. Rather than smugness, she saw calculation in his eyes. He had plans of his own."

It caused her to pause and then back away from the confrontation.

"Try your food, Straga," she said. "It is very good."

"Excellent, a wise choice my dear," said Damien.

Cherine and Straga stared at each other pensively, each trying to discover any secret plans of the other.

"My husband, I want to thank you for this meal," said Nala suddenly to deter his notice.

"It's my pleasure, Nala. I've missed having quality meals while I was forced to travel this backwards world. How could I not share from my bounty with my beloveds?"

Straga smirked at his statement. Cherine simply continued to watch him.

A messenger came into the room and whispered to Damien. The calmness on his face changed to rage.

"It seems Aron can't understand when he's beaten," Damien uttered tersely. "It means nothing. He's too late. I'm already here. Straga, it seems you'll get your final battle with your Brutan cousins sooner than you anticipated."

"What have you been told?"

"Aron is pressing toward us in the wilds, but he has a relatively small force with him. I'm sure they were looking for speed in their pursuit. You'll have the advantage of selecting the site of your battle and you'll have superior numbers. It's really no concern of mine at this point. My plans will lead me elsewhere."

"Thank you, Damien. As you say, we've been arranging this fight to be at the best possible place for us. He covets Cherine, so he must come to us."

Cherine scowled.

"So true, Straga, I wish I could stay to deal with him personally, but my destiny demands I preserve myself for the future. It will be your duty to put an end to his arrogance. Afterwards, you're free to establish control as you are able. The world is in turmoil and like the sheep they are they'll follow anybody with a firm hand and a plan for them to follow."

Straga smiled at a prospect of his victory.

* * * *

Aron was quickly closing the distance in spite of slogging through daily fights. His opponents varied between skillful ambushes from Straga's Erati to generalized engagements with Damien's soldiers. His Uripean allies were getting accustomed to battle and to life outside of the swamp.

They were stopped for the evening when suddenly Enna and Biala came into camp.

Aron hugged both women.

"We were worried about you, ladies."

"Aron, we've fought with you for how long? You don't know we can take care of ourselves?"

Aron chuckled.

"Damien has gone back to his ancient building. Cherine is captive there. She has another woman with her who appears to be her friend. Damien has taken both of them. I don't know if he thinks to use them as pawns to hold you at bay. We had too few with us to try to free her. They watch her constantly so she's never had a chance to free herself."

"It's what I suspected."

"Aron, can you break into his metal fortress. I remember he had an invisible barrier to keep anybody out."

"Has he used that barrier?"

"Not that we could see. There is traffic in and out of his soldiers. We saw Straga too."

Barmon sat up, attentive.

"What armed forces does he have deployed?"

"He's ringed by his soldiers. Straga has taken his forces back to their homes not far away. I think they plan their great battle against you to occur there. I fear you're outnumbered by a great number."

"We've been outnumbered for the whole war," Aron replied. "Do you have any ideas about getting us close? I'm sure Damien is well aware we're here and I'm sure he has something planned."

"I don't. It's a different matter for a few to creep about undetected, but for a larger force, I think it isn't possible. When you attack, I think you'll need to do so from afar and then keep racing toward them. It's not much of a plan but

I'm no officer."

"You do just fine, Enna. I don't suppose you and Biala will stay behind here in the camp. This could well be a suicide mission."

"You're correct, Aron. We won't stay behind. You'll need every sword possible with what you'll be up against. Everybody dies. It's just a matter of when. We chose to take the risk. It isn't your choice, Aron. We chose for ourselves."

Aron looked at his leaders.

"I think we can't have two battles at once. We must either go after Straga and the Erati, or Damien. You know I prefer we strike Damien first. If he has his weapons available it could mean our end before we could ever face Straga."

Barmon bristled. "Aron, you know my feelings and why, but I won't stand in the way of your choice. If you choose Damien, I will follow you there."

The others nodded their ascent.

"I think too that we must move quickly. The more time Damien has, the worse it will be for us."

No one said anything.

Aron looked at the commander of the masters, Cherine's second.

"Cherine is our priority, Aron. She's our leader physically and spiritually. We won't abide her captivity a minute longer if we can strike at Damien. We've pledged our lives to ending his."

"I guess we have a decision. We just don't have an attack plan. If anybody has any ideas, no matter how outrageous they seem, now's the time to speak."

They simply stared at him.

"What I worry is charging ahead blindly could lead to senseless losses. We could stumble into a trap of his that could wipe us out without getting to him. I don't think it's a simple matter of breaking down his door."

"Unfortunately, he has no incentive to come out. We have no way to lure him because we have nothing he wants, Aron."

"I know that."

"Aron, we have to act," Brock piped in. "We face hazard and the risk of death everyday anyway. This is no different. If we attack his building, we'll do so cautiously, send in part of our force, and keep others back until we see what happens. For those in the forefront, it's a necessary risk, and yes there will be losses. It can't be avoided."

Aron grimaced.

"Life is precious, Brock. I'm not saying you aren't correct, but when it comes to asking people to die, it's a tragedy I take very seriously. We've been together for so long and faced so many things as brothers and sisters; it hurts to risk losing anyone. I don't want a single death on my conscious. If I were a better leader I should find a way to win this fight without killing off so many. Even our enemies are merely misguided citizens from abroad, lost inside our borders. They were led astray by Damien's lies and once they got here they feel they have no other choices."

"Perhaps we should speak to them, Aron," said Trent.

"I'll go with you, Aron," said Lilith.

The entire group smiled at her gesture. No one had any doubts about her reasons. Though she was showing great courage in going to an enemy camp, her endgame was obvious. Aron looked at her with consternation. She was making another public show of affection and in a sense trying to stake her claim to him.

She looked at him before continuing. "You all know of my great love for Aron. I'm no fool to ignore he's engaged to Cherine. I accept that. This attack we propose to rescue her, it's not a guarantee for us or for her. If for some reason we fail and don't recover her, I want Aron to know he'll have another option. He's been alone too long and that's a crime. He deserves a loving wife and children."

Her impromptu speech had a surprising affect. No one scoffed or laughed at her. They didn't judge her worthiness to be Aron's mate. They only noted her genuine feelings and brave act.

"I don't ask for your approval or even your understanding. I'm just speaking the truth to quell all of the rumors. I'm not a woman gone mad. You've stood at my side in battle. You know me."

There was a murmur of ascent. They looked at Aron as if the moment required his response.

"Ah, Lilith, I'm gratified by your offer and the support you've given me. I'm not prepared to look in any other direction than getting back Cherine. I don't discount what you're saying and I respect you on the field of battle and in camp as a friend. You've earned your place here as well as your maidens. I can't give you anything else at this point."

"I asked for nothing, Aron. You've pleased me by saying you'll at least consider my offer. It's enough for me."

Aron shrugged.

"I guess trying to talk to Damien's soldiers is worth a try. Obviously that doesn't include Straga and the Erati. There's only one outcome there."

The Brutans roared and bashed their shields loudly.

"I'll go this evening," Aron continued.

When Aron walked into the first enemy camp under a flag of truce, he wasn't immediately attacked.

"You're Aron, their leader," said the camp commander in surprise. "Why have you come?"

"We've talked and it makes no sense for us to fight you any longer," Aron explained. "Our enemy is Damien and if you're honest, he's your enemy too. He misled you and everyone else into this predicament. You're here dying for him but can you honestly say for a good reason? You heard what he said about his plan for mankind, but then you saw what he did. Who sends women and children in the first wave of attacks as sacrifices? What kind of person could do that? You saw his personal habits, how he saw every other living being as his pawns for his use. No one had any worth to him other than to be used. I'm sure you've talked about these very things amongst yourselves. Why stand against us now when our only goal is to attack him and rescue those he holds as captives?"

The officer looked at his soldiers. Their faces showed they agreed with Aron.

"I don't know the condition of your homelands after the war," Aron added, "but I think we can all agree you need to return. You need to plant crops, rebuild homes, and heal from the death and destruction. Damien is finished, one way or another. He won't be coming back to bother you. I'll give you my guarantee of that fact."

"I'd say that's beyond generous, Aron. You're right, we've stood behind Damien, and as I look back now, I can't understand why. None of what he promised was ever going to come true. He would only have replaced our former masters with his own version of dominance. We've lost so many brave souls in this war. We're all tired of fighting. We watch so many from our army passing by going out of here. I think it's our turn to leave. Whatever waits us back home couldn't be worse than dying here."

"We have no further quarrel with you, commander. I'd appreciate if you'll stop at the other camps and tell them what I've said. I just don't have time to go see them all. We need to attack Damien now."

"I'll do it, Aron. Thank you and good hunting. I'll pull back my patrols and we'll be packed up and be gone by morning."

"Avoid Straga. They won't be happy to see you leave."

"We will, Aron, and thank you."

Lilith smiled at Aron with great pride.

"I could kiss you right now," she said.

He chuckled. "That won't be necessary, ma'am. Let's get back to camp."

His men cheered when he told them about his successful speech to the enemy troops and their decision to leave peacefully.

"That's leaves us with our real antagonists," said Brock. "We have Damien and we have Straga. I like our chances much better now."

Everybody cheered again, but Aron worried about potential overconfidence in his troops. Nothing regarding Damien had changed in their favor. He was still holed up in a seemingly impregnable fortress.

Lilith brought him a mug of ale.

"You can relax for one night, Aron. The battle will still be there tomorrow."

"I'm not going to get drunk, Lilith."

"Of course you won't," she replied with a teasing smile. "I'll watch over you, darling."

"That's not going to happen, Lilith." Aron scowled and glanced at her ruefully.

She laughed heartily and took a long swig of ale and then looked at him playfully.

"Don't be such a coward, savior of the world. I'm not so scary. You can drink one mug. It will calm your nerves."

"Just one," he groused.

"Excellent," she chirped.

"To Aron," she shouted. She got a resounding shout from the men as they all decided to follow her lead of an adult beverage. Her maidens were right there to join with the men.

Aron made a point to wander over to Brock, Trent, and the others.

"Keep an eye on me, brother?" he asked.

Brock looked at him and a grinning Lilith mirthfully.

"You're a big boy, Aron. Maybe you should cut loose for one night. We never know if it's our last."

"Brock, keep an eye on me."

"Sure."

Lilith was toasting with Trent and both of them were already red faced.

Her maidens were suddenly very popular with the men as they let down their hair a bit drinking together, joking and carousing. Each maiden was suddenly surrounded in concentric rings of males. Battle was the last thing on their minds for a night.

"I think I'm going to regret this," Aron muttered to Brock.

"I'm not," said Brock. He swept up Lilith in his arms and started to dance with her. The camp celebrated as if they'd already beaten Damien. Another mug of ale quelled Aron's worries and soon Lilith pulled him out to join the dancing. She was a very skillful and provocative dancer.

Erati scouts sat nearby watching the inexplicable transformation.

"Have they gone crazy?" asked one of the scouts. "Has there been a defeat for our side we don't know about?"

Savior

"We must report this to Straga," the other replied.

He slipped away and went to Straga's camp.

* * * *

Coraline felt strange going back into the royal suite. The palace needed a great deal of cleanup but structurally it was intact. She was surprised to see her wardrobe untouched, but when she looked at her bed, the thought she'd never see her husband again struck her painfully. They'd quickly retrieved his head and planned a quick state funeral. His skeletal remains were buried with his head in a place of honor.

The queen asked her to take the king's quarters, but she refused. After her prompt public abdication and Coraline's anointing, the burden of ruling crushed her instantly. There was nothing in the city which didn't require her hand as it all needed rebuilding and rectifying. Marin's fierce presence steadied her as she grappled with the problems. Nobody wanted to contend with him, but of course Granor was in the background consolidating his base and poisoning as many as he could against Coraline's leadership.

Rather than a formal royal wedding, they opted for a simple ceremony to bind them together, so Marin moved into the vacant place of the crown prince beside Coraline in the royal bed.

It was bittersweet for Coraline in that she had no problem loving Marin. Those feelings had been growing for a long time, but being the center of attention and the object of the schemes around her was taxing and unpleasant.

Coraline didn't know it for a month, but her wedding night led to her first pregnancy. She would start a new line of royal heirs. It was a development very upsetting to the queen's children who were being dispossessed of their places in the hierarchy.

Marin was beside himself with joy when she told him. His genuine happiness was very gratifying for Coraline. He didn't think about her in terms of the throne, only as his wife and soul mate, and soon to be the mother of his first child. Marin had no desire to become a king. He was content to let her be the ruler of the realm.

People flooded back into the city. It was amazing how many of them had survived Damien's occupation and with Coraline's inspiring words of hope they worked together to put back the city to livable conditions. The commerce and the economy would be a work in progress, but a spirit of mutual sacrifice and sharing appeared seemingly overnight. People realized they had to work together or none would survive.

The last residue of Damien's invading army, those who'd stayed behind to become brigands, were attacked and pursued vigorously by the reconstituted royal command. The criminal element was expunged from Nephora after which conditions began to improve rapidly.

Former servants who'd been slaves to the monarchy returned.

"You're free to make your own choices," Coraline ruled. "If you choose to work in the palace, it won't be as chattel. You'll be paid workers and partners to us."

They flocked to her after that. A job in the new palace hierarchy was a highly sought position. They could feel esteem at last rather than shame at the lives they lived there.

The queen spent all her time with Coraline, the new queen.

"Please don't call me, your majesty," said Coraline.

"Why not, it's your proper title. I'm very comfortable with it. What you've accomplished in a short amount of time is incredible. I knew it was the right choice. Had I tried to rule, I would have been vulnerable and soon overthrown. There are still dissenting elements about, as you know."

"I didn't want this job, but since I have it, I want to do my best."

"This kingdom has a chance, at last, for a peaceful and prosperous state we've never approached or achieved. You should be proud of yourself and I'm immensely proud of you."

"Thank you, my queen. It's kind of you to say that. I don't feel I deserve it, but I appreciate your kind words."

"Coraline, you can be one of the greatest rulers ever. Trust in your decisions. You have a knack and the people have bonded with you quickly. I'm afraid my husband and son set such a low standard they expected nothing good from their leaders. You've pleasantly surprised them, my dear. Now that you carry a child, the people are very protective of you. I've been told the few people who try to speak ill are dealt with on the spot very harshly. I never experienced that in my whole life."

"That's good to know. I hope I warrant this faith they have in me. I've sent word asking Galean to return from Arreck. I can think of no better counselor than he. I thought I'd install him as my prime minister."

"He'll decline."

"I know, but I won't accept it."

The women laughed.

"So you wish to push men around, Coraline?"

"In a sense, yes I do."

"This is truly a new world and I think it's a world I like much better."

"What's the condition of the king?"

"I hold out no hope he'll recover. He withers by the day. If it's an illness, I hope it's not contagious. This is a terrible way to go."

Savior

"You've felt no signs of it. Am I correct?"

"Yes, that's true. Thus far I've been spared. I have chosen to sleep apart though. I have a physician checking the king and I'm nearby in an adjoining room."

"I'm sorry for the burden you're forced to carry, my queen."

At that moment Marin walked in.

"Majesties," he said with a bow.

"The queen tells me the future of the king's health is in doubt. She's forced to sleep separately to avoid the malady."

"I have associates I trust to assign as your personal protectors. The king's corps was destroyed in the war. Though you've ceded rule to Coraline, it isn't wise to have you lightly guarded. Will you accept a man I can send to you? He's highly trained and fully competent."

"I hadn't thought about it, Marin."

"Remember, Cherine and Aron were caught off guard by Lilith. That risk is still there. Low quality people are always about."

"I defer to your opinion, Marin. Thank you. Send your man to me and I'll accept his protection."

"His name is Ardrick. He will not fail you. I want to give one bit of explanation. He'll keep close to you at all times. Enemies seek out our weaknesses and most vulnerable moments to strike. Do you understand what I'm saying?"

"Oh my," she answered, slightly flustered. "You're talking about the situation you were in when Agar assigned you to safeguard Coraline. I understand, Marin."

"You're a fine looking woman still. You were younger than your husband. You shouldn't feel your life is over and you're destined to sit in obscurity with no further role in our society. If you have concerns about propriety…"

"I don't, Marin. Those matters aren't foremost in my life at this point, but I wasn't planning on sitting in a corner. I know what you're trying to tell me without saying the words. I can handle having your man on familiar terms. I want to say, my husband is alive and I'll do nothing to dishonor my commitment to him. If he's destined to pass away, I'll look at other options at that time."

"You've had time to grieve his loss, your majesty. No one would expect you to have a lengthy period of widowhood to satisfy convention. It's a needless waste. Whatever choices you make, we'll support you."

"I'm not being naïve. I'm really not, Marin. Coraline and I have spoken in private about our lives and our choices. I'm not a perfect person."

"Nor am I," Coraline echoed.

Chapter Seventeen
~Mortem Obire~

Once the area around Damien's compound cleared of his former soldiers, Aron moved in close.

"Is the barrier restored?" asked Lilith. "I can't tell."

"It's not visible to the eye, generally, although it can waver and fluctuate. I think he's probably sealed us out, Lilith."

"What can we do?"

"I'm not sure. I always left it to Galean to deal with those kinds of questions."

"Does he know we're out here?"

"I'm sure he does, Lilith."

"That may work in our favor. Although he's cautious about taking risks personally, the chance to strike at you might be strong enough for him to take some sort of action. To do that he'd need to lower the barrier."

"That's true, but it isn't something I can plan for. If he made a move, we'd only have time to react to whatever he did. With his devices, I'm sure he knows where we are and what we're doing. We're still at his mercy."

"What we do know about him, Aron, is his vanity and his arrogance. He thinks he's invincible. Arrogance is a flaw."

"I agree."

Lilith looked at him. "You're thinking about her. Is she looking at you this moment hoping you can break in to save her?"

Aron shrugged. "This is as close as I've gotten to her since the battle in Nephora. It's frustrating to have no move I can make."

* * * *

Inside the building that was exactly the case. Damien smirked as he focused his cameras on Aron and Lilith. Cherine and Nala were seated on each

214

side of him watching the monitor.

"Here is your love, Cherine," he chided. "It would appear your time apart has driven him into the arms of another woman and interestingly I know her. That's Lilith. She tried to pledge to me, but proved to be a very faulty vessel. What a fitting piece of irony that Aron's failings in the area of romance lead him to the bottom of the barrel with that loose woman. It seems no other woman would have him. You're so fortunate to be my wife. You'll live at the top of the new society worshipped by the masses. Associating with Aron demeans you. He always aspired too high. He's such an average man. He has few notable qualities. I don't call stubbornness a virtue."

Cherine was on the verge of attacking Damien. His guards had moved very close at Damien's request.

She looked at Aron and her heart ached. She was angry at herself that Damien's taunt affected her. It was silly to think of Aron as being unfaithful. Daily, she was the victim of, but still also the intimate partner of Damien. She had no room to feel aggrieved about Aron's alleged actions. She'd never coped with her unjustified feelings of being on some level an accomplice to Damien's lusts. It wasn't a rational conclusion and it wasn't accurate, but often feelings aren't logical.

"Although it's entertaining to watch him take futile action time after time, it's time we prepare for our next step, ladies. It isn't a matter you can take prized possessions into the future. I'm afraid that only our naked bodies can be preserved in stasis. Nothing else can be in the chambers."

Cherine felt panic. Damien looked directly into her eyes.

"I know you're having some foolish thoughts, wife. It will be the last time that you'll need to worry about such distractions."

Cherine felt Nala touch her leg secretly. She stood up as if she accepted Damien's instructions.

Suddenly Nala hit icons on the screen which caused warning lights and sirens.

"What have you done?" shouted Damien in rage.

He sat down to try to reverse the entries, but inadvertently without having any idea what she was doing, Nala had lowered the outer barrier.

Aron reacted in an instance when they heard the sirens, saw the barrier suddenly appear cloudy and then disappear.

They raced the short distance into the building. Entry was automatic as they were transported inside. Damien couldn't reverse the error fast enough.

Damien had far too few guards inside and they were quickly felled by Aron and his fighters.

Straga had learned how to exit the building and vanished before Aron could arrive.

Damien raced to the room holding the stasis chambers and frantically started to program the device leaving the women behind. Escaping Aron's wrath was his only concern.

Cherine reacted coming out of her daze after the shock of Nala's brave act. She knelt down as Nala held her side from a bloody swipe from a guard's sword.

The guards followed Damien and tried to stand their ground there.

Aron raced into the control room and swept up Cherine and a fierce embrace. She sobbed on his shoulder in relief at her rescue at last.

"I feared we'd never be together again," she whispered. "Aron, this is my dear friend Nala. She saved us. You must get her to the physicians. She has a serious wound."

"I will, Cherine. Where's Damien?"

"I think he went to that thing to preserve his life into the future again."

"How did you bring down his barrier?"

"It was pure chance. Nala just pushed buttons on his screen."

"Cherine, stay with your friend and get out of this building. We'll go after Damien."

"Aron, be careful."

They hugged again before he raced away with Trent and Brock, and Barmon. The masters flocked around Cherine and escorted her away from danger to freedom. She quickly changed out of the skimpy dress and back into her uniform. She donned her weapons and felt a whole person again at last.

Nala's wound was deep, but it wasn't life threatening.

Meanwhile, Aron ran down the hallway to the room he remembered so well to the place where Damien had lain preserved for countless ages.

Damien's guards fought, but it was a forgone outcome as they fell before the rage and the fearsome skill of Aron and the angry others.

They burst into the room to see the cover close on the machine. Damien was already in the chamber.

"It's too late, Aron," he shouted through the window. "I'll awake again in a new age. You'll be just another lost cause on the trash heap of history."

Aron bashed at the cover, but it was impervious to physical damage from fists or even swords.

Damien laughed at Aron's futile attack.

"You come up short again, Aron. I'd have given Cherine paradise in the world of the future, but she chose poorly. I leave her with you to live out a pathetic life. Perhaps some of your issue will procreate through the ages and I'll take a distant descendant of yours as a bride."

Aron simmered and stopped a moment to think. He thought about Nala's actions and went over to the control console.

Aron started to push icons hoping to reopen the cover and give them access to Damien. Again, it was pure chance that Aron entered a sequence that started preset reactions in the chamber.

Aron had no idea what the language meant that appeared on the screen nor did he understand the words he heard over the speaker. The warning siren and blinking red alarm lights frightened him that he'd put his group in danger.

The words on the screen mirrored the words being spoken, "Unidentified contaminant, begin purge sequence." The warning repeated over and over again.

The glowing lights of the stasis machine changed from blue to red and a low whine sounded.

They heard Damien screaming, "No, no, no." He pounded on the cover without effect.

They heard a whooshing sound and saw the inner chamber quickly fill with a cloudy gas. Damien screamed again but this time in pain. It didn't take long to execute the system purge. The cloud cleared away to reveal the blackened charred remains of Damien's body. Suddenly the cover opened and the entire chamber turned to roll the body out onto the floor. There was a terrible odor of charred flesh and strong chemicals.

They stood by looking on in horror.

"You earned this ending, Damien," said Aron.

His men wrapped the body in a blanket and they took it outside.

"It's all over," said Aron to the crowd that had assembled.

Cherine walked over to look at the remains, as though she needed to see for herself he was dead and gone before she would believe it.

Aron put an arm around her.

"Thank you, Aron," she said. "I need to tell you…"

"No Cherine," he replied, cutting her off. "I know it was bad for you so it isn't necessary to tell me anything."

"I do need to tell you some things, but you're right it should be at a different time."

* * * *

Far away in the mountains of the Arreck, the drone suddenly re-emerged from storage, activated, and launched into the air.

It had been called forth by the energy emanations from Damien's complex. The drone glided quickly to a point near the building. The automatic defense system at the complex activated sensing the approach of a threat.

217

Fortunately, Aron's people were all outside the building to listen to his address to the troops.

Pulsar batteries rose up from within the building and commenced firing at the drone. It was undamaged behind its energy shield.

The automated battle was terrifying especially being so close.

"Flee," shouted Aron as they raced away from the danger.

It was like the drone was waiting for them to move out of the way before unleashing an overwhelming assault.

The building shimmered brightly as the power of the drone struck. The defensive barrier suddenly fractured and the building erupted in a massive detonation. There were numerous secondary explosions that went on for over an hour before it stopped. The drone kept firing until the building was totally destroyed.

It stopped, turned, and flew back to the mountains. When it arrived it went back into storage and went dark and inaccessible.

Aron's guards crept cautiously back to view the wreckage. It was hot to the point the metal was in a molten state.

"Leave it," said Aron. "We'll come back another time to bury it."

* * * *

Aron chuckled at the mass of people approaching him. Cherine looked herself again dressed in her military uniform, but the masters refused to allow her to move without them being there too, in force.

"Are you invading with your army, Cherine?" he joked.

She hugged him again. "Let's get out of here. I just want to forget that part of my life."

"How is your friend?"

"The doctors say she can travel. It will take time for the wound to heal. It was a serious cut. She was no warrior but showed such courage to take action against Damien."

"I'm thankful she did. I'm sorry, Cherine, but I'm afraid we have unfinished business here with Straga. You can certainly go with Nala back to Nephora."

"Oh, Aron I'm sorry. I've been stuck in that other life for so long I wasn't thinking. Of course I'll stand with you in that fight."

"I don't know, Cherine. It's been a while and if you've lost your edge in a fight, I'm not willing to take that risk. This will be a serious battle facing the Erati."

"I'm fine Aron. Those skills are not something you lose. I think a good fight is exactly what I need to get back to normal."

"If you fight, you stand right beside me, do you agree?"

She laughed. "Yes, master."

"I'm not your master and you know exactly what I mean."

"Yes, master," she repeated. "I agree to your terms. Can I fight?"

"I'm only agreeing because I suspect the masters won't allow any enemy fighters to get near you."

"That's probably true."

"Okay, we'll go after Straga tomorrow."

"I just want you to know I'm itching for a fight, Aron. I have a lot of pent up rage I need to release. Being helpless to Damien for so long, it affects you."

"Just be careful. Nothing about battle has changed. We can feel we're too good to fail, that we're invincible, but a lucky sword stroke, a stray arrow, an adverse situation can take us out at any time."

"I know that, Aron, but my feelings aren't changed. I want to fight. I'm going to go sit with Nala for a while and talk, okay?"

"Of course, you don't need my permission to comfort your friend."

Cherine smiled and kissed him gently.

"It's going to be good for us, Aron. I promise you that."

"I never thought otherwise, darling. I'll see you later."

Lilith walked up to them and overheard their remarks.

She smiled smugly at Cherine. "Yes, Cherine, go to your new friend. I'll stay with Aron. We've become quite close while you were away. Someone needed to step up to fill your vacancy. Aron has suffered enough."

Cherine got an amused smile. Aron looked perplexed and embarrassed.

"Lilith…" he complained shaking his head in consternation.

"Aron, don't worry," she answered. "I'm not unhappy Lilith offered her friendship."

"Close friendship," Lilith corrected.

Both women chuckled.

"Am I missing something?" asked Aron in confusion.

"Not at all," Cherine replied.

"I wish to meet her, this new friend of yours," said Lilith.

"Of course, you'll like her. Perhaps you'll see something of yourself in her, Lilith. She was forced to be self-reliant and it formed her into a savvy independent woman. I think it's a good thing."

"Interesting, Cherine, I'd thought you had little regard for me."

"Quite the contrary, Lilith, in spite of our prior travails, I always respected you as a female force in the world. We have too few of those."

"Thank you Cherine. I hope we can be close friends, like Aron and I are close."

The women laughed heartily. Aron shook his head having no comprehension of what they were saying. They were on a wavelength that eluded him.

"I think I'd like to have a long talk with you and with her, Cherine," Lilith continued. "We have a new world opening before us with great possibilities for those bold enough and talented enough to grasp those chances."

"I agree, Lilith. I think you're one of those who qualify for those opportunities."

"I am," she agreed boldly.

They laughed again and this time they hugged.

"Goodbye," she said. She winked at her and nodded to Aron.

Aron almost didn't want her to leave. Lilith's possessiveness of him seemed to be growing and inexplicably that didn't seem to bother Cherine.

Aron strode off rapidly. Lilith hurried to walk at his side.

"You can't escape your fate, Aron," she huffed, as his stride was meant to silence her. He muttered unintelligibly and scowled.

Barmon was animated when they walked over to him.

"At last, Aron, this fight with Straga has been too long in coming for my liking. He must answer for his sins as Damien did. I won't have him alive in this world to threaten my wife any further."

Brock and Trent came to join them.

"Easy, Father," said Brock. "Keep control or we play into Straga's hands."

"Don't worry about me, son. I won't let you down. I don't want to die but there is a task we must complete. You know that. Sirina could have chosen to remain with him but she chose us. Straga refuses to accept it. There can be no other outcome."

The chief of the Brutans approached them.

"We'll move out at dawn," Aron advised.

"Aron, you know this is a ritual battle for us. You must not interfere. I know our ways in some areas are repulsive to you, but realize the Erati are no better. What we do, they would do to us. Each tribe looks to eradicate the other. That means no Erati would surrender as no Brutan would ever surrender. This is a fight to the death, literally. Neither tribe would have it any other way. I would even say, the Black Fist and the masters have been our brothers and we have a blood bond with you, but this kind of fight, what you'd call barbaric, it may be one which you should avoid. What will happen at the end when there's one victor only, it will not be for the faint of heart. It's our way and I know you don't approve. Trophies are an honor to us, a symbol of our triumph and a way to shame our enemies. Their men must die and their women and children will be absorbed in the Brutan tribe. If we lost the same thing would happen the other way. My wife would become chattel to an Erati."

"We can't abandon this fight, chief. We have our own grudges with Straga, as you know. You're right that we don't approve of those things you do to the dead bodies. I'm not going to make it an issue. I hope if your arch enemy is gone you'll no longer find the need to live that way. I'm thinking about your young. If you teach them to live in a civilized way I'd say that's a good thing. From my perspective, we won't allow Straga to win."

"I have no objections to your terms, Aron. With this particular fight, no Brutan can be sure if he'll be a survivor. There are guaranteed to be heavy losses on both sides. I may not be around to see the dawn of this new age."

"That's true for everybody, chief. I can't get Cherine to back off either. She wants a fight, badly."

"We respect her a great deal. It's not the Brutan way for our women to bear arms, but with her example, and Lilith too, we've opened our eyes to other ways."

"Cherine has been an example for everybody, chief. I don't think she realizes how much she's changed people's views."

"The same could be said for you, Aron. You and she are the same in that you don't acknowledge your significance."

"Chief, what people don't understand is that we do realize it, but neither of us wants the acclaim. Neither of us feels worthy. You don't know how weak we really are inside."

"Your kind of weakness, we could use more of it in the world."

The chief laughed. Aron was amused.

"I don't see you laugh very often."

"We've learned this laughing from you, Aron."

"You're welcome, chief."

"Aron, it's a sign we've already looked at our way of life and some things have changed on their own without our conscious efforts. I know we can't go on living as barbarians. We'd always be a terrible threat to our neighbors. Perhaps we see eradicating our mortal enemies as a final act of our old ways. To civilized people one last horrific act as closure makes no sense. I understand that point of view, but I'm afraid this isn't an occurrence which can be avoided."

"That decision is yours, chief. You know my feelings. I don't agree you have to do it, but we won't let you have this fight alone. Straga is going to lose."

"We were hoping this is what you'd say." The chief laughed again.

"We'll be ready to move at the appointed time."

"I assume Damien will accompany us to the battle."

"Of course, Straga is welcome to have his master returned to him. He put too much store in Damien's invincibility."

"He'll learn the same lesson as his master. Your bad deeds come back on you sooner or later."

"I wonder if Damien's ancient enemies are looking down from the beyond, smiling."

"They're probably opening extra kegs of ale, Aron."

They both laughed heartily. "Chief, that is so wrong, I don't think they have ale in heaven."

"You don't know for sure, Aron," the chief joked.

"I do not, but I suspect I'm right."

"If I end up there tomorrow, Aron, I'll try to get a message to you from the other side."

"Chief, don't pass over tomorrow. I don't want any messages from the other side."

* * * *

Granor sent his men to execute his plan. He was very worried as it was fraught with risk. The royal children joined his conspiracy and what remained of the old royalty threw in with him too. It all hinged on this dangerous attempt he was already questioning.

They moved to their pre-arranged places, separate, but highly visible so if anything went wrong they'd have viable alibis.

Granor was the person with the most to lose. He'd be identified as the author of the plot. Regardless, he went to an appointment with the army staff he'd engineered ostensibly to discuss city planning and safety.

His men skulked to the royal suite the king and queen shared. She slept in another room and at this point in time she was away with Coraline and some other women at a tea.

The king was in his bed, awake, but unaware. The kidnappers trussed him up and hustled him away quickly. He followed them without question. His higher faculties were long since lost.

The entire operation was ridiculously easy. They took him away to a secret location and sent word to Granor.

Granor had been on pins and needles at the meeting. When he got a positive message he relaxed and returned to his former personality, self-important, and domineering. He wanted to race to the secret lair, but he spent ample time to be sure he wouldn't be implicated.

He was at supper when word spread about the king's disappearance. He was the first person Marin sought out.

"What's this, Marin?" he complained. "I've been occupied all day. There are any numbers of your friends who can verify that."

"Granor, this has your scent all over it, by why. The king no longer rules?"

"Exactly, there would be no motive. You'll have to ask the guilty parties when you catch them."

Marin studied him closely.

"Okay, Granor. You can go for now, but I'll have eyes on you."

"Perhaps your eyes should be directed at pursuing the culprits."

He returned to his suite, but slunk out a secret passage to go see the king who was oblivious and incapable of speaking to Granor.

"This is perfect. The king is lost, but now he'll have a voice in the kingdom again."

They started rumors the king secretly recovered and escaped his suite where an ambitious Coraline conspired with the queen to usurp the rule of the kingdom. It seemed a ridiculous premise, but with the help of whisperings, support from the nobles and bribes, the theory gained traction in the palace.

None of the common citizens paid particular attention, other than out of curiosity. If the king regained his mind, he was the proper authority and Granor had always been his spokesman.

"The king chooses to remain in hiding," Granor explained in his first public speech. "He's shocked and incensed his wife and daughter-in-law could turn on him in his weakness. Now that he's recovered he fears they'll take worse action even to the point of assassination. It's prudent he stay concealed for his safety."

When the nobles lined up behind Granor, and then the royal children denounced Coraline and their mother it created a tense and a dangerous situation. It was very fortunate Marin commanded the respect and the full support of the army. They couldn't be swayed to defect to Granor.

The queen was crushed and shied away from public. It left Coraline to stand alone against the poison of Granor's charges and subterfuge. Marin was her rock with Aron gone.

Marin kept his promise to shadow Granor, but Granor made no mistakes. He had no reason to see the king personally any longer. His invented proxy served his purpose. Amongst the former criminals who occupied the city there were plenty of recruits willing to follow Granor in return for spurious rewards and bombastic future promises.

Granor built a military force sufficient that he could defend himself. Similarly, the former nobles formed their own militias and in most cases reoccupied their former residences. They lacked slaves in the new society but there were so many people desperately poor, they lured staffs of the gullible to operate their mansions again working for a pittance. The nobles barely curbed their former abusive ways.

Granor and his ilk were busy at trying to rebuild and reintroduce the old monarchy.

The problems he caused were not easily resolved because there was such an entrenched mentality that accompanied the old guard that some accepted absurdity instead of standing up against tyranny. Nobody believed Granor wasn't behind a conspiracy. Coming on the heels of a near fatal war, the populace was weary of fighting and the uncertainty.

Marin worked to consolidate support behind his wife. The army didn't waver in supporting him. That was their great strength. Without them defecting, Granor had no chance of toppling Coraline, but he remained a serious problem nonetheless. His villainous actions behind the scenes built a consensus of poison.

The development of dire events Granor orchestrated led to a culmination in confrontation where he attempted to force Coraline and the queen to appear before a council of his handpicked nobles to answer questions about their alleged conspiracy. It was a sham and merely an attempt to add credibility to his position as the king's voice.

"I will put an end to this charade," said Marin, as Coraline was dressing for the occasion.

"I'm sure Granor is banking on that, husband," she replied. "We must find a better way to deal with it. If you marched in and bullied them it would add to his diatribe."

"I don't pretend to be a scholar to debate with Granor, but I know enough that he can't be allowed to continue on this path unchecked. His lies are starting to take root. There are plenty of people who fall for this misinformation. No one wants Granor in power, but they also wonder if what he says is true, that the king is recovered and in hiding."

"That's ridiculous. The king will never recover."

"We know that, but people who haven't been around him don't know. The nobles want to be back in power. That's the real risk."

"The queen is distraught."

"Coraline, you're the queen now. You've got to acknowledge it. They'll use it against you if you continue to defer to her. She abdicated, otherwise they can make the case the king can assert his rights through his proxy."

"I, eh…"

"There's no other way. I know you didn't seek the throne, but at this point there's no turning back."

"What do you think I should say?"

"I suspect Granor isn't looking to claim the throne. He's not stupid. The throne would never be his. I think what he wants is acknowledgement and a place of prominence in your administration. He'd like to have his old job back and be your prime minister."

"I could never deal with him, Marin. He's repulsive to me. With what the crown prince wanted in the old days, he didn't mince words. He spoke it right out. He was wrong and came to regret it later. Granor on the other hand tried to work in the shadows, to impose on his victims that they'd accede to his demands without revealing it to the public. He wanted to have his way but have no consequences. Do you see the difference?"

"Of course, Coraline, I'd be happy to administer his consequences."

"I wish it was that easy, husband. We have the army and we have the people, but it doesn't protect us from the secret attacks from Granor and the nobles. I must stand against them. The queen is too fragile to shoulder the burden."

"If that's your choice, I want you to know I don't agree and I won't allow them to harm you. If they take such actions, I will step in and I tell you they won't survive."

She smiled and embraced her husband.

"Your strength heartens me to the possibility I can be brave also, Marin."

She went to the council chamber an hour later. It was a strange feeling walking into the familiar room. The old banners had been salvaged and re-hung. They reflected the supposed exploits of the king and the former crown prince with vast tapestries depicting battle triumphs. One of them showed Aron being driven off by the royal army.

The drafty castle was perpetually cool. The pennants moved with the constant air currents.

Granor didn't have the temerity to sit on the throne, but he did pick a seat of prominence at the table flanked by nobles and his staffers.

"Greetings, Coraline," he said glibly. It was an intentional snub not using her title.

She thought for a moment if she wanted to start with a fight.

She looked at the faces of the inquisition. They were uniformly stern and disapproving, like she was still the farm girl from the border.

"Please take your seat," Granor continued, nodding to a prisoner's chair.

Again she pondered how best to respond to the affront. She decided she needed to issue her own challenge. She walked up to the throne and sat there. The counselors murmured and scowled at her.

"Granor, ask your questions."

"I must say, I'm surprised you didn't bring Marin and his army friends,

Coraline."

"Should I have brought them? You claim you want to get to the truth. Play your game. We both know the truth."

He gave her an amused smile.

"I assure you, I'm not playing a game here. If you don't understand the seriousness of these proceedings I must tell you otherwise. The king has a much different view of you trying to take his throne. There are consequences for those who do ill and try to thwart the law."

"Yes, Granor, those are definitely consequences for our actions. That applies to all of us."

"We'd asked for the queen to attend. Where is she?"

"She's not up to the stress. Having her husband spirited away has harmed her spirit."

"That's a convenient excuse, Coraline. You expect us to make our judgment based solely on your testimony? There are serious charges you're at the center of a conspiracy to usurp the throne."

Coraline simply looked at him.

He smiled smugly and looked at his collection of vipers.

"If that was meant as a threat to intimidate us, madam, know we're determined to do our duties regardless of any risk. We're the righteous representatives of his majesty, the rightful ruler of the kingdom. We don't acknowledge what you've done. We don't acknowledge you as our sovereign. The queen has inside knowledge of the events of this nefarious affair. We won't be mollified by your obstructionism."

Coraline felt genuine anger, but she realized Granor was counting on that, hoping she'd respond with an ill concerned rant. She closed her eyes a moment to collect her wits and calm her rage.

She smiled at Granor. "You're certainly entitled to your opinions, Granor. Because you speak these words doesn't make them true. As I said, play your game, but if you try to threaten her again, there will be consequences, as you said."

Granor eyed her with a calculating look.

Chapter Eighteen
~Battles~

Two completely different kinds of fights loomed. Coraline faced the plotting of Granor and Aron faced the final battle of the Brutans and the Erati.

Both could be blood baths but in much different ways.

Aron got up early. Cherine was at the hospital with Lilith seeing Nala and spent the night there. When the men assembled she showed up in full uniform.

"You and Lilith can sit this out," Aron explained.

"No, Aron, we can't. We're going, so drop it."

Aron shrugged.

The Brutans painted their faces and bodies and looked the part of deranged barbarians.

"Chief," said Aron, as he walked up along with Trent and Brock.

"Where's your father, Brock?"

"He's going to be in the middle of the Brutans. He's going straight for Straga. That's a grudge fight he can't be talked out of."

"Straga will have protections. The Erati may not let him get close enough to fight Straga personally."

"My father will have protections also."

"I must prepare the masters, Aron," said Cherine. He nodded as she turned and left. Lilith smiled at Aron before following Cherine away.

Her maidens were joining the masters in surrounding Cherine. Aron looked at her, the consummate warrior woman. She looked her old self, daunting and imminently competent.

The Black Fist crowded around Brock staring at Aron.

"There's not much to say. You all know we have a chance here to put an end to the war. Damien is gone forever and his army is leaving the kingdom to go to their home countries. Straga is the last of the enemy forces we need to deal with. You know how to fight and to protect each other. This time, we have a chance to give this land a new opportunity. We can aspire to have peace, to have wives and children of our own. I don't have any doubt we'll prevail today but it will be deadly dangerous out there. The Erati are fighting for their lives and they won't go easily. They won't surrender so it's a fight to the last man. I hope the Brutans don't go to excess with, well, you know what they do to the defeated. I can't really control them, but the chief says they want to change their ways. We'll give them a chance to do what they say they want to do. I would say we should do what we can for their women and children afterwards. Make sure they aren't drawn into the horror."

The men stood in silence.

"It's been my great honor to lead you all these years. We've faced so many situations where people didn't think we could survive. We beat all of the odds and here we stand. Let's do this one last time and be done with warring."

Aron noticed the Uripean contingent eased close and he'd put fire in their eyes too. He nodded to their commander. They gave him a salute with a loud martial shout.

The allied army moved toward the Erati lands at a brisk pace. They had no illusions the Erati didn't know they were coming.

It annoyed Aron that Cherine didn't ride at his side as he requested. She rode at the head of the masters riding behind Aron's Black Fist contingent.

The path to the Erati was one trap after another between snares and ambushes. They were forced to slow their pace to keep from unnecessary casualties. The Erati even managed to herd a pack of predators into their path. It was a serious fight because those animals were trapped with the Erati goading them and the allies in front.

The Erati stayed long enough to engage the allies until the predators were either killed or driven off before they receded.

"This won't be the last of Straga's schemes," said Brock.

"Let's go," Aron replied as they ambled forward.

With no element of surprise and with the sun rising on the horizon, both sides would have a clear view of each other.

As they drew close to the Erati border, they heard them in the distance screaming and banging their drums building battle frenzy. It was frightening to hear. Aron looked at the Brutan chief. His eyes smoldered with his own battle frenzy. His men were equally committed.

The Erati chants grew in sound as they drew nearer. Aron could hear them banging their shields as their leaders incited them.

Aron took a deep breath as they formed up to assault the Erati camp. He'd overwhelmed them before, but that was long ago and the stakes were much different. This battle was not a sure thing even with his superior numbers and numerous highly skilled allies.

Aron looked for Cherine. She was out of sight deploying the masters and Lilith's maidens to a different part of the battlefield.

The Erati shouted defiance and insults at them.

The Brutan chief raised his arm and the Brutans began their own ritual chants which were equally terrifying. Neither side had used them in the war previously. This was special to both sides. This was the day of death or triumph. The families of the losers would pay the price.

The cacophony of noise was deafening. Aron never heard the Brutan chief yell the order to charge. He just experienced sudden movement all around him. He rocked into motion more from momentum than from conscious thought to act. He pulled his sword and shouted along with the rest of his army.

Straga had built numerous hazards from breastworks, sharp pointed barriers, and covered holes to fall into, etc. It was a deadly approach to his skirmish lines, of which he had multiple tiers.

Aron worried about Cherine, but the battle consumed him quickly. He could only worry about surviving the individual fights. Wherever she was at that moment he couldn't see her.

Barmon was a demon fighting in the midst of the Brutans driving inexorably forward. He fought like one of them, but the Erati were equally ferocious selling out completely to take down as many as they could. This was a day of death on both sides.

Straga could be seen running from pressure point to pressure point, redirecting his men to the best possible effect. The allies fought their way through the hazards until they reached the first line of defense. At that point it became a meat grinder as casualties mounted with no change of position. The Brutans stubbornly attacked despite their losses. They were extracting a heavy toll from the Erati but those lines held nonetheless.

When the Uripeans launched a new attack at one of the Erati flanks, Straga sent reserves to meet the threat and achieved a stalemate at the new point of attack.

Aron led the Black Fist along the line and picked a point of lesser Erati personnel concentration to add another attack point. Straga had reserves ready to surge to the point. Still, no one could penetrate the line.

Cherine launched her own attack at the other flank of Straga's defense with her masters and Lilith's maidens. Again they couldn't rupture the line.

In any of the incursion points if the allies rallied to climb up the obstacles, they were thrown back by the Erati.

Aron couldn't use his superior numbers to advantage with the restricted space in the battle zone. Straga selected the perfect spot to make his stand.

The day ground along with the impasse as the sun traveled across the sky and perched barely above the horizon.

Aron sent word to pull back. No one had eaten since morning. The Erati cheered and jeered at their retreat back to camp. It angered Aron who strode back forward with a white flag of parley.

He went with Brock, Trent, the Brutan chieftain, and Barmon.

Straga came to stand on top of his defense wall to look down at them.

"Aron, what's this? Have you had enough? Do you wish to throw yourselves on our mercy?" His troops laughed derisively.

"No Straga. I've brought your master back to you."

They unfurled the wrap and let Damien's body flop onto the ground. It shocked Straga and his men.

"What did you do to him?"

"Damien engineered his own demise. We simply helped him with it. His machines consumed him. It was a terrible death. You thought he was invincible."

"If you think this will frighten us into surrender, Aron, you're sadly mistaken."

"I didn't think anything, Straga. His body was stinking up my camp and I wanted to be rid of it." He noticed Straga not only looking uncomfortably at the body but also staring at the animal hatred in Barmon's eyes.

"I can't save you, Straga. It's too late for that," Aron said in conclusion.

"You will steal no other man's wife, ever again," Barmon hissed.

Aron turned and walked away. He felt incredibly vulnerable as they were well within range of Straga's archers.

Straga's camp quieted after Aron's gambit. They were barbarians that had no remorse about killing or the same butchery as the Brutans, but the condition of Damien's body terrified them, as if Aron did it to imply he had Damien's ancient weapons at his disposal.

Aron went to his camp to look for his fiancée. He saw her at the physician's tent.

"What happened?" he asked in concern.

"It's nothing, Aron. A small nick, the kind we get in battles. I've had plenty of them before."

Aron frowned as he looked at a red line on her side. The doctor put a bandage on it and spoke to her. "I'd tell you to take it easy until this heals, but I know you wouldn't heed my advice."

"Listen to your doctor, Cherine," said Aron.

"As if you'd avoid a battle for a minor wound, Aron..."

"I would."

"Don't lie to me. I'm not some weak blushing school girl. Battles test us. I'm up to that test."

"Aron, I'll ward her," said Lilith.

"Perhaps we should re-align our forces so I can ward both of you."

Lilith chuckled and Cherine smiled.

"Men," said Cherine.

"Indeed," Lilith agreed.

Aron glanced behind them at some movement. The women turned.

"Nala, should you be up and walking about?" asked Cherine with concern.

"I need to regain my strength, Cherine. I can't lie about while all of you risk your lives."

"You're no warrior," Cherine pointed out.

"Nevertheless, I can support you."

She walked up to Aron.

"I've heard a great deal about you."

"Is that a good thing?"

She laughed. "I understand you, Cherine. He's a wonderful man. I've not known many of those in my life. To answer your questions, Aron, yes it's a good thing. You're renowned amongst your enemies as well as your friends. That's a remarkable thing."

Aron glanced at Brock and Trent who were smirking.

"It's nice to meet you, Nala. I understand you were a dear friend of my fiancée during your captivity. Thank you for that. Someday I'll find a way to repay you."

"It's enough for me if you allow me to continue my friendship with Cherine. She is a high woman and I'm far beneath her. It's been a great honor to be held in esteem. Being around her has put me in the center of momentous events. Without her, I was nothing to Damien."

"Nala, you're beneath no one," Cherine chided. "You have great worth and I'm honored you call me friend."

"You're injured?" asked Nala, noticing Cherine's bandage for the first time. "Cherine you can't take these risks? I won't allow it."

Aron laughed. "Thank you, Nala. I can see you being my great friend too. If Cherine heeds your words, you help me with my greatest problem."

All the women smiled at Aron.

"Has the doctor released you from his care, Nala?" asked Cherine.

"He says he'll check me until it's fully healed, but yes it's true."

"Then you'll come to stay with me and Lilith. We're camped with the masters."

"Your force of elite fighters," Nala mentioned rhetorically.

"You'll be safe with us. During the fighting I'll have people watching you. I won't allow harm to come to you."

Nala looked questioningly at Aron.

"You don't need my permission, Nala," he said, though it seemed to him there was something else she wondered.

Nala glanced at Cherine.

"We've not had much chance to be alone to speak," she explained to Nala. "I told him there are things I wished to say. He dismissed it without hearing me out. We'll talk about it later. You're welcome here amongst us. That's what's important."

Aron had no idea what she meant. Nala glanced at him again before the women left to go back to the master's place in the camp.

Aron looked at Trent and Brock in confusion.

"Don't ask us for answers," said Brock. "You notice neither of us have a woman. They're incomprehensible from my point of view. I suppose once this war is done I'll have to allow one of them to woo me."

They laughed heartily.

"That's a sight I'd like to see," said Trent, "Brock being wooed."

Aron laughed in amusement, but he was curious about the women. Every woman he'd ever known always seemed to have some aspect in secret which he couldn't decipher. Whether it would pan out to be a worrisome issue, he had no idea, but at this point the fact there was an issue of any kind bothered him.

His 'bride to be' wasn't acting badly toward him, but after his misadventures with Tasha, Coraline, and even Liani, he was accustomed to distress when it came to women. He could only hope for the best.

Nala was surprised about something and now Aron was very curious what it was. Cherine choosing to sleep elsewhere irked him now too. She'd said it wasn't time for her to act as his wife. She needed to resume her martial state to execute the battle plans at the highest level. It wasn't a satisfying answer for Aron, but he didn't feel he had any say in the matter.

His old anxieties receded but never disappeared. It was too easy for him to think the worst. Cherine and Nala lived a long time with Damien, intimately with Damien. Could that have turned her against Aron in some way? It was a troublesome thought he couldn't dismiss.

He lay down to rest for the next taxing day of battle, but his mind punished him with unfortunate thoughts. What if Cherine found him weak after he failed to rescue her promptly?

He sat up in the night and looked around for his sentries. They were all at their posts. The Erati camp was quiet too.

Savior

It took him so long to fall asleep. Brock had to shake him awake the next morning. "Come, brother. It's time."

They ate a quick breakfast and drank considerable coffee before assembling the troops.

* * * *

The Brutans were already creeping forward in the semi-darkness of pre-dawn. Barmon was right beside their chief. The chief made a signal and suddenly archers launched waves of fire tipped arrows into the Erati wooden structures. The arrow's tips were wrapped in flammable clothes soaked in oil. It took a time but the sharpened logs and spikes caught fire and flames spread rapidly. The Erati couldn't extinguish the blaze and it forced them back away from the skirmish lines.

The Brutans eased closer and closer and both sides showered each other with arrows.

They waited until the burning wood structures started to collapse and fall apart. The charge came so suddenly Aron was caught off guard. He led the Black Fist to try to catch the Brutans who were screaming insanely and racing at full speed.

The Brutans hit the barrier bashing open gaps and racing past. The Erati were arrayed just beyond and charged immediately to keep the Brutans from establishing a foothold. It was ferocious hand to hand fighting for inches of ground.

Aron and the Black Fist pushed through the barrier to see the Erati massing to push the Brutans back against the flaming obstacles. They charged immediately to steady the line.

Eratis shouted his name and he became a target of their wrath. Brock, Trent, and the others rallied to defend Aron from death. Again he could think of nothing. He could only react to each blinding sword stroke. The Uripeans poured in behind the Black Fist and pushed ahead to bolster the attack. Still the Eratis held them at bay.

They began to make slow progress. The Erati fought bravely, but now the numbers weren't in their favor. They were squeezed backwards incrementally.

The fight went on for many hours. There would be no pauses this time. It would end in defeat for somebody before the sun set.

They moved ahead to the point Aron could now see the other points of the battle. The Brutan spearhead was a focal point for Straga's fighters. The chief was another target, but Barmon was his personal protector. There were none who could kill him.

Aron looked a moment farther along and saw the uniforms of the masters.

They were in a similar state making slow progress. He even saw a flash of Cherine. She was a dervish of flying sword strokes, a killing machine too. Lilith was fighting right beside her.

Aron didn't see Straga though. The man's absence worried him.

Suddenly the Erati dropped to the ground at some pre-set signal leaving the allies to face a sudden launch of a barrage of arrows. Not everyone was able to elude the shots and it put them momentarily off balance for the Erati to strike.

Aron fought against three as he was suddenly separated from the others.

"I will take your head," one of the Erati taunted. They tried a simultaneous attack from three different points, but this was how Aron had trained. He was a man singularly ready for this fight. His instinct took over fighting for his own life. It was the supreme challenge against these deadly opponents. He wasn't even aware when his strokes picked them off one at a time. He became aware when they were felled, but to his horror he heard a great shout from the other side where Cherine had been similarly cut off from her men and was facing multiple attackers too. She was too far away for Aron to race over to save her. She was in desperate trouble and it appeared she would fall. Suddenly, it was Lilith who broke out of the pack to strike at the ring of attackers.

Cherine was knocked to her knees, vulnerable to the beheading stroke already swinging at her when Lilith pummeled bodily into the man knocking him to the ground. She rolled over beside Cherine and the two women stood up fighting back to back to survive.

Moments later the masters battered through the Erati line and surrounded their leader.

It was a critical point as the hope of the Erati to wipe out the allied leaders and to especially crush their spirits by taking Cherine's head off failed.

Aron screamed in rage and charged forward. The allied army answered his call and they began a frenzied surge which the Erati could no longer contain.

The remaining Erati executed a calculated retreat and pivot to center their remaining men. They were attacked mercilessly from all sides. Suddenly Straga appeared and raced straight toward Barmon. The two met in an incredible state of fury unleashing their hatred in feral attacks that would have killed most.

This was the part of the fight Aron despised. The Erati were starting to fall with greater frequency and the outcome at this point was no longer in doubt. None of the allies showed any quarter. The Erati sought death so that was what happened.

Aron started to work his way around as the battleground condensed.

When he finally reached Cherine she nearly attacked him.

"Aron?" she asked.

"I thought I was going to lose you," he replied.

"No, Aron. This was not my day to die."

They engaged back into the fighting as Lilith was being driven backwards by multiple Erati. Aron and Cherine ended that danger.

"Aron?" asked Lilith. "What are you doing here?"

"Saving you," he answered.

"I had them under control," Lilith huffed.

"I could see that. Nonetheless, I acted on your behalf."

"Thank you, Aron."

The fight pushed ahead as the remaining Erati were driven away from Straga. That fight continued oblivious of what was happening all around. Neither man could gain an advantage.

Brock tried to step to his father's side.

"No, son," Barmon shouted. "This is our fight alone. Back away. One of us must die today."

Brock grudgingly acceded to his father's wishes.

The fight resumed but Aron got a sense Straga no longer looked to prevail, like this was his inevitable end.

They fought hard and furiously, but Barmon wasn't going to be denied. He made a feint and suddenly smashed a fist in Straga's face knocking him to the ground, his sword falling out of his hand. Straga lay for a moment panting before getting to his knees.

"Make it a sure stroke and give me a clean death," he said.

"I take no pleasure in this, Straga. I promise I'll be a good father to your boys. They'll pay no price for your crimes."

Straga suddenly looked stricken. He closed his eyes and leaned over exposing his neck.

Barmon struck before Aron could intercede. Straga joined Damien in death.

The battle turned ugly as pockets of Erati fought to the death.

Barmon looked truly upset. Brock walked over and consoled his father.

Aron went up to the Brutan chief.

"Go to your people. This isn't the time to savage the dead. Those widows and children of the Erati need to see kindness from the Brutans. It's time right now to change your ways."

The chief nodded in agreement. The terrible battle drained him of frenzy.

Aron went to be among the first to enter the Erati village. The women and children were cowering in terror.

"Come out," said Aron gently.

They hesitated before a couple of brave ones started to move. Once they were all around him he spoke to them.

"I'm sorry we had to disrupt your lives. Straga would have it no other way. Please accept our regrets. We want you to know this isn't the end for you. We're going to offer you places amongst us. The Brutans aren't going to make you slaves. If any of you wish to join them to find new mates, you can do so. The rest of you may join me to return to Nephora. You can make new lives and find new husbands."

They stared at him in silence.

"You're Aron?" asked a young girl.

"Yes, child," he answered.

"They said you were a monster that killed little children."

Aron walked over and knelt down in front of her.

"I'm not a monster. I'm your new friend," he said softly. "Everything is going to be fine. We'll take care of you." He kissed her forehead.

She looked up at her mother who was conflicted after having all their men wiped out. She looked at Aron and then her daughter.

"Come, Ana," she said. "He won't hurt you."

Aron stood back up.

"We have food in our camp. Pack up your things and join us. We'll be going soon."

The widows and their children started to move to their homes to pack their valuables.

"You did well, Aron," said Lilith. She walked up close to him peering deeply into his eyes.

"Thank you, Lilith."

He looked over to see Cherine talking with Nala and looking at him. He wasn't sure if there was a problem. Lilith was always affectionate with him. Whether Cherine wanted him to curb it, he wasn't sure. He didn't get that impression as Cherine's attention seemed focused elsewhere. She and Nala were involved in a heavy conversation, one which excluded him. It evoked his feelings, again.

"I'm very impressed, Aron," Lilith continued. He'd tried to step around her to walk over to Cherine. Lilith took a step to block his way.

"What's going on, Lilith? Are you supposed to keep me away from them?"

"They're having a private talk, Aron. Don't concern yourself about it."

"Lilith, she's supposed to be my future wife."

"That hasn't changed. You need to remember Tasha and Belisa coming out of a captive life. They needed time to sort things out. In those environments you're forced to make compromises. Coping with those adverse choices isn't easy. I know that very well from my life. I did things I wouldn't have chosen, but I had no choice. Do you hear me?"

"I have no idea what you're trying to tell me, Lilith. Maybe you should say it right out. Does she hold it against me because I couldn't rescue her?"

"Only you'd come up with such an idea, Aron," she replied chuckling. "You put you in the center of every issue. I don't know why you try to take on so much guilt. Cherine and Nala became very close as Damien's wives. They had their own compromises to deal with. Trying to sort that out and create a new life is not easy. One doesn't just shed long term feelings like taking off a coat."

"I don't understand. I've never said they can't still be friends. I've never said anything about it. Are they putting words in my mouth?"

"No, Aron. You have no blame here, so you should stop trying to invent blame. There's no blame to anyone. It's best you leave them to talk it out and come to a conclusion. When they're ready, they'll come to you."

Aron shrugged.

Cherine and Nala turned and walked away although their conversation continued. They were both very expressive in their points, whatever they were.

* * * *

Meanwhile Coraline bristled at the tone and the lack of respect she was receiving from Granor and his people.

"Would you care to share your version of events, Coraline?"

She pondered the trap and how to respond.

"My version?" she questioned. "Are you implying I'd tell you something other than the truth, Granor?"

"My role here is to ascertain the facts, nothing more. I can't guess about the motives of another person. You must realize his majesty has told us some very disturbing things. Frankly I was shocked at what he says occurred. I can only follow the evidence regardless of where it leads."

"Does it matter what I say? The more I sit through this, the more I realize you have an agenda and an end game. The fact you've chosen to take such a colossal risk tells me you're determined to follow spurious paths and desperate measures. I find that very disturbing. There isn't a person in the entire kingdom who doesn't know I didn't want the throne. The queen insisted."

"Yet, you tell us the queen can't attend to verify this, how convenient, Coraline."

Coraline looked at the faces of the panel. They had predatory looks as though she was easy meat.

"The truth is the truth, Granor. You're not here to ferret out the truth. You have some leverage that emboldens you. Why waste any more time. Tell me whatever it is you brought me here to hear."

"Are you refusing to speak in your own defense?" he asked rhetorically. "Are you saying we should make a judgment based on what the king has told us?"

"I've had enough of this, Granor."

"I must tell you, I'm surprised. I take no pleasure in what I must do next. Since you have no answer to the facts as presented by his majesty, the true ruler of the realm, I tell you we don't accept you as our sovereign. As his majesty's duly appointed minister, I'll temporarily assume the duties of managing the kingdom. All of the noble's former rights and privileges are hereby reinstated as well as their places of authority in the realm. You're being formally charged with treason and conspiracy against the crown. I must remand you into custody pending a trial to deal with the crimes and your potential punishment."

He nodded and his personal soldiers marched up and laid hands on her. She was in shock he would do such a thing.

"You won't get away with this, Granor."

"I pray for your soul, Coraline. Take her to the prison."

It happened Marin was away in the city that day so he wasn't there to intervene. The palace corps wasn't sure what to make of their beautiful new queen being dragged away to the dungeon accused of being a criminal conspirator.

Coraline was in shocked disbelief when they closed and locked the cell door. It was the last thing she would have anticipated from the hearing.

Granor's silent coup continued when he sent another force to secure the former queen and drag her also to the dungeon. It was a dangerous gambit, but the main characters weren't there to intervene.

The news raced through the palace like a wild fire and with no one present who could challenge Granor's actions he grew bold. Granor ordered the palace guards to close the building and resist Marin when he returned at the end of the day.

Granor went into the throne room and sat down on the royal seat, smiling smugly to gloat at the ease of his success.

The nobles all quickly announced their support for Granor as the temporary regent on behalf of the king. It confused the army captains into inaction while they waited for their commander to instruct them.

Marin received word late and raced back to the palace. When the guards refused to open the palace doors, he called up the army.

Granor came out to face him. A huge crowd assembled to hear the exchange.

"Behold citizens, this is husband to the woman his majesty has charged with serious crimes of treason against the state. His majesty fears their further treachery so he chooses to remain in hiding to preserve his life. You all know me as his appointed representative. He's asked that I manage the kingdom until this sorry matter is resolved and it's safe for him to emerge again. I do so with a heavy heart. I was duped just like all of you. I called Coraline and Marin friends. I'm appalled at their vile ambition and their reprehensible behaviors. Here stands Marin preparing to assault the palace, but on what authority? He received no appointment or position from the king. He was the common man of the late crown prince, but it's widely suspected he took advantage of the assignment to safeguard the crown prince's wife by compromising her female weakness and taking her to his bed shattering her wedding vows of faithfulness. It's despicable and unseemly. Now we're expected to simply accept his word they're all innocent? Hah! We're not so gullible. Now they're wed after the crown prince was out of their way? How ironic his tragic brave death was a lynchpin in their scheme to usurp the throne. They're all commoners. They had no right of birth or crown decree. They're mere interlopers on the throne, but his majesty won't stand for it. We will put this crime to right. We will see proper authority restored and our glorious kingdom rebuilt. As you can see, all of the nobles stand behind the king and me as his representative. The king's children are also firmly behind me in this unfortunate matter."

The army officers looked confused, unsure what to make of the charges.

"You men of the royal army, you're sworn to preserve the kingdom against all enemies foreign and domestic. I order you to stand down until we can adjudicate this dire matter. Those who are guilty will pay the price for those crimes."

Marin walked up to Granor. Granor's men drew swords.

"If you lay one hand on her, I promise you'll curse the day you were born."

"Don't threaten me, Marin. You're a common soldier still while I'm anointed to be a leader. You have a chance to assume a place in society, but not as a co-conspirator."

"I'm not a fool, Granor. Don't waste my time and don't think I can't take action. I'll give you this moment, but realize you are a dead man walking. I promise you that on my life."

"Citizen's, you heard it from his own mouth. What else would a guilty man say? He threatens the rightful authority when his schemes fall down around him. I'm clothed in rightness, therefore I do not fear."

Marin turned and walked back down the steps. The army pulled back and established positions all around the palace.

Chapter Nineteen
~Return to Nephora~

Aron assembled the Erati survivors and placed them in the center of his army for traveling back to the capital city. Those survivors gradually realized with time Aron truly meant them no harm and they began to let down their guard. It amazed him to see how the children of the Erati mingled freely with the children of the Brutans. There was no animosity, though the widowed women were not quick to forgive.

Going back the way they'd come across the border into the farmlands, Aron noticed farms were being re-occupied along with the local villages. When he went through his home village he saw friends and acquaintances taking up residence again and was happy they'd found a way to survive the invasion and the terrible war. It was heartening to imagine life could return to normal, new growth out of the destruction. Aron's parents were still in Nephora waiting for him there.

They traveled in an arc bending toward the great swamp to release the Uripeans back to their homes.

Enna and Biala refused to stay there though.

"We're going with you, Aron. Rumors are that there's trouble ahead. I think you'll need our swords."

Aron smiled. "I really do love you, ladies."

They smiled warmly and hugged him.

"You know our feelings, Aron."

It made him feel good. Cherine was still occupied with dealing with the unnamed issues of her captivity. Nala stayed with her along with Lilith, though Lilith tended to seek out Aron's company a great deal.

Enna and Biala noted the schism and joined the women to discover the problem.

Savior

Aron decided rather than fixate on an issue out of his control he spent considerable time with the Erati refugees. It was a wise move that went a long way towards eliminating potential problems with them. There were Erati women who still had a thought to take revenge for the battle that killed their men. They were easy to spot and Aron sought them out. He listened patiently to their feelings and talked about healing and new beginnings, freely sharing his own tortured past.

"I can't bring them back. I wish I could. It was such a needless choice deciding to die and leave families behind. I wish I'd had time to reason with them. Straga made a personal decision but it dragged all the rest of the Erati along with him."

"They weren't just husbands, they were fathers and brothers," said one of the women.

"I know that," Aron replied. "If they'd won and the Brutans were sitting in your predicament, would that be a good outcome? Would your men have shown mercy to the Brutan women and children? You know the answer. They would have become slaves. We made a choice to make your lives better. None of us expect the bitterness and the pain of loss will go away quickly. We just ask for you to bear with us. I'm not lying when I say you can make new relationships and find new mates. There are so many widows and widowers after the carnage of the war, there are no lack of chances to re-connect. Take care of your own, but keep an open mind. There are many among my army who will turn to the idea of starting families. They sacrificed for me but it's time they have some good in their lives. Is it so difficult an idea to consider? What do you have to lose? There are worthy men in this world that will cherish you."

Enna and Biala joined him when he moved on to the next group.

"You're very good with them. I'd have thought it an impossible task to sway the women of the Erati to rational thought."

"Thank you," said Aron. "I think everybody gets to a point where you must be realistic. They waited to see if I was lying, if we would turn to abusing them at some point in time. I think they feel confident now there can be a good life ahead."

"That makes sense. We can't argue with the success you're having, Aron. This is what's so impressive to others. You don't do it for accolades. You do it because it's the right thing to do. It's part of your nature."

"I don't know about that. I don't think of it in those terms. It seemed to me something needed to be done, so I did it."

* * * *

The trek across the countryside wasn't testing but it was steady. Aron

241

wanted to get back to the city as soon as possible. He'd heard some concerning reports about the state of things there.

He left the matter of Cherine alone waiting for her to come to him. That finally happened just as they left the frontier and entered the more populated regions leading up to Nephora. Nala came with her, but behind, like she was an intruder.

"Ladies," he said. "What can I do for you?"

Both women looked daunted and looked at each other.

"Is this a good time for us to speak, Aron?" asked Cherine.

"Anytime is a good time."

They came over and sat down, but beside each other facing Aron rather than sitting beside him.

"I wanted to talk about some things which we experienced."

"I told you, Cherine, I don't need to hear the details about what Damien did. It isn't hard to figure out. I've had some experience with these kinds of traumas. It didn't change things with Tasha and Belisa. Maybe they felt better coming clean, but I didn't require it."

"Please listen, Aron. It isn't about what Damien did. As you say, it's obvious. He pretended we were his wives and exercised husbandly prerogatives. None of that was meaningful to us. As a matter of fact, he was a joke he was so completely lame as a partner. Nala and I laughed privately after he left so full of himself that he'd impressed us. It was a game for us misleading him."

"What is it then that's troubling you?"

"We were in a relationship where it was three of us. That leads to feelings and dependencies. Without Nala, I'd have been seriously affected by that life. We bolstered each other which worked in essence to save us both. You've never been through it to understand what I'm saying. Nala is closer to me than any other woman in my life. I lost my mother early, so I never had a female role model or serious companion. As we've talked about our past to ponder our future we've struggled. I've pledged to become your wife. If that means I must part with Nala, I must tell you it's possibly a test beyond me. I love you, Aron, but I also love Nala. Do you see what I'm saying?"

"I'm not seeing what the big problem is, Cherine. Of course you can still be a close friend with Nala. Why would you think I would object to that?"

They got an uncomfortable look on their faces.

"We were Damien's wives, both of us."

"Yes, what am I missing here?"

"We weren't his wives, eh, separately. We were in his control and subject to his whims and also his excesses."

Aron still looked confused. "I guess I would say I'm not a novice about relationships. I know about different choices other people make. I don't hold whatever he made you do against you. Maybe you think it didn't apply to some areas. Cherine I want you under any circumstances. The past is the past. I say let it rest."

"Aron, what we're saying is I have the chance for a life with you. Nala has been a part of my life as I have been for her. She doesn't have the same opportunity as I. Leaving her adrift is a thing I can't do. Also, I don't want to miss out on a part of my life I've come to cherish."

"Are you asking me to step in like Damien, being husband to both of you?"

They looked at each other. Cherine spoke. "No Aron, that's not what we want. I guess I'm asking if you'll allow us to have time together. She is your friend too, but we'd like to do some things we've spoken of. Visit some places of interest and so forth."

"I may just be too stupid to figure out what you're saying. I'll stand on what I've already told you. I want to marry you and the sooner the better, Cherine. Whatever space you need, just let me know. I hope I can do a better job than Damien if he was such a bust as a man."

Both women laughed. "Thank you, Aron. I'd like to marry as soon as possible too," Cherine added.

They smiled warmly, like the weight of the world had been lifted off their shoulders.

"Aron, you're a rare man," said Nala. "If you change your mind about having two wives, just let me know."

"Keeping two women happy, I think you're asking the impossible from me. Let's go with the first plan."

"We agree."

"Do you still need to sleep apart from me?"

"No, that's over, Aron. I'll take the place where I should have been all along. I'm sorry you had to put up with me. We'll go get our things and be back shortly."

Aron stood up, stretched, and looked around smiling.

"Apparently everything went well," said Brock. "I'm glad. Maybe you can try to be a little optimistic from now on."

"I'll try. Things always seem to happen to me."

* * * *

Coraline worried a great deal when she spent the first night in her cell. It meant Marin had somehow been barred from getting into the palace to free her.

It seemed impossible with the army at his back that Granor could hold him out. There was no sound of fighting outside, although the prison cells were well recessed in the bowels of the palace so it would be difficult for sound to get down there.

It was late when Granor came down to her cell.

"I'm sorry we can't provide a more comfortable place for you, but circumstances being what they are you had to expect the worst. Stealing the throne is the most serious of offenses."

"Granor, there's no one else here. Save your lies. You came here for something. What do you want?"

"Coraline, I fear you don't grasp the gravity of your plight. Your husband hasn't come for you as you expected. What do you think that means? Perhaps you need to rethink your position to more reasonable views while you still can."

She said nothing in response.

He gave her a sly smile. "Fortunately for you, I'm a reasonable man. I don't want to minimize your risk, but I'd hope we could reach a mutually beneficial compromise. In return I promise I'll leave no stone unturned to investigate this serious matter. If I discover evidence to vindicate you, I'll be happy to do so. It pains me to see you here in such distress. I think I'm the only friend you have. The people were shocked to hear about the king's charges. They aren't your sheep following you blindly any longer, and you know they're like any other mob, thirsting for blood. You're so beautiful you'd draw every man, woman and child in the kingdom if you were sentenced to beheading. It's strange how people react to things. The prettier you are, the more they want to see you separated from your head. You should think hard on this because it's a real possibility here. I'll give you a night to think about it. Perhaps you'll have an offer for me tomorrow night when I return."

Coraline was genuinely terrified. The prior day she was the queen. Today she was at Granor's mercy and she didn't doubt his threat.

"You didn't try to threaten me," he said reflectively. "That's a good sign you understand you have no power here, and that I'm the only way out for you. I think a night of contemplation will bring a solution to mind. I'm sure you can figure it out."

He smirked before turning to leave her, content to leave her to percolate in helplessness.

Coraline felt alone. The queen was housed elsewhere in the dungeon so she couldn't talk with her. It wasn't difficult to understand what 'solution' Granor had in mind. He'd approached her in the past with it. Going through what Cherine had, and Tasha, and Belisa, it chilled her to the bones with revulsion that it seemed to be her turn to go down that vile path. She'd seen other women dealing with it, but she'd never personally been subject to it before. The reality of it was far worse than any imagining.

"Now it's your turn to find courage within yourself," she murmured. "Others have been through much worse than this. Marin will find a way to get through to me. I must just hang on until that happens. Granor, I hate you so much."

Outside the palace proper, Marin called a meeting of the army commanders. It was a difficult gathering because they were conflicted between loyalty to Marin but at the same time loyalty to the crown.

"I know what you're feeling because I'm one of you," he started. "The only reason I haven't bashed down the palace doors is because I don't want to lend credence to Granor and his lies. I personally saw the king throughout the war. I don't believe he's recovered his faculties. My opinion is Granor has exercised a scheme to reach his goals. None of those goals would be good for the kingdom. You've seen him in action before. You know what to expect, a return to the old ways and the old abuses but with new faces. Did any of you trust him in battle or in council? Of course not, the king himself dismissed Granor from his role before he deteriorated. Isn't it strange his majesty stays hidden while Granor speaks on his behalf? The motives of the nobles and the royal children are clear. They lost their places and positions, so they heeded Granor's call. I tell you this; I will not allow Granor to harm my wife, our queen. If any of you chose to side with him, say so now."

They looked amongst themselves a moment before a general spoke. "Marin, you own the respect of the army and our support. We all struggle with the dilemma. I agree Granor is probably orchestrating this whole sorry event, but on the small chance the king is recovered, we don't feel we can join you in attacking the palace. I'm very sorry to tell you that."

"I understand. None of you will ever be my enemy. I respect your position but I think that sooner or later you're going to be forced to choose a side. If Granor feels he's overplayed his hand and gets backed in a corner, he may take serious actions and as I said, I won't allow him to harm Coraline. He's dangled the threat of her execution. That's not going to happen. I pledge my life on it."

The general answered, "I find it hard to imagine he would take such a step."

"I wouldn't have thought he'd do what he's done already. I'm not going to make assumptions about his thinking."

"What are you going to do, Marin?"

"I'm going to tighten the noose. I'll cut off all deliveries of supplies going into the palace. It will force him to take action sooner than he wants."

"We won't interfere one way or the other," the general answered.

"I would ask for you to increase your patrols around the palace. Granor's right that the populace can be unstable and fickle about these issues. Executions are a draw some demented people would welcome. I can't have unrest unsettling the plans I put into place. The carnage of the war has warped some people into dangerous states of mind. It's something we would have been forced to deal with at some point in time. Granor plays on the weakest parts of humanity without conscience."

The general nodded in agreement. "We'll revise the duty rosters right away, Marin."

"Thank you, gentlemen..."

* * * *

Aron reached the outskirts of the city without realizing the seriousness of the crisis Granor created. Where they would have raced toward the palace had they known, they stopped and set up camp to rest before going into the city.

Aron was in a good mood with Cherine living with him again at last. It skewed his usually skeptical viewpoint toward an uncharacteristic mellowness. His happiness spread throughout the camp. Even the Erati survivors dropped much of their hesitance and resistance. The long trek brought no adverse consequences for them so they believed Aron's words of healing and cooperation.

The city was still in shambles. Rebuilding homes and returning to old neighborhoods had begun for the city dwellers, but there were considerable holes as so many died in the war and the occupation by Damien's minions.

Replenishing their supplies here wasn't doable. The people still had very little and the shops weren't restocked and reopened yet. They sent out hunting parties to garner food and stayed put.

Coincidentally, another party was making its way to Nephora. Galean, Liani, Wu Hang, Belisa and her parent's and a considerable contingent of the Arreck army had a different mood as word of Granor's treachery hastened them along. The allies' families were a part of the pilgrimage. They reached the northern outskirts of Nephora soon after Aron arrived from the west.

Royal army couriers advised them of Aron's position. Belisa rode with a column of Arreck soldiers as quickly as they could to get to him, but it wasn't close enough for them to get there rapidly.

The following day they raced into his camp rousing the attention of the soldiers.

Brock was the first to meet Belisa. "What's happened?"

She jumped off her horse to embrace him. "I'm sorry to tell you Granor has caused severe trouble at the palace that requires our intervention. Where's

Aron?"

"He's with Cherine. They don't get up too early."

"I must see him now. This is urgent."

"My lord, there's an urgent matter," shouted the messenger outside of Aron's tent.

"We'll be right out," he answered. They hurriedly dressed and crawled out into the sunshine.

"Belisa?" he asked in surprise.

She embraced him firmly and then embraced Cherine warmly. "I'm happy to see you two together again. I'm sorry to disturb your tranquility, but there's a crisis we must see about. Granor has raised charges against Coraline. Apparently the king was taken away, though Granor claims he escaped from where Coraline held him captive and tried to usurp the throne. He claims to speak for the king and they're holding her in the prison with a threat of beheading."

"What!" he shouted in shock.

Lilith, Trent, and the others of Aron's officers came over to listen.

"Aron, this doesn't surprise me about Granor," said Lilith. "He's always been too ambitious to raise his status in society. He can be a dangerous threat. We need to get to the palace quickly. He knows he has limited time, so we must hasten before he does something dire."

"Break camp," said Aron. "I want us in the saddle within an hour."

Later when they started their ride Belisa rode beside Aron.

"It's been reported by our spies Marin couldn't simply slay Granor. There was enough of a possibility the king could be recovered that the army didn't feel they could act."

"We'll deal with Granor," Aron replied tersely. "I can't believe he would threaten Coraline."

"She was placed on the throne. He had to take action against her to achieve his scheme. I'd have thought he was looking to grab his old job as counselor, but now I wonder if he wants to install one of the royal children on the throne he could control. Obviously the nobles would support him for self-serving reasons."

"I guess I was naïve to think our troubles were over," Aron commented. "It must be my lot in life to struggle with endless challenges."

"There's no lack of weak people, Aron."

"I never liked that guy. He always seemed like trouble."

"I don't know if we can arrive at the palace soon enough to intervene. It's too far away. It's going to fall on Coraline to find a way to survive until we can get there. Granor has his own weaknesses I'm told. I think Lilith can explain to you his particular character flaws. She's had dealings with him in the past."

"I'll talk to her. I hadn't planned on making any stops other than very brief ones."

"Our people are contacting Marin, but as I said, whatever Granor does will happen before we can arrive."

Aron looked back. Lilith was never far away from him. She saw him look and rode up beside them.

"We're trying to figure out Granor," he said.

"He's a snake."

"Belisa said you know his weaknesses, Lilith."

"He has plenty of flaws, but stupidity isn't one of them. Coraline is a breathtaking beauty so I'm sure he'd like to take advantage of her. Obviously her husband wouldn't let that crime slide so he's probably tried to maneuver a situation where he can act in secret. I don't believe he wants to kill Coraline, but if he felt he had no other choice, he'd do so. There's nothing more alluring for the insane than the prospect of a stunning beauty executed before their eyes. It could cause problems for any force trying to intervene. I'm sure this is part of why Marin is held at bay."

"I never suspected he was capable of such a bold and a risky gambit."

"He was shocked by what I did kidnapping you and Cherine, Aron. I think in a way I'm partly to blame for this because he felt marginalized and a man like him can't stand that. He thinks he can match my temerity with his schemes. He's an idiot to go against you."

"I really don't have a plan for when we get there. I would just march up to him and have at it."

"Very shrewd, Aron," she laughed. "Perhaps we should think about a better approach. The problem for Marin is the same one we'll have. Granor has powerful enough friends in the nobles that there's some credible risk to us. Their long term prospects aren't good, but in the short term they can still wreak havoc. My thought is to discern his next moves and thwart him there. If we cut off his avenue of escape, perhaps find where he's hidden the king, we can shut down this operation before it can go any further."

"That's good thinking," said Belisa. "My spies have been looking for the king already. Perhaps they'll have information for us we can use against Granor. Unfortunately, there's nothing we can do for Coraline. She's in a prison cell and no one is allowed to enter the palace."

"Does Granor know we're back in the city, Belisa?"

"I'm sure word of it is spreading, but we're moving faster than any potential rumor. I think we have an element of surprise on our side."

"Okay, I guess my idea of an immediate frontal attack will be our plan B. I won't wait long though. If things don't work out for us quickly, I won't hesitate to tear down the palace."

"Duly noted," Lilith replied with a smirk.

* * * *

Coraline sat in despair the following evening when Granor returned to hear her idea of 'compromise'.

"Good evening, Coraline. I trust you've thought about the situation. I'm anxious to hear what you're willing to offer for your life, and that of the queen."

"I know what you want, Granor. You've asked for it before. You're a vile man. For my own self, I would gladly go to the chopping block before I'd give you that satisfaction. I'm only thinking about the plight of the queen. You seemed to be convinced you can avoid the consequences of your actions. I'm not sure where you get that thought. Do you think my husband will let such a matter rest?"

"Your husband will never know, or else you'll get your wish to see the executioner along with the queen. Perhaps we'll let you watch her die first. The sight of her pretty head rolling on the ground with her dying heart spurting blood out of her severed neck can be a very sobering sight knowing that you'll be next. Thinking about it happening isn't the same as seeing it with your own eyes. She's someone you care about, so if you wish to test my resolve, I warn you I don't bluff."

Coraline frowned at her predicament.

"If I accede to your demands, what guarantee do I have you'll honor your bargain. You could simply kill us afterwards."

"You have none. You're a woman I treasure, Coraline. I wouldn't see you put to death if there was any way to avoid it. I'm a reasonable person. I'm sure we could work out some sort of place for me in the administration after this matter is resolved. As far as the nobles and the royal children, you already know you had to make some accommodation for them. They have rights and claims which must be honored."

"You couldn't simply come to me on their behalf," she said reflectively.

"I'd have had no leverage under those circumstances, Coraline."

"What footing do you think you'd be on with me after this?"

"You're a smart woman. You've proven it by rising from an obscure villager to wife of the late crown prince. You understand you're not in a position sitting here in that cell to threaten me, and how unwise it would be to do so. If you're thinking about your revenge afterwards, you need to survive to get to that point. There's no move you have but to make the obvious choice…you can rejoin your late husband in death."

She stared away into space.

"I think it's time for you to make your decision. We have a busy day tomorrow, one way or another."

* * * *

Marin assembled his personal corps. "You men know the army doesn't feel it can intervene, so it falls on us. Tomorrow Granor will call forth the public for his moment. If he thinks he can use an execution to advance his aims, I fear he'll do so. We can conquer his guards, but it would still be a fight to storm the execution spot. Granor will expect us to act so he'll have considerable soldiers there. He's banking on the blood lust of the mob to hamper us, and I think it would be a problem. We can't go there as a military unit. We need to blend in with the crowd and filter to the fore. When we strike, it must be quick and decisive. He'll try to save his hide and might hasten the beheadings. He'll also look to escape. We can't allow either to happen."

"They'll search us for arms," said one of his officers.

"I've gotten the cooperation of the army with that problem. They're tasked with searching the arriving crowd. They'll allow us in with our hidden weapons. We won't go close enough to draw the notice of Granor's soldiers until the last moment. Does anyone have any questions?"

They looked back solemnly.

"Be brave, but also be ruthless. We can't give them time to react. It will put Coraline and the queen in deadly danger."

"We won't fail you, sir," his officer replied.

Marin was immensely frustrated at the impasse, but he was savvy enough to realize he couldn't get away with simply storming the palace. He worried what his wife was facing as Granor's prisoner, but that concern was secondary to his fear for her life the next day. Already rowdy civilians were gathering with the lure of an execution. It was all he could do to keep from attacking them in his rage.

* * * *

The pieces were all in place for a pivotal point in history. The challenge to the 'villager queen' had been made and there was a real possibility of a dire outcome. As unlikely as it would have seemed, Granor pulled off a remarkable coup. His willingness to take drastic steps wasn't something anybody questioned, including Coraline as she gave Granor her answer and looked at his face for his reaction.

The following morning, the area surrounding the palace filled up quickly starting at dawn as the curious flocked to the bizarre stage to witness the spectacle. The idea of beheadings of the two beautiful queens gained traction and the excitement amongst the demented became a significant factor for Marin and the others to cope with, exactly what Marin anticipated. The mob acted as though they were rabid animals demanding their meat. Anything short of that could spark a riot and there were a great number of people to worry about.

When the guards came for Coraline, it didn't surprise her. Granor wasn't trustworthy and she also realized what he could gain here in notoriety by slaying her and the queen. He could establish himself as a force to be reckoned with and he might gain the support of the army using the king's authority as his lever. Her decision the prior night of either way would have led her to this same outcome. She was afraid, but also very sad. Her marriage to Marin was a joy that seemed to be coming to a premature end. She thought about the hardships that pockmarked Aron's life. Now she was experiencing it. Trying to be brave was nearly beyond her at that point with all she would be losing, including her unborn child.

She was led separately from the queen. They didn't see each other until they were led outside into the sunshine of morning. Her last meal had been a tasteless breakfast.

Tears filled the eyes of both women as they saw each other. They were both chained so they couldn't embrace.

The crowd roared at the first sight of them, the feral mob rabid for slaughter. Granor emerged and walked solemnly to the fore. He'd stationed his entire phalanx of troops in a defensive perimeter to fight Marin if he struck.

"Good morning, citizens. I'm sorry to meet you here for such an unfortunate occasion, but the law demands justice for our king who was wrongfully accosted by those closest to him. People he loved and trusted, people who proved to be traitors and vipers. I know it's difficult to imagine these women you idolized could do such foul deeds, but the facts speak loudly against them. His majesty has proclaimed their guilt. See, he is here to watch their punishment."

The crowd gasped as the palace doors opened to reveal the king standing in his full robes and crown. He didn't come out of the building and he was supported by guards on each side of him. He wasn't clearly visible to see if he was coherent. It was a very risky ploy, but Granor took the chance in order to cow the army.

"Before you stand the last two women anointed as queens of the realm. Our rigorous investigation revealed they're both guilty of the crimes for which they're charged. The king himself has announced their sentences of immediate death by beheading. Their bodies and heads will be placed on public display to demonstrate the penalty for treason and treachery. Their actions were shameful, so therefore their death repose will reflect that shame as they'll be stripped of all clothing to lie open to scorn and the righteous retribution of the kingdom."

The crowd roared at the titillation he promised, making it into a thrill for them instead of a horror.

The guards grabbed the women to rip off their clothes. It was too much and Marin gave his signal to attack. In spite of their attempting to be prepared for the fight, Marin's men scythed their way forward felling Granor's men like wheat. Marin himself burst through the defensive line and raced toward the execution site. The crowd was riotous at both the sudden battle, and the chance their prey could be snatched away from them. The helpless and bared women were both forced to their knees and bent over the blocks. They looked at each other in fear and in regret.

Marin was racing to save them, but the distance was too great.

Guards pulled back their hair to expose their necks and the executioners prepared to take the fatal swings at the very spot where Agar had died.

Suddenly in the distance they heard the horns and the screams of Aron's soldiers charging.

"Aron has come," shouted men in the crowd. "Protect the queens!"

The army responded in an instant attacking the palace guards and Granor's soldiers.

"Strike now!" Granor yelled at the executioners who hesitated. Their pause gave Marin time to close the distance. They had no chance against his feral attack, losing their own heads.

Granor turned and ran along with the survivors of his men. They went back into the palace and locked out the allies. They led the king away and headed for their preplanned exit point where horses were saddled and waiting. They rode into a secret tunnel which led them outside the perimeter.

Marin went straight for Coraline wrapping her up in a hug before quickly putting her clothes back on her. Servants quickly helped the queen too. Both women were surrounded by protecting guards, ten rows deep.

It took an hour before Aron rode through the palace gates. The rabid bloodthirsty crowd totally transformed to give him a hero's welcome.

Galean arrived soon afterwards with Arreck escorts.

Aron stood with Galean to address the crowd.

"I can't believe you allowed this to happen. Coraline is your legitimate queen. The king is being held hostage so Granor can pretend to have his authority. How could you allow it?"

Aron was livid. Galean saw he was about to go down a path of retribution, so he stepped in.

Savior

"You can understand Aron's ire. We all make mistakes, but the error of the mob here nearly cost you your future. If we're going to have a society, it has to be a shared burden. Every one of your leaders must account for their actions, but so do you. You must be defenders of the queen. Because there are those misguided people among you who cry for blood and sacrifice of the innocent, that doesn't mean you can't have an answer to that darkness. If one of you first says no to evil, then another will and another and so on. Those courageous few then grow into an invincible tidal wave of goodness. If you think it was the queens who were shamed here today, you're wrong. It was all of you. This must be a lesson you never forget. You can't allow lust to rule you ever again. Now you must pledge again to your sovereign, Queen Coraline."

The crowd went to a knee and shouted their answer.

"Long live Queen Coraline?" They did it three times.

Surprisingly to everyone, Coraline hadn't slunk away in embarrassment. Instead she stepped forward with her husband to stand beside Galean and Aron. She nodded to the throng as if nothing untoward had happened.

Chapter Twenty
~Resolution~

There was still a great deal of confusion in and around the palace. The palace guards were penitent for their role in Granor's power grab. Their captain met with Queen Coraline and her vindictive husband. The captain cowered in fear standing before them expecting the worst.

It wasn't a singular meeting. Aron, Galean, Belisa, Tasha, Radigan, Trent, Brock, Lilith, Belisa, Liani, Wu Hang, Abdurka, Enna, Biala, and the army staff were all there. Opinions about what to do varied a great deal. Marin's punitive thoughts were abundantly clear.

"You expect me to believe you couldn't act to protect your queen? It's your primary duty!"

"Marin, wait," said Aron. "He was in no different position than the army. They were sworn to the crown and nobody could disprove Granor, so he couldn't make an arbitrary choice that could have cost his command their lives."

Marin scowled grimly eyeing the captain murderously.

Aron continued, "I'm not excusing anybody for what was done, Marin. I'm just saying now is the time to cool our tempers. We've declared Granor a criminal. We'll find him sooner or later and bring him to justice. There was a city full of confused people out there for the execution. We can't punish everybody for what amounts to usual human weaknesses. Hopefully lessons were learned where it can't happen again. I think everybody knows now the king will never recover his mind, so that myth has been dispelled. It takes away Granor's only leverage. He's walking around on borrowed time."

"Aron, I don't want to seem unreasonable, but my wife, the current queen, and the former queen have been besmirched and shamed in public. That crime

254

demands retribution. I can't sit idly by while the guilty walk about freely. There are men among the palace guards who laid hands on them and stripped off their clothes to pander to the mob. You can tell me they were just doing their duties, but I saw the glee and lust on their faces. They took pleasure in that action and they would have cheered to see their heads lopped off. It's intolerable. I can't accept doing nothing. You want me to reply to such abomination with forgiveness?"

"Husband," said Coraline. "It was my shame and it's my burden to bear. I understand what you feel, but if I can live with it, perhaps you can too. I didn't lose my life, so I'm inclined to be forgiving. I have faced worse. Circumstances demand compromise no matter how wronged we feel."

Marin scowled and then walked up to the officer to get in his face. "Don't think I'll forget this. They may forgive you but I won't. I saw which soldiers did the deed."

"I'm sorry, my lord. I can't go back and undo the mistake. I'll accept your wrath because we're in the wrong."

Marin looked back reflectively at his wife. Her added comment piqued his curiosity about what she meant and what she'd faced. His immediate impression was something heinous from Granor while she was in her cell. That was a dark possibility that angered him further.

"Aron, you're right to say Granor is a dead man. I'll see to that personally."

"Marin, you'll need to get in line as many others have serious issues to rectify with Granor," said Lilith. "I'm at the head of that list. My plan upon returning to Nephora was to have words with him. My maidens and I have unfinished business. I suspect he won't survive that conversation."

Marin looked at her and smiled darkly. "I believe you, Lilith. I think you have past grievances for transgressions on his part which requires deadly consequences. I understand that. I think we should combine our efforts to find him and exact justice on behalf of many."

"I have no problem with it if your wife doesn't object and I'm sworn to Aron so I'd need his release to pursue this task."

"Lilith, I'd rather go with you," Aron replied.

"I'd rather go with you too, but it wouldn't work. Riding after Granor with an entire army would guarantee we'd never catch him. Marin and I can have a chance with our knowledge and with the proper size of our forces."

"I'd say be very careful, Lilith. We want you back to us safe and sound."

Lilith laughed and looked at Cherine. "I warned you he favors me. You'd better have that wedding while you still can or you'll be lacking a groom."

Cherine laughed. "I'd offer to add the masters to your quest, but as you say, greater numbers is a hindrance in trapping a fox. I won't hold against you your lusting for my husband-to-be, you shameless wench."

"I am that, no argument here."

"I'd like to join you," said Brock suddenly stepping forward. "I like to stay busy."

Marin shrugged nonchalantly and Lilith agreed.

Cherine turned to Aron. "Perhaps it's time we finally tied up the little matter of marriage."

"I've been ready forever," Aron replied.

"Galean, could we impose on you to perform the ceremony?" she asked.

"It would be my pleasure and my honor."

"Thank you."

* * * *

While Marin left his wife behind to ride out with Lilith and Brock, Aron prepared to wed. It caused him more anxiety than any battle he'd faced.

"Why are you so worried?" asked Abdurka. "The duties of a husband for his new bride aren't difficult, or unpleasant. It's something to treasure not to fear."

"I'm not afraid," Aron retorted defensively. "I just want it to be perfect for her."

"Neither of you are adolescents, and both of you have ridden that horse before, Aron."

"I know what you're saying. This is a culmination of a very long road for me. I think that's a part of what I feel. It was a painful process and it didn't work out like I would have thought."

"They were wonderful women, but they just weren't fated to be your wife, Aron. Now you finally have her. That's enough. Don't read all those past troubles into this. Just marry her and start your new life."

"I want to say I feel like I don't fully get some things about her. She has aspects or sides she keeps separate from me. I don't know if that's because of things I've done."

"Aron, you remain your own worst enemy. Shut up those bothersome thoughts and just be a good man to her. Everything else will work out if you do."

Cherine moved away from Aron, again, this time only until the wedding. They didn't want a big ceremony, but too many people refused to be ignored, so it grew by the day into a city wide phenomenon. Decorations went up, musicians came out of the woodwork, and a festive banquet was arranged.

They received no word from the field on the search for Granor, nor did they get reports from Lilith.

* * * *

Coraline proved to be very resilient after her near execution. She resumed all of her duties as queen and showed no sign her public de-clothing had any lasting effect on her. The former queen, however, chose seclusion and only gradually began to be seen in public again. She over-dressed as if she needed to show no part of her body as penance. As if she was responsible for what was done to her.

The only accommodation Coraline made after the incident was to dine in private with her former mother-in-law. It helped mollify her and gave an avenue to gradually re-assimilate into palace life.

"Coraline, I'm so fortunate to have you in my life. Thank you for looking out for me. I'm sorry to be so weak. When I had the king to deal with all matters I was sheltered and never faced adversity. This is unnerving for me. I was terrified when they came for me and dragged me to the dungeon. That brush with death nearly killed me on the spot from fright. I understand the hardship of the people now. I'm ashamed of what we imposed upon the weak. I closed my eyes to what was plain to see all around me. It was so wrong."

"We need to worry about the present. Marin has assigned top notch men to guard us but Granor may have allies here in the palace, so we must be cautious and on our guard at all times."

"I just want it all to be over."

"You must never go anywhere without adequate guard protections, even for just a moment. Marin's man will personally safeguard you so put your trust in his instincts about situations."

"I will, Coraline."

"With Marin gone, I'll stay here with you at night if you wish until he returns."

"It would be a great comfort, thank you again. Although my husband was lost it was still a blessing to have him nearby. I've never been a person who wanted to be alone."

"You won't be from now on."

"Marin's man, Ardrick has presented himself to me. I'm very pleased. His presence isn't any sort of hindrance and is actually a great comfort to have a man near at hand. It helps me with my problem of loneliness. Give your husband my thanks."

* * * *

The day of the wedding was bright and sunny. It brought out the throngs, again. The same people that thirsted for beheadings of the queens were now assembled shouting their love for Aron and the kingdom. Overnight, Coraline was again the beloved of the mob. They cheered wildly when she appeared along with the former queen to attend the marriage ceremony. The former queen was reassured with Ardrick at her side, no longer cowed by public appearances.

Galean donned formal robes to officiate the joining ritual. He stood bedecked in splendor like an ancient prophet called forth from on high.

Aron's desire for a small event was totally ignored as anybody of consequence in the realm elbowed their way to assume prominent positions at the front of the pack. It mattered not at all to him or to Cherine who stood where.

With the exception of Lilith, Brock, and Marin who were still searching for Granor, all his other friends were there. The women he'd favored through his life, Coraline, Tasha, Liani, Belisa, Enna, and Biala, they were all there smiling. It was comforting to him to feel he was finally at the end of his torturous road through mishap and mayhem.

With Brock gone, Aron asked Trent to be his best man and hold the rings. Aron noticed his mother had tears in her eyes. He walked over.

"The wedding hasn't started yet. Why are you crying?"

"It's a woman thing," she answered.

"It's supposed to be a happy occasion, mother."

"It is, son. I'm happy. I just feel like I'm putting down a heavy burden of worrying about you. I know you'll be fine now. Cherine will be a wonderful wife and will make you very happy. I felt your pain through all of the travails of your life. I'm glad it's over."

Aron hugged her tightly and kissed her forehead.

"I just hope I don't do something stupid to embarrass you, like trip and fall down in front of everybody. I didn't want a big spectacle with all of these strangers here."

"You'll do fine. Don't worry, son. This is a joyous day for both of us. You're among friends."

"With Cherine as a wife, it's a benefit to know your spouse is a world class warrior. My threat level is going down."

"You're so foolish," his mother replied as they both laughed heartily.

"I'm anxious to get this over with."

"It's time, Aron," said an aide as Galean took his position.

They played the anthem of the kingdom before switching over to a wedding march. Aron's heart thumped when Cherine emerged from the palace in her wedding dress. On this day, her femininity took to the fore. She was stunning to the eye. When Aron pulled back her cover to see her face, her warm smile evoked him. Mercifully, Galean's ritual was a short one and the bride and groom kissed for the first time as man and wife.

The masses cheered wildly as Aron and Cherine went to a waiting carriage to be whisked away to a place they could have some privacy and a short honeymoon. Aron had his bride at last pledged to him alone. Meanwhile the city celebration went on even with them gone.

* * * *

The event and the after times were a blur of happiness for them both. Their martial natures and pasts were put aside for a time to revel in love and total partnership. Aron had no other thoughts in his mind, including catching Granor. Nothing seemed important any longer with happiness in his grasp finally.

About a week into their honeymoon, they reclined in the morning after their breakfast.

"Aron, I'm happy beyond my wildest imagination. I hope you know I love you only. I've hesitated talking about Damien. Whether I like it or not, I spent considerable time along with Nala at his mercy. He called us his wives, but there was no mutual bond. It was simply his will imposed on us. I won't go into the details, unless you want to know."

"No Cherine, I don't want to know. If you were married and divorced the situation would be the same. I don't need to rehash the past. He's dead so it doesn't matter anyway."

"My point is we were forced to make compromises not of our choosing. I want to be honest with you because you have a habit of distorting things and taking them to absurd extremes."

"I'm an idiot, Cherine, but you already knew that. There must be something you're getting at."

"His tastes varied from yours, Aron. He wasn't a virile man of great pleasure to a woman. Therefore he demanded outlets with other actions. It shames me to say what we did."

"Cherine, really, you don't have to tell me. If you mean there's some residual effect or problem that's what we should probably talk about."

"We feared there could be, Aron, but that concern is diminished so I'm optimistic. I just didn't want you to think I was hiding something and withholding a truth from you."

"Our life now is together. The sooner you forget about Damien, the better. I don't have any worries and I certainly believe you love me. That's what matters to me."

"You're a good man, Aron. I'm a lucky wife."

"I'm going to file that last statement away in my memory and pull it out if we ever argue."

Cherine laughed and kissed him. "Fair enough, husband."

* * * *

Marin, Lilith, and Brock's expedition lengthened in elapsed time without cornering Granor. As a matter of fact, his trail cooled along with any new leads. He made no appearances although there were whispers he was working behind the scenes pulling strings.

The children of the king and the nobles began to return to disclaim any connection with Granor and his plot claiming to have been duped about the king.

It was an opportunity for Queen Coraline to exact revenge for what was done to her and she had strong feelings to teach them a lesson, but she thought about it a great deal and decided to extend mercy and the hand of friendship. It was a wise and prudent move that made her enemies beholding to her.

The former queen, however, was irate at her spineless children and refused to see them for an extended period.

She brought them to a small conference room along with Coraline and a large contingent of guards.

"You would have allowed me to be put to death," she hissed. "You complain that I never gave you respect. You didn't earn it! I try to imagine any circumstance where I would have done this to my mother and shudder I could have birthed such as you. Your queen is Coraline and you better get that in your heads. I would not have shown you the mercy she has. If you don't have it in you to live better lives, perhaps you should all pack up and leave the kingdom to find another home."

Her children were shocked. She'd never been a forceful woman before. They had trouble understanding her now though. They stood awkwardly waiting for the tirade to end.

"Leave my sight. I want no part of you. The daughter I gained through Agar's marriage cares more for me than any of you ever could. You disgust me."

They started to amble toward the door.

"What you did was very serious," said Coraline. "I'm of a mind to allow you a chance at redemption. Living better lives your mother spoke of, I'd like you to do that. I haven't banished you from the kingdom, but any further such miscreant acts will have a severe price for you to pay. Do you understand? When I was kneeling naked with your mother waiting for the death blow I felt so many regrets. I'm giving you a chance to rectify your mistakes and to change your ways to do good for others. There are so many in need. If you need to speak to me, I won't shun you."

"Thank you, your majesty," they all said going to a knee.

"Go in peace. I hope in the future we'll see each other as friends."

"Long live Queen Coraline," they said in unison, like a pack of recalcitrant parrots.

After they went out the door, Coraline looked at the queen.

"I think you've made a mistake. As long as you let them hang around, they'll be a threat. It's the same with the nobles. They're snakes that will strike if they see a weakness."

"We'll be careful. Perhaps they'll surprise you in a good way."

"I very much doubt that. Could you have allowed your mother to be sacrificed, Coraline?"

"I'm a different person."

"You're a normal person. There's some flaw in them I don't think can be corrected."

* * * *

Aron returned to the palace with his wife. Both of them resumed their military positions, though with the war ended there was nothing to do other than assist in rebuilding the kingdom.

Marin's quest ended without capturing their prey but it wasn't totally fruitless.

When they returned to the capital city, they found out the time in the field had nurtured a relationship between Brock and Lilith, as unlikely as it would have seemed.

A second startling revelation was Trent had taken an interest in Nala and romantic possibilities blossomed there too. That was very good news for Aron as Nalas' seeming dependence on her relationship with Cherine faded as she transferred her feelings to Trent.

Both new couples didn't wait long to marry.

The search for Granor continued, but now through field units of soldiers. Wherever he was hiding, they had no luck in finding him.

To avoid his punishment, Granor shrewdly kept a very low profile for a long time which impeded their attempts to apprehend him. His network of spies and confederates maintained his plots while he remained out of sight. He contacted the nobles, and even the royal children. As he expected, they were willing to listen to any scheme if they thought it would advance them. None of their 'crocodile smiles' in front of Coraline had been genuine or sincere. They were only gauging the danger they were in and their chance to escape consequences.

Coraline's kindnesses came across to them as weakness. They reflected the worse in humanity and were perfect relics of the excesses of the former regime. Being allowed to resume residence in the palace in their former suites was an unanticipated bonanza. Along with the nobles, they tried to resurrect the old customs, parties, and social life. At first they were careful not to go too far, but gradually their demands and requests expanded. Although palace servants were no longer slaves, they were still seen as lesser persons available for royal usage.

Coraline had a much depleted treasury to fund royal operations, but she still instituted employment status for palace workers. Their wages were modest, but certainly much better than what they'd received before which was nothing.

She put great emphasis on the recovery of the city, getting people back into homes and getting shops reopened. It was the main priority and with the army assigned to both protection against thieves and miscreants, and to assist with construction and repair of the damaged buildings, the work went rapidly. A fledging economy appeared seemingly overnight and flourished.

The grateful people were more than happy to share in their bounty with the queen and the treasury coffers began to fill.

Aron pondered his situation happily. He'd taken his time returning from a honeymoon which he'd extended. Although Cherine was anxious to take a role in the recovery, she warmly acceded to her new husband's request.

"Is it a problem, wife?" he'd asked cautiously.

"Of course not, Aron, I'm not in a hurry to leave your embraces, but we can do those in our home. I'm anxious to help build a better nation. From all I see and hear, Coraline is doing a remarkable job. I've spent my life fighting, destroying, and taking lives. If I can do some things to help build to offset the things I've done, do you see what I'm saying?"

"I do, Cherine. I'm being selfish. This is so idyllic a life with you as my wife I hesitate to give it up."

"You're not giving me up by going back home. You want these days of pleasure. I like them too, but we have responsibilities we must honor, Aron. I know what you've been through and believe me I want to give you the rewards you deserve from a loving wife."

"Is it a taxing matter for you? It almost seems you're saying being my wife is a duty you fulfill, as you did when you were Damien's wife."

"Aron, if you start that nonsense, I will knock you senseless. Nothing of this reflects on your old feelings. They were always wrong, but you've lived with them so long, they've gained credibility in your mind. I can appreciate where they came from, but I want to say, I'm not going to spend the rest of my life explaining and rationalizing to cull your worries. There was no problem, there is no problem, and there will be no problem, unless you create it. That's the last time I want to talk about this."

"Yes, ma'am, message received."

"Good, now get up out of bed and let's go do something constructive for the queen."

He smiled at her.

"No," she said.

"I didn't say anything."

"You didn't need to. We've played already this morning."

He sighed and arose from the bed. "I can see how things are going to be. I'll have no say in things."

"About those 'things' you would choose to have for our days where we only 'played'."

"What's wrong with that?" he questioned, laughing heartily.

She gave him an exasperated look.

"I'm coming, darling. I'll bathe and then pack our things. You win. I'm sure it won't be the last time."

"Thank you, husband, I realize I married an infant."

He laughed again.

* * * *

Life at the palace mirrored life in the kingdom in general. Everything gradually improved. It didn't take much to surpass the achievements of the former regime. It became clear to the populace their new queen was not going to revert back to the old ways and they felt trust in government for the first time.

It seemed impossible they could have stood screaming for her head not so long before but that sobering memory worked as a positive as they started to self-police. When Granor's divisive rumors appeared, they quashed them quickly and sought out the mongers.

Granor remained a threat, but at much reduced levels. Nobody wanted to see Coraline replaced. All of what remained of unreasoning loyalty to the old king dissipated and then disappeared.

It was Cherine who first started a trend as her unions with her husband produced a pregnancy. It was like a constraint was broken as promptly the other women started families too. Coraline, of course, was already pregnant, but now all of her women friends joined her in that state.

Brock was particularly proud he'd be a father and for once, he shut Lilith's mouth as she acted the compliant wife. Of course, that was only when she was with Brock in public. Behind the scenes with the other women, she remained the strong willed personality she'd always been.

Aron was genuinely happy. Even seeing Tasha was carrying Radigan's child only gave him a twinge of jealousy. He felt happy for Queen Coraline. Marin was a good man who he respected. Marin was another man who beamed with pride at impending fatherhood.

Liani becoming pregnant with Wu Hang's child was a cause for widespread conversation. With her petite frame and his massive size, many wondered if she could birth a giant baby.

Wu Hang was so much different a person. It seemed he'd finally found peace with his demons which haunted his life. His dark deeds of his past were never going to leave him, but with the contentment of a marriage and a wife to love and cherish, he could find the positives in life. He would never have a physical appearance which wasn't frightening and intimidating, but at least he could have a refuge to turn to. Liani was his treasure and in turn she gave him her love. It was a wonderful relationship stemming from the most unlikely roots.

Time passed as more babies were born. Though he didn't want the job, Marin asked Aron to be overall commander of the army. Cherine remained commander of the masters. The elite Black Fist swelled to a size of ten thousand warriors. Similarly the masters reached a comparable size.

Belisa married an Arreck noble, which wasn't a surprise with their closed society and insular beliefs. They were close allies with Coraline and the kingdom though.

Enna and Biala finally returned to the swamp and married within their people but they were frequent visitors returning to the palace even with infants of their own.

The former Erati women and children were assimilated seamlessly and were never a problem in society.

Aron was a busy man with having to travel all about the kingdom. He went with his wife and children, a son and two daughters, along with Brock's family, Lilith and two sons, back to their home village. It had been rebuilt and it was very prosperous. Cherine, the wife and mother, was such a different incarnation for who she'd been all her life. Finding gentleness for her little ones wasn't difficult at all. Similarly, Lilith was also a greatly transformed person raising her babies.

The fact legendary Aron was from there drew armies of sightseers. The village expanded to build numerous extra inns for the tourists. It was amusing to the brothers.

"Who could have anticipated this?" asked Brock.

"People are very gullible brother. Anybody who wants to see where you came from clearly is deficient."

They laughed along with their wives as they watched the children in the market playing with village children.

The mayor of the village came up to them with his wife.

"Would you be so kind as to grace us with your presence at a festival in your honor this evening?"

"Sure," said Brock quickly.

Lilith elbowed him. "Try to have a little dignity. The mayor will think you're only drawn by the prospect of free food."

Everybody laughed.

"Woman, you're the scourge of my life," he groused playfully.

"This is why I'm pushing out your babies, because I'm your scourge?" she replied scornfully. "I don't think so."

"How can I get any respect if you're always demeaning me?"

"You get what's coming to you, sir."

The wife of the mayor laughed hilariously. "I love this. I love that a woman can be her own person. It's about time."

"If you thought we were in charge of our marriages because of these fantastic stories told about us, I can tell you it was never true. We're ruled by our women," said Aron.

"This is why the kingdom is improving," Cherine chided.

This time it was the women who laughed.

"This is what happens when you let a woman wield a sword," said Brock. "Now I must go to shop to pick various colors of cloth. It's a sobering twist to be so shackled with such noisome tasks."

"Shut up, Brock. You're lucky I let you live."

"There, you heard it. Do you see what I mean?"

"Brock, you can't win. You should let it go before she does brain you," Aron said laughingly.

Brock muttered, but wisely dropped his complaints.

"We'd be honored to accept your invitation, mayor," said Lilith. "Thank you for your hospitality and your friendship."

"We'll see you then," he replied.

"It's wonderful to meet you," said his wife. She smiled at the two wives.

"I think you've created a new headache for the mayor," said Brock. "I think she's up to no good after hearing the two wives spout off."

"Brock," said Lilith threateningly. "I may end up a widow before this party tonight if you don't shut up. It would be a burden that I'm more than able to handle."

Cherine laughed hilariously. Aron smiled at Brock and shrugged his shoulders.

"I tried to tell you, brother."

* * * *

Aron's parents traveled to the palace to visit Aron, Cherine and their grandchildren often, but they'd opted to return to reside at the farm. They were able to hire workers to tend the fields and handle the livestock with their stipend from the crown. The farm had been rebuilt so it was almost unrecognizable. Similarly Barmon and Sirina returned to claim their old farm and rebuild it. Straga's two sons loved the life there and blossomed into wonderful young men well respected in the community. Barmon was a totally different man too. With his issues finally rectified he became the good man he was capable of being. He proved to be a good husband for Sirina and a good father for the boys.

After visiting in the village and then spending time with families, Aron's family continued their journey going into the wilds. It was no longer the dangerous place it had been. Although predators still abounded, the criminal elements had been either eradicated or absorbed into society.

It wasn't as if there were no remaining problems because there were, but Coraline's steady hand guided the realm toward peace and prosperity for all.

Going to the site of Damien's building was a difficult moment in spite of the fact that threat was over. The dark memories were difficult. Each one of them had their own feelings to cope with.

The destroyed site had been buried so there was no sign of what had been there. The ground was quickly overgrown by the aggressive plants that flourished in the wilds. It was just a hill in the middle of the forest now.

"Thank god we survived," said Aron. "He would have destroyed everybody everywhere."

"Galean never lost faith you'd find a way, Aron," Cherine replied. "When I was captured and held along with Nala, there were times when I nearly gave up hope. There were so many times when I dreamed about killing him, mostly with my bare hands. He always was on the defensive. It was uncanny how he could anticipate danger and find ways to avoid it. I can't think of those days without feeling revulsion at myself for being captured and neutralized."

"I think back of the idiot I was," Lilith added. "I was warped by my youth and the abuse I faced. I became so selfish a person I could only think of my wants and my needs. When I kidnapped the two of you, I thought I'd made such a great mark in the world. Women never accomplished important things, other than you, Cherine. I wonder how I could have been so stupid as to think either of you would accede to my offer of companionship."

"I thought about it," Aron replied.

"As did I," Cherine added.

"You don't have to humor me at this point," said Lilith.

"We're not," said Aron. "Actually it was gratifying you'd want me. Remember the romantic travails I had. I wasn't confident in that one area."

Lilith shrugged. "It all worked out for the best. Now I have this brainless lout to punish me on a daily basis as penance for my many sins."

She grasped Brock in a loving hug. "And now I have children and I'd never have believed I'd have that blessing."

Cherine embraced Aron. "Thank you, husband, there's no other man I'd wanted. You're perfect for me and for our kids."

"I feel the same way, Cherine. I think you got the short end of the stick in this marriage, but I've got no complaints."

"You're right, Aron," she replied mirthfully.

"Hey!" he objected. "I wasn't looking to get slammed."

They left the site of the demise of the scourge of the world to make their way back home. The great test of their age, the need to prove they deserved to survive, they'd passed it on behalf of all mankind.

The End

About the Author

Dennis Hausker is retired from a career as a medical insurance specialist for an insurance company. Post retirement he works part time as a financial consultant and he is the finance chair person at his church. He has been married since 1968. He and his wife met at Michigan State University from which they graduated in 1969. She is a retired teacher who volunteers helping adults with learning impairments. Dennis is a veteran of the Vietnam War. He served at Long Binh as a finance clerk paying field combat units. He loves to write with his preferred genre being Epic Fantasy, although he has the goal to also write books in other genres. He is very grateful for the business partnership he has established with Melange Books in terms of their professional support services and encouraging friendly atmosphere. His hope is his stories will be captivating, unique, and compelling for the reader.

www.denniskhausker.com

Other works by the Author with Melange Books, LLC

Mortus, Book 1 of the Faenum Quest Series
The Gathering Storm, Book 2 of the Faenum Quest Series
The Faenum War, Book 3 of the Faenum Quest Series
Stirring Sagas, an author anthology
Tales of the Heart, an author anthology
Twisting Fate in R.U.S.H. anthology
The Villager, Book 1 of the Shattered World Saga
Rebel, Book 2 of the Shattered World Saga